Trevennor's Will

Gloria Cook is the author of well-loved Cornish novels, including the Pengarron and Harvey family sagas. She is Cornish born and bred, and lives in Truro.

Also by Gloria Cook

Trevallion
Trevennor's Will
Listening to the Quiet

The Harvey Family Sagas

Touch the Silence
Moments of Time
From A Distance
Never Just a Memory
A Stranger Light
A Whisper of Life

The Pengarron Sagas

Pengarron Land
Pengarron Pride
Pengarron's Children
Pengarron Dynasty
Pengarron Rivalry

The Kilgarthen Sagas

Kilgarthen
Rosemerryn

The Roscarrock Sagas

Roscarrock
Porthellis

The Leaving Shades Sagas

Leaving Shades
Reflections

Gloria Cook

Trevennor's Will

CANELO

First published in the United Kingdom in 1994 by Headline Book Publishing

This edition published in the United Kingdom in 2022 by

Canelo
Unit 9, 5th Floor
Cargo Works, 1-2 Hatfields
London, SE1 9PG
United Kingdom

A CIP catalogue record for this book is available from the British Library.

Print ISBN 978 1 80032 818 1
Ebook ISBN 978 1 78863 644 5

Printed and bound in Great Britain by Clays Ltd, Elcograf S.p.A.

1

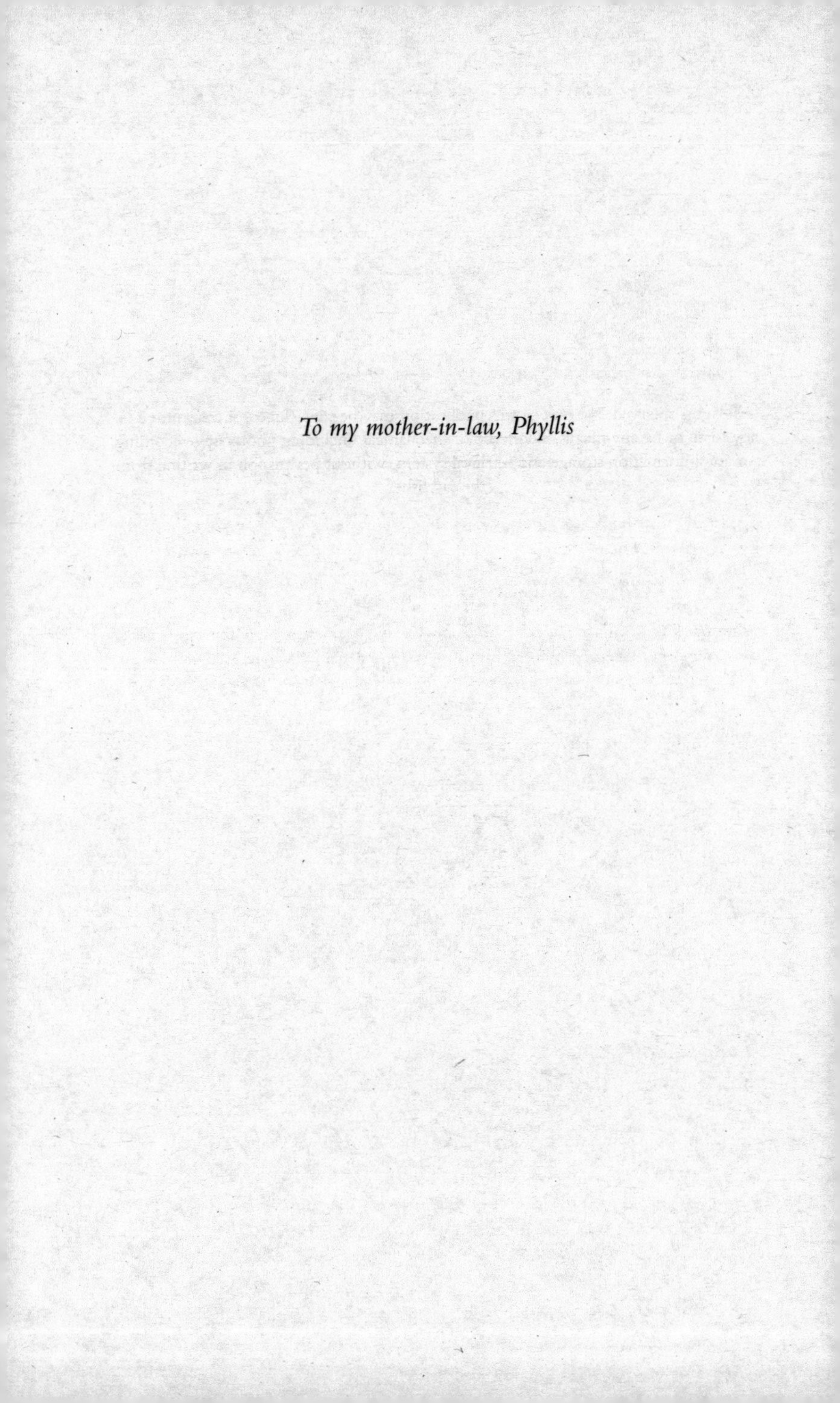

To my mother-in-law, Phyllis

Chapter 1

'Oh, do stop whimpering, Ginny!'

'But we're going too fast, Miss Isabel.'

'You've been fussing since we set out,' Isabel Hampton told her maid crossly.

'Slap her face,' the other person in the coach said spitefully.

'That won't help, Phoebe,' Isabel replied, frowning as she was forced to hold on to the seat. She looked out of the window, and saw the countryside rushing by. 'Ginny has a point, we are travelling too fast.'

'It was you who gave the order to get us there as quickly as possible,' Phoebe replied, raising her voice above the creakings of the vehicle and glaring at Ginny on the opposite seat.

The coach hit a rut and Ginny shrieked. She pressed her fists to her chest and screwed her eyes up tightly. The next moment her head rolled to the side. Isabel rummaged in her purse and produced smelling salts. Phoebe banged on the coach roof and shouted, 'Rickardson, slow down!'

Ginny came to with a panicky sob as Isabel leant forward and administered the smelling salts, having difficulty keeping her balance as the coach took a bend.

There came a sudden shout from the guard.

'There's rocks on the road!'

The coach jolted alarmingly and slewed to one side and Isabel was thrown against the door. She screamed as the door gave way and she was thrown out. She hit the ground, tumbling over and over, aware of the coach overturning, hearing it splintering and grinding, the horses whinnying in fear and their thundering hooves as they broke free, and the terrible screaming that seemed to go on and on. Isabel came to a halt in a bed of prickly gorse. She wanted to help the others but could not move. She tried to cry out but no sound would come. She lay still and listened and the noises grew fainter until suddenly they stopped.

Almost at once she heard a different noise, a thud of heavy feet and a gleeful mocking laugh. It was a looter. Isabel held her breath. The man was picking among the debris of the coach; she prayed she had been thrown far enough away not to be noticed, but moments later she heard him coming towards her. She tried to get up and run but overcome by shock and fear she blacked out.

–

Nick Nancarrow viewed the carnage and shook his head at the irony of what he saw. He had just come from Laurence Trevennor's deathbed, but he would not be able to carry out the urgent promise he had given to the old gentleman a few minutes before he'd died.

He had been drinking in the Basset's Cove Inn at Portreath when a groom from Trevennor House had brought him a message that his company was requested there at his earliest convenience. Nick had left the inn at once and was grieved to find that Laurence had not only taken to his bed, but he was apparently dying. The ageing gentleman's heart, weakened by a bout of rheumatic fever, was rapidly failing him.

Laurence Trevennor owned a large amount of Gwithian's 2,600 acreage, and surrounding land. He also had financial interests in a lucrative foundry works at nearby Hayle, supplying machinery for Cornwall's tin and copper mines.

Nick's father had been the Trevennors' head groom and coachman, and Laurence had taken a particular interest in Nick, who, as a robust, precocious, wild-haired child had been allowed to run the length and breadth of Trevennor House and its grounds. Laurence and Nick became close and trusted friends.

At Trevennor House, Nick was met with the unaccustomed sight of Laurence in a woollen nightshirt, cap and shawl. His sharp features were more pronounced, and his chest heaved as he fought for breath through his opened mouth, but his pale grey eyes still showed some vitality. A sweet sickly smell permeated the bedroom.

'Thank you for coming so promptly, Nick,' Laurence greeted him breathlessly.

Nick shook his weakened hand and sat carefully on the side of the bed. 'This day has come all too soon, Laurence. I'm only glad I happen to be back in the neighbourhood and your groom was able to find me.'

Laurence smiled at the young man of twenty-seven years whose height of six foot four inches and broad shoulders, knotted with taut muscle, gave him an advantage in the wrestling rings of Cornwall. His long sandy hair was tied back but still managed to look unruly; his clothes were of rough stout cloth, worn in a casual manner. His appearance might suggest a leaning towards slovenliness but there was nothing unguarded about Nick Nancarrow. He chose to shun the comforts of life and it showed in his hands; skilled at many jobs, they were coarse and tanned from continual outdoor life. His face was strong, confident and alert, etched with his lifelong belief that he was any man's equal. It was a face that knew little of indecision; his deep blue eyes, set under a wide, determined brow, were quick to register distaste and annoyance and he had a ready temper to match. Laurence had never seen the younger man lower his square chin and at times he saw a haughtiness in Nick that reminded him of the very person he wanted to talk about now.

'I knew you'd come to see me by and by but I wanted to talk to you as soon as possible.' He tapped his heaving chest by way of explanation, which made him cough. Nick waited patiently as Laurence wiped spittle from his mouth and took in several ragged breaths. 'It's about to give up on me, this old heart, and I have the weight of nearly five and sixty years upon me. Now before you say that you are sorry, I will tell you that I do not mind, in the least, the prospect of being with my dear wife again. But, Nick, it's a great comfort to have you here. I have little time left and I cannot leave this mortal body without confessing to you that I have a great worry on my mind.'

'Oh?' Nick drew in his straight fair brows. 'Is it something I can help with?'

Laurence beckoned Nick closer. 'I was hoping you would offer to help. I must tell you this quickly before one of the servants or the doctor returns. There are few people I trust as I do you and I believe you are the only one capable of what I have in mind…' Laurence glanced at the door and took a laboured breath. 'As you know, my dear wife and I were not blessed with children, but from my two late sisters I have a nephew and two nieces.

'My sister Prudence married a Mr Kempthorne, a gentleman of small means at St Ives, and produced Edmund and Deborah. Edmund is a wastrel, he's never worked for his own money and as and when he can get his hands on others', he gambles it away. Deborah is as unworthy as her brother and has been left bitter by an unfortunate marriage. After her husband left her she reverted to her maiden name. You may remember Edmund and Deborah from the few occasions they were here when you were a boy.'

Nick recalled the black-haired couple in their youth, the male a handsome beguiling wretch who cheated the local children out of their hard-earned pennies, the female a spiteful sour-faced individual who had looked down disparagingly on Nick. 'And the other niece?'

'Isabel.' Laurence's voice softened. 'Isabel Hampton. She is the daughter of my sister Eliza, who made a good marriage into a wealthy Truro shipping family. Isabel is everything her cousins are not – sweet, kind, loyal and caring. She is much younger than Edmund and Deborah and rather immature for her age of twenty-one. She's vulnerable, Nick, and I fear for her.'

Nick had no difficulty in remembering Isabel Hampton. Although he had kept away from Trevennor House when it received visitors, he had not missed sight of the plain gawkish little girl who shared Laurence's sharp features and grey eyes. Since those days he had heard she had turned out to be a simpering young fool.

'Since my wife died I had planned to leave my estate equally between my nephew and nieces, but because of the Kempthornes' behaviour I have changed my will entirely in Isabel's favour. In six weeks' time she is to be married to an upright young naval officer. At this moment he's at sea, not due back until just before the wedding day. When I'm gone, Isabel will be a double heiress. She will be young, wealthy, vulnerable and unprotected.'

Nick had no idea what Laurence was talking about. 'Unprotected from what?'

'From her cousins, Edmund and Deborah,' Laurence answered in a whisper.

'You're afraid they'll try to relieve her of her inheritance. Is that it?'

Laurence gazed at Nick sombrely. 'I'm very much afraid of more than that, Nick. Thanks to Edmund's wanton manner of living, he and Deborah are almost destitute. They are here constantly begging for money. The last time Edmund was here he demanded five hundred guineas on the strength of what he thought he had coming to him when I die. We quarrelled, and foolishly I informed him that I am leaving everything to Isabel and he and his sister will not receive a penny. Both of them have always been jealous of Isabel's closeness to me and Edmund made threats against her. I am worried that he and Deborah may go as far as to try to murder her.'

It sounded absurd. Laurence Trevennor wasn't usually given to wild fancies but being so close to death perhaps his mind was wandering and imagining things. Nick pressed a reassuring hand on Laurence's shoulder and looked away lest his face give away his thoughts. He poured a glass of water from the china jug on the bedside cabinet. When he tried to hand it to Laurence, it was waved away. Laurence was not fooled.

'I am serious, Nick,' he said, his breathing growing more laboured. With a trembling hand he pressed a cloth over the beads of sweat that had formed on his brow. 'I ask you to take me seriously. If Isabel were to die before her marriage, Edmund and Deborah, as her next of kin, would inherit everything – her wealth and mine. I believe they are unscrupulous enough to stop at nothing to get what they want.'

Nick nodded apologetically and put the glass down. 'Very well, what do you want me to do about it, Laurence?'

Laurence sank back on his pillows, visibly relieved. 'I've sent for Isabel and she will be on her way here now. I have ordered the servants not to inform Edmund and Deborah of my illness, but with my end so near they are bound to find out. Isabel has been staying with the Antiss family on their Comprigney estate, half a mile out of Truro, and will probably be travelling here in their coach with their daughter, Phoebe, who goes everywhere with Isabel. What I want you to do, Nick, is to leave here and meet the coach. I have very little time left to me and I do not want her to arrive here after I am gone because she would refuse to leave until after my funeral. I want you to tell her exactly what I have told you, then I want you to put her under your protection until her wedding day. After that she should be quite safe in the hands of her husband.'

'You know I'll gladly do anything you ask of me, Laurence,' Nick said, 'but why do you think I'm best suited to this task?'

'You have the intelligence and common sense, Nick Nancarrow,' Laurence said, 'and the sort of cunning that might be needed to keep Isabel safe for the next few weeks.'

'Have I, indeed?' Nick returned wryly. 'And what do you imagine I shall do with the young lady to keep her safe?'

'I'll leave that to you,' Laurence said, waving a shaky hand. 'I'm sorry to have to burden you, Nick… Isabel's fiancé has only two somewhat batty elderly aunts. I would have asked Sir Robert Antiss but he is a rather foolish man and could easily fall for Edmund's silver tongue. Moreover, Phoebe has taken a fancy to him.'

'Say no more, Laurence. Leave it to me. You have done much for me over the years, think of it as a favour being returned. But tell me, why should your niece, Miss Hampton, believe a word I say to her? How can I convince her that I have come to her at your wish?'

Laurence showed no concern on these points. 'I've spoken of you many times to Isabel and she knows that I trust you completely. I grant you she may take a little persuading to believe that her life may be in danger.' Laurence pointed to a drawer at the top of the bedside cabinet. 'In there is a ring that belonged to my dear wife. Isabel has one identical to it which I gave her on her twenty-first birthday. She knows I would not part with her aunt's ring lightly. Show it to her and remind her that I consider you to be one of my closest friends, that I trust you as I trusted your father before you. Take out the ring, Nick, and the pouch of money beside it. You may have need of it.'

Nick lifted out the ring, fashioned in a gold circle of two clasped hands. He placed it in the palm of his big rough hand and turned it over slowly with his fingertip. 'I'll do what I can for your niece, Laurence,' he promised solemnly.

The bedroom door handle turned and Nick had just enough time to slip the ring into his breeches pocket, the pouch of money into his jacket. The doctor, the curate and Laurence's housekeeper entered. Nick stood up and as they joined him round the bedside, Laurence coughed, took a deep shuddering breath, smiled to himself, and died.

Nick stayed for a respectful ten minutes before leaving. He was walking back through the village deep in thought and grief when a man ran up to him and thumped a hand down on his shoulder.

'Nick, 'tis good to see you again. Just got back, have 'ee? We must meet up in the Leg of Mutton later.'

Nick gripped the other man's arm firmly. ''Tis good to see you again too, Jimmy.' Jimmy Rowe was a boyhood friend who now worked as a shepherd for Laurence Trevennor. 'How's the family?' Nick was anxious to be on his way but he could not leave his friend without a few words of greeting.

'They'm all right,' Jimmy replied, becoming a little serious at Nick's solemn face. 'Marion's expecting our third any day now. I've come down on behalf of the other shepherds to ask after Mr Trevennor.'

'I've just left there,' Nick replied gravely.

Jimmy Rowe's wide, ruddy-complexioned face fell at Nick's tone. He saw the curtains were pulled across at the tall windows of Trevennor House.

'Oh no,' he groaned and Nick put a hand on his shoulder. 'Not yet, not Mr Trevennor. He wasn't that old, not really. What are we going to do without him?'

'It was very peaceful, about fifteen minutes ago. I'm sorry, Jimmy, but I have to be on my way. There's something I must do.'

Jimmy frowned and looked at Nick curiously. He waited for an explanation but none was forthcoming. Nick bade him farewell and hurried on his way. There was no time to waste.

A short time later he came across the wrecked coach.

–

There was no need to disturb the bodies. There was no doubt they were all dead. The coachman, a brawny, red-faced man with whom Nick had occasionally downed tankards of ale in the local inns, had received a broken neck. The guard's head was crushed. Both men had been robbed of nearly all their clothes and boots. The looter had not had time to disturb the women's clothing before Nick's arrival had made him flee. An overweight gentlewoman, whom he could just recognize as Phoebe Antiss, lay horribly mutilated under the coach. Nick felt a pang of compassion for a servant girl in dark dreary clothes lying at a twisted angle with one of the heavy back wheels flattening her face. For the strong work-toughened man it was not a hard task to lift the wheel and edge it slowly away from its resting place. He took care not to survey the damage inflicted on the human flesh as he let the wheel drop with a thud. Rubbing his hands on the rough cloth of his jacket he walked briskly to what had to be Isabel Hampton's body.

She lay crumpled face down and Nick looked down on her with no emotion. So this was the woman whom Laurence Trevennor had cared so much about. The woman he had wanted to leave his grand house and fortune to and whom he had believed to be in mortal danger. With the evidence of the pile of rocks at the bend in the road it was clearly not a coincidence that the uncle and niece had died on the same day.

He had had no firm thoughts in his mind as to what he would say to Miss Isabel Hampton. But with her dead at his feet it was no longer important; no matter how wicked they might be, Edmund and Deborah Kempthorne would inherit Laurence Trevennor's small fortune after all.

Nick decided to return to Trevennor House with the news of the accident and to return the gold ring Laurence had given him; he did not want to be accused of stealing it. But before moving away he bent down to the body, curious to see what Isabel had looked like.

His eyes travelled downwards from her shoulders, taking in the rips made in her dark blue travelling coat by vicious gorse spines. On the outside of her blood-stained gauntlet glove was a duplicate of the ring tucked inside his pocket. Her striped, pale blue dress and yellow, richly embroidered petticoat were thrown up above her knees, revealing long shapely legs in flesh-coloured stockings, which despite his gruesome perusal Nick admired. Sweeping his gaze back to her head, where a high curled wig of white human hair sat askew, he grasped her shoulder and pulled her round none too gently. His heart gave a queer thump as her body spun round with his hand, sat bolt upright and blinked at him out of huge terrified eyes.

'You're alive!' came his horrified reaction and he almost pushed her away from him. His innermost thoughts observed Isabel Hampton as a remarkably ugly woman. First glance showed her features had not changed, but Laurence's had been vole-like and kindly; here were signs of one used to winning arguments and issuing orders and her grey eyes possessed a startling clarity and directness. There was nothing delicate or feminine about her, and to Nick's mind, with her white-powdered and rouged face, she looked more like a harlot than the young lady of Laurence's deep affections. Her chin was quivering and, terrified by Nick's presence, she began to scream shrilly over and over again.

For some reason it angered Nick and he would have slapped her out of her hysterics if there hadn't been blood trickling from her nose and down over her chin; blood as red as the full painted lips that twisted and contorted and added greatly to her repulsiveness. Instead he gripped her shoulders and shook her violently until her teeth chattered and her screaming gave way to anguished whimpers.

'Shut up, woman!' he ordered, then added in a threatening tone. 'Be absolutely quiet.'

Isabel lapsed into a stunned silence. Her body quaked, her eyes were panic-stricken as they stared back into his. 'T-take anything you w-want b-but please don't k-kill me,' she pleaded. All courage and spirit had deserted her. Her once proud shoulders sagged, her refined voice had lost its fullness and could only beg.

Her whining tone struck at the end of Nick's nerves. 'I'm not a looter,' he said harshly. 'I'm not going to hurt you. I've just come from your uncle's house.' He pulled her unceremoniously to her feet, keeping a hand on her arm to hold her steady while he looked urgently all around. 'We must get away from here in case the looter comes back.'

'You have come from my uncle, Mr Laurence Trevennor? You are taking me to his house?' she asked, recovering some of her composure and with it her natural haughtiness. Her firm cheeks tightened and her chin lifted noticeably as she looked at Nick. It did nothing to reduce his instinctive dislike of her.

'No,' he said bluntly. He tightened his grip on her arm and yanked her along a few steps with him.

Isabel clutched his jacket and stood her ground. There was fear in her eyes again but it was accompanied by hostility and suspicion. 'Why not? I demand to know this instant! I refuse to go anywhere—'

A fierce look silenced her again. 'You're in no position to demand anything! Your uncle died this afternoon and just before he did he put you under my protection.'

'Dead! Uncle Laurence? But… but… I was on my way to him.' Tears were added to the powder, dust and blood streaking Isabel's face. 'I don't believe you.'

'I'll have no more argument, you're coming with me now,' Nick said unsympathetically. For some reason this lady with her shrill voice and ugly face brought out the worst in him. He dragged her along using long strides that made her stumble over her high-heeled shoes and caused more damage to her flesh and the hem of her petticoat from the merciless spines of the dead gorse.

'What do you mean by saying that my uncle has put me under your protection?' Isabel shouted at him, gathering her wits as she was hauled along. 'What do I need to be protected from?'

Nick's mouth was set in a tight stubborn line and realizing she was not going to get an answer, Isabel looked ahead. She saw they were heading for the cliff's edge and let out a terrified scream.

'What are you doing! Stop! Please! Please!' She clawed at Nick's body until he ceased walking 'I'm not going to throw you over the cliff, Miss Hampton,' he said impatiently. 'Although if you don't stop that bloody awful shrieking I shall be sorely tempted. What I'm going to do is make it look as though you wandered away from the scene of the wreck in a daze and fell over to your death.'

'Why?' Isabel screamed. 'Why do you want me to appear to be dead?'

'Because the coach going off the road was probably no accident,' Nick replied. He was anxious for them to be on their way.

Isabel looked back at a trail made of snatches of yellow cloth her petticoat had left on the gorse clumps. Pressing taut fingertips to her forehead, she closed her eyes. She could hardly believe what she was experiencing on this most dreadful of days.

She had been breakfasting with Phoebe Antiss in Phoebe's boudoir when she was told of her uncle's illness and that he was asking for her. Phoebe's father had arranged for the two young ladies, with Isabel's maid, Ginny, to travel immediately to Gwithian. Sir Robert Antiss was to follow on later in the day to escort Phoebe back to an important ball at Truro's High Cross assembly rooms and, if it was required of him, to help Isabel deal with her uncle's funeral arrangements.

Despite the plushness of the coach's pink satin lining and gold silk cushions the journey was most uncomfortable and Ginny had constantly fretted. Phoebe's light-hearted chatter had been unable to break through Isabel's morbid worries over her uncle's health. He had had heart attacks before, from mild flutters to serious failings, but this time Isabel knew he was unlikely to survive. She was desperately worried about him.

The roads had suffered severely during this winter of 1770. Hard frosts, deluges of rain and hail had made the ruts and potholes deeper and wider. Many times the coach had stopped and the guard had been required to make the roads passable.

The hard lurch as they'd rounded the sharp bend had given no warning that Rickardson, the driver, was losing control of the coach and a disaster was to follow.

Since then this brutish common man had not ceased to abuse her. Her whole body ached, her legs felt weak, there were sharp pains in her shoulder. An overwhelming numbness assailed her and she saw for the first time blood on her glove and became aware of the warm sticky wetness trickling from her nose. With a trembling hand she produced a handkerchief from a tiny pocket inside the lining of her coat and dabbed at the tender spot.

'C'mon, we've no time to waste,' Nick said irritably.

'But there is so much I do not understand,' Isabel retorted, looking straight at him. She was a tall woman, nearly five feet ten inches, and held herself at her fullest height even though it hurt her back, but her tilted chin came only to the base of his throat and she felt at an acute disadvantage. For a moment he glared back at her. It was long enough for her to see he had eyes of the same deep sapphire blue as the gems of the necklace Phoebe Antiss wore at important social functions. Phoebe! She had been so preoccupied with her own predicament that she hadn't asked how Phoebe and the others had fared.

'My friend, Miss Antiss...?' Isabel looked round at the wrecked coach and took a step back towards it.

'She's dead,' Nick said unkindly and gripped her arm, forcing her onwards again.

Isabel was horrorstruck. 'Wh-what about Ginny?'

'If you mean the servant girl, she's dead too.'

Isabel's voice rose and sobbed, 'And Rickardson?'

'And him. The guard also.'

They were now inches away from the cliff edge which had an almost sheer drop. Isabel shuddered as a sudden blast of salty air stung her face and buffeted her wig. It was as cold as the shock of learning she was the only survivor from the accident. She reached up to straighten her extravagant coiffure and shrieked as Nick ripped a large piece off the back of her petticoat and tossed the silk over the cliff. She clapped a hand to her throat, swallowing hard as the fabric disappeared from sight, quite unable to look down at the barbarous rocks and the hissing sea that raged about them.

''Tis caught about a third of the way down,' Nick said, satisfied. 'Should do the trick.'

Isabel forgot about her predicament and bridled as the cold draught of air blew her shift onto the back of her legs. 'You are no gentleman,' she uttered angrily.

Nick glanced at the familiar landmarks of Knavocks Point with St Ives beyond it, and in the other direction at St Agnes Head and its namesake Beacon. Then he turned to face Isabel.

'Well, that hardly matters, does it?' He enjoyed the outrage on her sharp white features, which heightened considerably when he swept her up in his arms.

'How dare you! Put me down at once! I may have minor injuries from the coach accident but I am quite able to walk!'

She fought against him as he walked off to the east, the opposite direction to which she had been travelling in the coach. He said gruffly, 'I'm not in the least bit concerned about your injuries. I simply do not want you to leave another trail of yellow cloth as if the gorse was budding early.'

She was light in his arms and Nick did not mind having to carry her. Some of her class habitually over-perfumed themselves but Isabel Hampton smelled of a pleasant light rose fragrance. Nick liked it and kept his nose close to her neck. Isabel tried to keep her face away from his warm breath, but to keep herself steady as he strode along she was forced unwillingly to put an arm round his broad shoulders and over his long sandy hair.

'Where are you taking me?' she asked, trying to hide her helplessness and humiliation in a superior tone.

'To a friend's home,' he told her grudgingly.

'Is it far from here?'

'No, only to Reskajeage Downs.'

'I've never heard of it,' Isabel sniffed, implying the place must be insignificant as Nick was in her view. 'I want to go back and collect my hat and find my purse.'

'You can't, they were taken by the looter. Anyway, you won't be needing them or the rest of your fine clothes for much longer.'

Isabel's face burned. She gulped and stared at the bare scenery of the cliff and the field of ploughed earth that now separated them from the road.

'Who are you?' she demanded suddenly.

Nick had a good mind not to tell her but decided not to risk a fresh outburst of hysterics. 'My name is Nancarrow.'

'Nancarrow? That's familiar to me... I have it, Uncle Laurence's coachman was called Nancarrow.'

'My father,' Nick said shortly, in a tone that forbade further questions.

Isabel made an indignant noise. How ill-mannered this wretched man was. She hated being in such close contact with him, this common creature who treated her so disrespectfully. Why couldn't he tell her exactly what his intentions were? And what had taken place between himself and her uncle? Was Uncle Laurence really dead? She remembered him talking fondly of Nancarrow the coachman's son – this man, evidently – and could not understand why he had liked and trusted him.

She stole a quick look at Nick's stern face, noting its strong planes and angles, straight proud nose, square jaw and perfectly proportioned cheekbones. She found his ruggedness and overt masculinity somewhat overwhelming, but she knew he would have appealed to the amorous appetites of Phoebe Antiss. Poor dear Phoebe. Her mother would grieve for the rest of her life for her only child. If Uncle Laurence truly was dead and she herself had died in the accident, who would grieve for her? She shook off the morbid thoughts and stabbed again at Nick.

'Tell me, why does my uncle believe I need protecting and why did he ask you to take charge of me? I have cousins at St Ives and friends at Truro. Why did he not ask them?'

Nick sighed heavily. 'Did you know you are the main beneficiary under your uncle's will?'

'Yes, he mentioned it to me,' Isabel answered cagily. 'What has that got to do with you?' She could not deny that if her uncle had related the details of his will to this man, Nancarrow, he must truly have trusted him. But could she, should she, trust him?

''Tis your cousins, the Kempthornes, that Laurence was worried about. He firmly believed they mean you a mischief, that they will do away with you to get their greedy hands on your inheritance.'

'Edmund and Deborah? Do me harm?' Isabel snorted. It made her nose bleed again and she dabbed gingerly around it to stem the droplets. 'We have never been close, it's even true to say we don't like one another, but they are all the family I have left now. I cannot believe they would wish me harm. I demand that you take me to Trevennor House immediately!' She tried to wriggle down onto her feet, but Nick retaliated by squeezing her until her ribs felt they would break. She angrily submitted and became still.

'Laurence believed you could be in danger and he asked me to keep you safe until you are married and under your husband's protection. I promised him I would and although I do not relish the prospect I intend to do precisely that.'

'Then you do so against my wishes!'

'I don't give a damn for your wishes, woman!' Nick snarled. 'Only Laurence's. And it seems he might have been right in what he feared. 'Twas no accident that the coach overturned. A pile of rocks was deliberately put on the bend in the road. Your cousins could well be responsible. Laurence was worried enough to ask me for my help and you'll come with me now and do exactly what I say even if I have to beat you into it!'

'You vulgar-mouthed man! How dare you speak to me like that!' Isabel shouted back, her voice so highly pitched it competed with a few excited gulls circling overhead. 'And it's Mr Trevennor to you, not Laurence. You have no right to be so familiar.' Abruptly Nick dropped her to her feet, making no move to steady her as she staggered. He stuffed his fist into his breeches pocket, took out the ring and held it before her glaring eyes. He was absolutely furious.

'Laurence was my friend,' he said through gritted teeth. 'He gave me this ring to show to you, so that you might know you can trust me. He said you were a sweet child, kind and caring. Fate certainly went wrong somewhere while you were growing up into this ugly distasteful woman I have before me. Laurence couldn't have seen the creature you really are, Isabel Hampton, an ungrateful little rich girl who's not worth protecting for any reason. If I had my way I'd give your rotten cousins all of Laurence's money on a silver platter!'

Isabel fainted.

Chapter 2

Charlie Chiverton handed Nick a battered tin mug containing a dark earthy coloured liquid and sat down beside him on the steps of his home, a small one-roomed shack. Dark grey clouds were ominously building up out over the churning sea; soon they would obliterate the glowing slash of orange-pink that proved there was a sun about somewhere in the lowering sky. Charlie sniffed the air.

'Went be no rain tonight though, I d'reckon,' he said conversationally.

It made Nick grin over the dubious contents of his mug. Charlie had not mentioned a single word about his sudden arrival with Isabel Hampton who was lying on Charlie's lumpy rag-stuffed mattress after fainting a bare two feet from the shack. It was as though it was no unusual occurrence for him to appear suddenly with a painted Jezebel of genteel birth dressed in splendid but tattered clothes and spattered with blood.

'Wind's pickin' up though,' Charlie added. ''Twill be ruddy cold tonight.' He threw a piece of foul-smelling mackerel to some gulls who were hopping about at a short distance, sending them into a frenzy to reach it first.

'She didn't even notice your shack,' Nick said incredulously, slowly shaking his head. 'Nor you putting wood on the fire there.' He pointed a finger at the blaze crackling under the tripod, hook and kettle from which Charlie had obtained the hot water for the drinks. 'She was too mad at me for calling her uncle by his Christian name.'

'What uncle's that then?' Charlie asked, finally curious, wiping his damp fishy fingers on his greasy stained neckerchief, then gulping from his own mug.

'Laurence Trevennor. He died this afternoon, about an hour ago,' Nick replied sadly. 'I rescued her from a coaching accident a short while after. There's quite a carnage on the road back-along above Deadman's Cove.'

'Oh? Accident or highwaymen? Tedn't unknown in these 'ere parts.'

'I disturbed a looter picking the area clean, and 'twas obvious by his build who he was – Gyver Pengelly. You can make a safe bet that he was responsible for putting that pile of rocks on the bend in the road. I reckon the driver saw the rocks and pulled the wrong rein as he took the bend. The roads and tracks are a lot worse this winter with the heavy frosts we've had, even on the coast. There's bodies and wreckage scattered everywhere. The roof was yards away in one direction, the box and steps in the other. The coach took a terrible tumble, probably travelling too fast. She in there,' Nick thumbed at the shack behind them, 'was the only survivor.'

Charlie noisily sucked in his breath at the enormity of the accident. 'I know who she is now you say Mr Trevennor was 'er uncle – Miss Isabel. He was very fond of'er, you know, always spoke 'ighly of 'er, 'e did. She'm a strange sort of woman if you ask me, never knew 'ow to take 'er meself when I saw her about the village. Still, after all that's 'appened, poor maid.'

Nick grunted his disagreement. He did not care about Isabel Hampton. 'Just before Laurence died he asked me to look out for her until her fiancé gets back from sea – he's a naval officer.'

Charlie tossed a stick of driftwood onto the fire. 'What about taking 'er to the Bassets? They respected Mr Trevennor and would be glad to 'elp and keep 'er safe till this strange business is all sorted out.' Many years ago Charlie had set up his shack here on land owned by the Bassets, one of Cornwall's foremost noble families. They had allowed him to stay here on the condition that he informed them straightaway of any shipwreck along the North Cliffs, to which they had the right of plunder.

Nick shook his head. 'Laurence asked me to take care of her and it wouldn't be right to ask the Bassets with them in mourning. I got a job over there at Tehidy actually, 'tis why I'm back in these parts.'

'Went be much left of that coach when word gets around,' Charlie said, knowing it was no use to pursue the subject of what was to be done with Miss Isabel Hampton.

'They're decorative enough, some of these gentry coaches, but they aren't made of much,' Nick said. 'Not well-crafted and strong like the wagon I once had. The Antiss coach was all right for Truro's streets, the meeting place of the county's fashionable people,' he added scathingly, 'but not for narrow country tracks and rough coastal roads. My wagon stood up to everything.'

'You'll 'ave one again, boy,' Charlie commiserated. ''E'll be missed,' he went on sadly, referring to Laurence Trevennor. 'Was a good man, did a lot fur the locals, speshly the young 'uns. He liked to walk the cliffs and he stopped many a time to 'ave a word with me when I was out tin-streamin' round the mouth of the Red River. Treated the missus like a lady, 'e did. Not like most of they wealthy buggers who went give 'ee the time of the day and would rather drive 'ee under their coach wheels then give 'ee time to git out of the way. 'Twas Mr Trevennor who bought me new tools back-along to go down the mines when Gyver Pengelly stole 'em. 'E kept me workin' on the copper when I wus fit enough to go down the shafts.'

'Aye, he was one of the best,' Nick agreed, pictures of bygone days of himself exploiting the pleasures of hide and seek in Trevennor House flashing through his mind. 'The parish won't fare well under the fops who could inherit from him.'

'She must be one of 'em.' Charlie tossed his head backwards to indicate the woman lying on his bed.

'Well, she'll be the only one if I can keep her alive for the next few weeks.'

'Aw, aye?' Charlie raised a bushy eyebrow in his peculiarly ugly face. He always reminded Nick of one of Laurence's favourite dogs, a stubby, old wrinkled bloodhound he had kept about the house many years ago. Charlie's weatherbeaten looks suggested he was much older than his forty-two years.

'She's the main one to benefit under Laurence's will. He cut out his other niece and nephew, Deborah and Edmund Kempthorne, and then he feared they would do her harm after he died. People have killed and maimed for less and Laurence said they were always pleading with him for money. Isabel Hampton's got her own fortune as well and the Kempthornes are impoverished. They're an unlikeable pair, could've been them who arranged the coach accident, but whether they'd go as far as that I don't know. That's something I'm going to have to find out.

'Anyway, before he died, Laurence was worried enough over the Hampton woman that when he heard I was back round here he sent for me to protect her until her coming marriage. I was going to try to persuade her to return to Truro and let me keep a watch over her there, but after the events of this afternoon I plan to keep her out of sight. I've made it look like she fell over the cliff to her death. So, you haven't seen me or her, right?'

'Fair enough. 'Tes no one's blamed business who I d'see comin'along 'ere. Don't see many folk, of course, way back from the cliff path as I am. You'm the first in many a week. Can I git 'ee a piece of fish, boy?'

'No thanks,' Nick said, remembering the odious smell of the mackerel thrown to the gulls. Charlie kept rows of dried fish and meat inside the shack. They made his home stink and although he did not seem to mind or notice, Nick could never bring himself to eat any of it. He took a swig from the mug cradled in his hands and screwed up his face.

'You could get the Frenchies to run a better tasting coffee than this, Charlie. No point in risking your neck running contraband that tastes like bilge water and is likely to poison you.'

‘’Tes the way I like it, ’tes the way my missus made it,’ Charlie said, giving a canine grin. ‘You prob’bly don’t know how to make it, you young bugger.’

‘Neither do you,’ Nick grinned back and received a playful punch on the arm.

‘We’ll ’ave a drop of summin’ stronger drekkly. A nice drop o’ rum. Weren’t too much of it in one tub I brung up the cliff, mind you. Damn Frenchies! Can’t trust none of ’em. Could’ve done with a strong pair of arms like yourn the other night. Brung up such a load up ’ere fur me customers, nigh on broke me ruddy back. Tell ’ee what, Nick, there’s a big run comin’ in the night after next, over St Agnes way. Gyver Pengelly’s runnin’ it from land so keep yer ’ead down, lessun thee don’t want to git it blown off. If I was you, I’d keep away from un. ’E’s a cruel man and gettin’ worse.’ Charlie choked up a ball of phlegm and spat it expertly to land and sizzle in the flames a short distance from their feet. ‘There, that’s what I d’think of ’e.’

‘I won’t forget the sight of Pengelly running away from the coach, he’s like a great shambling tree trunk. If he had found the Hampton woman alive, he’d have used her cruelly and probably bashed her head in. I’m not afraid of him,’ Nick said dismissively. ‘He may have beaten me by cheating with his knee in my groin in our last wrestling match at Redruth,’ Nick’s face took on a sudden harshness, ‘but he won’t do it again and one day I’ll have my revenge.’

‘Aye, ’tes rare to ’ave a stickler umpiring a match worse the wear on cheap gin or else Pengelly wouldn’t ’ave got away with it. You’ll ’ave un one day, never fear. The tide don’t go out lessun it comes back in again. But if they Kempthornes put Pengelly up to making that coach go off the road then you’ll be in some danger from ’e.’

‘One thing’s for sure. If Pengelly is innocent of what happened to the coach, he would have stayed around to challenge me and carried on looting. He didn’t stay because he was hoping he wouldn’t be recognised.’

Charlie carefully opened a long, narrow, hand-carved wooden box he had on his lap and took out a white clay pipe. It was the only thing he bothered to keep clean. Before lighting it he looked at Nick.

'I know you want to keep she inside out of sight, but what exactly are you doing along here, young Nick? You aren't takin' she along the cliffs fur the fresh salt air.'

'I've worked out a plan, Charlie. I'm hoping folk will be fooled and believe Isabel Hampton is dead. I'll root around when I go back to Gwithian for Laurence Trevennor's funeral. Hopefully I should get more of an idea whether she's really in danger or not then. I need your help to carry it off.'

–

Isabel lay on Charlie's lumpy and foul-smelling mattress staring up at the dull grey spots of sky visible through a number of holes in the flat roof. The shack was made entirely of ship's planking and other plunder from the maritime graveyard along the shores and coves at the foot of the treacherous cliffs. Charlie had obtained most of it in his younger days, climbing down parts of the granite few other men would have attempted. The shack boasted other items that he had secreted from the mines he had worked down. The dog-faced old miner was proud of his home but to Isabel it was just a lot of old rubbish and smelled horrible.

She had no idea where she was nor how long she had lain here. She could hardly bear to think back over the events that had brought her here, a place not fit for animals to live in.

Isabel closed her eyes and tried to ignore the revolting unwashed smell of Charlie Chiverton's bed and relax her aching body, but Nick Nancarrow's face came to haunt her. She could see the cruel edges of his wide mouth as he had told her that her uncle had died. Even without the accident she would have been too late to be there at the end of his life and Nick Nancarrow had seemed pleased by the fact. How could her uncle possibly have liked and respected such a wretched man? If he really was a friend of her uncle's, how could he justify the way he was treating her, the niece Laurence had adored and left his worldly possessions to? Uncle Laurence would not have approved of Nancarrow's rough behaviour, he would have been terribly upset and she meant to point this out to that smug individual.

She could hear him talking outside with another man, someone older whose Cornish accent was so much broader she hardly understood a word he said. Were they talking about her? Was this other man part of a plot to abduct her? But she couldn't ignore the fact that Uncle Laurence had thought very highly of Nick Nancarrow, and Mrs Christopher, Trevennor's housekeeper, felt the same way; so too did all the villagers of Gwithian, to her knowledge. It was most unlikely he wished to harm her. He had shown her her aunt's ring as proof of her uncle's trust in him. She must cling to that; how else was she going to survive this ordeal?

Isabel sat up stiffly. She rubbed at her aches and pains and looked at her hand. Her ring was still on the blood-stained glove, it had not been stolen – at least not yet. She pulled it off and then removed the glove. She studied her hand and wrist; they were badly bruised and bore the prints of Nick Nancarrow's fingers.

The sound of someone climbing the steps outside made her scramble nervously to her feet. The door of the shack was pushed open to let in the afternoon light and the welcome smell of fresh salty air. Isabel yelped at the sight of Charlie Chiverton, unkempt and ugly as he was, but she swallowed her fears and held herself upright and proud when Nick gently pushed him aside and faced her. His expression showed distaste and hostility.

She said, at her haughtiest, 'I don't believe for one moment that my cousins wish to do me any harm. I demand that you take me away from here at once and straight to Trevennor House where, if my uncle really has died, I can mourn for him.'

'You can demand all you want,' Nick retorted, 'but I made a promise to Laurence and I intend to see it through to the bitter end.'

He was blocking out the light and the relief from the shack's horrible smells. He was overbearing and despite her outrage Isabel was intimidated.

'I... I won't be—'

'That's right,' Nick shut her off. 'You won't be anything.' He ignored a prick of guilt. He knew he had treated her abominably since discovering she was alive. Laurence would have been mortified and disappointed in him that he could not show his beloved niece even the smallest respect due her station in life. He could sense Charlie looking curiously at him. 'I'm taking you to a friend's house at Crantock,' he told Isabel moodily. 'We'll need to travel without arousing too much interest so you'll have to change out of those clothes.'

'And if I refuse?' Isabel said, incensed at the very suggestion and clutching protective hands to her coat front.

'You only have Hobson's choice in the matter, woman, and you know what that means,' Nick snapped, finding that he was enjoying the mirth Charlie was taking no pains to disguise at the turn of conversation. 'My friend here will lend you something to wear.'

Isabel stared at Charlie Chiverton, aghast. 'I am not going to wear anything of his!' She shuddered as Charlie winked at her.

'Not mine, ma'am,' he said, surprising and galling Nick by giving Isabel a perfectly executed bow. 'Yer too tall fur my things to pass fur a boy. I got a few things 'ere which belonged to my missus.'

Isabel found she could follow most of what Charlie said now she was face to face with him. She acknowledged his salute with a curt movement of her head and hoped she had found someone of a kinder spirit.

'What did you do that for?' Nick hissed at Charlie while nudging him with an elbow.

'Nothin' wrong with a few manners, boy,' Charlie chuckled. 'Mistress Trevennor was a fine lady and I always belonged to be respectful to 'er, and 'er niece shall git the same. Now git yerself back outside and I'll find the young lady 'ere some clo'es to wear 'n' leave 'er to change in peace.'

Nick frowned heavily at Charlie and turned to Isabel. 'Make sure you take off all that finery, and I mean everything, your shift, stays, everything. I don't want anything left on you that could give us away. Make haste, I want to get on. And wash all that muck off your face.' He left the shack.

With her face a bright red under its mask of white powder, Isabel pounced on Charlie. 'Please help me. That man, Nancarrow, hates me, I fear—'

Charlie broke off her anguished plea by shuffling her aside to rummage in a small chest at the head of the bed.

'There's nothin' I can do fur 'ee, Miss Hampton, but you got no call to be in fear of Nick. He's a good man, a damned good man, went find none better in my reckonin'. Yer uncle thought so too, don't 'ee forget now. Nick'll see 'ee all right. 'E promised Mr Trevennor afore 'e died an' Nick'd die 'imself afore 'e'd break a promise. You'll be all right just as long as thee do what 'e says.'

Isabel wrung her hands in desperation. 'But he is such a beastly man. He hates me.'

Charlie looked up from the chest from which he was tossing items of shabby female clothing onto the low bed. There was a cheeky sort of grin on his weathered face and Isabel got the impression she was looking into the face of an impish child.

'Nick hates all the gentry, the only one he could abide was your uncle.'

'It seems I have no choice but to obey him and go along with this ridiculous scheme,' she said mournfully.

'Aye, 'twould be wise, lessun 'e comes back in and strips thee naked,' he nodded at the clothing, 'puts some of they on 'ee and drags thee along by yer 'air. 'E's a straightforward man and don't take to bein' messed about.'

The thought of the big powerful man outside doing such intimate and outrageous things to her caused Isabel to clap her hands over her mouth to stifle a squeal of horror. It would not have been so bad for Phoebe Antiss. She would probably have seen the whole terrible situation as an opportunity for an adventure. If only she had survived the coach accident. They would have been in this together. Oh, why think of Phoebe now? She could not help her and was beyond help herself. Isabel knew she ought to be grateful to be alive but she wished she had some of Phoebe's extrovert personality. Thoughts of Phoebe brought on tears which she choked back.

'Are those the clothes?' she asked Charlie, putting her hands to her cheeks to hide their redness.

'My late wife's. They're all I've got left of 'er.'

'I will do my best to look after them and as soon as I possibly can I will have them returned and my own clothes collected.'

'She never 'ad much in the way of clo'es,' Charlie said quietly, smoothing his grubby palms over a brown calico dress, 'but take what you want. Wrap yerself up warm, miss. 'Twill be ruddy cold tonight.'

Isabel shivered and suddenly realized she was very cold; her predicament seemed only to escalate. With all that had happened, she was now to be forced to disrobe completely in this cold squalid building and put on some rags belonging to a dead woman who had probably cared nothing at all about personal hygiene. She shuddered violently. If the clothes were anything like the bed, they might be crawling with lice.

Charlie went outside and she heard him talking to Nick. She crossed the few feet of planking to peep out through a crack in the door to see which way the two men were facing. She could see their backs and gulped with relief that neither were peeking in at her. She must hurry. Nick Nancarrow was as impatient as he was horrid and might walk in on her at any moment.

There were no bows, ruffles or lace on the two dresses Charlie had put on the bed. The other one was a dull blue and looked as if it was made of sailcloth. A black knitted shawl was unexpectedly soft and warm to the touch. All the clothes, including an off-white muslin tucker and a pair of rolled-up thick stockings, smelled of the same unpleasant odour that filled the shack. There were no shifts or petticoats and Isabel did not relish the thought of having the coarse material of either dress against her skin.

She found it difficult taking off her own clothes. All her life she'd had a maid to attend her and her long tapering fingers were cold and agitated. She was fearful that one or both men would come in before she was reclothed. She reluctantly laid her coat and dress on the dirty bed. They had been worn only once before and she hated to see them ravaged by the accident and the gorse. Taking off her stays, she pulled her shift down over her shoulders and arms then held it up across her breasts while rapidly inspecting the numerous abrasions and bruises she had received.

She picked up the brown dress because it looked less worn and put it on. It was not as rough on her skin as she'd feared; it had been given a warm soft lining, presumably to keep out the cold. Pushing her shift down over her feet, Isabel wore nothing now but the late Mrs Chiverton's dress. She felt particularly vulnerable, as though she had left her familiar cosseted life behind her for ever and been plunged into a hostile new world that promised nothing but hardship and possible danger. When she'd put on the rest of the shabby clothes, she carefully folded her own. Not wanting Charlie to touch them, she placed them with her wig in the chest.

There was just her face left to wash. Looking about the dingy room, its walls blackened by tallow candles and pipe smoke, she located a chipped bowl half filled with water. It looked clean and she hoped it was. A precautionary sniff, then she washed her face thoroughly with her hands, shivering at the icy contact but finding it soothing to her grazed lip and tender nose. Returning to the chest, she gently dried her face on her petticoat then ran stiff fingers through her hair, now hanging long and free.

She would have liked a mirror to see how she looked and with a sinking feeling she realized that however she looked now, the first time Nick Nancarrow saw her she must have looked even worse. Then she was angry with herself. Why should she care what that vulgar man thought of her?

'You 'aven't got much daylight left,' Charlie was saying as she stepped outside.

Both men turned and stared at Isabel. Apart from the obvious fact that she had changed her clothes, she looked quite different. Her hair was a dark honey-brown; thick and shining, it fell in soft waves to below her shoulders. With the powder, paint and blood washed off, her skin, though pale, glowed clear and smooth, making her eyes appear a bright deeper grey. Her features seemed to have lost their sharpness. Her nose was small and pert, her eyebrows curved like a true aristocrat's, and although she could not be said to be beautiful, her face was enhanced by full red lips; slightly pouting and sulky, they tilted gently upwards, and looked to Nick to be baby-soft.

Devoid of her hooped clothes, she stood tall and straight on the top step of the shack, hands held firmly together, head up to reveal a slender white throat under an arrogant well-practised expression.

'Is this satisfactory?' she asked sarcastically while looking directly at Nick.

He ignored her.

'We'll 'ave to do summin' 'bout they shoes,' Charlie murmured, tweeking his ear. Isabel's painted kid shoes were clearly visible under his wife's dress. 'I got none left from the missus.'

'They'll have to do until we get to Portreath,' Nick said irritably.

Isabel looked down at her shoes as she stepped onto the iron-hard ground, glad she did not have to sacrifice them too. She made eagerly for the fire, holding out her hands to the flames which bent this way and that now the wind had picked up.

'It's freezing up here on the cliffs,' she said to Charlie.

'What do you expect in February?' Nick snapped. He pushed past her, took the three steps in one leap, disappeared inside the shack and immediately reappeared carrying her bundle of clothing and wig.

'What are you doing with my clothes?' she demanded, trying to wrest them away from him. Nick raised them up out of her reach, his eyes travelling over her ears, wrists and throat.

'Where's all your jewellery?' he asked suspiciously. 'What have you done with it?'

'I have only the ring my uncle gave me,' she said, quickly hiding her hands under the shawl.

'Give it to me,' he ordered, thrusting out his hand.

'No!'

Her protest was of no consequence. He pushed the clothes into Charlie's arms, pounced on her, wrenched her hands from the shawl and pulled the ring off her finger. Spitting in fury, Isabel slapped his face.

'Don't you try that too many times!' he growled.

'What do 'ee want done with these then?' Charlie said from behind the clothes, his hooded eyes twinkling as he gazed at Nick's livid red cheek.

'Throw them on the fire,' Nick replied in icy quietness.

He stopped Isabel's lurch towards Charlie by tightly holding her arms and she watched horrified as Charlie dumped her clothes on the ground and obediently threw her petticoat onto the flames.

'My missus never wore none of this,' he said, holding up her stays and shift in either hand.

Isabel was outraged at these men touching her intimate apparel; she felt as though they had violated her. 'No! How dare you do this! Don't you dare destroy any more. They're all nearly new,' she screamed, struggling to free herself from Nick's grip and raking long nails across the back of his hand.

'Never mind,' Nick hissed into her ear, 'you can buy a whole lot more with your inheritance – if I can keep you alive.' He laughed when she called him a heathen, and seemed not to care when Charlie looked disapprovingly at him.

Nick knew he was going too far with his cruel behaviour but he could not help himself. Her continual outrage at his actions to protect her exacerbated the hatred he felt for her class, and added gall to the fact that he had no wish to be her protector. As the clothes burned, he let Isabel go and watched her unfeelingly while she grimaced as Charlie smashed the whalebone hoop and tossed the pieces into the blaze. The very air between Isabel and Nick seemed to crackle like tread on hoar-frosted ground.

'What have you done with my ring?' Isabel shouted at him.

'Nothing yet. I'll find a suitable hiding place or throw it over the cliff. I don't want any evidence of your being… a lady, the same as I don't want anything to show you have been here,' he said, looking at the fire.

'I see, and the ring which my uncle gave you?' she asked pointedly.

Nick was angered by her tone. 'I have no intention of selling it, if that's what you're getting at! The first opportunity I get I shall return it to its original place in Laurence's bedroom.'

He suddenly snatched one of Isabel's wrists and before she could execute a second slap across his face he grabbed the other to look critically at her fingernails and then the marks left on his hand. 'Your nails are too long. Bite them off or I'll do it for you. Your hands are too clean but I daresay they'll get dirtied soon enough.' He let her go and she stormed off a few paces and turned her back on him.

Nick looked at Charlie and held out a hand in friendship. 'Thanks, Charlie,' he said sincerely. 'I'll make sure you get your wife's things back.'

''Tes a bit 'arsh, takin' she across the cliffs, Nick. Can be an 'ard journey this time of year, 'twill be damned 'arder fur a lady.'

'I know it sounds dramatic, Charlie, but after the coach accident I feel I must keep her out of sight until I can find out if Laurence's suspicions about her safety were well-founded. If anyone suspects she's still alive they'll expect her to take refuge in an inn or comfortable cottage somewhere, travelling by road. The last place they'll expect her to be is up on the cliffs.'

'Aye, I s'pose yer right. Mind 'ow you go then.' Charlie grinned impishly. 'Both of 'ee.'

'Please accept my thanks too.'

Nick had not expected this from Isabel and he stared at her again. She moved towards Charlie, her hand extended. With much embarrassment he wiped his dirty hands down the sides of his even dirtier breeches and gingerly shook the proffered soft hand.

'Where are you taking me?' she asked Nick, as if he was the lowest of servants.

He did not hide his hostility in the reply. 'I've already told you, woman, we're moving on to Crantock.'

'My name is Miss Hampton,' she said condescendingly, as if he was too stupid to have comprehended before that she should be addressed as such. 'And how are we to get to Crantock?'

A look of gloating satisfaction crossed Nick's face. 'We walk,' he said.

'What? Crantock must be over thirty miles away!'

'More like twenty across the cliff top,' Charlie offered consolingly as he passed Nick a packed canvas bag.

'The cliff top?' Isabel looked wildly from one man to the other. Nick was gazing at her as if she was stupid. 'You don't really expect me to walk across the cliffs? They're dangerous! And it's nearly dark! We cannot possibly travel across the cliffs at night.'

'We'll manage,' Nick said lightly. 'And the sooner we start the sooner we'll get there. A gentry coach is a rare sight and a damaged one is as good as a wrecked ship, the area will be crawling with people dismembering it and someone might come along this way to talk to my friend here about it.'

Isabel shuddered at the thought of the coach being pulled apart until nothing was left of it. She had heard many coloured tales of what the wreckers could do to a sailing vessel unfortunate enough to be swept onto the perilous shores. She had seen for herself, while out with her uncle, what a ship looked like after it had been done over. She had visions of a swarm of human ants carrying off even the smallest piece of the coach for firewood or trophy, and of the undignified treatment the four bodies they had left behind would receive, but her upbringing forbade her to show her distress.

'Can we not hire horses and travel by road? I am an accomplished horsewoman.'

Nick would not have believed it if the words had not come from her own lips. Isabel Hampton looked the kind of lady who found half a dozen steps from carriage to doorstep overtaxing.

'We couldn't travel incognito that way,' he said gruffly. 'I'm well known along the roads and villages. Folk don't expect to see me with a woman holding me back and the moment you open your shrieking great mouth your voice would give us away.'

Not waiting for a response he threw the strap of the bag over his shoulder and bade Charlie farewell. Ordering Isabel to follow him, he started off walking east. Isabel stamped her feet, gave Charlie a look of helplessness and followed angrily in Nick's wake. Charlie watched them, a cold wind beginning to snatch at his clothing. The same wind carried the sound of Isabel's protests to him long after the warring couple had disappeared from sight.

Chapter 3

Edmund Kempthorne sat in his late uncle's favourite armchair, slouched and content, before a roaring log fire in the parlour of Trevennor House. Wood smoke curled from the flames and filled his nostrils with a pleasant scent; he felt utterly satisfied with life.

He had removed the adjustable lectern on the chair's worn leather arm, which Laurence had used for reading, and placed his own arm there in its stead, his hand holding a glass. Between sips of the excellent brandy, he triumphantly studied the finer aspects and ornamentation of the room. The furniture was all English, mostly walnut and made that century. The walls were covered with paintings and tapestries of Greek tragedies. On the mantelshelf and tables were several silver and bronze candlesticks and his aunt's silver spoon collection. Edmund took in everything at his leisure. To the marble busts of his uncle and aunt on top of a bookcase he raised his glass and gloatingly drank to their ill health and its consequences. His gaze rested on the elaborate plaster overmantel of the fireplace, which looked as if it belonged in a much larger room.

The woven firescreen was put aside and lying behind it were two young bloodhounds. Not sharing the same contentment as the man who believed he was their new master, they glanced up at him often and nervously. Edmund had tried to put his feet on one of the dogs but it had moved out of his reach and the other dog had lain down fretfully beside it. Edmund had laughed heartily. He had had such good fortune today, no one, and especially not two humourless dogs, could upset him.

Daylight was shut out of the room by heavy black silk curtains, pulled across at every window to show the house was in mourning. Edmund had angered the servants by insisting myriads of candles be lit in the parlour so he could recline there; they believed he should be keeping a long vigil of prayer in the deathbed chamber at the side of his dead uncle. Edmund hated the dark, and he particularly hated death, but it was not for those reasons he felt no urge to mourn. He was delighted that Laurence Trevennor was dead.

Edmund's sister came into the room and he held up his empty glass and grinned wickedly. 'Get me a refill of the old man's delectable untaxed brandy, sister dear,' he said in his velvety voice, 'and don't look so miserable. I'm not grieving over our dear departed uncle, and with that silly flit of a girl from Truro being so conveniently killed on the same day, all of her fortune and,' he opened his effeminate hands to encapsulate the house and its contents, 'all of this is now ours. It couldn't have worked out better if we had planned it ourselves. Our dreams have come true all on the same day. What more do you want, Deborah?'

'Some civility from the servants in this house for a start, especially that Christopher woman!' Deborah snapped, but it was sympathy she was looking for from Edmund, her chagrin was never directed at him. 'They would do well to remember that they are our servants now and if they want to stay in our employment they should not speak to me like a lackey! It's enough to bring on one of my headaches.' She put the back of her hand dramatically to her forehead. Deborah thought mistakenly that such gestures gave her a delicate femininity.

'Don't worry, Debs, when everything is finally settled we'll move to Truro,' Edmund said brightly.

Deborah refilled Edmund's glass, and helping herself to a small port wine she gave the bloodhounds a disapproving look as they scuttled away under a distant table. She sat down sedately in the chair opposite Edmund and rubbed her fingertips over her taut forehead. When no blinding pain threatened to materialize and spoil the afternoon, she smiled at her brother.

'That's better, Debs. Just think, no more freezing half to death in that garret of a cottage at St Ives. This is our life from now on.' Edmund slipped even further down in the green upholstered chair with a look of sweet contentment on his deceptively handsome face.

Deborah looked at him fondly. At thirty-six she was four years his senior and from Edmund's birth she had treated him as a doll-like creature to be played with and fussed over. Edmund had also been adored by their mother, the female servants and Laurence Trevennor's wife, who could see no ill in him. Not unexpectedly he grew up taking it for granted he would be treated in the same way by every woman who crossed his path. With his soft brown hair, dark eyes, clean-cut features and ever-ready charming smile, he was rarely disappointed.

After their parents died, Deborah had pandered to his every need, but Edmund's profligacy had quickly left them penniless. Deborah had not the face or disposition to secure even a second-rate marriage but she took up the offer made by an unwise middle-aged office clerk who believed he would further his position by marrying a kinswoman of the gentry. He would be the source of a regular, although small, income to the Kempthornes, and to the clerk's horror, instead of him moving into their comfortable large house on the outskirts of the fishing village, they left it to be sold to cover some of their debts and moved into his cramped and austere cottage closer to the heart of St Ives.

Within a month of Deborah's constant complaints of having to live at such close quarters to the hardworking fisherfolk, and realizing he would soon be bled dry of his humble savings, the lawyer's clerk salvaged what he could and abandoned his wife, leaving her and her parasite brother destitute.

The couple spent the next ten years living on their wits and Edmund's expertise at cheating at the card tables. The earnings of prostitutes contributed too; the women were happy to help keep him in fine wines, good food and fashionable clothes in return for introductions to wealthy clients. Deborah was fiercely jealous of any woman he was involved with but she found that if he was kept in reasonable luxury and did not have to lift a finger to work, she could manipulate the greater part of his life and keep him living with her.

She took pleasure at the sight of him now. Although they had barely kept their heads above water over the last few years she had always managed to pay Edmund's tailor, a remarkably talented Jewish man who lived in a quiet street in Hayle. She liked to see Edmund well turned out. His natural elegance was evident even while he lounged in the chair. The silver-plate buttons of his full dress coat and waistcoat of indigo watered-tabby silk shone like stars in the candlelight. His linen shirt was graced by ruffles of needle lace, and the buckles on his shoes, won in a card game, were real silver.

Deborah had stinted herself and allowed the cottage to fall into a serious state of disrepair to enable Edmund to enjoy his excessive lifestyle. She attempted to look like a lady of fashion by having alterations made to cast-offs of wealthy gentlewomen, but nothing could soften her severe face or make her stout, big-boned body appealing to the eye. She wore a black saque-backed dress, altered so badly that the wide pleats falling from her broad shoulders at the back hung crookedly, giving her bulky form an off-balanced look. Her hair, muddy in colour and darker than Edmund's with no glossy shine, was streaked with premature grey and piled high under a white lawn cap tied under her wide chin.

'Yes, Edmund, we have been fortunate today,' she said, allowing herself another rare smile. 'We came here today to beg mean old Uncle Laurence to pay off one of your gambling debts and to lend us a few measly pounds, only to find that he had passed away peacefully just an hour before. Then we learn that the sole beneficiary under his will, Isabel Hampton, has also met her end in a tragic accident.'

'You don't look very tragic, Debs,' Edmund observed, with a twinkle in his lazy eyes.

Deborah's expression changed and her true nature showed itself in full venom. 'Now things will be as they should have been years ago. The old man and that haughty miss treated us like dirt! Us! Their only relatives. Oh, St Ives was not good enough for the gracious Miss Isabel Hampton to visit us there. There was too much of a smell of fish for her high tastes. Well, she's got what she deserved. Smashed on rocks and rotting in the sea! There won't be any grand wedding next month for us to be overlooked at, to be paraded only as the poor relations. There will be no alliance with the Grenvilles of Falmouth for her to boast about while we slowly waste away unprovided and uncared for.'

'She always seemed a delicate little thing to me,' Edmund said thoughtfully. 'A little taller than the average woman perhaps but I thought it added something to her proud bearing. I liked that about her, that and the way her body moulded its way deliciously in and out.' He moved his free hand in a slow figure of eight, picturing it wandering over Isabel's body.

'Really, Edmund.' Deborah had never liked his indelicate talk.

'I planned to take her one day, hopefully while still a virgin. It would have been exquisite.'

'I can't see why. In my opinion she was most unattractive.'

'No virgin, especially no young virgin, is unattractive, my dear. Besides, after I had seduced her I could have demanded a pretty sum of money to be kept from telling Richard Grenville that he had married soiled goods.'

'And what if she had not fallen for your fatal charm, Edmund?' Deborah said tartly, but again the sharpness was not aimed at him. 'That little bitch was too mean to give anything away.'

'I daresay I could have got round her for a tidy allowance every year. She probably wouldn't have wanted to live in this house, not with a huge residence at Truro and the home Grenville would have provided for her. I'm sure she would have allowed us to live here.'

'You are being too kind to our cousin's memory, my dear,' Deborah demurred. 'Your charm may not always get you what you want. Let's not forget that it did not make much impression on Uncle Laurence. He was very cruel to you, disapproving of you having a game or two of cards. You were born a gentleman, what else did he expect you to do with your leisure hours? Most of the best of society play the tables. If he had had the goodness to settle a substantial sum of money on you and provide us with a respectable income, you would never have been tempted to keep on gambling to cover your debts.'

'Mmmm, it is a pity I cannot play a false card occasionally in the grander clubs, but I could never get away with it like I can with the fools around St Ives. One has to be careful; the best of the professionals play in the grander places and some of them get very ugly if they don't lose fairly.'

'Quite so, but there is no reason Uncle Laurence should have disapproved of your owing money to an establishment such as Almack's of London. Only the leading members of society are allowed in through its doors. Well, now we will be able to settle all our debts, rent out the cottage at St Ives for a good sum of money and live here in luxury, as two dignitaries of this little parish, until we can move up to Truro. That is where we belong, the place where the country's fashionable people meet, an important coinage town and port. I can see us now, walking down its wide streets together. Let's go there in a few days' time, Edmund. We can see the shops, eat at the Red Lion Inn, mingle with those we are now equal to.'

Edmund coolly stared his sister in the face and wondered what she would say if she knew his debts amounted to several thousand pounds more than the estimated value of their uncle's estate. It was a good thing Isabel Hampton was dead and her wealth was at his disposal. He found it amusing to think of the famous London gaming club's debt collectors scouring for the nonexistent Cornish baronet, Sir Francis Rashleigh of Launceston, the pseudonym he had invented for himself along with a clever disguise to gain entry there. It was most useful, he reminded himself, to have acquaintances in the acting profession to teach you different voices and how to use powder and paint skilfully to change your appearance.

'Mmmm, I'm comfortable here. No, let us stay here for a while,' he said languidly, tapping a manicured fingertip on his straight white teeth.

'Very well,' Deborah said doubtfully, 'as you please. But those wretched servants will dance to my tune or they'll be out on the streets.' Her small shrewish eyes fell on the two bloodhounds, another source of irritation to her. 'Those creatures can go out in the stables. I won't have them spreading their fleas and leaving their revolting smell in the house.'

Edmund looked at the dogs who both hung their heads and looked nervously away, sensing Deborah's dislike of them. He pursed his smooth pink lips and stroked his cheek, a gesture that sometimes presaged a tantrum.

'Oh, I don't know, Deborah. They aren't hurting in here. Dogs, particularly bloodhounds, are a part of Trevennor House.'

It was decided. The dogs would stay in the house.

'Have you sent to St Ives for our things?' Edmund asked.

'Yes, my dear, but only for our clothes and personal effects. We'll let the cottage furnished. I don't want any of that cheap and gaudy stuff in here letting us down when people call on us.'

'And Mary Ellen? Have you sent for her?'

'Don't be foolish, Edmund! I will never understand why you desire the company of that common little trollop and that bastard child of hers.'

'That child is also my child,' he answered coldly. 'A pretty little girl of three years old and her name is Morenwyn.' His features took on a cruel edge. 'I'll thank you, Deborah, not to refer to her by that label ever again.'

This was one thing that Deborah continually fought against and over which she was prepared to risk her brother's wrath. 'How can you be sure the brat is your child, Edmund? And even if she is, the girl knew what she was doing when she lay with you. No man can be held responsible for the consequences of that type of liaison.'

'Oh, Morenwyn is mine, most definitely mine. She is the living image of me. I want her and Mary Ellen here with me. Besides,' he added in a sultry voice, 'Mary Ellen satisfies me in a way no other woman can. I like to see her often.'

'It's only a few miles from here to St Ives, Edmund,' Deborah argued, battling against what was coming next.

'It would do no harm to have them here,' he persisted.

Deborah leaned her ungainly body forward. 'As servants or equals?'

'I think somewhere in between.'

'We would be talked about,' Deborah warned.

'I don't care a jot about what any narrow-minded little nobody in this nondescript village might say about us. I'll soon have them all weighed up – the men who are prepared to have a wager behind their wives' backs, the women who are prepared to do… other things behind their husbands' backs. Mind you, Debs,' he went on seriously, 'we were not popular in St Ives. The churchgoers spurned us and they are the ones who carry the weight in any place. So I suppose it would pay us to be nice to the local people of Gwithian. I want you to be able to entertain the ladies to tea, to be respected. It might be to our advantage to carry on some of Uncle Laurence's charitable works.'

'In that case we had better go upstairs and weep over the disgusting remains with the curate when he comes back. With the church just across the road and the curate's house next to ours, we ought to try to make friends with him and that scrawny wife of his. And I suggest you leave that lady to favour only her husband. But if we are to be on good terms with the curate and his wife,' Deborah added artfully, 'don't you think it would be unwise to install your mistress and her child in this house?'

'Not if we are seen to be offering a respectable home with good Christian principles to an unfortunate homeless widow and her child,' he answered back.

Deborah tightened her thin lips, tossed back her head and inwardly admitted defeat – but only for the time being. She was not going to share Edmund with anyone else for long.

'We had better put on suitable mourning faces,' she said. 'That fat Antiss woman's father will be here quite soon. He will pass the wrecked coach on his way here and I'm afraid it is your duty to inform him that his daughter is dead.'

Edmund shuddered and cursed his brandy glass for being empty. He had forgotten about the other corpse in the house, laid out in the bedchamber next to their uncle's.

'This house is full of death and the stables are no better. I shall be glad when Antiss has carted his daughter and servants back to Truro where they belong. Pity about Phoebe though.'

'Oh?' Deborah said sharply. 'Why do you say that?' Edmund smiled, very slowly, and his face slipped back into contentment. 'She visited Gwithian with Isabel last year, and while our cousin was out riding with Uncle Laurence, I happened to pay a call here and found Phoebe alone. She entertained me exceedingly well.'

'I do not wish to hear any more about your rapacious appetites, Edmund. Come,' Deborah said, rising to her big flat feet. 'We must prepare ourselves for our visitors. We will have a stream of people calling here to pay their respects to the old man.' Edmund stood up, just an inch taller than his sister, and picking up his malacca cane he rubbed the brass top with his thumb. 'Phoebe would have been a good catch if I had taken her to wife. I think she found me most agreeable and I found her humour very stimulating. I always found it rather odd that she befriended our more serious virgin cousin.'

'They're all the same, that sort,' Deborah said spitefully. 'If you've got enough money and property it matters not at all if you are as fat as a cow or as sharp-faced as a rat, you fit in. If you have no money or property, you're shunned, as we have been all our lives. Anyway, Phoebe Antiss is dead and you don't need to marry anyone for their money now.'

'I suppose she really is dead.' Edmund said, in a sudden moment of panic.

'Well, if she isn't who do you suppose the mangled heap lying upstairs is?'

'No,' Edmund said impatiently. 'Not her, Isabel.'

'Why do you say that?' Deborah asked in alarm.

'Well, it's just a thought. I… I suppose her body will be washed up in a few days' time.'

'It was seen on the rocks at the bottom of the cliff,' Deborah said. 'The man who brought the news told Mrs Christopher so.'

Edmund looked comforted. Deborah knew he would not be able to bear their new life of wealth and comfort suddenly being snatched back from them. She clenched her fists and made a fierce silent vow that she would never, never be poor again. Then holding up her head proudly, she stalked out of the room and shouted fresh orders at the servants.

Chapter 4

Nick walked briskly, keeping alert for signs of anyone coming towards them or moving up behind them. Isabel lagged a long way behind, her constant complaints lost in the roar of the Atlantic Ocean that stretched three thousand miles from the foot of the cliffs.

They were travelling along a narrow, well-worn path, trodden smooth by generations of villagers from Gwithian and of Portreath, the tinners and copper miners, the bands of cautious but efficient smugglers. It was a fairly straight course over flat, stark cliff top, moving into the teeth of the wind. Isabel felt worn and buffeted and was constantly in fear of being blown off the cliff edge. Ominous dark clouds were building up on the sea's horizon and inland to the south over the granite mass of Cam Brea which could be seen for miles with its castle perched on the top.

Clutching her shawl under her chin to protect her cold ears, Isabel tried unsuccessfully to keep up with Nick. Her high-heeled shoes were torturing her feet and making her steps clumsy and unsafe. The dress she was wearing was a poor fit and chafed the tender skin under her arms and she heartily wished the wind would blow away the offensive mouldy smell left on the clothes from Charlie Chiverton's shack. To add to her misery, her pleas were being ignored.

'Will you please slow down!' she shouted at Nick's hostile back. She saw his shoulders stiffen, but he kept up his striding pace.

Isabel ran a few steps and screamed across the divide he deliberately made, 'Don't keep ignoring me! I told you to slow down.'

Nick stopped, turned and scowled. 'Were you asking me something?'

'I want you to slow down and I did say please the first time,' she snarled back, furious and exasperated, walking as fast as she could to close the gap between them.

Nick gave an offensive grunt and carried on, slowing his steps only very slightly. Isabel sighed heavily to stop herself from shouting abuse, the results of which she knew would use up valuable energy and impede her progress.

Reskajeage Downs was soon left behind and a short time later Isabel slumped to the ground, her breath laboured and her head reeling. The ground was hard and freezing cold and there was nothing to shelter her from the biting wind that chilled her to the bone.

Nick had gone round the outward curve of a small headland and waited impatiently for Isabel to come into sight. He had spent most of the time since leaving Charlie's shack mulling over where they would spend the night. There was half an hour of daylight left and at the rate Isabel was holding them up they would not make Portreath, which was only two and a half miles away, before dark. It would be possible to walk safely by the aid of the lantern he had with him but a light bobbing its way down off the high platform of cliff into Portreath would arouse unwanted interest. Folk would be curious about any woman in his company, and him a man well known for the wanderlust in his soul, who fought shy of human responsibilities. And if they heard Isabel Hampton speaking in her irritating cultured voice they would be the talk of the North Cliffs for weeks. If Edmund and Deborah Kempthorne got to hear of it, they might well come to the correct conclusions.

A short distance before Portreath there was a cave halfway down the cliff. Better to spend the night there and move on to

Portreath in the early morning. It did not matter if it took a day or two to reach Crantock; all that was important was to keep the woman out of sight as much as possible.

'Where is that damned woman?' Nick muttered under his breath, craning his strong neck for sight of her. 'Probably fallen down a rabbit hole.'

He marched back and came upon Isabel slumped on the ground. He ordered her crossly to get up.

'I cannot go any further,' she said, her face lowered and voice muffled in the shawl. The coach accident had taken more out of her than she had realised and she was disappointed with herself. As a fit horsewoman she had thought she would cope rather better on this enforced trek.

'We have less than thirty minutes of daylight left to walk a couple of miles and climb down a hundred feet of cliff. Now get up and let's get on, unless you want to spend the night out in the open.'

Isabel's head jerked up and Nick's impatience was not lessened by the anguish on her face.

'But I cannot possibly climb down a cliff, not in these shoes. My feet are hurting terribly as it is. Surely we can go on and spend the night at the nearest inn or even go back to that dirty little man's shack.'

'Have you no brains at all, woman? Must I explain everything to you over and over again?' Yanking Isabel to her feet, he dragged her along. Her shawl fell from her head and the wind whipped her hair across her face. 'You are supposed to be dead!' he shouted in her ear. 'Your life is believed to be in danger and we can't afford to attract attention to ourselves, which we surely will if we're seen coming down off the cliff at night. Folk will take us for smugglers for one thing and for another we are not going to go back to my friend's home and put him at possible risk. Do you understand?'

Isabel fought him off as she was hauled along and he let her go. 'How dare you! I will not be spoken to in such an outrageous manner and don't you dare touch me again!' Her highly pitched voice grated on Nick's nerves.

'You've got no ruddy choice if we want to get on.' He prodded her onwards as she stopped to pull up the shawl and Isabel turned sharply, bringing her hand up to slap his face. Nick caught her wrist and twisted it until she cried out in pain. 'You're far too free with your slaps and orders, woman. I'm trying to save your life, for God's sake!'

She let out a choked sob and followed him, miserably keeping her eyes firmly on the path for safety while trying to keep up with his impatient strides. It was getting dark and she was very frightened at the prospect of having to climb down a cliff. And always, always there was the rush and boom and thump of the sea. She wanted to put both hands over her ears and shut out the awesome noise but it would mean denying herself the warmth of the shawl. The sea was a brute! She wanted to scream at it to stop, that she could no longer bear it. She wanted to run away from the hostile cliff and the mighty rocks out in the sea standing there like sentries, holding her prisoner on the cliff above them. The rocks all had names and a story behind them, which would have made them seem friendlier had Isabel known this, but she did not and only wanted tó run away and never take sight of them again She wanted to escape from the chilling wind and the vast expanse all around her under a foreboding sky, but her legs were stiff and wooden, her feet blistered and growing more painful by the moment.

Most of all she could not bear to be with this terrible man who had so unfeelingly told her the news of her dear uncle's death and that her cousins could be plotting her murder. Nick Nancarrow was a bigger brute than the sea.

Isabel wanted to be with Edmund and Deborah Kempthorne in Trevennor House sitting before a roaring fire, wearing sedate and comfortable clothes, grieving with them over their uncle's death, and having them smile softly at her and put comforting arms about her and tell her their uncle's suspicions were utterly groundless. It was a cosy picture, and an unattainable one, not least because she knew the Kempthornes despised her.

Nick had stopped. When she reached him she saw they were on the top of a promontory and were looking down a long steep drop with a fast-moving stream at its bottom running seawards down into a little rocky cove. On the other side of the stream the cliff rose sharply again.

'Where are we?' she asked, looking down anxiously.

'This place is called Carvannel Downs. Go down the drop sideways,' he advised brusquely and abruptly set off.

Isabel watched numbly until he was halfway down. She felt dizzy, the wind was making her eyes water and suddenly her vision blurred. She wiped her eyes dry, determined not to call him back to help her. She took the first uncertain step downwards, heeding his advice to keep her foot sideways. The ground was not firm and she was nervous. Each step jarred her whole body, making her grind her teeth and once painfully biting her tongue.

At the moment she felt a little more confident, she fell. She did not scream, her mouth was clamped shut as she bumped and rolled over and over, passing Nick and stopping only against the raised bank of the stream with a hefty thud. One arm flopped into the icy water.

Nick bounded down the rest of the way to reach her. He knelt and swiftly pulled her arm out of the water. Then he moved his hands up and down her limbs and over her ribs, worried that he would find broken bones.

'Can you speak?' he asked.

Isabel blinked and moaned, then coughed. 'I… I…'

'All right, don't try to talk. You don't seem to have broken anything. Can you move your head?'

She was almost too afraid to try but made small movements to each side and lifted her chin up and down. Nick would never know how relieved she had been to feel the firm searching pressure of his hands over her body. It proved that she was not paralysed. Her father had died paralysed from a stroke and she had a horror of not being able to move freely.

Then suddenly she was furious with Nick. If he insisted on taking responsibility for her safety, he should have made sure she did not fall. She pummelled his broad chest with clenched fists as he leaned over her but she did not have the strength to bawl the recriminations she wanted to at him. Nick grasped her flailing arms as gently as he could, forcing them to the damp ground above her head. She became still, her chest heaving for breath. She closed her eyes tightly as a wave of nausea overwhelmed her.

Nick gathered her up in his arms; he would carry her the rest of the way. He had chosen to ignore the fact that she had been hurt in the coach accident and felt a small measure of guilt at forcing her to walk so far. He had been asked, and he had promised, to keep her safe, but if she kept having accidents there would be small chance of that. He hoped there would be no lasting effects from the fall. Isabel lay quietly against him, dazed.

He carried her across the stream, over the length of ship's planking put there by Charlie years ago so his wife would not have to leap over and to give himself safer passage home after a night's drinking at the Basset's Cove Inn at Portreath. Wild garlic grew on either bank of the stream and the wind blew the strong smell over them. It caused Isabel to stir and as Nick skilfully made his way up the other side, she gazed over his shoulder at the green water of the stream that ended in a sheer waterfall and cascaded onto the rocks and beach far below. There was just enough light to see the spray that leapt upwards in a fine mist.

Isabel longed to sleep but fought her fatigue to stay alert. She did not want her wits dulled. Nick was taking long fast strides and she was jolted continually against his chest. She wondered if he found her heavy, but if he did she did not care. It was his fault she had fallen and he had no right to take her on such an arduous journey in the first place. There must be an easier, more comfortable way of giving her his protection and keeping her out of sight of other people.

Ten minutes had passed when he stopped walking and put her carefully down on her feet, holding her until he was sure she was steady. They were very close to the edge of the cliff. Far, far below, Isabel saw a small sandy beach where two massive slaty rocks stood side by side like the walls of a semi-demolished house. A channel of raging sea surged in and out between them. One rock was attached to the main cliff wall, the other was topped with a jagged edge. Isabel had a fearful image of a luckless person plunging down and being impaled there.

'Is it down there?' she gulped nervously. 'Where you want us to climb down?'

'About halfway down, but 'tis a brave drop,' Nick replied, for the first time making a point of looking at her when he spoke to her.

'I'm frightened,' she admitted in a small voice.

'There's no need to be. 'Tis risky but not dangerous if you know what you're doing.'

'But I don't know what I'm doing and it's nearly dark,' she said desperately. 'Oh, please, please, can we go somewhere else?'

Nick took her arm and guided her several feet away from the cliff edge. He heard her long deep sigh of relief.

'See there?' He pointed to a deep depression in the scrubby ground. 'If you don't know the cliffs as we locals do you would plunge to your death walking over that. The gorse and rough grass have grown over the shaft of a disused copper mine. That's how we're going down to the cave.'

'You mean we don't have to climb down the cliff? We can arrive at this cave by climbing down a disused mine shaft?'

'Aye, it'll give us shelter for the night.'

'But isn't it just as dangerous?' Isabel felt the jitters bite at her insides again.

''Tis easy as hell,' Nick assured her grimly. 'We're going to climb down inside the cliff to the cave. The cave has always been there, the miners tunnelled out from the shaft to meet it to provide ventilation. It's been used as a smugglers' hide ever since, even when the mine was a working concern. The goods are landed by rowing boats that meet a ship out in deeper waters. Then they're unloaded on the beach and hauled up on ropes into the cave, which is roughly halfway down the cliff. The goods remain dry, hidden and safe until they can be brought up the shaft.'

'That's incredible,' Isabel said, impressed. She knew about smuggling – it was every other Cornishman's second occupation – but she had no idea it was so well organized.

''Tis a welcome place for us to sleep in tonight,' Nick said.

A sudden thought seized Isabel. 'You don't mean to keep me down there until Richard arrives back in Cornwall, do you?'

'Who's Richard?' Nick asked, without real interest, as he crouched himself down to light the lantern he had taken out of the canvas bag.

'Captain Richard Grenville, my fiancé.'

'No,' Nick answered. 'The cave will be used long before that happens, there's a good deal of free trading going on along this stretch of the coast. And how you do forget. I'm taking you to Crantock, remember?'

'Oh, yes, of course.' She hated the way she appeared to be so foolish before this uncompromising man.

With the lantern lit, Nick pulled aside a huge mat of gorse to reveal a gaping black hole. Just visible below its rim were the top rungs of the first of many wooden ladders that went down and down.

'I'll go first and light the way. You'll be quite safe if you hold on tightly. The ladders are kept in good repair. Take each step slowly and don't look down.'

Another fear beset Isabel and she clutched Nick's shoulder. 'What if there are smugglers down there now? What if someone wants to smuggle something in tonight? I've heard they do not like to be disturbed or recognized.'

Nick pushed her hand away. ''Tis not likely. Charlie knew of no run coming in tonight and even if there is, they'll know me.'

He turned and lowered himself into the hole until his feet located a rung. He climbed down until only his head and shoulders were visible. Then he called for Isabel to follow him.

She glanced around the cliff scenery. The sky was dark blue with only a strip of light on the horizon over the sea. She felt as if she was about to volunteer her early presence to her tomb. Taking a deep, deep breath, she turned as Nick had done, lowered herself onto her knees and, clutching at the harsh grass, fearfully let a foot down inside the shaft. When it made contact with a rung, Nick called to her that she was doing well and to try the next foot. Although her heart seemed to be in her mouth, she knew there was no room for argument, nowhere else to go. She obeyed and shakily made a few steps down until her hands were gripping the top rung of the ladder. Nick had not moved and she felt a little safer to be cocooned by his body and have the lantern level with her face.

In this way they climbed down and down and down, stopping often to rest so Isabel could keep a firm grip on the ladder and not tire out. Exertion and fear of falling brought her out in a cold sweat. Nick was impressed by her courage and made every effort to make the long descent easier and less frightening for her. He had assumed he would have to bully her down; in fact, having seen men run away in pure fear of the terrible depths and the blackness of the underground, he had thought he might even have to knock her out and carry her down unconscious.

After what seemed like an eternity consisting of thousands of rungs, Nick stopped and spoke quietly so as not to startle her into a precarious movement. 'Look over to your left and you'll see a wooden platform jutting out from the rock. It leads straight to the cave. I want you to move your body across and step onto it. Don't worry, I'll hold you so you won't fall backwards. First, put both your hands on the side of the ladder. Can you do that?'

Isabel nodded. By now she was so fatigued, her head so light she felt as though she was in a weird dream. Instinct alone took over and told her if she obeyed this strong male voice behind her head she would soon be on firm ground again, safe and able to sleep. How she longed for precious, dark, silent sleep. Very slowly she edged her taut hands across the rung she was gripping and transferred them to the side of the ladder.

'Good, good,' Nick encouraged her. 'There's a hook just here which I'm going to hang the lantern on and I'm going to put my arm round your waist. I want you to reach out with your left foot and step onto the platform then move your other foot beside it. I'll hold you tightly while you swing across and you'll only have to walk forward and be perfectly safe. You have nothing to fear. I won't let you fall.' In any other circumstances but these Isabel would have been petrified or become hysterical. But she trusted the husky voice and did as Nick told her. An instant later she was walking into the cave after passing through a few feet of low tunnel, with Nick behind her lighting the way. The cave's mouth was a roughly circular hole about five feet in diameter through which a bitterly cold draught poured and chilled her to the marrow. Isabel was disappointed that the wide expanse of the cave's belly was empty; she had expected to see tubs of rum and brandy and bales of silk, and hopefully warm blankets to wrap herself up in for the sleep she wanted so desperately. The roof of the cave was a bare inch above Nick's head.

'Come on,' he said, 'there's a turn to the right along here where we can get out of the cold wind.' He held the lantern high and led the way.

'Do you know this cave well?' Isabel asked, her eyes rooted to the uneven ground lest she trip. 'Do you take part in this smuggling business?'

'Nothing that I'd admit to,' he answered gruffly. The turning led to an area that showed signs of use: coils of thick rope so high and wide they could be sat on, tarred torches set high in nooks and crannies of the walls, empty wooden crates, a discarded broken clay pipe and a piece of a man's scarf. Isabel sat down wearily on one of the crates and rearranged the shawl so the cold wet part that had fallen into the stream was not touching her arm. The muscles at the top of her legs ached and twitched wildly. On her face she felt a welcome heat and a prickly tingling feeling from the barrage of the wind. Her heart thumped in her chest and pounded in her ears.

Nick, too, was relieved the climb down the ladders was over. He had lied about it being easy. It was a long way down and certain death if you fell; he had seen more than one man plunge to his doom, left at the bottom of the shaft to rot, during the occupation of a smuggling run. Now they were safely in the cave he realised it would have been foolhardy to have attempted to carry Isabel down if she had refused to cooperate. He wiped the sweat from his face and put his bag and the lantern on the crate next to Isabel. He lit two of the torches and blew the lantern out.

'You hungry?' he said, over Isabel's bowed head.

She looked up and thought he was actually smiling at her. She blinked and his face was as stern as ever. His question made her realize she was very hungry.

'Yes, I am,' she replied softly.

'Charlie put some food in my bag for us. Don't know what it's like though; his wife was a good cook and always insisted on filling my pockets with hunks of bread and hevva cake. He doesn't do any baking but has kept up his wife's habit of giving me food when I call on him. I'll get us something else in Portreath tomorrow.'

'Anything would be welcome at this moment,' Isabel said truthfully.

'You may not say that when you see what it is,' Nick said, remembering the piece of stinking mackerel Charlie had offered him. He unstrapped the bag and put his hand inside and pulled out a large packet wrapped in a red handkerchief. 'Hope this is clean,' he said doubtfully, unwrapping the cloth, then, 'Bloody hell!'

'What is it?' Isabel asked, half afraid to be told and frowning at his bad language.

'A pasty. 'Tis a beauty too, nearly a foot long. Well, I'll be damned. Charlie must have gone into Portreath himself earlier today. This is one of Mundy Cottle's I'd reckon and her baking is legendary.'

'It was very kind of your friend to give us his food. He must be so terribly poor, living as he does in such squalid conditions. I hope he won't be going hungry for our sakes.'

Nick eyed Isabel with deep suspicion. Except for Laurence Trevennor, all the wealthy people he had come across cared little or nothing at all for the poor, but Isabel's expression seemed sincere.

'The pasty smells good,' she said, wetting her dry lips in anticipation.

Nick held the pasty under her face so she could see it. 'There's no need to be concerned about Charlie. Like me, he lives the way he chooses, but when I get the chance I'll repay him for his help.' Isabel was staring longingly at the pasty. 'I'll break it in half,' he said.

'No you have a bigger part of it,' she said, looking up and meeting his eyes.

He raised his brows. 'Why? Why on earth should I do that?'

'Because men need to eat more than women do. Mrs Sweet, who cooks for Uncle Laurence, always says so.'

It struck Nick as a child-like thing to say. 'Well, Wenna Sweet is entitled to her views as the best cook in Gwithian, but tonight we'll have equal shares.' He broke the pasty in half, gave Isabel hers in the kerchief and sat down on the next crate. She thanked him and ate a mouthful, chewing it slowly, then gazed at it solemnly.

'Mr Nancarrow?'

'Mmmm?'

'Is… is my Uncle Laurence really dead?'

Nick swallowed what he was chewing and answered softly, 'Yes. Apart from his concern for you, his last moments were painless and peaceful.'

With her body hunched over and the pasty gripped in both hands, Isabel cried quietly.

Nick glanced at her then looked away. She seemed so small. 'Eat up, you'll feel better.'

Isabel ate in painful gulps then folded the cloth which Nick put back in the bag. A great weariness overtook her and she longed for sleep, to shut out the muted noise of the ocean and escape her tortured thoughts, her aches and pains and troubled future. The slats of the crates were too widely spaced to sleep on; she moved stiffly from the crate and sat on the cold hard ground that was to be her bed for the night. Pulling the shawl over her head she leaned back against the crate and closed her eyes. Nick watched her and came to kneel in front of her.

'Your feet are swollen and bleeding,' he said. 'You'd better take your shoes off.'

Isabel was too tired to care and made no protest when he did it for her but she gasped to see the pebble-sized blisters and the skin rubbed raw from the edges of her shoes. Nick pulled off his neckerchief. Tearing it in two he carefully bound each foot in turn.

'That should help,' he said, glancing at her under his long fair lashes as though he required her approval.

Isabel was cheered that his mood had finally softened but when he raised his head and looked at her fully, his handsome face held all of its usual harshness.

'It does, thank you,' she replied, looking at her feet bandaged in plain blue cloth, then closing her eyes again.

'The best way to keep warm for the night is to huddle together.' He thought this would provoke a barrage of protests. But Isabel was too worn out to feel any sense of impropriety and in her wretchedness she welcomed the prospect of being close to another person, even this dreadful man who it would seem hated her for no good reason. At present he was the only source of warmth and security in her nightmare world. Thoughts of right and wrong could be left until tomorrow when she would feel fresh and have regained her strength and full senses.

Nick sat close beside her and drew her towards him so she was resting comfortably against his chest. Instinctively she nestled in closer, the sound of his heart beating drowning out the sound of the sea, his warm unique smell taking the place of the odour of the clothes she wore. She was deeply asleep before she could feel the strong capable arms he put round her.

Chapter 5

Nick gazed down at Isabel's sleeping face. Hers was a child's face at that moment, soft, warm and slightly flushed, framed with tiny damp tendrils of honey-brown hair. She looked absurdly young and Nick could see why Laurence Trevennor had thought her young for her age. She had said some rather naive things yesterday, yet she could argue and order like a self-assured adult. Nick traced her soft red lips with a light fingertip and wondered what would come forth from them when he woke her, the tired vulnerable femininity of last night or her usual self-righteousness and indignation. Her breathing was regular and deep, her body warm and pliable against his. He liked the feel of her in his arms and thought it a pity she didn't possess a more pliable nature. Then the task of lugging her across the cliffs and through the villages and coves to Crantock would be less cumbersome.

Picking up one of her hands he rubbed his thumb over the edges of her bitten-off nails and marvelled at the neat job she had made of it. He decided not to wake her yet and lowered her gently onto the cold hard ground, then made his way to the cave's mouth to see what weather the early morning had brought. As he stood there in the cold light of day he found it difficult to believe in Laurence's worries over Isabel's safety. The more likely danger was that Edmund Kempthorne would try to sweet-talk her out of her inheritance. And given that the coach accident was almost certainly caused by Gyver Pengelly, who was a greedy man and valued no one's life, only their possessions, it was probably a coincidence. If he wanted no witnesses to his misdeed alive, however, then Isabel's life was in danger from him and it was better Pengelly thought she was dead for the moment.

Isabel began to come to, instinct warning her that she had lost her source of warmth and protection. She woke with a terrible start and found herself looking up at the damp cave roof. Horror engulfed her as she realized her worst nightmare was real but she quickly forced it aside. With a struggle she got up on her heavy legs and sore feet. Her fear that she had been abandoned and left trapped a hundred feet below ground dissolved when she saw Nick's bag lying on the crate. She sat next to it and considered her feet and whether her shoes would fit over the makeshift bandages.

She bid Nick a good morning when he reappeared but he shrugged it off as an unnecessary pleasantry.

'There's a heavy mist coming in from the sea spreading over the cliff so we should be able to slip into Portreath unnoticed.'

'Will we find the way there in the mist?' Isabel said, concern making the dimples on either side of her mouth more pronounced. 'We might lose our way and fall over the edge of the cliff.'

'When will you learn to trust me?' he said tartly, but wondering why he had not noticed her enchanting little dimples the day before. ''Tis a mist, not a fog. The cliff path will be quite visible as we tread the way and I know my way over the North Cliffs blindfolded.'

'I'm delighted to hear it,' Isabel responded mildly, determined that from now on she would ignore his ill humour. After all, he was no more than an ignorant common oaf.

'I have been thinking. I want you to take me to the estate of Menadarva which is set a little way back from the cliffs in this area, or if you insist that we go to Crantock, I want you to take me on to Trewinton. The Bevilles there will gladly give me refuge.'

'Not in those clothes they won't. They wouldn't let you in even by the back door. They'd probably set their dogs on you.'

He threw the bag over his shoulder and said at her angered face, 'Let's get things straight once and for all, Miss Isabel Hampton. I promised Laurence I'd take care of you until your wedding day and unless I can see that no one anywhere offers you any danger, that's the way it's going to be. Do you understand that? Have I made myself perfectly clear this time?'

Isabel sprang to her feet and glared at him. 'Perfectly,' she snapped contemptuously, then pushed past him and began the walk back to the ladders.

Nick grinned to himself at her anger and said, speaking to her back, 'We'll go up the same way we came down so you don't have to fear you'll fall down the shaft, and when we get back to grass I'll carry you. I'll get you a more suitable pair of shoes in Portreath. It's no trouble to me getting you through the mist and down into the village.'

Isabel wanted to ask if he could also walk on water but kept the sarcasm to herself. He was a persistent boaster as well as a vulgar boor. She said, over her shoulder, 'And what is to be done with my shoes?'

'I'll throw them down the shaft. They'll never be found.' Nick prodded her shoulder and she whirled round to voice her objections but he spoke first. 'Just one other thing. When we're in company I don't want you to speak. I'll say you were born simple-minded, so just stand about looking idiotic. I'm sure you can manage that easily enough.'

Isabel did not rise to the bait. 'That won't be necessary,' she said, with a small smile.

Nick wasn't amused. 'I won't allow you to be difficult with me. You'll do as I ruddy well say.'

'I used to spend hours talking to Ginny, my maid,' Isabel explained sounding patient with him but looking superior. 'I can mimic her perfectly.'

'Talk to me on the way to Portreath and if I'm satisfied you sound convincing then maybe I'll let you speak.'

Isabel found the reach to the ladders from the platform truly terrifying but the climb up a lot easier than the one going down.

The air on the surface was bracing and damp and helped to wake up her tired limbs. As Nick made tidy work of replacing the shaft's concealing cover, she listened to the sounds of the sea. It seemed quieter with the mist masking it from view, and not so threatening. Nick lifted her none too gently into his arms and set off, looking dour. Isabel found she was quite comfortable and with the wind coming from behind them his big body shielded her from the biting wind. She looked around but could see only a few feet in any direction in the white hazy world.

She waited a while then began the mimicry of her maid. 'I'll have to become a new person, Mr Nancarrow, have a new name,' she said, in a soft Cornish accent. 'My housekeeper at Truro had a little niece called Jenna. 'Tis such a pretty name I've always believed. How about Jenna Trelawney? Has a nice ring to it.'

Nick was impressed by her accent, there wasn't a note of her own unmistakable educated voice, but he did not tell her so. 'Trelawney's too well-to-do,' he said stiffly. 'Think of something more ordinary.'

A few minutes thought, then, 'How about Stevens? My first nursemaid was called Stevens.'

'It'll do.'

'What shall I say if I'm asked why I'm with you?' she asked in her own voice.

'Tell them you're my woman.'

'Your wife, you mean?'

'My woman,' Nick corrected her. 'Folk know me for a man who won't put a noose round his neck. From now on use the other voice and don't call me Mr Nancarrow.' He lowered his voice into a deliberate seductive tone. 'The women I sleep with call me Nick.'

The last remark had the effect Nick desired. Isabel blushed and turned her face quickly away. 'I... I... don't have to sleep with you. I won't!'

'You did last night,' he said, to prolong her embarrassment.

'We did not do anything!' Then Isabel saw through the satisfied smirk on his full wide mouth and rallied. 'You said yesterday that people would think it strange if you were in the company of a woman.'

'I've been thinking about that,' he said, so close to her ear it sent shivers down her neck. His next sentence added to his bawdy theme. 'I'll tell folk I've decided I want my creature comforts more often and readily to hand.'

Isabel ignored this. 'And where am I supposed to have come from? You cannot tell people I just materialized from out of thin air.'

'That's simple enough. I've only just got back from up north, around Bude, where I was training coach horses. We'll say I met you up there and brought you back with me. I keep my private life to myself and folk will assume I'll want to try to keep you out of sight. Collecting you from somewhere quiet will account for my sudden disappearance from your uncle's house and Gwithian.'

'In that case we don't need to skulk about like two people who have or are about to commit a crime.'

'We still need to be inconspicuous. The less known about you and me the better. And don't forget your new voice. Think of yourself as Jenna Stevens from now on, because when we've climbed down this high platform of cliff we'll be at Mundy Cottle's cottage at Portreath.'

–

Mundy Cottle looked Isabel over once then beckoned her to sit down at the huge scrub-top table in her kitchen. She viewed Nick with a definite air of disapproval and did not extend the same welcome to him. Isabel sat down gratefully on the first chair she had seen in nearly twenty-four hours. She looked curiously from Mundy Cottle's reproachful glances at Nick to his deliberate look of assumed innocence as he stood warming his back against the fireplace, his head between two black beams of the low ceiling.

The cottage was wonderfully warm and filled with the delicious aroma of freshly baked bread. The furniture was dark and serviceable. There were snowy white runners on the tops of shelves and a chest of drawers. Framed against all four thick walls and edged with lace were many embroidered Bible texts. The numerous cupboards and shelves were bursting with jars of dried herbs, preserves, pickled fruit, vegetables and eggs, and crudely carved and cheap paste ornaments. Lanterns lit by seal oil stood about. Clean linen and stacks of perfectly pressed children's clothes lay everywhere. Some of the ornaments looked as if they had been made by children's hands. The children responsible for them were quietly watching Isabel from a polite distance.

'You're lucky to find me home,' Mundy said, tight-lipped, looking at Nick. 'I always attend a preaching down in the harbour at five o'clock. 'Tis the only way to start a day.'

'We would have waited for you,' Nick returned, with a smile full of charm.

Mundy sniffed. 'I'll get 'ee a bite to eat, maid,' she told Isabel. 'I'm fasting today but there's no need for thee to go hungry.'

'Thank you, Mrs Cottle,' Isabel replied, speaking as her alias. Her mouth was watering at the sight of two neat rows of warm barley bread in front of her.

'Don't come from round these here parts telling by your accent,' Mundy said, cutting a thick slice of crusty bread and buttering it. 'Here, have this to be going on with. You d'look famished to me, you poor little soul. I'll put some bacon on for 'ee, you look like you could do with a good meal.' She snorted and turned to face her other visitor. 'Well, out of my way, Nick Nancarrow. Can't cook with a great ox like you standing in the way.'

Nick grinned and moved to sit in the window seat which looked out down over the fine yellow sand of Portreath's beach.

Immediately the Cottle children swarmed over him, sitting on his lap, draping over his shoulders, hanging on to his arms.

'Well, you lot still like me,' Nick smiled at the children, while looking meaningfully at their busy mother.

'You know my views on living in sin,' Mundy said, slamming a pan down on her brick oven. 'If a maid's good enough to be used she's good enough to be made a wife. Mr Westley would never approve of such goings on. Do you some good, boy, to hear un preach one of these days. Look at her,' she pointed at Isabel who felt as guilty as if she had done the thing she was being jointly accused of. 'She's just a maid. Taken in by your fine fair looks, I shouldn't wonder. Won't get her very far, will it, eh? Not to the marriage altar. You should be ashamed of yourself, Nick Nancarrow!'

Mundy Cottle was dressed as severely as her censure. Somewhere in her forties, her short fat body was modestly draped from chin to toes in dove grey and covered with a voluminous white apron. Her greying hair was scraped up at the back of her head in a bun and topped with a floppy untrimmed cap. She bustled about her kitchen until breakfast was prepared and on the table.

'Well, come on, young man,' she ordered Nick. 'I don't suppose the good Lord will mind me feeding a sinner.'

'You're a fine woman, Mundy Cottle,' Nick said lightheartedly, picking up his knife and fork as he sat opposite Isabel. 'There's not a better cook than you in the whole of Cornwall, I always say.' He wound a thick slice of bacon round his fork and before biting into it he inclined his head at Isabel. 'Jenna's had a bit of trouble with her shoes, Mundy. Can you help?'

Mundy looked under the table and saw Isabel's feet swathed in Nick's neckerchief. When she looked up, Isabel was saying grace over her meal and Mundy's chubby red-cheeked face was transformed with a look of approval on it.

'There's hope for you yet, m'dear,' she said, brushing a straying lock of Isabel's hair from her eyes in a motherly movement. 'You obviously come from a good home.' Nick snorted over a mouthful of bacon. Mundy pulled in her lips and turned her back on him. 'Never mind him, Jenna. So that's your name is it?'

'Aye, Mrs Cottle. Jenna Stevens.'

Isabel ate delicately until she received a hard nudge from Nick's boot on her leg and a pointed nod from his head. She frowned at him and piled her fork higher with food.

'Where d'you come from then, maid?' Mundy asked, standing back with her rough red hands clasped under her bosom, watching Isabel.

'Um, up Bude way.' Isabel blushed at the lie and straightaway told another one. ''Tis where I met Nick.' She hoped Mundy Cottle knew no one from Bude because Ginny had come from Falmouth and the accents differed.

'More's the pity for you then. Leading a young maid into temptation, teaching her the wicked ways of the world. He's been up to no good ever since a small boy. Lets Satan get the better of him. Mr Westley would soon sort un out. I'll find out when he's down this way next, you'd enjoy listening to him preach. Mind you, I say that, but I can tell you myself, you're on the way to Hell and suffering if you don't mend your ways.'

Isabel ate shamefaced, longing to be able to tell Mundy the truth of her association with Nick.

'Got a drop of ale, Mundy?'

Nick's question made Mundy whirl round as if she had been stabbed in the back. 'You know there's no Devil's brew to be found in this house, Nick Nancarrow!'

'Some of your lot do drink in moderation, Mundy,' Nick pointed out, waving his fork at her.

'Well, I don't hold for it, one drink d'lead to another,' Mundy retorted stiffly. 'It don't do to give the Devil a foothold. I'll pour 'ee both up a cup of herb and honey tea.'

Nick laughed heartily. 'Then get on with it, woman. We've been here half an hour and thirsting to death.'

Isabel stared open-mouthed at his rudeness, but she wasn't unmoved by the way his laughter had lit up his sapphire eyes and made his perfectly moulded mouth powerfully attractive. How could she think of him like this? She jerked her head back to the remnants of her meal and tucked into it.

Mundy poured hot water onto a mixture of dried rosemary and honey in two huge mugs and placed them, stony-faced, on the table. She squealed when Nick squeezed her tightly to him and planted a hearty kiss on her puffed cheek.

'Come on, Mundy, you know you'll always love me whatever I do.'

'Nick Nancarrow! Whatever will you do next! You're enough to get on my gidge.' Mundy clasped a hand to her heaving bosom. Her brood of children giggled. Nick laughed. And then Mundy was laughing herself and smoothing Nick's hair with both hands. 'Look at the state of you, hair all to lerrups and never tied back properly, buttons missing on your coat, always half clothed. I'll get 'ee another neckerchief while I'm out getting the maid a pair of shoes. Julia Triggs should have something for you both in her used boxes. I'll go now before the cove becomes alive. Now you let go of me and if Jenna wants another drink, just you make one for her. You know where the things are kept. There's no need for her to stand up on they poor feet till she gets some proper shoes to put on 'em. Oh, and there's some porridge left in the cauldron if you want some.'

Isabel watched the interchange in bemused silence when Nick playfully slapped Mundy on the bottom. What liberties he took, this handsome, common man, yet Mrs Cottle seemed to be very fond of him. Nick had taken her to two people he referred to as friends of his, and he planned to take her to another. Someone who doubtless liked and trusted him as much as Charlie and Mrs Cottle did. Uncle Laurence and Mrs Christopher felt the same way too. It was warm and comfortable in Mundy Cottle's home and Nick clearly belonged here. She wished that, now she was lacking all the things dear and familiar to her, she could feel a part of Mundy Cottle's home too, that she could make friends with his friends. But that could never be so, because Nick Nancarrow hated her and she was only passing through.

She desperately wanted to tell Mundy that she and Nick were not lovers and never would be. But now she had something more pressing she needed to ask her, something of the utmost delicacy, and she wished Nick and the children were not there.

'Let's have a look at they feet, maid,' Mundy said, after she put on her shawl and bonnet.

Isabel obeyed self-consciously, holding her feet out from under the table, and received an immediate tittering of small faces. She had always felt uncomfortable with children and they continued to stare when she whispered something in Mundy's ear, while blushing furiously. Mundy whispered back discreetly after shooing the children away. She judged Isabel's feet to be about the size of her eldest daughter Martha's, took a handful of coins from Nick to pay for everything and left. Isabel was relieved her children went with her.

'They're only a few of 'em,' Nick said, after the door closed behind them.

'A few of what?' Isabel asked, finishing her tea and taking the liberty of helping herself to another slice of bread and butter. The sea air had always increased her appetite when she'd stayed at Gwithian and after the harrowing events of yesterday she was ravenously hungry. She took a bite of bread and shifted about uncomfortably on her chair, wishing with all her heart that Nick would go out too.

'Mundy's children,' he explained. 'The eldest is about my age, the youngest about three. The curious thing is, though I've known her all my life – I used to play with her older children as a boy and I've visited her every time I've been back in these parts since I grew up and left home – I've never seen her husband. All I know is that he's a stone-mason and worked on the harbour wall put up in the cove ten years ago.'

'Who is Mr Westley? Presumably not her husband.'

'Oh, she means John Wesley, the preacher. The Cottles are staunch Methodists. Mundy's been trying to get me 'saved' for years.'

'I see,' Isabel said stiffly, becoming withdrawn.

'So do I,' Nick said, amused. 'You're one of the Anglican brigade that strongly disapproves of Methodism. Well, I've got a lot in common with John Wesley and his brother, Charles. We've slept in barns and the open air and are energetic in what we believe in. We're loyal to our friends and causes. They've done better than the lawful Church in most places, restoring Christian fellowship like it ought to be.'

'Have they really?' Isabel said grittily. 'Well, they're given only a quiet reception at Truro.'

'Maybe so, but without the strength of enmity they used to get. 'Tis said the Wesleys are as brave as lions. Do you think I am, Isabel?'

Isabel ignored the question. He was mocking her again and using her Christian name as though they were close friends.

Nick got up and poured hot water from Mundy's great kettle into their mugs then added spoonfuls of rosemary and honey. 'Sorry there's no sugar to put in it. Mundy won't have it in the house. John Wesley preaches against it because of the cruelty of the slave trade. Did you know that?'

'I don't approve of making men slaves either,' Isabel snapped. She looked at the steaming liquid in the mugs and urgently, but as graciously as she could, rose to her sore feet. 'I… I'm going out the back.'

'Good idea. Mundy keeps a nice earth closet out there – nearly good enough for a lady to use,' Nick said, then adding without tact, 'You'd better get on with it, it's not good to hold yourself for so long.'

Isabel swept past him but halted when he said, 'Watch out for Mundy's pig. He's a good mater but very fierce. He's been known to try to eat folk before now.' He gulped down his drink and reached the door before she did. 'I'm going down into the cove to see if the news of Laurence's death and the accident is abroad.'

Isabel was vexed. If she had waited one more minute she would have been spared her embarrassment. She rushed to this small wooden closet put up amid the vegetable patch of the back garden. Inside she hurried herself because there was no lock on the inside of the door and she had a horror of someone bursting in on her. As she hastened back to the cottage, she looked warily about for the pig. There wasn't one to be seen and she wondered crossly if Nick had amused himself again at her expense.

Chapter 6

Deborah Kempthorne was also up early that morning. She was walking self-importantly into Gwithian's church in the company of Charlotte Thomas, the curate's young wife, to say prayers for her deceased uncle and cousin. She was smugly pleased when the few villagers that were about curtseyed or touched their forelocks to her and she gave a gracious nod to those who expressed their condolences and made a suitable display of being grief-stricken.

Inside the church she spent the time thinking over how she was going to spend her double inheritance rather than asking the Almighty to have mercy on her relatives' souls. With a scrap of black lace clamped to her face she allowed Charlotte Thomas to take her arm and lead her out into the cold misty air. Deborah spied a woman gazing down at a grave near the church door.

'Would you be so kind as to leave me to have a few moments to myself, Mistress Thomas,' Deborah said, sniffing into the handkerchief. 'I would like to spend a little time at my dear aunt's grave. I can make the walk back across the road by myself.'

'Well, if you're quite sure, Miss Kempthorne,' Charlotte said, giving Deborah a little pat on the arm. 'I don't mind waiting outside the churchyard for you.'

'No, please go on home. You have a young family to attend to. You have been very kind and have already given far too much of your time.'

'I will call on you again this afternoon,' Charlotte said, before going quietly upon her way.

Deborah scowled at the younger woman's trim back. It had taken her only a short time to hate Charlotte Thomas. Hate for her slim figure despite the fact she had borne four children within the last five years, hate for her angular grace, her pretty face with its clear complexion and firmly rounded chin, her bright animated brown eyes. Hate for her being happily married and settled in a life that suited her, where she was loved and respected by those around her. Deborah decided to draw Edmund's carnal attention to the physical attributes of the curate's wife after all and made a wish that she would fall readily for her brother's charms. Then she could try looking Deborah in the face with that hypocritical concern of hers!

Deborah moved her heavy body round the church to scowl down gloatingly at the grave Laurence Trevennor would share in a few days' time. She was still feeling the sense of elation that had overwhelmed her when she had first learned of the two deaths of her wealthy relatives and that she and Edmund had come into their fortunes.

She had not slept a wink last night in her excitement. It had been with a great surge of triumph that she had climbed into the bed Isabel had used when staying at Trevennor House. A roaring fire had heated the room through and through and instead of rushing to get between cold sheets as she did in the freezing cottage at St Ives, she had made the unfortunate maid who had waited on her take her time preparing her for bed. When she had thrown the crying maid out of the room after threatening to dismiss her for pulling on a tangle in her hair, Deborah had settled back on plumped-up pillows and hummed happily to herself.

Edmund had not been able to sleep either. Deborah had heard him pacing the floor in the chamber next to hers. She knew he was just as excited as herself, but his main reason for pacing the floor was because he was missing Mary Ellen. In the morning, Deborah had gone to him and found him asleep across the bed with his soft dark hair splayed on the coverlet and about his face. After gently pushing the hair from his face, she'd kissed him tenderly and laid out his clothes. She wanted to do everything for Edmund herself and vowed over his sleeping form that Mary Ellen would never hold a claim on him; she would find a way to get rid of the whore and her child.

The air of death laying claim to Trevennor House was considerably lighter this morning with Sir Robert Antiss having removed Phoebe's and their servants' bodies last evening. Sir Robert had shown his contempt for the Kempthornes quite plainly and declared he would not leave his daughter's body under the new owners' roofs a minute longer. The baronet had left the parlour in tears and Deborah had had to nudge Edmund to prevent him from laughing out loud. Now they had only to get rid of their uncle's dead bones.

Deborah had overheard the servants talking and she knew that Nick Nancarrow had been at her uncle's deathbed. Mrs Christopher said he had been deeply grieved over Mr Trevennor's death and although he had suddenly left Gwithian, he was sure to be back for the funeral. Deborah smiled like a cruel cat. She knew that despite her new-found wealth, few of the gentry would look in her direction. She had heard about the tall sandy-haired man and vaguely remembered him as an ungracious youth. He had been a trusted friend of Uncle Laurence's, but was that loyalty or the hope of receiving a legacy one day? If Nick Nancarrow turned up for the funeral, she'd look him over and find out where his true heart lay.

'My sympathies to 'ee, Miss Kem'thorne,' a scratchy voice said at her side. 'Mister Trevennor was a fine man.'

Deborah did not look up from under her black net veil, knowing full well that the woman who had been looking at the grave by the church door would move round to speak to her.

'You did well, Nellie. Here is your payment. Take it and give it to your man. He will give you your share.'

Deborah dropped another handkerchief she had with her and the woman, a scruffy creature who had boasted a young pretty face only five years ago, picked it up, swiftly took out a pouch tied inside it and handed the handkerchief back. Deborah tucked it away and looked at the woman.

'I went straight to un, jus' like you said, Miss Kem'thorne, after I'd told 'ee about Mister Trevennor bein' so ill an' sendin' fur Miss Isabel. 'E said 'e knew exactly what 'ee wanted 'im t'do.'

'He did well too, Nellie. I'm very pleased with both of you. Now, listen closely,' Deborah said harshly. 'You are not to say a word to anyone about this and must not even discuss it with your man. Do you promise me?'

Nellie smiled proudly from behind her vacuous colourless eyes. She said eagerly, 'Oh, yes, Miss Kem'thorne. I'd do anythin'fur you. Mister Pengelly, 'e do say you are a fine lady and 'ave bin some good to un.'

'Off you go then. I daresay Mr Pengelly will treat you to a sweetmeat out of the pouch. Remember that you must not open it yourself.'

'I promise upon my soul, Miss Kem'thorne.' Deborah watched Nellie skip away through the graves. She had been an ordinary young girl living with her bedridden grandmother, hoping one day to meet and marry some young man, until the night five years ago when Gyver Pengelly had met her in a quiet lane. Nellie had been hurrying home with a jug of ale for her grandmother when Pengelly had assaulted her then beaten her so badly her mind had never been the same again. Soon afterwards her grandmother had died, somewhat mysteriously it was rumoured, and Nellie had emerged from her ordeal as a cheerful simple-minded girl who thought Gyver Pengelly was her friend and whose every whim she obeyed. She had borne him two children, offspring his own ill-treated wife could not bear him. People said it was a blessing that both babies had been stillborn. Nellie had thought they were nasty dolls who had given her belly a terrible pain and she was glad Mr Pengelly had taken them away and given them to some other little girl.

Gyver Pengelly would do anything if the price was right and with Nelly's limited intelligence they were useful to Deborah's schemes.

Deborah made her way quickly to her new home. She saw Nellie stroking and talking to a large grey cat sitting on the parsonage wall next door. Nellie spoke to no person unless Gyver Pengelly told her she could, but what was she saying to the cat? Deborah was thoughtful as she entered Trevennor House's dignified door.

–

Isabel sat close beside the cheerful fire at the Cottles' hearth and held out her chilled feet to be warmed through. Looking around the kitchen, which she realised served as the only living room of the cottage, she marvelled that so many people could live in such cramped conditions and so tidily. The room was smaller than the dressing room of her mansion house at Truro. Being here reminded her of the gardener's cottage in its grounds, which she had visited often as a child, when her life had been cosseted, unthreatened. Like the gardener's cottage, Mundy Cottle's home had an atmosphere of normality and security. Isabel wished she could stay here and be waited upon until her fiancé arrived back in Cornwall and put an end to her nightmare.

She willed herself to shut out all thoughts of her predicament while she had the cottage to herself. She closed her eyes, listening only to the gentle crackle and hiss as the flames burned up dried furze and driftwood, hoping no one would be back for hours. But she was given little time to drift away and pretend nothing was wrong. Mundy Cottle soon returned, but without the children.

'Feeling better, my handsome?' she asked kindly, putting her purchases on the table.

'Yes, thank you, Mrs Cottle,' Isabel said, remembering to speak as Jenna Stevens and swallowing her disappointment at not being left alone for long.

'You don't seem the sort of maid to take up with Nick,' Mundy said, taking off her shawl and bonnet. 'You'm too polite, for one thing.'

'Yes, he can be very rude,' Isabel agreed, alert for Mundy's probings.

'And you're just an innocent.' Mundy gave her a cheery smile and added bluntly, 'If you haven't let un bother you yet, don't you let un. He might not be too pleased about it but Nick's not the sort of man to force himself on a woman.'

Isabel felt Mundy could see straight through their deception. She wanted to confide in the dumpy little woman but knew Nick would be furious if she told her the truth. Unable to meet Mundy's direct looks, she changed the subject. 'It looks like it's getting mistier outside.'

'Aye, 'tis as wet as rain. Could last for hours. The weather's getting worse. If you ask me, there's a storm brewing up for later on. I just hope there's no sailing vessels out at sea round here, this coast is a proper ship's graveyard. I know folk are grateful for the pickings, been glad to have a thing or two myself over the years. But all they souls lost! Don't bear thinking about if they're not heading for the Lord.' Mundy unwrapped her purchases. 'Come here and look what I've got for 'ee m'dear.'

On the table was a pair of black leather shoes, scuffed across the toes but sturdy and with plenty of wear left in them. Next to them was a pair of woollen stockings, a blue spotted neckerchief and some food. Picking up the shoes, Isabel thanked Mundy and took them to the fireside, then crossing one leg over the other she began to unwind Nick's old kerchief from one foot.

'I'll get 'ee a drop of warm water to bathe them afore you put on your new stockings,' Mundy said, watching sympathetically. 'I'll put in a bit of salt to help heal the sores and blisters. My man picked up a barrel of salt two year ago on the beach down there and it's lasted we all that time.'

'Thank you,' Isabel said, wincing as the bloodstained neckerchief and stockings pulled at her tender flesh.

'Give they to me,' Mundy said. 'Might as well burn them, went be no use for nothing else. Some funny business, if you ask me, dragging a maid across the cliffs, all quiet like. But I'll say no more about it. 'Tis none of my affair. You must have been so cold last night.' Mundy looked up from the blaze the bloodied rags had caused.

'I'm used to it,' Isabel lied, as she gingerly slipped her feet into the bowl of warm salty water provided for her.

'Are you now?' The other woman sounded unconvinced. 'I've got a cloak in my bedroom. Belonged to one of my daughters. She died about five years ago of the malignant sore throat. You can have it if you like, she were quite tall like you, it'll help to keep 'ee warm.'

'But what about your other children?' Isabel protested. 'Wouldn't one of them be glad of it?'

'Margie was rather special to us all. Born simple-minded, she was, and always like a littl'un. I'd rather not see any of my others wearing it. Memories, you understand. You're welcome to it, m'dear.'

Isabel was touched by Mundy's gesture and thought it was a pity that Nick Nancarrow couldn't be as kind and pleasant as his friends were. 'I would be grateful for the extra warmth but won't it be painful to part with it?'

'Well, better to let it be put to good use. You've got nothing in the world but what you stand up in, have you? And Nick.' Mundy moved to her bedroom door and then turned and said quietly, 'Jenna, whatever you're running away from, don't forget there's always One up above who's watching over 'ee.'

A short time later, wrapped in Margie Cottle's long brown cloak, the deep hood pulled over her face, Isabel left the warmth and security of Mundy Cottle's cottage with Nick. He held her arm and guided her down a narrow sloping pathway into the cove of Portreath itself. He pulled her away from a line of pack mules loaded down with copper ore making for the harbour, built by the Basset family who gave the local inn its aristocratic name. A ship was moored up waiting to take the ore to South Wales, but it would not set sail until the weather cleared. A strong wind blew sand at them as they passed the length of sandy beach and soon they were climbing again, leaving behind Portreath with its ruddy copper-stained river that ran into the ocean.

The ground was not hard and dry as the day before but wet and slippery. The climb was heavy going for Isabel but when the cliff levelled out, the stiffness in her legs had eased and she felt fit and able to cope with the next stage of the journey. There was nothing, no trees, vegetation or rocks to give shelter and the mist swirled around them, driven by the wind. Nick let go of her arm and told her to stay close in case she became lost or fell down a disused mine shaft.

''Tis a shame you can't see the splendid scenery today,' he said. 'From now on the coast is broken up into many interesting uninhabited coves. We're making next for a large one that has lots of people living there. Porthtowan, a copper mining community.' Nick was not bounding along today and Isabel could comfortably match his steps.

'Will we stop there?'

'No, we'll go straight on to St Agnes.'

Isabel was pleased Nick seemed to want to hold a conversation. It helped to make the walk go along faster and keep her mind off her worries. With the unlikelihood of anyone being about, she used her own voice. 'I think Mrs Cottle is suspicious about me.'

'She is, but not for what you might fear. The news is out about Laurence's death and all, but Mundy doesn't think for a moment that you're his niece. She had a right old go at me when I met up with her in the cove. She reckons you're the daughter of some rich man I've slocked off to turn into a loose woman. She said, "A fine parcel of trouble you're making for she!" 'Tis a good story to put about if someone seems to be on to us. Mundy reckons you'd be quite at home in the company of the Bassets over at Tehidy.'

Isabel was pleased that her breeding had shown through. She looked hard at Nick to try to see what he might be thinking but his face was unreadable.

'Do you think Mundy will say anything about us?'

'No, Mundy is a deeply religious woman. She never gossips and refuses to listen to any.'

'I feel a lot warmer now, thanks to this cloak Mundy very kindly gave me, and these shoes she got for me are quite comfortable. You seem to have some very pleasant friends.'

Nick did not respond. He seemed to have exhausted his inclination to talk and their conversation died. Isabel felt hurt. Why was he so hostile? She fell out of step with him and followed a little way behind.

As she trudged along, she kept her eyes on the marks his boots left on the muddy track. After a while it occurred to her his boots were made of very high-quality leather, far too expensive for the means of a working-class man. Further study and she realized they were somehow familiar to her. Then she remembered. On one of her last visits to Uncle Laurence he had been polishing the very same pair of boots with great care and attention. She had remarked that they looked at least two sizes too big for him and he had told her they were to be a gift for a special friend. So Nick Nancarrow had been that special friend.

She was so deep in thought that when Nick stopped suddenly and turned to her she ploughed straight into him. Isabel blushed to the roots of her hair.

'I was going to tell you to keep close because the mist is thickening but I can see I don't need to,' Nick said. Isabel raised her chin. He found the movement unexpectedly appealing and pulled in his lower lip with his teeth before going on, 'We have two more steep drops to climb up and down like the one you fell down yesterday. I'll help you up and down but if you'd rather I carry you, you only have to say so. How do you feel at the moment?'

Isabel was surprised at his concern, which for him had been expressed kindly.

'I have a few bruises left from yesterday but I'm quite used to this walking now,' she replied.

He nodded and grinned, showing his teeth, and she was suspicious of him again.

The slippery ground made it difficult to keep a firm footing as they descended and scaled the two valleys. Nick held Isabel's hand firmly to stop her from descending too fast and hauled her up beside him as they climbed. He was panting himself when they reached the top of the second slope. He gave Isabel the flask of water. She missed the warm roughness of his big hand.

''Tis fairly straight walking from now on till we climb down into Porthtowan,' he said.

'I'm glad to hear it,' Isabel said, trying to regain her breath. 'Then we go on to St Agnes and presumably Crantock after that.'

'In a manner of speaking. We have to go through Perranporth and Holywell Bay as well as some other small coves and coombes before we reach Crantock.' Isabel looked around but her vision was limited to about two feet by the grey-whiteness of the mist as it billowed about them wetly. It muffled the sound of the rolling surf two hundred and fifty feet below. The stillness of the morning made it seem far away. 'I hope we can rest along the way.'

'I'd be there by now if I didn't have you holding me up,' he said stonily.

'I have no wish to be in your company either,' Isabel said crossly, turning sharply away from him.

Nick walked on and she waited a moment before following and found his big frame was already eaten up by the mist. The ground was stony and his boot tracks hard to make out but she had no intention of calling to him as though she was lost or frightened.

A figure appeared and she assumed it was Nick coming back for her. But this man's outline was broader and when he suddenly stood barring her path it made her scream in terror. He was shorter than Nick, about thirty years older, with a huge girth of swollen stomach instead of a waist and a thick neck that grew out of his chest. His eyes were close set either side of a broken nose, below which grew a full black beard that was as curly as his wild corkscrew hair. His clothes, including a ragged knee-length waistcoat with all its buttons missing, were filthy and from several inches away Isabel could smell stale ale and sweat. He looked like one of the old-time privateers who had once haunted this part of the lonely coast. Isabel had heard stories of their heinous crimes, of the terrible degrading things they did to the women they captured. He took a step towards her with an evil leer on his face and she screamed again.

'Well, bless my soul. The mists 'ave thrown me up a fairy princess all fur meself,' the man sniggered. 'Thee didn't oughta be up 'ere all by yerself, my lovely. 'Tis a good thing fur 'ee I jus' 'appened t'be comin' along at this very moment. Most opportune, I should say.' His voice was as thick as his neck.

Isabel could not move but did find her voice. 'Nick! Nick!' The man grasped her shoulder and yanked her in against his huge belly, laughing like the booming of storm waves entering a deep cavern. She tried to beat him off with her fists and kept up her screaming. 'Nick! Help me!'

'Now, there's no need fur all that, princess. You be nice and obliging to me and I'll be more 'n' the same to thee!' He brought his face down to Isabel's and she thought she would faint at the stinking breath from his black mouth and rotten teeth.

'Let her go, Pengelly!'

The man was startled by the sudden harsh command. His grip on Isabel loosened. She wriggled free and ran round him straight into Nick's arms. He clamped her protectively to him and she did not miss the look of hatred he shot at the man who had terrified her.

'Well, well, well and well again,' Pengelly sneered. He stared at Nick then looked Isabel up and down. 'Don't tell me, Nancarrow, you've finally taken up with a reg'lur woman! Thought you was too much of a fly bastard fur that. Mind you, I can see why you 'ave with this one. She's a cut above the whores you usually lay with, even that rich man's piece you beds down with at Crantock. This one is yer woman I take it, or can any man make 'ee a bid fur 'er?'

'She's mine all right, Pengelly, and if you ever touch her again I swear I'll kill you!'

Pengelly roared with laughter which made his belly and massive shoulders shake. 'You ain't fit t'spit on me, Nancarrow. Be the other way round, more like it.'

Although he was shouting at Nick he kept up his scrutiny of Isabel. It terrified her and she clung to Nick, her hands pushed inside his jacket and clutching the back of his shirt.

'My name is Gyver Pengelly, princess,' Pengelly said menacingly. 'I daresay you'll be seeing me again.' He rocked with mocking laughter, then turned and bounded away down the steep hill they had just climbed, shouting over his shoulder, 'One day I'll wrestle 'ee fur 'er, Nancarrow!'

'I've never been so afraid in all my life,' Isabel said shakily. 'Something about that man was so… so savage.' She pressed her face to Nick's chest. She could hear his heart leap in anger while her own thumped with fear. He did not let her go and she did not want him to. He rested his chin lightly on her head and rubbed his hands over her back to calm her quaking.

'You have good reason to be scared where he's concerned,' he said as though he'd eaten something bitterly sour. 'He's a big man with a little brain who struts and fumes about the North Cliffs. He's nothing but scum, a savage, like you said. I saw him at the scene of the coach accident and I'm almost certain he was responsible for the pile of rocks being on the road. From now on, keep very close to me.'

They walked on, with Nick checking often that Isabel was close behind him. She could see enough of the track to realize they were moving over some very rugged coastline and then her ears picked up a strange symphony of noises: clanking, whirrs, hisses and booms, and after a while human voices. As she tried to determine what it all meant, Nick took her arm and led her away inland. The noises died away and the mist thinned. They were now walking through a rough field.

'What were those noises back there?' Isabel asked. 'I heard similar sounds before, much further back, but then I thought it was the roar of the sea and wind.'

''Twas a copper workings. The Wheal Prospect-Rose. The one back-along was the Porthcadiak Mine,' Nick explained. 'I'm keeping you out of the way, don't want you seen unless it's inevitable. St Agnes Beacon is over to our right, all six hundred odd feet of it, but you can't see it in this mist.'

He found the well-worn cliff path again, which pleased Isabel as it was easier to tramp along. They reached the high cliff overlooking Porthtowan without further incident and again he helped her down the tricky climb to firm ground. She looked back up and the top of the cliff was lost in the mist. It was just as steep and much higher than the drops they had conquered before, and she thought again that under normal circumstances she would have refused to do it. Nick nudged her and she obediently walked beside him at a fast pace through the village. They avoided the simple cottages and homesteads and passed over the sandy beach where the ebbing tide had left a long line of stones. There was yet another climb, although not so high, to take them on to St Agnes.

The wind was blowing harder here and clearing the mist, revealing snatches of St Agnes Beacon, the wild physique of the rocks and a raging high sea. With better visibility, Nick no longer checked his long athletic strides, and Isabel battled on after him, wishing she could stop and rest awhile.

Nick kept them mainly to the paths which for the most part were flat, but saved time by keeping in a straight line rather than following the path if it ran round a headland. Since the encounter with Gyver Pengelly, neither he nor Isabel spoke a word. The improved visibility did not last long as the weather took a turn for the worse. The sky grew darker and the sea became wilder. A blast of wind hit Isabel's back and sent her scuttling forward. Nick caught her deftly and steadied her. The wind howled so loudly he had to shout to be heard.

'A storm's blowing up. We'll carry on to St Agnes Head, go on a bit further and slip through Trevaunance Cove then go on beyond it to a little coombe I know where we can find shelter. There's an old cottage there. No one lives there now because the locals believe it's haunted.'

'Can't we shelter in St Agnes?' Isabel shouted back.

'No, 'tis over half a mile inland, 'tis market day today and the people are so friendly we'd have to answer a lot of questions. Besides, 'tis where Gyver Pengelly lives and I don't want to bump into him again – yet.'

They scrambled down into and up from another small cove and made their way around St Agnes Head. None of its usual abundant birdlife was to be seen. Trevaunance Cove, too, was deserted and soulless. Then it was up a stony slope onto the bare cliffs again. It was three hundred feet high in parts and Nick moved them inland as far as was possible to get away from the punishing winds whose awesome strength buffeted them about and hurled grit in their eyes.

Nick held Isabel firmly round the waist to keep her close and aid her stumbling passage. She grumbled to herself that it was bad enough being forced to make this journey without these adverse weather conditions adding to her discomfiture. But when Nick stopped a moment to put the canvas bag over his other shoulder, she could not help but marvel at the natural beauty of the colours of the cliff face that veered out in front of them. There were rich buffs and browns and, in places, the purple-blue of high-quality tin ore. She could see distant mine buildings and was drawn to the dark brooding silhouettes of the engine houses. They no longer seemed ugly or boring to her as they had been in the past, or foreboding as in the mist, but important and majestic somehow.

Nick hugged her waist again and they fought their way on until at last they descended one more steep hill where scant vegetation grew alongside a bubbling wide stream that wended its way over a rocky bed to give itself to its master, the sea. Nick carried Isabel over some stepping stones, putting her down to follow the stream's course inland. The rise on the other side of the valley shielded the two lonely figures and then Nick announced they were in Trevellas Porth.

Isabel longed to reach the cottage he'd promised would be there and didn't care how many ghosts haunted it. She wanted only to get out of the terrible wind, the biting cold. As they neared a low, thick-walled building, icy stinging rain suddenly lashed down on them. Nick grabbed her hand and raced with her towards the sanctuary of its dark door.

Chapter 7

Gyver Pengelly burst his way into the Basset's Cove Inn in a foul temper. The rain glistened on his beard like dew on a spider's web. He glared around the taproom with his screwed-up bloodshot eyes. They alighted on and leered at the landlord who tersely nodded to him, then on a nervous young serving maid and five male drinkers who were loafing there. The inn had been grandly decorated, proud and hopeful, when built fifty years ago. Since then it had deteriorated into a draughty drab-roomed place with dirty windows, moth-eaten curtains, drink-stained tables and a mud-encrusted floor. A few candles were lit against the gathering darkness caused by the stormy weather.

Pengelly shook himself and sent drops of water flying from his greasy hair and long waistcoat, his only protection against the weather. He didn't seem to feel the cold and never wore a coat. He roared his order for a brimming tankard of best ale and leaving a puddle at his feet stalked through the pungent smell of burning tallow candles and the fug of the other customers' pipes. He snatched up the tobacco pouch of one of the drinkers, glared a threat at him against making a protest before arriving at the counter for his ale. The serving maid gasped and choked and ran out into the back room. Pengelly spat after her then gave a thunderous roar of laughter. The landlord didn't raise an eyebrow. Pengelly and the girl went through this ritual every time he entered the inn. The landlord just hoped Pengelly would never catch her alone.

Pengelly settled his bleary eyes on his host. 'Is it ready or no!' he bellowed, referring to his drink.

The landlord may have allowed his establishment to slip in standards but he was proud of the dozen new pewter tankards he had acquired recently and at Pengelly's entry had hastily hidden them under the counter. He served Pengelly's ale in an old battered tankard. It was two inches taller than the others but he charged the same amount of pennies as for the smaller measure. It usually worked to keep the brute who terrorized the North Cliffs in good humour with him. Not that he was particularly worried about his personal safety; as one of Pengelly's best contraband customers he was not normally the target of the other's cruelty.

Pengelly lifted his ale and quaffed half the contents in one gulp, which left a wave of froth on his beard. He wiped it away with a dirty hand. 'The weather's gettin' worse, so tonight,' he winked a heavy-lidded eye as he threw down the money for his drink, 'went be on. Be in a couple of days when all's settled down again.'

'I'll be glad of it.' The landlord leaned over the counter and whispered, 'Me cellar's getting low. But a boat would have to be mazed t'brave these seas. Have the next drink on me, Mr Pengelly.'

Pengelly liked to be spoken to in respectful terms. He nodded and took up his second tankard of ale and pushed his bulk through the tables in the taproom, spilling the ale of those drinking at them. No one dared to complain. He was looking for entertainment. He peered down the five dusty steps into the next room which was separated from the taproom by a high banister and quickly found what he was looking for. Settled at a table in front of a crackling fire were two travellers, a man and a woman of middle age eating a meal of goose and plum pudding. Pengelly leaned his cumbersome weight on the shaky banister. The landlord suddenly remembered he had something important to do elsewhere and disappeared after the serving maid.

'Af'noon to 'ee. Welcome to Portreath,' Pengelly shouted at the newcomers, his booming voice sending chills down the backs of the other drinkers. 'Bet 'ee are glad t'be out of the perishin' cold, eh?' He rubbed his free hand over his beard then tapped out a loud pitter-patter on his tankard with black fingernails.

'Good day to thee, brother, and on my wife's behalf may I thank you for your welcome,' the man said, standing up and smiling pleasantly.

Gyver Pengelly pawed his massive chest uncertainly. He had been about to toss the travellers from their warmth and meal, but as his eye fell on the food, his stomach grumbled in hunger and he decided to eat it off the table. If he cast folk away from a table he invariably overthrew it and its contents ended up on the floor. He looked at the woman to see if she had a pretty face and was not disappointed. She inclined her bonneted head demurely but looked unsure of him. Then her husband did something she was to regret bitterly.

'Please do come down and share our fare, sir,' he said, holding out a hand in invitation.

After gulping a noisy throatful of dark bitter ale, Pengelly bounded down the steps. He stood beside the man at the head of the table and glowered over him and his wife. They both wore dark, simply cut clothes, the woman showing no neck or bosom, without decoration or jewellery. Pengelly summed them up with a creaking grimace on his huge face.

'Methodies, are 'ee?' he roared.

'That is correct, brother,' the man replied, smiling widely. 'Both saved these last twenty years, praise the Lord.'

'Then good fur you!' Pengelly said, slapping him soundly on his narrow shoulder which brought him down on his chair. 'And I don't mind if I do, share yer meal, that is. 'Tis some good of 'ee to offer an' much 'preciated on a day like t'day, when a man's innards could sore do with fillin'.'

Pengelly rounded the end of the table and plonked himself down close to the woman on her bench, forcing her to move well away from him. She looked most uncomfortable, an anxious frown pleating her forehead. Her husband smiled at her encouragingly although he, too, could smell Pengelly's sickening odours.

'Damme, if this isn't jus' the thing.' Pengelly pulled the goose carcass in front of him. It was still liberally covered with flesh and picking it up in both hands he bit out a chunk of breast.

'I am Andrew Fairweather and this is my wife, Amorel. We have recently attended a love feast at Camborne,' the man said, pleased that he could not offer his hand again with his guest grasping the goose.

Pengelly glared at them both. 'Yer both fair of face but when 'ee came this way thee should 'ave brought fair weather with 'ee like yer name.'

Andrew and Amorel Fairweather gave polite laughs.

'Can I buy thee folks a drink?' Gyver asked, chomping noisily, grease dripping off his beard. This was a question aimed at causing trouble.

Amorel Fairweather stammered their thanks and declined Pengelly's offer. She was looking flustered and begged her husband in a silent look not to say anything that would aggrieve this bad-mannered man. There was something wholly dreadful about him and she wished her husband was not given to gestures of spontaneous hospitality.

'What?' Pengelly roared, waving the carcass about in one massive hand. 'You refusin' my 'and of friendship!'

'No, no, no,' Mr Fairweather interjected hastily. 'Good sir, we meant no offence. What my wife meant was that we do not partake of hard liquor. We would be most grateful for a dish of tea if the landlord could be prevailed upon to supply us with one.'

'Tea!' Pengelly said derisively. ''Pon my soul.'

'And without sugar served, if you please. We do not encourage the practice and ill-treatment of slaves.' Andrew Fairweather was oblivious to the storm building up inside the inn. Amorel's heart sank rapidly. 'Mr Wesley—'

'Who cares 'bout they or cares 'bout 'e?' Pengelly snarled, thumping a greasy fist down on the table. He might tolerate this couple's company – for a while. He would not tolerate sermon talk from them.

'The Lord does,' Fairweather replied, ignoring his wife's urgent warning looks and the fear building up in her pale eyes. He smiled confidently at her. He was sorry she had turned a curious shade of puce, but her discomfiture would have to be endured for the moment. He had made an opening to talk about the Gospel and it was his duty to perform the glorious work allotted to him.

'We are all equal in God's eyes, old and young, male and female, noble man and servant, and there should be no need to enslave a man, woman or child, of any colour or creed. The slave of the Bible was a different thing altogether to the way it is done in this day and age. Do you, by any chance, know the pardoning grace of the Lord, know and love the Lord Jesus, brother?'

'Never mind 'bout 'e neither! Don't want to 'ear none of that prattle! An' don't call me brother! The only brother I 'ad 'ad 'is guts ripped out by a Frenchie in a fight over a 'alf anker of brandy bein' smuggled in. Is that why you invited me feat with 'ee? To fill me 'ead with yer bloody salvation talk, eh? Shut up an' order me another drink!' Pengelly slammed his tankard down on the table and Amorel blinked and started with fear. Andrew Fairweather looked anxiously about for the landlord but he was still absent.

Pengelly devoured the remains of the goose and wiped his hands on the wide thighs of his breeches. He belched, and seeing his hosts had lost their appetites, grabbed the whole plum pudding which quickly went the same way as the goose. He belched several times more, leaning over Amorel to do the last one, then laughed uproariously.

All was tense in the inn. The other drinkers had drifted away and only one new customer ventured in.

The landlord crept back and served the newcomer. Fairweather called unobtrusively for service and debated whether to try again to save the soul of the other man at the table – he was obviously in Satan's iron grip. His wife looked as if she could not bear another moment there. She was too frightened to tell him that Pengelly had his hand on her leg and was rubbing it up and down.

'I'll tell 'ee what I think 'bout this Westley!' Pengelly roared. 'I 'eaved a ruddy great rock at un at St Ives back-along, when 'e first begun all 'is preachin' down this way. 'It un too, I did. Do 'ee think 'e forgave me?'

'He surely did,' the woman piped up unexpectedly, and then leapt off the end of the bench.

'Then 'e's a bloody fool!' Pengelly bellowed. 'I'll kill any man who as much as gives me a black look.'

Andrew Fairweather rapidly joined his wife who was now sobbing at the foot of the steps. 'Well, if you will excuse us, sir. My wife needs a rest before we go on our way.'

''Bout time too, yer was gettin' on me bleddy nerves! I'm a man who likes t'eat in peace.'

The couple scuttled away and Pengelly laughed mockingly after them. The landlord brought him a large jug of ale and retrieved the platters from the table before Pengelly swiped them to the floor. Then he went after the retreating husband and wife to apologise profusely and offer them his best room, free of charge, for them to rest and recover in. Pengelly looked about for his next victim but couldn't find one. There was only the solitary drinker in the taproom, a man who wasn't afraid of him. It was Charlie Chiverton.

'Af'noon, Charlie.'

'Af'noon yerself, Gyver. 'Ow's things with you then?'

'Not so bad. 'Ad some good sport jus' now.'

'So I 'eard and saw. They'm a charmin' couple, good as gold. Do anythin' fur anyone, they would. They pass this way occasionally and don't do no 'arm to no one,' Charlie said, lighting his pipe with exaggerated care and looking Pengelly straight in the eye. 'The man's a fine preacher, believes in what 'e's doin' and what 'e says and lives up to it. You were out of order there, Gyver.'

'Go to 'ell,' Pengelly scowled and poured more ale. He was wary of picking a fight with Charlie Chiverton who was quick on his feet and skilful with the knife he kept hidden in his belt. Pengelly had seen Charlie despatch three Frenchmen, bigger and stronger, in the same dispute that had cost his brother his life.

'Bloody weather's put paid to me run tonight,' Pengelly said moodily. No one ever spoke to him by choice and he liked a conversation if he had a captive audience or someone who was not afraid to stay put and listen to him. ''Ad a nice little lot comin' in round Trevaunance Cove. Gotta keep me buyers 'appy. If 'ee can't deliver reg'lur, they'll go elsewhere. 'Ow 'bout thee comin' along an' 'elpin' me t'bring in the goods when I'm in bizness again, Charlie?' Pengelly talked quite openly about his smuggling runs. No one would ever dare to inform on him and the local Revenue men had learned to stay out of the inns if he was inside or risk a broken neck.

'I'm 'appy with me own arrangements,' Charlie answered. He hadn't smuggled with Gyver Pengelly since the fight with the Frenchmen many years ago. It had been Pengelly's attempt at a double-cross that had caused the bloodshed. ''Tes fair rough at sea today. Glad I'm not out on it. The Revenue men will reckon to 'ave a quiet night anyway.'

'Well, if there's no run, there might be other pickin's,' Pengelly said, rubbing his giant's hands eagerly.

'Aye, there might,' Charlie said grimly. He had gone to the scene of the coach accident soon after Nick and Isabel Hampton had left him the day before and it had been picked cleaner than an old bone. The four dead had been left naked. He knew Gyver Pengelly must have come back soon after Nick had dragged Isabel Hampton away and he knew he would give a wrecked ship the same irreligious treatment.

Pengelly remembered something and grinned evilly. ''Ere, saw an 'quaintance of yourn this mornin', up on the cliffs 'tween 'ere an' Porthtowan.'

'Aw aye. Who was that then?'

'That Nancarrow swine!'

'Nick Nancarrow, eh? I 'eard 'e was back in these parts.'

'Aye, got back jus' in time to see 'is gen'leman friend, old Trevennor, give up the ghost yesterday.' Pengelly laughed maliciously. 'Course, you must know what 'appened to that po-faced kinswoman of Trevennor's, the fancy piece from Truro. Her coach was turned over and smashed to bleddy pieces up near where you d'live. You must've 'ad good pickin's from un. Must've thought 'twas Christmas and feast days rolled into one!'

Charlie got up and joined Pengelly, sitting on the opposite bench. 'I managed to get a few pieces of wood out of un.' Charlie's bloodhound eyes watched Pengelly's face closely, wondering if he had seen Isabel Hampton with Nick. 'Looters got there first though, took all the best stuff, cushions, tools, even the wheels had gone by the time I got there.'

'Pity I missed un,' Pengelly said with mocking eyes. 'I 'eard the bodies were a proper mess, all 'cept Trevennor's niece who's said to 'ave gone over the cliff. Bit of her dress was seen down un.'

'Aye,' Charlie shook his head. 'A double tragedy.'

'Yah,' Pengelly scoffed, raising a greasy dismissive hand. He picked up a discarded toothpick from the floor and dug away at his rotten teeth. Looking shrewdly through the gloom of the afternoon, he pushed aside the candlestick, the only item gracing the bleak table, making the flame bend precariously. 'Who's the fancy piece of woman'ood with Nancarrow then, Charlie?'

'How d'ya mean?' Charlie said, giving nothing away but knowing he ought to show a keen interest.

'The wench Nancarrow 'ad with 'im. Told me she wus 'is woman. 'Twas passin' strange, I thought.'

'Nick?' Charlie feigned surprise. 'With a woman? She went 'ang on to 'im fur long, 'e's too fly-by-night fur that. Well then, what's she like?'

Pengelly made a rude gesture. 'A comely piece right 'nough. Bit on the thin side fur my tastes but rounded in the right places I d'reckon with 'er clo'es off. Tell 'e one thing, Chiverton, she's got good blood in 'er, she's no common trollop.' He rubbed his thick black beard, making a rasping noise, and slobbered coloured moisture from the comers of his fat lips. 'Reckon Nancarrow got in there first. Wouldn't mind 'avin' a piece of 'er meself when 'e's taught 'er what's what 'n' passed 'er over.' Pengelly pushed his ugly face forward. 'Thought you would 'ave seen 'er yerself by now. Calls on 'ee, don't 'e?'

Charlie stared back, not intimidated by Pengelly's direct look. 'I'll see un soon enough and knowing young Nick 'e'll 'ave got rid of this woman by then.'

'Well, if 'e 'as, tell un to send 'er along to me!' Talking of the woman he'd seen with his old enemy made Pengelly wish he had time to go on to Gwithian and visit Nellie, but he had to see his smuggling cronies and make plans for another run. Nellie thought he was good to her. It was him who had gone for help when her grandmother had been taken suddenly ill – well, after he had fed her poisoned oysters and left it too late to save her. Nellie was good to him, she didn't blab about their bedding together and if he hit her she took it as just punishment. Pengelly thought it a good idea to render all women simple-minded so they were inclined to do a man's every wish without argument. Nellie would look after the money that Deborah Kempthorne should have given her today with her life and not spend a penny of it, and he would just have time to slip home to St Agnes and spend some time with his barren wife, another woman he had moulded to his ways.

Pengelly drank the last of the ale straight from the jug. Then he grunted at Charlie and burst his way out of the inn, slamming the door in a wood-splintering movement.

The serving maid poked her meek head nervously round the wall of the taproom and seeing the man she feared above all others had really gone, went about her duties once more.

Charlie sighed and stretched his feet out to the hearth. He had been to Gwithian that morning and he'd seen Mrs Christopher out in the village. Mrs Christopher had told him it had been Pengelly who had called at Trevennor House with the news, three hours after the event, of the coach accident, and said he'd watched Isabel Hampton's broken body being washed away at the foot of the cliff. He'd obviously lied about seeing Isabel Hampton dead to be sure of being paid for ambushing the coach. It was a good job, Charlie thought as he put his splendid pipe carefully away in its carved box, that Gyver Pengelly was not as intelligent as he was brutal or he would have pondered a little bit more deeply on just who the woman was he had seen with Nick earlier in the day.

Chapter 8

Isabel was astonished at what she saw inside the one-roomed cottage. She stood and stared by the door as the rain pounded down outside. Nick moved into the room and banged his head on a rafter. He cursed it soundly. He turned on Isabel to challenge her to remonstrate with him but she seemed not to have heard. She seemed frozen for a few moments, then she moved inside, scrutinizing everything closely. She was in a fully furnished room with ornaments on the mantelshelf, kindling wood laid in the hearth, cheap cloth for curtains pulled back at the two shuttered windows and bedding rolled up on a wide bench that served as a bed. The small square table was laid ready for two people.

The cottage had obviously been empty for years. Everything in it was shrouded in layers of dust and cobwebs. It seemed sacrilege to disturb anything. In every crack and crevice of the walls, rags were stuffed to keep out the draughts. The thick walls kept out the worst of the cold and muffled the sound of the wind which was now howling like a demented wild animal.

'How long has it been empty like this?' she asked, many more questions poised on her lips.

'Three or four years.'

'I would have thought the common people would have taken everything out of here long ago,' Isabel stated wonderingly, gingerly pulling a dish towel from the string washing line tied across the hearth. It brought down a confusion of dust and made her cough. When the dust had settled, she used the towel to wipe thick dust off a stool and sat down on it. 'Some of the furniture looks well made and there seem to be some other nice pieces in the room.' She looked up at Nick and her heart froze. There was a tempest forming outside and from the expression on his face there was one raging inside him. 'What's the matter?' she asked.

'Clear up the rest of this mess,' he growled. 'You're a woman so there ought to be some sort of house cleaning instinct in you. I'll light a fire and we'll eat.'

'Won't people be curious to see smoke coming out of the chimney?'

'Not many folk come past this way and if someone does I'm counting on them being too scared of the ghosts to investigate. They won't come in without knocking and you earn hide behind the door while I send them on their way. Now get on with some work!'

Isabel shot him a look of sheer loathing. His rudeness appalled her. She got up and rubbed her icy hands together to get her circulation flowing and tried to recall what her housemaids did while cleaning a room. Deciding they would probably first ensure there was a usable table, she denied herself the warmth of her cloak to work more efficiently and began wiping the table down. She cast uncertain glances at Nick as he used terse movements and swore in even worse language until he got a small blaze under way. He stood up and bumped his head again which resulted in him angrily kicking a tin jug out of his way. Its clattering jarred on Isabel's nerves.

'What on earth is the matter with you?' she snapped.

Nick grabbed a broom and thrust it at her. 'Sweep the floor,' was his moody reply.

'Nick.' Her tone was softer, coaxing, as she left the table and accepted the broom. She was suddenly weary and did not want to quarrel with him. 'Have I done something to upset you?'

'Said,' he rapped back.

'Said? Then pray tell me what it was I said.' She tried a small friendly smile but he wasn't interested.

'If you want to eat, woman, get this place clean, and quit jawing on me.'

Isabel flinched under the icy sting of his words. Shaking her head she set about sweeping the floor. The dust rose and made her choke and she could feel Nick sniggering. It took a real effort to ignore him. She went back over every word she had spoken since they'd plunged through the cottage door. She had not said much before he'd become silent and angry, only a remark about the ordinary people not taking things from the cottage. But she had not used the word ordinary, it had been common. Was that what had upset him? She had not meant to sound patronizing, or superior, or to make a reference to their different stations that was offensive. He was such a prickly man. How was one to take him?

When the room was a little less dusty he suddenly pushed the canvas bag into her arms. 'Mundy put some food in there, put it on the table,' he ordered her.

Isabel gritted her teeth. She dearly wanted to put the broom about his back or strangle him with the neckerchief Mundy had bought for him.

When they were sitting, she on the stool, he on the only chair, warmed by the crackling furze fire, eating pilchard pies off the wrappings Mundy had put the food in, Isabel broke the stony silence.

'I did not mean to cause offence when I made the remark about the "common people" to you, if that is the reason why you are angry with me again.'

'Your sort never miss a chance to show how much better you are than us more ordinary mortals. Better houses, better clothes, better manners,' Nick snarled, breaking off a crust of pastry and pointedly ramming it into his mouth.

'You are very touchy about the subject.' Isabel looked at him squarely. 'Are you ashamed of your station in life? Perhaps you secretly hold the desire to be rich or a gentleman yourself.'

Nick remained completely unruffled which put Isabel on the defensive. 'No, you just remind me of all that's bad about your class.'

'Oh? And what is that?'

'Let's begin with injustice. Not paying a labourer or servant his worth. Enclosing the common pasture land so folk can no longer rightfully graze their livestock. Sending a child to prison for taking a rabbit to save his family from starving—'

'We're not all like that I'll have you know,' Isabel broke in.

Nick guffawed and his scathing expression told her he singled her out particularly in his accusations.

'It would help if people didn't spend so much of their earnings on liquor,' she said quietly, trying not to show how upset he was making her.

'It would help more if some of the landowners who grumble about that didn't insist on paying part of a labourer's wages with cider.'

'It would help if the public-house keepers did not allow men to become credited with an ale account they cannot afford to pay.'

'It would help more if those who are better off really cared about the working folk having a better standard of living and provided more educational places where they could learn how to better their lot.'

'You're impossible,' she countered, resisting the impulse to hurl the pilchard pie wrappings at him. 'You try my patience, Nick Nancarrow. You know as well as I do that the Bassets have provided scholastic facilities.' Then her tone softened, 'I don't have to bother with you but if I have to endure your company I would rather it was on congenial terms.'

Nick was staring at her lips and she couldn't contain the colour that was creeping up her face. She found it disconcerting, his habit of only briefly holding eye contact while they conversed then dropping his dazzling eyes to her lips. Why did he do it? Because he wanted her to stop talking or – and this was what was causing the blush – because he wanted to kiss her?

'I… what I had meant to say was that with so many ordinary people being so poor and in need, I was surprised they had not taken some of the things left in the cottage. They need them so badly. A wrecked sailing ship is rapidly stripped of its assets so why not an abandoned cottage? I wasn't criticizing the people.' She waited hopefully for a positive reaction from Nick.

He opened a bottle of ale he had bought at the Basset's Cove Inn and took a mouthful, wiping his mouth on his shirt sleeve. 'Is that so?'

'Yes, it's the truth… Why don't you like me?' she asked, looking at her food then at him.

'Why should I?' he asked levelly.

Isabel shrugged her graceful shoulders. 'You liked my uncle…'

'Why should that mean I should like you?'

'It doesn't!'

It was nearly dark in the cottage, with only the firelight illuminating Isabel's face. She had turned angrily from him. The flames gave the side of her taut face a creamy-golden sheen to add to the roses put there by their recent exertions. Nick couldn't believe now that he had once thought her sharp-faced. She had a delicately shaped but proud chin which combined with her straight nose and smooth brow to give her a fine aristocratic profile. She turned to pick up the water flask.

Nick watched her lips as she drank demurely. He wondered how many men had pressed their lips to hers, had felt their softness. Something inside him stirred and caught him unawares. He had kept control of his baser instincts in this young woman's company, telling himself he could never desire such a creature, but he was suddenly caught with his guard down. Damn the firelight! He was not a romantic man. No woman had had that effect on him before. Certainly not a haughty madam like this one. She was angry with him. He had upset her. It made her grey eyes darker, almost black in the shadows of her face. Nick got up and moved away from her.

Isabel finished her food and stood up to shake the crumbs from her lap. She pushed the stubborn ones down off her dress and Nick, whose eye had caught her movements, was reminded that all there was beneath it was a pair of gloriously long legs. He winced and finished off his ale. Damn the woman! Didn't he have enough to put up with without her arousing his carnal feelings?

'I see Mundy has put some muffins in the bag. Do you want some?' she asked him, keeping her voice mild.

'No, thank you,' he replied shortly. 'That long black fork standing in the hearth is the toasting fork,' he informed her, a trifle grudgingly.

'I know how to toast muffins,' she said, piercing a muffin and holding it out to the hot embers. 'The king and the queen toast muffins in their own chamber.'

'Then you are in good company even in a tin-miner's cottage,' Nick said dryly, keeping to the other side of the table.

After finishing her muffin, which she found delicious despite not having any butter to lavish on it, Isabel spotted a wide-toothed comb on the mantelshelf. She took it down and scrutinized the wooden object for signs of lice. After wiping it furiously with the dish towel, she began to ease the comb through the tangle of her hair.

'That probably belonged to the bal-maiden murdered by Billy Noone on that very spot. That's her bloodstains you're standing on.' The tone of Nick's voice chilled Isabel as much as his remarks did. She backed away hastily and stared at the floor but could see no marks or discoloration on the stone slab floor.

'What are you talking about?' she demanded.

Nick returned to the chair and settled back to enjoy himself. 'Billy Noone was a tinner. Bit daft in the head, he was, daft enough, too, to fall in love like any other man. But the girl he'd set his heart on, Annie Visick, a pretty little thing who worked at the same mine, had a mind to marry another, a hostler from St Agnes. Anyway, the story goes that Billy lured her here to his home. He was proud of his little cottage. As you can see, he done it up all nice and believed any maid would feel honoured to be his wife and live in it. But when Billy Noone told Annie Visick of his love, she laughed at him and,' Nick paused for greater effect, 'and he went berserk. Turned her into a right bloody mess with his mining pick, right where you were standing. He was so distraught at what he'd done he picked up her body, carried it along to St Agnes Head, and plunged them both over the cliff.'

He got up and moved to Isabel who was rooted to the spot, and in a lower, huskier voice, went on, 'She haunts this place, does poor Annie Visick. 'Tis reckoned she don't realize Billy Noone is dead too and she comes back regularly to get her revenge on him for cutting off her life so young and in its prime. You can hear her wail in fury when the wind blows and her spirit whips up the sea to such a din like you never heard before. She rattles on the door and bangs on the window to get in and take her venom out on Billy Noone. But Billy is never to be found here. If anyone else is, well, heaven help 'em, because no living soul will.'

He said the last words straight into her ear. Isabel was trembling. He had more to say. 'Some folk are said to have mysteriously disappeared after coming up this way, never to be seen again, and no beast nor bird will come within spitting distance of this place. That's why everything in the cottage is just the same as it was when Billy carried Annie Visick out. Not even the most ardent looter will take a single thing for fear of Annie's revenge.'

'Not even that dreadful man we saw up on the cliff? You said he lives not far from here,' Isabel breathed.

'Not even Gyver Pengelly.'

A gust of wind tore up a handful of stones and hurled them against the door outside. Isabel gasped loudly and put a hand to her thumping heart. 'Do… do you believe it? This terrible story?'

'Aye. Billy Noone was really mazed. He killed the girl all right.'

'Then why is it you are not afraid to stay in his cottage?'

'I knew Billy well. We used to get roaring drunk together, used to wrestle and seek the favours of women together. There was nothing wrong with the man, not until he fell in love. I reckon if I only seek shelter in his home and take nothing out of it, his ghost nor anyone else's will hurt me.'

'You don't believe the girl haunts this place?'

'No, but she wouldn't hurt me anyway. Annie was a comely wench and very obliging where I was concerned.'

Isabel hated it when he spoke coarsely. 'Billy Noone would not have liked that!' she said accusingly. 'You, with the girl he loved.' She flung back her head and her hair turned to deep golden in the firelight as it rippled over her shoulders.

Nick turned away. The firelight did dangerous things to this woman. Angry thoughts were racing through his mind. I could have you too. Crush, bruise your lips and mark your precious white skin with my rough hands. I bet you've never had hard calloused hands running over your body before. It'd make a change from the smooth fingers of a naval rake and any others who might have had the pleasure.

Isabel leaned sideways so she could see his face. His thoughts were written clearly on his harsh features, living thoughts of sensual lust. His breathing had quickened, his hands trembled. He met her gaze and his eyes flashed naked desire. She knew his feelings were held on a razor's edge.

She tried to stay her ground and beat him down. But this was no ordinary challenge. This man, with his primitive sexuality, wanted to use her. Not from a mutual attraction or simply because he had taken a fancy to her. He hated her. He hated her because she had been born in superiority over him. He wanted to exert his authority over her, stamp her down, degrade her. He was too overpowering. The terrible feelings, the longing he exuded filled the room. She dropped the comb and moved out of his reach.

Nick picked up the comb. He stepped behind her and spoke in a grazed voice, his breath warming her hair. 'Shall I comb it for you?'

Isabel gulped and panicked. He had once more reduced her to a quivering ninny. She was terrified she would not be able to speak and he would take her silence to mean acquiescence. And if he touched her…

Painfully she cleared her throat. 'N-no… thank you. I can do it.' She felt the comb pushed into her hand, then he went to the window and opened the shutters a little and stared outside into the gathering storm.

Isabel retreated to the makeshift bed and sat on it with her legs curled under her body. It was colder away from the fire, but darker, which she welcomed. She combed her hair while keeping a watch on Nick's back, ready to stop the instant he moved. Somehow this once ordinary everyday action, one she usually had someone do for her, had taken on a deeply intimate tone.

When the tangles were gone and her hair was flowing free, she returned the comb to the mantelshelf, using the pattern left in the dust to place it exactly where she had found it. Next she carefully pulled off her shoes and massaged her feet, not daring to disturb her stockings or the bandages Mundy Cottle had wrapped round them for fear of making her blisters sore again.

With his face wet and icy cold, Nick closed the shutters tightly and came back into the body of the room. He ignored Isabel huddled by the fire in the chair. He located some dips, the tallow candles Billy Noone had worn round his neck and used lighted on his hat to see his way underground and lit them, tipping melted grease to secure them around the table and mantelshelf. Isabel welcomed the extra light but as Nick moved restlessly about, his head bent under the low rafters, he cast ominous shadows. The weather howled and threatened outside, but at least Nick kept away from her. Slowly she relaxed and before she knew it she had dropped off to sleep, where she sat.

A terrified scream woke her, bringing her rigidly to her feet with a scream from her own lips. She shot fearful looks at the door and windows, half expecting to see the vengeful spectre of Annie Visick come hurtling at her throat. Another cry and a profane oath told her it was Nick who had screamed.

'What is it?' she cried, rushing to him where he sat on the bed, shaking his hand furiously.

'A rat! A rat ran over my hand!' he gasped, horror clear on his face in the candlelight.

They heard the rat scuttle across the floor and Nick sprang back further on the bed and lifted his feet up high. Isabel saw the rat's eyes twinkle in the firelight and dashed to the broom. She snatched it up and brought it down squarely on its pointed brown head, killing it with one blow. She was surprised, shocked and horrified.

'It's dead! Oh God, I've killed it!' She looked at Nick. He lowered his feet and put his hands to his face.

'Ugh, I hate the bloody things! Can you get it out of here, Isabel? Please.'

Taking a piece of rag from a crevice in the wall she marched up to the rat, lifted it nervously by its long tail and threw it, with the cloth, out of the door. With the storm shut out once more, she returned to Nick.

'Are you all right?'

He blew out deeply, puffing his cheeks. 'I am now. Well, Isabel Hampton, lady of gentlefolk, means and leisure, I shall see you in a different light from now on.'

She was greatly pleased. In his terror of the rat, he seemed a little more human, more ordinary. She wouldn't be quite so overawed by him. 'Like you, the creature was not afraid of Annie Visick's ghost,' she said. 'For some reason I have never been afraid of mice, but rats...' she shuddered. 'If you had not been frightened I'm sure I would have been the one to scream.'

Nick ran his fingers through his hair and smiled at her sincerely for the first time. Isabel had surprised him with her courage in killing and disposing of the rat. She was also kind enough to try to salvage his male ego for him. He got off the bed.

'I need a drink. Thank goodness I bought two bottles of ale in Portreath but I wish it was brandy instead. You want some?' he asked, pulling a bottle out of his jacket pocket.

'I have never tried it,' she said doubtfully.

'Do you good, put some blood in you,' he said, giving her a wide smile.

How could she resist a smile like that? The ale was bitter on her tongue but she managed to swallow two mouthfuls before giving it back to him. She felt good at last. She had won his admiration and respect. Sharing his ale meant she could perhaps gain his friendship.

'Thank you, Nick, but I prefer mead or Madeira,' she said, returning his smiles.

'Ah, women's drink,' he laughed, and downed the remainder of the bottle. 'That's better. Thanks, Isabel, for getting rid of the rat. Damn thing! I've hated them since I was a small boy, when one nearly bit my toe off. Maybe I'll show you the scar one day.'

Nick had kept the fire well built up and the whole room was warmed through despite the wind and rain battering the outside walls. Isabel took her cloak to the bed and curled up comfortably on it.

'Are we going on with our journey today?' she asked.

'No, as long as I keep you out of sight there's no hurry to get you to Crantock. I just have to be sure to get back in time for Laurence's funeral.'

Isabel thought about her uncle's body lying in his bed at Trevennor House as the county's gentry paid their respects. She hoped that if Edmund and Deborah Kempthorne had taken over the house, they would allow the villagers inside to do the same. Her eyes filled with tears but she didn't want to show Nick her mourning. Now that he was being friendly, she wanted things to remain that way, almost on a cheerful note, to make her grief and what might lie ahead more bearable.

'You were obviously very fond of Uncle Laurence from your childhood,' she said, blinking back tears.

'He was always very good to me, treated me as an equal.'

'I was wondering, if I may ask, what kind of a boy were you, Nick?'

He was a man a woman could take pleasure in simply looking at and she treated herself by doing just that as he considered his answer.

'Very wild, carefree and invariably up to my neck in mud, blood and sand,' he said, with an element of pride. 'And you, I should imagine, always prim and proper and never once with grubby hands or a torn dress.' He perched on the table, stretched out his long legs and folded his arms loosely, looking at Isabel with a gleam in his eyes.

Isabel was pleased that he was interested in her childhood too. 'No, I wasn't. Actually I liked to run free too. Uncle Laurence used to call me a tomboy and I liked to go to Gwithian because he and my aunt used to let me run about.'

'I can hardly believe that of you,' Nick said, 'not from the way you looked yesterday.'

'Yesterday seems so long ago now,' Isabel said, thinking of how she must have looked with her powdered, rouged face and painted lips, the extravagant wig and her endless protests. 'I suppose I did rather allow myself to come under Phoebe's influence these last years. Uncle Laurence did not approve, he was afraid people would think me a Jezebel. But then, appearances can be deceptive, wouldn't you agree?'

'Aye,' Nick laughed heartily, 'and if the news ever gets round that Nick Nancarrow was frightened of a rat and had to be rescued by a lady I'll never be able to hold up my head on the North Cliffs again.'

Isabel laughed with him. He liked the sound, like bells tinkling in harmony, not shrill as her voice had been. He thought about that. Her voice had dropped to a new softness, had lost its irritating highly-pitched edge. It was as feminine as she looked now, bereft of unbecoming finery. Surprising what the threat of danger and a bit of rough treatment can do for you, he mused.

'I promise I won't tell anyone our secret,' she said, realizing that this bound them together on a personal level. She hoped it would make things between them easier from now on.

'I thank you for that at least.'

'That's good. If you don't mind me asking you another question, how do you earn your living? I think you said you train horses. You're not a farm worker, a miner or a fisherman to my knowledge.'

'I've done a little of those three things and more besides. I like to travel around, keep on the move, I can't bear to be tied down in one place for long. My main occupation is breaking in and training horses to pull coaches.'

'I see. Have you thought about getting married one day, raising a family?'

'Not me,' he replied emphatically. 'Horses are my first love. I was a post boy as a young'un, till I grew too tall, then a packman and a waggoner. I had four horses of my own at one time, old nags two of 'em were but the other two were young and sturdy. I've delivered goods all over Cornwall, prided myself on getting through in all weathers and on all roads when others wouldn't travel. Now I train horses for the gentry. It pays well because it's a skilled job. I've got a good reputation and can demand a high price. While you were growing up in Truro as a fine lady learning to embroider silk cushions and play the spinet, I was roaming all over the county and beyond.'

'You make it sound romantic put like that. It certainly sounds fascinating. But where do you live, where do you go back to at the end of each of your travels?'

'Nowhere.'

'But surely you have somewhere to stay at Gwithian? You were born and raised there.'

'Laurence always used to invite me to sleep in Trevennor House but I preferred the stable loft,' he said simply, then after thought added, 'I suppose I do make my way back to Gwithian every now and then.'

'I can almost see you,' Isabel said enviously, 'a free and happy spirit, pleasing yourself, friends wherever you go, never having to bother to dress up, your hair always untidy.'

'You are beginning to know me, Isabel,' he grinned. 'Is my hair untidy now?'

'Yes, it is, very untidy.'

He took the comb from the mantelshelf and stood before her where she sat on the bed, saying softly, 'Comb it for me.' His eyes looked into hers in a warm caress as he took her hand and put the comb into it.

She was quite unable to keep looking into his eyes in case he reached down into her soul and read the attraction she felt there for him.

'You… um… will have to sit down,' she gulped.

He did this and she stood behind him, hoping he could not hear the wild beating of her heart. With shaking hands she gingerly pulled away the piece of cord with which he tied his hair back. She worked quickly, surprised to find few tangles in the shoulder-length sandy hair. It felt fine and silky and smelled of the fresh outdoors. Gathering it together, she retied the cord firmly then reached hastily round him and dropped the comb back into his hand. Afraid of what he would do next, she scrambled to the sanctuary of the corner of the bed.

'Thanks,' he said, feeling the smoothness of his hair at the back. He got up and put the comb on the table, giving his head a small shake as he did so. His hair fell naturally to its usual untidy state. Isabel watched him as he banked down the fire for the night and blew out all the dips. She could hardly see him in the darkness.

'Might as well settle down early and get some sleep and rest,' he said. 'Can't do much else with the storm raging.'

Although it wasn't late, Isabel still said, 'Good night.' She lay down facing the wall, wrapping herself in her cloak. She thought the bench much better than the cave floor but she missed her canopied bed which took three steps to climb into. She put her hands together. They were tingling from touching his hair, as if he had passed on some form of energy to her.

When Nick approached the bed, she sat bolt upright. 'You aren't going to sleep here?'

'As you said before, Isabel, I am no gentleman,' and she could detect the mocking amusement in his voice. 'Surely you don't expect me to sleep on the cold floor?'

'No… no, I suppose not, but…'

'Well, there's nowhere else for me to sleep.'

The bench was narrow, hardly big enough for two. Isabel shunted herself up as tightly as she could to the wall. Nick lay down beside her but not with his back to hers as she'd expected, hoped. She caught her breath as he moved in close, very close, on his side. He pulled Billy Noone's rolled-back rough blanket over them both and put his arm firmly round her.

Isabel held her breath but couldn't find the words to tell him to take his arms away.

'What would your fiancé say about this, eh?' he whispered through the darkness with his face close to the back of her head.

Isabel had forgotten all about Richard Grenville. With the reminder of him, the man she was due to marry in six weeks' time, she thought she ought to be feeling disturbed to be lying in another man's arms, but she did not. She did not answer Nick. She closed her eyes and shut out all thoughts of past and future, concentrating on the warmth and security of being so close to Nick. She breathed in his raw masculinity. It stimulated some strange unfamiliar senses, something new that was awakening in her. It was threatening yet she was not afraid. It was drawing her to the brink of another world. Should she, could she, risk entering it and leave behind, even if only for a moment of her life, all that she had been born and bred for, all that she had held dear and thought important? She had never been this close to a man before. If she turned round and stepped over the boundaries, would this new world welcome her into it?

Chapter 9

The storm blew itself out before first light the next day. But not all folk stayed warm and snug in their beds for the duration. Cheated of his smuggling run, Gyver Pengelly had stayed up all night in the hope that the violent weather would give him other bounty from the ocean. He'd spent the time on the waterfront of Trevaunance Cove, lumbering back often to shelter in the lee of the rocks there. Now that things were calmer and there was a little tentative daylight, he scrambled up the cliff a short distance to Newdowns Head to scan the high seas, hoping for sight of a stricken vessel losing its fight for life. There was nothing to be seen but surging waves and hissing spray slamming the hazy outline of the rocks of St Agnes Head and thundering into Trevaunance Cove and Trevellas Porth a little way yonder.

Pengelly was bitterly cold and as hungry as a hunter. His unfortunate wife had failed to satisfy another of his appetites the day before and the beating he had given her for failing in her duty had not snapped him out of his ill temper. He had threatened to sell her to the highest bidder at the next market and the folk who had heard him bawling at her hoped he would do just that for the poor woman's sake.

Pengelly was furious there was no ship offering good pickings out there. He pounded the cliff and made up his mind to steal a huge length of warm cloth from his next smuggling run and get his wife to make him up a coat for the colder nights he was abroad. When he got home he'd have the biggest breakfast ever and if she couldn't make a better job of being a good and faithful wife, he'd beat her again and go over to Gwithian to see sweet little Nellie. If only a wreck would happen to come along this minute. He might even get a nice piece of cloth for a coat – but God help anyone who made a jest that he was giving into old age because of it.

He was suddenly out of patience. If there was a crippled ship, he would hear of it soon enough and his brutal nature would ensure he got the best pickings. He stamped a gigantic foot in temper and started for home. But he was peeved because if there was a wreck he liked to be the first to see it.

It was at that moment that Gyver Pengelly thought the kind of prayers he was wont to say were being answered. Lumbering into sight from Trevellas Porth, dipping and lurching in the trough of the waves, came a large two-masted ship, her sails tattered and in considerable peril. Pengelly laughed in pure happiness. The tide was running high and there was a reef of treacherous rocks under the waters before the beach was reached at Trevellas Porth. The ship would surely strike them and the plunder would be his! Pengelly watched in elation. He was too far away to hear the desperate shouts and screams of the crew on the ship, the tearing apart of the vessel itself. It had been fighting to stay afloat for some time and was moving inexorably onto the reef.

Before the rest of Trevaunance Cove woke up, Pengelly ran off to pull his brutalised wife out of her bed and make her fetch a barrow, and to wake up his smuggling cronies to help him in the work ahead.

–

Isabel lashed out with her elbow and the cry Nick let out woke them both. She turned round sharply to find him lying on his back, rubbing at his stomach.

'What is it, Nick? What's the matter? Are you in pain?'

'You elbowed me in the guts,' he moaned.

'I'm very sorry,' she said, pulling his hands away and rubbing her own in their place.

'Stop,' he groaned, with a different sort of pleading in his voice.

'This will help.'

'Isabel, will you please stop!' Her hands were soft as they moved in light massaging movements on the outside of his shirt just above his breeches waistband. Nick caught hold of her wrists tightly and held her hands away from his body.

'I'm sorry, was I hurting you?' She wriggled to sit up and looked down on him, making out his twisted features in the crack of pale light that filtered through a window shutter. He kept hold of her wrists. 'Nick?'

'No,' he replied huskily. 'You weren't hurting me, Isabel. I liked what you were doing too much.'

'Oh!' She prayed he could not see the flush of embarrassed colour washing over her face or sense the thrill shooting through her that she could affect him in such a way.

Nick wasn't sure if she was aware how much she had aroused him. He lay still, breathing in slowly to gain control of himself, yet at the same time wanting her to make a move and fulfil his need. He had to speak to disguise his double agony. 'What was wrong with you anyway to make you lash out like that? Did you think you saw the ghost of Annie Visick?'

'No,' and she shuddered at the memory, 'it was not that. I had a nightmare about that Pengelly man.' He let go of her wrists and lifted her hair back where it had fallen forward, hiding her face from him. 'Don't worry about Gyver Pengelly. I won't let him or anyone else hurt you. Do you trust me now, Isabel?'

'Yes, Nick,' she replied softly.

They stayed silent, looking keenly at each other. He put his hands on either side of her face. Isabel wanted him to pull her close to him. He rubbed a thumb gently under her eye and she closed her lids. He took it to mean she had shut herself off from him and the moment he was hoping for was gone.

'Might as well rest a little longer,' he murmured, 'then we'll set out for Crantock.'

Isabel didn't know he was as disappointed as she was and made to resume her previous position but he pulled her down and gently laid her head in the hollow of his shoulder and held her lightly. His body was firm, warm and alive. His chin rested on her head and he wound her hair round his fingers. How could she sleep now? She listened to the strong, sturdy sound of his heartbeat. After what seemed a timeless period but was only a moment she realized that a sound she had grown used to was missing. 'Listen,' she whispered.

'What to?' he whispered back, moving so his cheek rested against hers and she could feel the light stubble there.

'The storm has gone, it's all quiet. How quickly the weather changes.' She had her hands clasped but moved one and laid the palm on his chest.

'Aye, the storm eased off a while ago but the sea will still be riding high. I pity any vessel out there if it's got into difficulties.'

'Deadman's Cove, the place where the coach went off the road, is very dangerous. Uncle Laurence called it the graveyard of ships.'

'Him and many others. You surprise me with what you know,' he teased, bringing his hand over hers. 'The same's true of the Stones, a reef of rocks off Godrevy Island, and Hell's Mouth, and all round that area. The names speak for themselves. Many a ship's foundered in my lifetime. 'Tis nearly as dangerous round this part of the coast too.'

'I've heard some terrible stories about the deliberate wrecking of ships. Are they true, Nick?'

'No, malicious slander most of 'em, but I can think of one man who'd have no conscience about carrying a lantern or lighting a bonfire to give false directions and lure a ship onto the rocks or strand it on a beach.'

'You're talking about Pengelly.' Isabel gave a small shudder and Nick wrapped his arm tighter round her shoulders. He felt her hand move under his and he interlaced their fingers.

'You can be certain he's among the first in the rush to plunder a wreck clean, but the savage truth is that wrecks are so frequent in the winter there's no need to do it purposely. Folk race to a wreck like a swarm of ants. A few to save and help any survivors, the rest to salvage. I've seen Revenue men, gentry, even clergymen picking over a wreck.'

After the harshness of the period since Nick had arrived at the scene of the coach crash, and now she had won his respect and friendship, it was idyllic being held in his arms, to be this close, enjoying a conversation. She wanted to live just for these moments, warm and safe. And she wanted to know all about Nick. Only hours before, she would have been glad to see the back of him for good. She would have remembered him as an uncouth, liberty-taking common oaf who had dealt with her grievously. Now she could stay this way for hours, for ever.

'Have you ever picked over a wreck, Nick?'

'Of course!' Nick sounded astonished. ''Tis part of a Cornishman's living, like free trading, to make use of what the sea is merciful enough to leave behind. Folk like Mundy need whatever they can get. I've brought in many a survivor. Sometimes you have to be quick and it's risky, but not many will stand by and let another drown.'

'You are brave,' she said.

'Am I now?' he laughed. 'I suppose I've been used as the answer to someone's prayers. I suppose also I'm something of a bloody-minded cuss.'

'Yes, you are rather,' and she laughed too.

He moved and his unshaven cheek grazed hers. She made to dip her face away but he brought his hand up and held her chin. Their lips were so very close and Isabel closed her eyes. This time Nick did not misread her.

A sudden noise came, so loud, so unearthly, it froze their hearts. It lasted several seconds and left a threatening silence.

'Wh-what was that?' Isabel breathed.

Nick put a finger to her lips so he could listen. Another ear-splitting, gut-tightening sound sent him hurtling for the door.

'My God, 'tis a ship on the rocks! We should never have been talking about it, it's brought bad luck.' Nick shot Isabel a harrowing look. 'I'm going out to see if there's anything I can do. Isabel, whatever you do, stay in the cottage because there'll be wreckers. They won't come up here. Get ready in case I bring back any survivors.'

He was gone and she shouted after him to be careful. It had happened so quickly she felt stunned. Gathering her wits, she opened a shutter a little way to let in some light then folded the blanket that was still warm from the closeness she'd shared with Nick. She placed it on the table in case it was needed.

She looked out of the window and saw a bleak scene outside – the two high bracken-strewn banks that sheltered the lonely little cottage, the path and stream that led to the sea and the vessel foundering upon it. Isabel tried not to think of the fear those on the ship must be facing. She could do nothing but wait for Nick to come back. Returning to the table, she sat with the outward appearance of calm born of years of training to act always as a lady.

–

Nick ran nimbly over the rocks that ran the course of the stream. The storm had swollen it until it reached the top of its banks, hurtling noisily over its pebbly bed, its stepping stones completely submerged. Visibility over the sea was poor, but Nick saw the tilted shell of the ship, its masts and sails missing, heaved by the tearing waters. His ears were filled with the appalling sound of timbers breaking as the ship was hurled again onto a tall outcrop of jagged cliff several hundred yards away from where he stood.

Instinct made Nick look up behind him and he saw a large group of people running along the path he and Isabel had taken the day before. Gyver Pengelly was unmistakably the front runner and his smuggling gang were hot on his giant heels. Nick knew his unfortunate wife, probably with two black eyes, would be plodding along somewhere behind with a huge barrow to take the plunder home in.

He scowled and scrambled down a high bank of rock onto the stretch of dull beach not yet covered by the tide and ran to the water's edge where the waves were surging in. He could see bodies tossing about in the water. He looked wildly about but it was too dangerous to swim out to see if there were any survivors among them. Breaker after breaker swept in and snatched at everything in its path, bringing it closer to the shore and taking it back again.

White surging sea almost smothered the ship, its devouring tongues taking with it the mahogany timbers that were its cargo and tossing them about contemptuously like matchsticks. Pieces of ship were bitten off and tossed in all directions. The crew still left on the ship clung desperately to whatever would help them hold on to life for a little longer. But one by one they were being lost overboard.

Sometimes when the sea receded, Nick could see the low rocks that made up part of the beach, leaving momentary pools and exposing the places where he had gathered mussels and winkles as a boy. In some areas the rocks were only a few feet under the water and bodies were bobbing about over them among the wreckage. But then Nick thought he saw one of the men raise his head. Was someone alive out there? If he could make his way over those rocks and get to the bodies, relying on the surf to wash him back in if he got into any trouble, he might just be able to haul a survivor to safety. It would be a desperate thing to attempt, but a man could still be clinging to his life, like the few remaining screaming for help on the ship, and they were more desperate than he was.

The ship shuddered under the next onslaught of incoming tide. It righted itself then keeled over on its side seawards. Nick knew that men were being spilled out of its guts, howling in fear. It was a ghastly sight and Nick's numb lips muttered words of prayer. He knew they stood no chance of survival on that side of the ship.

He had to take the risk and see if there were any survivors among the floating bodies. And he had to be quick about it;

Gyver Pengelly would soon be on his back. He pulled off his boots and tossed them beyond the reach of the sea. He made his way into the surf, clambering and sliding on the ridged rocks under his feet, using all his strength against the water to get out into the sea. His hands were cut, his breeches ripped out at the knees, but soon he was half swimming through the waves. He had forgotten for the moment the responsibility Laurence Trevennor had given him.

He reached a huddle of floating bodies and snatching at their heads saw that all were dead. Another body was entangled in the legs of a dead companion and as Nick reached for the black sopping hair, the sailor lifted his head. Nick wiped the stinging salt water from his eyes and looked again to make sure they were not playing tricks. The exhausted sailor, who had been swimming for his life and had grabbed the other seaman's legs to rest, stared at Nick in abject fear.

'It's all right!' Nick shouted above the surge. 'I'm come to help you! Give me your hand!'

Some Cornish folk held a belief that a stricken ship could not legally be called a wreck unless every living soul, fowl and beast on board were dead. It was not unknown for survivors to be murdered to accommodate that belief. The sailor looked doubtful but reckoned his best chance of survival was to trust this stranger. He raised a feeble hand and Nick clutched it. At the same moment a piece of flying timber narrowly missed the back of the sailor's head and struck Nick in the face, cutting his cheek and showering both men with splinters. They both cried out and their hands parted.

Nick acted quickly. He pushed the dead body away from the survivor and grasped his shirt. A breaker hit them and tossed them several feet towards safety but their ordeal was not over yet. The undercurrent took them back almost as far but Nick still had much of his strength left and a good grip on the sailor. A broken piece of timber, about five feet in length, was floating near them and Nick grabbed it with his free hand. Manoeuvring it lengthways, he pulled his body over it. The sailor, who was showing no signs of panic, grappled in the water as they were tossed about until he put himself over Nick's back. Nick waited for the next big wave and the two men rode the surf over the rocks until they were in shallower water. Nick thrust the timber out of their way, grabbed the sailor and pulled him along, gasping for breath, falling again and again, till at last they were safe.

They lay weak and sodden, staring out at the broken ship. A horrendous noise sounded the ship's death knell. Nick and the sailor watched in a fascinated stupor as the remains were broken apart. Both men muttered snatches of desperate prayer and then, quite unashamedly, they wept.

Nick's main concern now was to get the sailor back to the cottage before they found themselves among the wreckers. He coughed and spat out a mouthful of salt water and turned to the other man.

'I don't think we can help anyone else,' he said hoarsely. 'We have to get away from here. Wreckers are coming and there's some among them I don't trust. There's a cottage not far from here. Do you think you can make it?'

The sailor was a man of Nick's own age, not as tall and muscular but with a well-developed chest and arms telling of his years of hard labour at sea. There was a gold earring in each of his ears. 'Aye,' the sailor answered, panting heavily, 'just give me a hand to get on me land legs.'

Nick was surprised at the sailor's accent. 'You're a Cornishman! Were there other local men on board?'

'Only me,' the sailor answered. ''Tis why I didn't panic. I know these parts well though I haven't set a foot on 'em for several years. When the captain shouted, Every man for himself, I jumped overboard and let the tide bring me in. Was in the drink for ages and losing my breath when I grabbed a body, and when I looked up I couldn't believe my eyes in seeing you there.'

Nick hauled the sailor up and shakily they started to climb the high bank of rock and head for the cottage, Nick retrieving his boots on the way. The sailor thrust out a hand. 'My name's James Leddra. I'm a St Ives man. I owe you my life. I've thanked the Almighty for sending you along to me today.' Nick shook James Leddra's hand as they strode along. 'I thanked Him for sparing us both. Nick Nancarrow. Born and raised at Gwithian.'

They pushed on in silence, their weakened, bruised legs stumbling, each reaching out automatically to save the other from falling on the rocky ground. Nick glanced up and saw Gyver Pengelly had reached the cliff edge and was about to make his way down to them. Pengelly's eyes were on the wreck and Nick hoped they would stay there.

He took James Leddra's arm and pointed inland. 'Run like a hare up that way. The wreckers will be down here any moment and 'tis better they don't see you. You'll come across a cottage. No one will go near it because 'tis reckoned to be haunted so you'll be quite safe. You'll find a girl in there, tell her Nick sent you and make sure she stays there till I get back. I'll head off the wreckers so they won't be looking your way.'

'But what about you? The wreckers—'

'I can look after myself. Get going!' Nick pushed James Leddra roughly onwards and watched as Gyver Pengelly slipped and slid his bulk down towards the shore.

–

Isabel shrieked as the young seaman crashed through the cottage door minutes later. She grabbed the broom and brandished it defiantly in his face. She trembled as much as he did, her nerves set on edge by the sounds of the ship's death throes.

'Who are you?' she challenged him in Jenna Stevens' voice.

The sailor bent over and gripped his legs above the knees, panting painfully. 'James Leddra's my name… Your man sent me… said his name was Nick… said to tell you that… says I'm t'stay here till he gets back.' He was shivering violently, his face flushed and bruised, his feet bare and clothes torn.

Isabel dropped the broom. 'Is Nick all right?' she asked anxiously.

'Aye, he's heading off the wreckers, to give me the chance to slip away unseen.'

'How many wreckers are there?' Isabel asked fearfully.

'Not many yet as far as I could see but there'll be hundreds when word gets around. Nick says no one will come near this place because it's haunted.'

Isabel nodded but her relief was small. 'I hope they don't hurt him.' She picked up the blanket. 'Come and sit down. Put this around you. I'm afraid the fire's gone out. How many more survivors are there to come?'

'Don't think there's any,' James said numbly. 'Just me… and if it wasn't for Nick… I hadn't much strength left when he swam out to reach me.' He sat hunched over with the blanket round him, water dripping from his loose dark hair onto the floor.

Isabel held out the water flask to him. 'Have a drink of water. It will make you feel better.'

'Thanks, a drop of rum would go down better but you don't feel too choosy when you've just nearly lost your life.'

Isabel viewed the dejected figure with sympathy. Two days ago she would have seen him as only an underling, one of the common people. They died regularly in large numbers, from mining accidents, drownings at sea, fires sweeping through their tightly-built hovels, a variety of fevers and illnesses. It was expected of them. They were used to it. It had not really mattered. She shuddered at how she had grown up, prejudiced by such views. She saw things differently now, after knowing Nick, his ugly friend Charlie, Mundy Cottle and her brood of children. She held out a hand. It hovered, hesitated, then with resolve she placed it on the darkly tanned skin of the sailor's shivering shoulder, exposed by his torn shirt.

'I'm so very sorry. They call it the bounty of the sea. Some do even believe that God sends them the wrecks – people poor enough to be glad of anything.'

James Leddra nodded grimly. 'Aye, you're glad of it if you're starving.'

He drank down the last of the water then looked at Isabel. Even in his distress he could see she was no ordinary working-class young woman.

'We was caught out at sea in the storm. Thought we'd make a run for shore but then the wind dropped and we were at the mercy of the strong tide and sea. Cap'n couldn't keep her off the rocks out there. We'd have stood a better chance if we could have beached at Trevaunance Cove. We was tossed around like a cork and I lost my little dog, saw her float away and there was nothing I could do. I was only saved because I know these parts and jumped off the ship. Took a chance on keeping my head and the tide washing me ashore. There'll be good pickings of timber for the wreckers. Cap'n was a good'un… went never find one to sail under like he again.'

'I'm sorry,' Isabel repeated, tears pricking her eyes. 'What was the name of your ship?'

'She was *The Bountiful*. I was the mate. She was my third ship since I ran away to sea about fourteen year ago.' James wiped away fresh tears and braved a smile over chattering teeth. ''Tis awful cold in here. Can't light a fire with the wreckers crawling about but would you happen to know if some dry clothes are to be found in here? I take it from the thick dust and your man saying 'tis s'posed to be haunted you don't live here.'

'I'll see what I can find.' Isabel felt disinclined to repeat the tragic story of the cottage's previous occupant but she was worried about its curse as she rummaged through the room for Billy Noone's spare clothing. In a cubbyhole beside the bed she found a well-worn darned serge shirt, a pair of rough black breeches and a holey pair of hose. It occurred to her that Nick would also be wet through and wondered whether she shouldn't keep something back for him to change into. But another quick look at the clothes told her they would not fit him and she handed them over.

'Bless you,' James Leddra said when she laid them on the table. 'You a local maid?'

'No, I'm from the north of the county.' She did not want to be questioned and tried to appear busy.

'I'm a St Ives man myself.'

'Really?'

'Haven't set foot in it these last seven or eight years. I've got a sister there, Mary Ellen. I heard she's got a young'un, a cheeil by the name of Morenwyn. Know 'em, by any chance?'

'No,' Isabel said blandly but she was feeling uncomfortable. It was unlikely that this man knew anything about her real identity but her cousins, the Kempthornes, had a notorious reputation in St Ives and she hoped the sailor would not mention them. If he went home and heard they had moved on to better things and got talking about them and his shipwreck and the man who had rescued him and the woman waiting in this haunted cottage…

She went to the window and looked out anxiously for signs of Nick. She kept her back to James Leddra as she heard him tugging off his wet clothes. She could not blame him for wanting to change straightaway, he risked pneumonia if he didn't, but she couldn't help feeling it was improper of him not to wait for Nick to come back.

'You Mrs Nancarrow then?' he said to her stubborn back.

'No.'

He kicked his wet clothes away and sat down again, still shivering but much more comfortable. He discarded the blanket too which his clothes had soaked. 'You can turn round now.' He was watching Isabel curiously. 'You aren't Nick's sister, are you.' It was more of a statement than a question.

'No,' she replied without turning round, ashamed of what her answer would imply. 'My name is Jenna Stevens.'

Nick's intention was for the wreckers to see him and not James Leddra running away inland. He was not afraid he would be mistaken for a survivor; by his clothes he was not a seafarer and he knew many of the wreckers. As they scrambled into the coombe, the majority of them ignored him and raced off to be first at the scene of the wreck, whooping and cheering each other on. Some hailed him by name as they rushed past him. Their leader had stopped in his tracks. Gyver Pengelly stood with coils of thick rope over massive shoulders, a hatchet and crowbars in his hands.

'Got here first, I see,' he shouted at Nick. 'By the look of'ee you've 'ad a dip in the sea. Been fur a nice little swim, 'ave 'ee, Nancarrow? Didn't 'ee realise 'tes a mite too dangerous fur that today?'

Nick clenched his fists. 'I thought I'd see if anyone could be saved.'

Pengelly gave a sly sideways grin. 'All dead, are they?'

'Aye, Pengelly,' Nick said savagely. 'But she won't be easy to salvage.'

Pengelly was sweating, his bleary eyes were red-rimmed and swollen from looking all night into the wind, his large lips were purple-blue. 'Not after the pickin's yerself?' he asked suspiciously.

'No, got better things to do.'

Pengelly would have stayed to badger Nick but was eager to be in charge of the wrecking. 'That maid of yourn must be good in the sack!' he bellowed, leering, then ran on.

Nick turned his back on the big man and walked quickly to the cottage. He found Isabel and James Leddra talking quietly.

Isabel ran to him, taking in his wet and torn clothes and the trickle of blood from his cut cheek. 'Are you all right, Nick?'

'I'm fine, Jenna,' he said, glad she had remembered to use her new character. 'Get packed up,' he added in a serious voice.

'I want to be on our way before that crowd spreads out over the cliffs.'

'But you're soaked through and hurt.'

He pressed his fingers to his stinging cheek and glanced at the blood on their tips. 'I'll see to it later and I'll soon dry out.' He turned to James Leddra. 'You'll be all right as long as you stay in here till dark and head inland.'

'I thank you again, Nick Nancarrow,' James said humbly. 'I won't forget what you've done for me this day.'

'I'd be grateful if you don't tell anyone you've seen me or her,' Nick said, picking up his canvas bag.

James glanced at Isabel who gave him a brief smile. He nodded. 'My lips are sealed, you have my word on it.'

Nick hurried Isabel to the door. She looked back uncertainly at James Leddra sitting in Billy Noone's clothes. 'Don't take anything else from the cottage. It's supposed to be unlucky.'

Nick led Isabel at a fast rate further inland, following the stream along a rocky path to avoid the cliff area. A few lazy twists and turns and the silhouette of a mine workings came into view. The sound of the sea was gone, the thump, thump of the engine house taking its place. Isabel saw distant figures of bal-maidens, mine boys and the older men dressing the ore on the surface for the stamping machines. The sound of their shovels and hammers knocking out the tin from the rock carried clearly on the chilly morning air.

'The folk of this mining community live way back behind the works. They haven't got word of the wreck yet or they'd be swarming this way,' Nick said grimly, taking Isabel's arm and heading back to the cliffs.

Chapter 10

Edmund Kempthorne was out walking that morning. He sauntered through Gwithian village dressed in elegant black clothes, his velvet eyes looking out jauntily from under his tricorn hat for any suitable female with whom to pass a pleasant hour or so. The village seemed deserted, the windows of every cottage and house draped in black in mourning for Laurence Trevennor. Edmund was disappointed. He had spent a less troublesome night knowing that Mary Ellen was arriving at Trevennor House later in the day, but that was not until the afternoon, and it seemed a long time away.

Deborah wasn't at all pleased with the arrangement. She'd pleaded with Edmund to wait until after their uncle's funeral. But Edmund had thrown a violent tantrum and insisted Mary Ellen and their daughter Morenwyn, come today – his needs were more important than risking the disapproval of any narrow-minded villagers. If they didn't believe the story that Mary Ellen was a poor unfortunate widow about to be evicted from her home, whom he and his sister had taken under their wing, he didn't care! He intended to move into Isabel's residence at Truro as soon as possible anyway, when all the legal arrangements were completed.

Edmund saw no one but the landlord of the local inn, the Leg of Mutton, putting his empty ale barrels outside in his yard. Edmund accepted the landlord's offer of refreshment and listened patiently to his regrets about 'dear brave, Mr Trevennor's death, God rest his soul,' until he realised there were no serving girls about who might be willing to oblige him. He drank up, thanked the landlord and left to saunter back down the village on the other side of the road.

He made a quick perusal of the churchyard but there was only the sexton tidying up the graves and grass verges to make sure it looked its best for Laurence Trevennor's funeral in three days' time. The sexton nodded his head in respect and Edmund walked on. He smiled and his features relaxed at what he saw next. A woman was coming towards him. She was quite alone and although she had a somewhat ragged appearance she looked young and reasonably comely from a distance.

Edmund increased his pace so he could meet the woman away from the houses. Drifts of sand lay across the road and at the grassy banks, blown there by yesterday's storm. The woman didn't seem to notice his approach and gave a cry when he presented himself in her path.

'Good morning,' he said with a friendly smile, lifting his hat. He was disappointed she was not as pretty or as young as she'd first looked but he thought she was better than nothing. She would whet his appetite before Mary Ellen provided him with a feast.

The woman backed away, but when his good quality clothes and refined voice had coursed their way through her usual mental fog, she curtseyed awkwardly and looked vacantly at him.

'G'mornin' sur.' She made to skirt round him but Edmund moved in the same direction. He was even more pleased she was dim-witted.

'Do you live in the village?' he asked pleasantly. 'Ais,' then she frowned and thought about it. 'But not really. Back-along there, along a little path, a little way after the bridge.' She turned and pointed the way she had come and Edmund moved in closer to her. She was startled to see him looming over her.

'Do you live there with your family, my dear?'

'Um, n-no sur. There wus me granny but she died.' Edmund licked his lips. This was getting better and better.

'Do you know who I am?' he asked softly.

'No, sur...' The woman thought hard. 'Yes, sur... I think p'raps you'm Mister Kem'thorne, brother to Miss Kem'thorne in the Big House. Mister Trevennor was yer uncle, 'e wus some nice gen'leman.'

'I'm so pleased to hear you liked him,' Edmund drawled, and assuming every man's disposition was the same as his, he wondered just how nice Uncle Laurence had been to her. 'I adored him, of course,' he went on, rooting the woman, who looked most uncomfortable and was fidgeting to be on her way, to the spot. 'I shall miss him dreadfully. I will make sure to be just as kind to the villagers as my dear late uncle was. Tell me, my dear, what is your name?'

'Nellie, sur.' And Nellie blinked and tried to clear her blank mind and remember where she had been going before this handsome gentleman had stopped to speak to her.

'Now, Nellie,' Edmund purred, keeping his eyes glued to hers, 'I'm sure you're a very good girl and would have done anything to please Mr Trevennor. I want to make friends with the villagers, and Mr Trevennor, I'm sure, would have wanted you to help me. I would like to see your home and the conditions you live in. If I find them wanting I will arrange to have the necessary work done on them. And for your help I will give you a shiny new shilling.'

Edmund Kempthorne had not met Nellie far enough down the road to be unobserved. From an upstairs window in the parsonage, Charlotte Thomas had seen him walk past and the moment she had seen why he had quickened his pace she had flung herself out of the room and down the stairs. She had nearly knocked her husband, who had just left his study, off his feet. The papers he'd been carrying were strewn all around them.

'What is it, Charlotte, my dear? Has one of the children—'

'Nothing is wrong with the children, Perran,' she said hastily, stooping down and thrusting a piece of paper at him. 'I'm sorry about that. I have to go out for a little while, dearest. There is something I must attend to and it cannot wait.'

It couldn't even wait long enough for the Reverend Perran Thomas to be given his customary kiss. His wife rushed out of the door without even tying the ribbons of her hat and cloak.

Charlotte attended to her ribbons as she marched down the road towards Edmund Kempthorne and Nellie and she was absolutely fuming. She had had just about enough of the way men like the abominable Gyver Pengelly and this lecherous, smooth-talking dishonest gentleman used Nellie. The poor soul possessed a child's mind because of Pengelly's brutal ways. She could not tell the difference between right and wrong and was quite unable to protect herself. It was time to do something about it!

'Good morning, Mr Kempthorne, Nellie,' Charlotte said loudly as she approached them.

They both swung round. Edmund looked angry but lifted his hat politely. Nellie looked guilty and confused. Charlotte had heard her say in a panicky voice, 'But Mr Pengelly wouldn't like it!'

'Run along to the parsonage kitchen, Nellie,' Charlotte said. 'There's some work for you there and Cook has a nice big breakfast waiting for you. Tell her I sent you.'

'Th-thank 'ee, Mistress Thomas,' Nellie blurted out. Gyver Pengelly allowed her to speak to Perran and Charlotte Thomas, but only lest they object to her silence and try interfering in her life. She took to her heels and ran all the way to safety.

'Are you taking the morning air, Mr Kempthorne?' Charlotte said coldly to him.

'Indeed, I am, Mistress Thomas,' he said, employing his voice softly. 'That strange young woman stopped me and said she was sorry about my uncle's death. She said it over and over again. I couldn't get away from her.'

'I'm glad you could see that poor Nellie has only limited mental faculties. I like to keep a keen eye on her. I'm afraid of people taking advantage of her, you see.'

'That would be most wicked!' Edmund exclaimed, feigning indignation.

He had swept his eyes over Charlotte Thomas and found her most attractive. She was about twenty-eight, and he had to agree with his sister's unusually glowing accolade of her yesterday. Looking at her, he knew why Deborah had spoken in that way: she wanted him to seduce and disgrace the curate's wife because she hated Charlotte Thomas for having all the things that Nature had denied her. Charlotte's skin was clear, her thick dark hair tumbled down about her slender shoulders owing to her haste, her brown eyes shone and her cheeks glowed. Edmund thought she was a woman who could be aroused to many passions. How fortunate for the curate, he mused. She obviously didn't deny him since she had presented him with so many squalling brats. It would be a pleasure to find out what the young parson was receiving in their private moments…

Charlotte had a good idea what was going on inside his head. She decided to retreat before she couldn't stop herself from smacking his face. 'Please give my regards to Miss Kempthorne. If you'll excuse me, I have things to attend to at home. Do enjoy your walk, Mr Kempthorne. May I suggest a walk along the cliffs? The cold fresh air will do you good.'

Edmund smiled and bowed to her and then watched her darkly as she walked sedately away from him. His mouth twisted as he thought about the morally upright woman. His observations would make good pillow talk with Mary Ellen later in the day.

From an upstairs bedroom window next door in Trevennor House, Deborah Kempthorne, too, had been watching her brother. Her face was coloured by hate. Edmund had not let her down and had made a good start with what she wanted for Charlotte Thomas, but she was unhappy about the smarmy little curate's wife's interest in Nellie. Nellie had to be got rid of before she talked in one of her feeble moments.

–

Nick and Isabel walked in silence for some twenty minutes. Then Isabel, slipping back into her natural voice now they were alone, asked solemnly, 'How many perished on *The Bountiful*, Nick?'

'Was that her name?' he answered, sighing heavily. 'About thirty or forty, I reckon.'

'Those poor people,' Isabel said, knowing it was an inadequate statement.

'Aye, 'twas terrible to hear their screams...' They were back on the coastline, tramping over patches of dead rust-coloured heather, the sea two hundred feet below. This was some of the wildest terrain Isabel had seen, with no way down to the virtually shoreless bottom of the cliff. There was always a headland, in front or behind them, stretching out fat fingers of land.

The clouds lifted and a determined sun shone down warmly and helped dry out Nick's clothing. Isabel pushed back her hood and let the warmth, the fresh salty winds, and the secure feeling of being with Nick, sweep all worries and melancholy away. She was getting used to the sea – its vastness, its sounds and smells, its multitude of shifting colours, its many mysterious rocks rising out in various shapes from its depths.

'Where are we going next?' Isabel asked.

'Perranporth – 'tisn't far. We're going round Cligga Head now.' He stopped to study some driftwood and ship's rigging bobbing pathetically in a narrow inlet of dark blue water at the bottom of the cliff. 'That probably comes from another ship,' he said, pointing it out to Isabel. 'There hasn't been time for wreckage from *The Bountiful* to get here yet.' Gazing up at the sky, he smiled at the sun. 'You know, I think after yesterday's storm we're in for a fine sunny day.'

The wreck of *The Bountiful* was put to the back of their minds. Isabel had no difficulty scrambling up and down the drops they met, except for one which was sheer and steep, covered in loose scree which shifted under her feet and trickled away in front of her. She froze.

'Move down in sidesteps or run down and I'll catch you,' Nick called up to her.

In the end Nick good-humouredly climbed back up and carried her down. Near the bottom he slipped and they landed in a heap of hysterical laughter.

They entered the sand-driven tract of Perranporth from part of the cliff called Droskyn. They passed the pilchard seine boats pulled up there for safekeeping through the winter months and entered the hamlet itself down a steep winding road. Nick bought pasties, bread, cheese, ale and water from the shops and street hawkers. A young girl approached laden with a tray of food almost too heavy for her to carry and he bought two sweet-pigs. He gave one to Isabel as they strode along. She had never seen a sweet-pig before and studied the pig-shaped pastry case, its belly filled with plump currants, with a child's delight before eating it.

Nick spoke to a chapman. He didn't want to buy one of his pamphlets full of popular tales and scandals, but chapmen were a good source of gossip. He found out that the news of Laurence Trevennor's death and Isabel's assumed demise was fully abroad. Nick gave the man a farthing for his trouble.

From there he and Isabel trudged along under the foothills of Perranporth, on fine golden sands, two long miles of it. The cliffs here were dark, honeycombed with caverns. After Isabel stopped to shake the sand out of her shoes, they started climbing again.

'I've never climbed up and down so many times in my life!' she exclaimed.

She marched on without complaint and Nick silently admired her long-legged strides. She could now recognize rabbit burrows, molehills and badger setts. She chatted about St Piran, the county's patron saint, of how his eighth-century oratory, the first cell he built after crossing over from Ireland on a millstone, was about half a mile inland, buried somewhere in the sand towans they had just left behind. Uncle Laurence had told her about it when she had become interested in a similar oratory on a site at Gwithian. Nick said he knew about that, of course, and she asked him if he also knew that a whole town was buried under Gwithian's sand towans and a village was buried under Perranporth's – bones were continually coming to light. Nick replied that he thought he had heard about it somewhere and teased her that she wasn't as soft-brained as he thought.

They talked easily as they walked, sharing their knowledge of local history and legend. Everywhere they looked they saw only a marvellous beauty, awesome in its loneliness. The sense of mystery, myth and legend touched the roots of their Cornish blood.

Nick pointed to a long rugged headland out in front of them. 'That's Penhale Point with the Gull Rocks out at sea. Just before that there's a little sandy cove. No matter what the weather's like, 'tis sheltered from the wind unless it's blowing in from the sea, which it isn't today. If you want to freshen up you can do what I'm going to do, swim in the sea. Can you swim, Isabel?'

'No, I cannot,' she answered, frowning, wishing she could.

'Well, you can splash about on the shore.'

'But surely it's too dangerous to swim in the sea so soon after a storm.'

'You're right,' he grinned. 'Worried about me, are you? I won't swim but I do intend to strip off and roll about in the water.' He waited for her to blush but she only raised an eyebrow and smiled a little. He touched his cut cheek. 'Got a few cuts and bruises to clean up.'

It was a tricky climb down to the cove. The path sloped sharply, zigzagging back and forth on itself and was but a foot wide and covered with tough foliage which they had to take care not to stumble over. At the bottom they jumped the last three feet down onto soft sand warmed by the sun. The cove swept round in a typical semi-circle. It was about five hundred yards long and stretched to about the same when the tide was out. The tide was out now.

'This is surely a smuggler's cove,' Isabel said enthusiastically.

'Aye, a bit obvious and rarely used for that now.'

'It's like being in another world.'

Nick tossed aside his bag and jacket and pulled off his boots. Isabel laid her cloak out carefully and sat on it. She took off her shoes and stockings and discarded the bandages. As she rubbed her feet and looked for fresh blisters she said, 'Oh, for a hot strong dish of tea.'

She looked up to see Nick running towards the sea and clapped her hands over her face. His strong muscular body was completely naked. Moments later she peeped between her fingers and watched him leap into the waves then lie down near the shoreline to allow the gentler waves to lap over him. She put her hands down. He was too far away for her to see anything improper.

Laying aside her shawl and tucker, she pulled the rough material of her borrowed dress down over her shoulders to let the sun warm her exposed skin. She gathered up Nick's clothes which he'd discarded in a line leading to the sea and left them in a heap so he could dress at a more discreet distance. Even so, she thought she ought to move further away. Picking up the cord with which he tied back his hair, she walked slowly to the other end of the little beach, enjoying the feel of warm sand massaging her feet.

She used the cord to tie up her own hair and stopped to pick up pretty spiralling shells, the like of which she had never seen before her flight. Eagerly she took in the fascinating habitat of the seashore, the small narrow world that lived between land and water. The seashore, the most dangerous of environments, was pounded daily by waves, scoured and damaged by sand and stones, harsh cold winds, and fresh water from rain and streams. Despite the harshness of the tidal zone, all its little creatures had adapted themselves to withstand its natural hazards. After what she had been through, Isabel felt at that moment she could adapt to whatever the future held. Brought up as she was, she had never known adventure, had never owned an adventurous spirit. With Nick, and because of Nick, she had experienced so many new things. It had been terrible and frightening at first. But the incident with the rat and a night in Nick's arms, the heady knowledge that he desired her and she herself could flame that desire so quickly, gave her a strong sense of her own unique femininity. She knew now that she was more than just a passive mate required to do her duty in an unexciting marriage bed. Here in the little cove she felt carefree for the first time in her life. And she wished she could spend one more night like the last up on the cliffs with Nick Nancarrow.

She stood on the firm wet sand and gingerly let the water lick at her feet. It was foam-topped, icy cold. She shivered, but slowly she walked a little further into the sea, and a little more, lifting up her dress in stages until the water was up to her knees and the dress up to her thighs. Far, far out a long strip of turquoise green caught her eye, such a beautiful colour, as though the sun had illuminated it with a long beam of extra-terrestrial light. Isabel waded, then ran, in and out of the waves becoming giddy with exhilaration and abandoned delight.

Then she noticed that Nick was watching her.

Chapter 11

Isabel became still and turned her head very slowly. Nick was a few feet behind her, clad now in his breeches, and he was staring at her legs, his expression full of appreciation. Isabel's heart quickened. She lowered her skirt a few protective inches. A breeze swirled about her, pushing the material to mould round her legs and show off their perfect shape.

He raised his eyes and looked right into her. His body glistened, his hair hung wetly at the nape of his neck. He looked like a legendary god, utterly desirable. Isabel caught her breath and wondered what it would be like to feel his strong bare arms round her, to be pressed against his broad chest without the barrier of his shirt. She did not want the spell to be broken, but the strength of feeling he was sending across the short stretch of water separating them forced her to speak.

'You'll get cold like that.'

He grinned mischievously. 'No, I won't. It feels wonderful.' He bent to scoop up handfuls of water. 'Try it.'

'Don't you dare!' she laughed.

Cold water lightly stung her face as he splashed it over her. She shrieked and ran from him, dropping her skirt which immediately became soaked to the top of her legs, screaming and laughing as he chased her and sprayed her over and over again. She tried dodging him but it was impossible; she had her back to the sea and he held her captive.

Isabel stopped, turned and fought back, batting water at him, until playfully she begged him for mercy. He stopped splashing and stayed still, and for one heart-stopping moment she thought he would come after her and dump her fully into the waves. With a grin he turned and waded back to the shore.

Isabel followed him and when her feet were on the sand he chased her back across the beach. Laughing until she thought her lungs would burst, she stopped at the edge of her cloak and held up her hands in submission.

'You're a beast, Nick Nancarrow!' She held out her wet dress. 'Look what you've done to me.'

'Well, take it off and lay it over the rocks. There's plenty of strength in the sun, it'll dry in no time.'

'How can I?' she pouted. 'I have nothing else to wear.'

'You have your cloak.' She hesitated and he winked saucily. 'Don't worry, Isabel, I won't watch. I'll get the rest of my own clothes.'

Isabel knew the wet dress would be too uncomfortable to insist on wearing. When his back was turned, she hastily struggled out of the wet dress and snatching up the cloak wrapped it tightly round herself. She stretched the dress out over the rocks to dry as Nick came back with his own clothing.

'Here,' he said gallantly, laying his jacket on the sand. 'You can sit on this.' He dropped the rest of his clothes in a pile beside his jacket and flopped down on the sand. He gulped down a bottle of ale and handed Isabel the water flask.

'Is it time to eat?' she asked. 'I am ravenously hungry.'

'That's sea air for you. We'll have the pasties but I doubt if they're as good as Mundy Cottle's.'

'It's like being a child again,' Isabel said as she ate. 'Running about on the sand and splashing in the sea, eating out of doors. What a pity we put so many restrictions on ourselves when we grow up.'

Nick looked her up and down, wrapped in the cloak from neck to toes. 'Your legs aren't like a child's.'

'Uncle Laurence used to take me to play on the beach at Gwithian.'

'I like a good pair of legs on a woman.'

'Once we walked across the beach very nearly into Hayle.'

'And you've got the best pair I've ever seen.'

'We took a picnic basket and although we had a long rest, the walk back seemed much longer.'

''Tis a welcome sight to see something like that under a woman's skirts.' Nick handed her a piece of cheese.

'Uncle Laurence picked me up and carried me most of the way home on his shoulders.'

'They're your best feature, you should be proud of them. Long smooth legs, shapely ankles, graceful feet and straight pert toes.'

'Nick.'

'Yes?'

'Eat your cheese.'

He chuckled and pushed a lump of cheese into his mouth. 'I like the colour of your hair too, reminds me of summer.'

'Thank you, kind sir,' she said, glancing at him then looking away hastily.

No man had given her compliments like this, so very personal and said so sincerely. She had been told many times that she looked beautiful when attending balls and other social functions, and once even enchanting. But what lady didn't look her best clothed in Paris silks, her hair dressed by highly trained maids? Her fiancé, Richard Grenville, had paid her the expected compliments the few times they had met since their marriage had been arranged, the words rolling easily off his tongue. She doubted if he or the other gentlemen she mixed with would give her more than cursory attention in her present state, wearing clothes borrowed from poor people, with no powder or jewels.

She gazed at the sky, the rushing sea, the lazy golden sand indented with their footprints, tilting her head back to look at the overhanging cliff behind them. 'I wish we could stay here for ever,' she sighed softly.

Nick moved, edging himself in close behind her with his knees raised. 'Lean back against me and relax. We don't have to hurry away, doesn't matter as long as we reach Crantock by evening.'

Isabel leaned back, but hardly touched him. He seemed not only behind her but all around her. 'It's like a summer's day today. I didn't realize it could be so warm in February.'

Isabel picked up another of the tiny conical shells and looked at it intently. She traced its orange-red spiral pattern, such a delicate fragile thing in a brutal world; its survival in its complete and beautiful form gave her a feeling of security and hope. It had once been a cosy home for a small creature; it helped her to believe she would find such a place again. But for now she wanted only to stay here.

'It looks even more beautiful under water,' Nick said quietly, close to her ear. He hoped his words would not break her contemplative mood. He felt as she did. That the real world was miles and ages away. That they did not belong to it and it could not break in on them here and hurt them. It was as if they had snatched a precious moment of eternity, a gift that belonged only to them.

'I've seen so many beautiful things, so many wonderful sights and views in the past two days.'

'I always have to come back to it,' Nick said, his voice huskier than usual.

They slipped into a natural quietness. She felt him move closer and she allowed herself to lean back against him without restraint. It was what she wanted. To be as close to him as she could.

Time passed slowly. Waves ate away eternally at the rocks, pounding and caressing them. The sun gained in strength and moved its position in the sky. A gull scrutinized them from the rim of a rock pool but finding them uninteresting took wing in a white flash and soared up against the slanting blue sky.

Nick pulled at Isabel's cloak but she held it tightly at the neck. 'Let the sun warm your skin,' he said, very softly.

She allowed the cloak to fall back from her shoulders but it was not the sun but his breath that warmed her flesh.

'Your bruises are healing,' he said.

'I had forgotten all about them.' Isabel reached up and felt the tender places.

Nick kissed her fingers and moved them away to kiss each shoulder. Isabel shivered in delight. It was improper for a lady to display her shoulders in public and the kisses were as intimate as if he had placed them on her lips. She wished he would. She wanted him to hold her in his bare arms and kiss her softly on the lips, gently, understandingly. She wanted to feel the rough stubble of his chin on her skin and his mouth behind her ears. His mouth, wide, moody, sensuous, would be hers. When would he kiss her fully? Should she turn to him, or wait?

He tugged at the cloak again, trying to pull it down further and reveal more of her back. 'Isabel, let go,' he murmured into her hair. He lifted the cloak up over her legs. She didn't like this and fought to hold it down, to keep her dignity. Her body tightened and a thrill of fear ignited inside her, replacing her elation.

'Nick, don't…'

'It'll be all right, Isabel.'

She did not like the new deepness in his voice; its raw intensity frightened her. There was nothing right any more about being in his arms. She felt sharp, almost angry movements as he pulled the cloak down to reveal the full length of her back. He slid his lips down, down over her spine and Isabel panicked and struggled.

'Don't Nick! Please stop!'

'Why?' he demanded harshly, letting her go. 'Tell me why. What have I done wrong?'

She covered herself and scrambled away. Her face was livid red, her body trembling with a mixture of emotions. 'I didn't know you were…' she gasped on the words. 'I…, I didn't know you wanted to…'

'Then what the hell did you think I was doing?' Nick got angrily to his feet. 'Asking you for the next dance at a Truro ball? Damn you, woman. How dare you lead me on like that then change your mind!' His face was as red as hers and Isabel stepped back.

'It was not me who started it,' Isabel angrily defended herself. 'I thought—'

'Just what did you think?' His eyes shot bolts of fury at her.

'That… that perhaps just a kiss—'

'Oh, now I understand! I'm not good enough to lie with. Too rough for you, am I, Miss Isabel Hampton? Too common? You only give it to the gentry!'

His fury stung her. She was hurt and humiliated. What was he saying? Why was he so angry? What right had he to expect her to give herself to him then become so cruel when she refused? Perhaps it was something deeper than just damaged male pride at being spurned but it was a side of life she knew nothing of.

Holding up her head, she said coolly, 'I have never lain with anyone. Why do you presume that I have?'

'I know your sort,' came the blistering reply, 'going from one rich man's bed to another's to amuse yourself while you wait for a suitable marriage alliance to be made for you. Then taking as many lovers as you please afterwards. And then there's the company you keep.'

'What do you mean by that?' Isabel hissed, shocked at his words.

He leaned towards her. 'Phoebe Antiss, she'll do for a start. Remember how you and Laurence would go riding while she stayed at Trevennor House with a headache? Oh, she used to have headaches all right. The sort cured by an hour with a good man.'

Isabel was cut to the quick of her soul. She could not smash a hand across his face as she wanted to because she could not deny that Phoebe had been obliging where men were concerned. It was something she had put to the back of her mind, but Phoebe had been her friend.

'Don't you dare talk about Phoebe like that. Have you no respect for the dead?'

'Well, it doesn't mean that she's suddenly turned into a saint.'

Isabel stared at him, her face now very pale. She had to know.

'And presumably... you were one of those "good men".'

'Me and every willing stable boy and no-good gentleman, including your cousin, Kempthorne. He followed me one afternoon.'

'You disgust me,' Isabel said, fighting back tears of shame. 'But all gentlemen are not like you and my immoral cousin. Uncle Laurence wasn't and I'm thankful to be betrothed to Richard Grenville who is a true gentleman.'

'Huh, I doubt if you love him or ever will.'

'It's none of your business!'

'No, of course it isn't. I mustn't forget myself, must I, m'lady?'

She could no longer bear his spite and hatred and turned away, tears scalding her eyes.

'Get your clothes on, the sooner I get you to Crantock and off my hands for a few days, the better.' In misery she pulled on the clammy wet dress. She buried Nick's jibe at Richard Grenville by thinking of the things she liked about him. She had met him only a year ago and seen him half a dozen times during a month's shore leave. Her uncle had been staying with her at Truro at the time. He was favourably impressed with Richard and generally in favour of the proposal of marriage he'd issued with the support of his family. Isabel had thought Richard the best suitor she had had. She did not want to be smothered by a husband's presence and liked the idea of having one who was mainly interested in his naval career. Richard also had good manners, a kindly smile, a good sense of humour. He would make a most suitable husband.

Isabel hoped that Crantock was not far away and she would soon be left there while Nick went about his own affairs. A sour thought besieged her. According to that dreadful man, Gyver

Pengelly, there was a whore at Crantock who didn't refuse Nick her favours and Isabel felt she could wager her life it was to her she was being taken.

–

The sky was pale blue, the horizon a deeper blue. The waves were still wild and rebellious on the ocean. Except for small patches of short-stemmed primroses, the cliff was stark. The feathered remains of a small bird lay at the mouth of a rabbit hole where perhaps the predator had hoped for a larger victim. Smoke rose in a straight line from a solitary cottage sheltered in a distant nook. Before the shameful, humiliating incident in the tiny cove, Isabel had begun to take an interest in these things.

She tramped along tight-lipped at a good distance from Nick, hating every step that brought her damp dress to rub against her legs, hating the reminders of the reason for the dress's condition and the remarks, which she now thought of as crass, that Nick had made about her legs. Her emotions had been exposed and felt as raw as the windswept cliffs. The pain of her uncle's death overwhelmed her again, as did the deaths of the four people on the coach. The horrifying sounds of the shipwreck haunted her too, and so did the encounter with Gyver Pengelly.

She hardly noticed when they left the cliff and passed over the sands of Holywell Bay. Wearily she trudged up and down its sand dunes where marram grass caught at her ankles and stung her flesh. When they reached firm cliff again, she allowed Nick to move further ahead. They walked round the edge of a ploughed field and down into Polly Joke, a deep sandy cove where cattle from common ground, which led away from the beach, had come down to drink from the stream that flowed to the sea. Then up the cliff again, and round a headland where Nick stopped.

He watched the sea racing up to a long beach of golden sand with high dunes behind it. Behind the dunes was the village of

Crantock and their journey was nearly at its end. A fresh wind tousled his unruly hair and the few tiny lines around his eyes creased as he took its force. He had looked at scenes like the one now before him innumerable times but he never ceased to be amazed by them.

Long steep banks of waves headed for the beach, spume flying off their tops as they rolled and broke, the water spraying backwards in white lacy flags, making Nick think of knights on chargers riding into battle. One wave rode on the back of another, racing to be first to bombard the black cliff on the far side of the beach, sending up mountains of cascading spray. The water then surged on, filling up the tidal river of the Gannel that snaked its way along the New Quay cliffs. Then the eye was drawn back to the indigo blue ocean to watch the assault begin over again. It was exhilarating and terrifying. A beautiful savagery.

Isabel was stunned by the sight, likening the spray to yards and yards of the most exquisite lace billowing in the wind. She stood beside Nick and they watched, eyes shining, mouths dry, hardly breathing.

A gigantic wave thundered in, crashing on the rocks below them, its spray reaching for the heavens, spreading out and showering them in a fine wet mist.

'We'd better move back,' Nick said. 'The cliff has given way here with the winter rains.' Mesmerized, Isabel did not hear him. 'Isabel.' Lightly he touched her arm.

She glanced up at him and a strange silent look passed between them and they knew they had shared another unique experience on this unwanted journey that fate had handed them.

It was not a simple cottage he took her to. It was not like Charlie Chiverton's hovel or Mundy Cottle's small square building. Situated behind the dunes and overlooking the River Gannel, it was a large whitewashed house with a thatched roof, a well-kept vegetable garden, flower verges, a granite rockery and trelliswork waiting for the summer's rambling roses.

Nick led the way up the straight ash-strewn pathway to a freshly painted green door, either side of which were opened windows with shutters. He rapped once on the door, opened it wide, stooped to enter and called out 'Kitty!'

'Don't look like she's in,' he informed Isabel after a moment and beckoned to her. 'Come on in.'

'Won't she mind?' Isabel asked, burning to know more about this place, who she was to stay with and what they were like.

'Kitty won't mind me inviting myself in.'

Isabel eyed Nick coldly. He was boasting again. 'And will she mind me entering her house uninvited?'

Nick studied Isabel from the doorway. She had undergone a remarkable transformation in the past three days and two nights.

'Kitty will like you,' he said huskily.

He ushered her through a hall into a big clean kitchen where a kettle simmered on a hook above a hearty fire. 'She's not far away,' he said. 'Kitty never stays away from the house for long. Sit down and make yourself comfortable. Your walking days are over. If Kitty agrees, and I'm sure she will, you can stay here for a few days while I go back to Gwithian to see if your cousins really mean you harm. You'll be practically living the life of a lady again.'

'Where are the servants?' Isabel asked, taking in the fully-equipped and well-furnished room. Everything was of the finest quality. 'I assume this Kitty has at least one or two.'

'Actually, she has none. Kitty comes from humble stock and hates the idea of other people skivvying for her. She does her own cleaning though she sends out things like laundry and dressmaking.'

'But why should she allow me to stay here? And why did you choose to bring me here?'

There was a marked twinkle in his eye as he answered. 'Kitty is my friend. She's always ready to help me out and she'll take good care of you and if necessary protect you. She's as strong as an ox and has an evil temper when riled. She also enjoys a challenge. We can tell her the truth about you, but don't forget that from now on, apart from when we're with Kitty, you're Jenna Stevens.'

Isabel sat down beside the hearth in a chair with plush embroidered cushions. It was obvious Kitty lived alone and had furnished and decorated the hall and kitchen in a decidedly feminine and tasteful. There were no bad smells to offend her and Isabel could not detect what her Uncle Laurence would have termed 'a definite unfriendly feeling about the place'. Would he have approved of this house and its owner? She supposed he would, knowing the way he'd trusted Nick. Anyway, she hoped that whoever this Kitty was, she would indeed allow her to stay.

There was a sound in the hall and Nick went to investigate. Isabel heard every word of the hearty exchange between him and the female who had entered the house.

'Nick Nancarrow! So the wind's blown you this way again, has it! About time too, I should say.'

There was a long silence and a bolt of cold steel shot through Isabel's heart; she knew they were kissing. Did this other woman, a common trollop by the sound of her voice, have her arms about Nick's neck? The rustle of her dress said she did. Were her lips moving under his, as only a short time ago she had hoped hers would?

Feeling an intruder, she stood up to face the woman who was to be asked to be her keeper for at least the next few days. Barely able to cope with the ache in her heart, Isabel raised her chin and looked squarely at the open doorway.

She heard Nick say, 'I've got someone with me, Kitty.'

'I know, there are two tracks leading to my door, one a lot smaller than yours,' Kitty replied. 'Well then, I suppose I'd better meet her.'

Chapter 12

When Nick returned to Gwithian he made straight for the snug rough-walled cottage of Jimmy Rowe and his extended family. Apart from his pregnant wife, Marion, and two small children, there were his father, crippled and unable to work from a miner's lung disease, and his mother who was a tiny energetic woman with the sharpest of tongues. It was evening and Jimmy was outside working on his garden patch.

'What are you going to put in that bit of dirt?' Nick called out teasingly as he leaned on the gate.

Jimmy threw down his spade and ran to the gate and pumped Nick's hand. 'A few potatoes. Where the heck have you been these last few days?' he demanded, opening the gate and pulling Nick through the wide opening. 'Mother and Marion have been baking each and every day and there's been no one with an appetite like yours to devour it. Mother's pretty mazed with you, Nick. You'll hear all about it, I can tell 'ee.' Before Nick could reply, Jimmy shouted, 'Mother! Marion! He's here at last! Get the kettle on the boil.'

A moment later a small darting figure of bird-like movements was out of the house and standing in front of the two men. Jimmy Rowe's mother, looking like a magpie in a black dress and long white apron, glared at Nick reproachfully.

'And where have you been? Keeping a body waiting with a cupboard full of good food baked and waiting all ready for 'ee? Didn't think you'd have the gall to stay away from your friends for so long. Well, speak up, Nick Nancarrow, or I'll have 'ee straight back out that there gate.'

Nick threw down his bag and lifted Meena Rowe up to his face and kissed both her shiny apple-red cheeks heartily. Jimmy was bent over laughing and other chuckles came with the slower arrival of the heavily pregnant Marion and her weakened father-in-law as they leaned on each other for support. Meena Rowe struggled against Nick with all her might and when he put her down the tiny woman looked as if she was about to burst.

'I should have remembered ye've got some mighty strange habits, Nick Nancarrow!' she shouted, pointing an agitated finger at him. 'Picking up a little frail old woman and making jest with her!'

'There's nothing frail about you, Meena,' Nick said, bending down and putting his hands on his knees as if he was talking to a child. 'You're beautiful. Beautiful! If I'd been around in your maiden days you'd be called Meena Nancarrow by now.'

Meena gazed back at Nick with her lips pursed. 'Mmmm, we'd have seen.'

'Don't I get a kiss back?'

'No, I'm not in the mood to give you one – at the moment.'

'Well, in that case lead me to this mountain of food you've prepared for me.'

'No manners!' Meena marched off, head down and tail up. She took her husband with her, and although he was much bigger and taller than herself, without lifting her head she patted him vigorously on his back. He had succumbed to a bout of coughing. 'See what you've done to Father,' she accused Nick over her tiny bony shoulder as she headed back indoors. 'Don't know what your mother would have said, she never brought you up to be such a sinner.'

Nick kissed and hugged Marion Rowe. 'What have I done?' he said innocently, nodding after Meena.

'You know you can't do anything wrong in Mother's eyes,' Marion said, giggling and leading him after her parents-in-law.

Jimmy picked up Nick's bag, shaking his head. 'I don't know how you do get away with it. If I said just one thing like that to she…'

Inside the talk changed to the sad and serious subject of Laurence Trevennor's funeral.

'Course when I was asked to be a pallbearer I put your name down at once. Said Mr Trevennor wouldn't rest easy if you weren't one of they chosen to bear him to his grave,' Jimmy told Nick as Meena laid the kitchen table for supper.

'Aye, I would have had something to say in this village if you'd been left out,' Denny Rowe contributed to the conversation from his high-backed chair at the hearth.

'As if they'd listen to you,' Meena snorted, ladling out steaming chicken broth. 'Here, Father, you can eat at the table tonight.'

Denny obeyed at once, getting up so Meena could lift his chair to the table's head. He received an affectionate tug on his once proud shoulders from her when he was settled again.

'Aw, I don't know, Mother,' he said, always slow to answer, picking up his spoon. 'There's been a time when even you did listen to me.'

Meena responded with a loud 'Huh!' and beckoned to Marion. 'You sit down next, m'dear then we'll see what room we have left round the table.'

Nick bowed his head while Denny asked for the food to be blessed. He was happy to be back at this table again, in the company of good-natured Jimmy and his gentle Marion, who was devoted to her husband, enjoying the banter of Meena and Denny that was pitted with sarcasm that was never meant.

'If you'd come half an hour ago you'd have seen Boy Jimmy and little Mary before Mother put them to bed,' Jimmy said.

'I'll see them and, by the look of it, the next one before I'm off on my travels again,' Nick said, smiling at Marion as he broke a slice of bread in two. 'I'm back this way because I've got a job at Tehidy.'

A disapproving grunt was heard from Meena's direction. Not because Nick had said he had a job at Tehidy but because Meena thought it unseemly to refer to a woman's 'delicate condition'.

Marion bent her head, her face warm and pink, over her bowl. Meena had had only the one child and Marion felt her mother-in-law didn't quite approve of her being on her third so soon after the birth of the last one. Nick wasn't embarrassed. 'You'll soon have a large happy family like the parson and his wife.'

Jimmy puffed up with pride.

'That'd be nice,' Denny said, pushing his bowl forward for a second helping.

Meena did the serving, sat down again and gave Marion a brittle smile.

To change the subject Marion said, ''Twas a terrible tragedy about Miss Isabel.'

'Aye, I heard about it a couple of days after it happened,' Nick said.

'Surprised you didn't see something, Nick,' Jimmy said, suddenly looking up from his meal. 'You were walking that way when I saw you the day Miss Isabel and Mr Trevennor died. Thought you would have seen the coach either being wrecked or passed it on the road.'

All eyes were on Nick. 'I didn't go that way,' he said, looking squarely at Jimmy.

''Tis Nick's business where he went and why,' Meena finished the discussion. 'Now, Nick, where are you going to sleep tonight?'

–

Laurence Trevennor was laid to rest in Gwithian's churchyard under a sulky grey sky with a tormenting sharp wind snapping at the mourners' hats and scarves. Nick was one of the six bearers who solemnly carried Laurence's mortal remains, in a much admired dark oak coffin, across the road from Trevennor House into the church. He and Jimmy Rowe walked in the middle, arms across shoulders under the coffin.

After a moving service, in which the Reverend Perran Thomas held up Laurence as the respected Christian gentleman he truly had been, they carried his coffin outside into the churchyard to share his wife's grave beside an ancient granite Celtic cross. Nearly all three hundred and fifty inhabitants of the parish turned out to pay their last respects; many of them, including some of the men, wept openly.

Nick nodded at Charlie Chiverton who was standing at the back of the crowds and then put his own grief aside and turned his attention to the Kempthornes. They had followed importantly in the coffin's wake, making a point of talking graciously and smiling grimly at the young curate and his wife and those of the county's gentry who were in attendance. While Edmund managed a few brief exchanges with the village folk, his sister contemptuously ignored them.

Deborah noticed Nellie hanging about shyly at the edge of the crowd in her usual shabby state. She had spoken to Nellie the day before, asking her to tell Gyver Pengelly that she wanted to speak to him urgently. Deborah couldn't help a little smile as the cortège passed the site of the paupers' graves. If Gyver Pengelly did what she required of him, and she now had the funds to pay him well for his services, there would soon be one more added down there.

As the Reverend Perran Thomas said a final prayer for the soul of Isabel Hampton, asking the Lord to send up her body from the deep to be given a Christian burial as befitted her, Edmund, wearing a black armband and a black silk scarf three yards long, put his practised eye to use, unobtrusively perusing the younger females among the mourners.

Nick did not miss Edmund's sexual reconnaissance and while he was thus occupied, Nick turned his attention to his ungainly sister. Deborah Kempthorne was standing on the other side of the grave to him, her face masked by a heavy black veil. When the last 'Amen' had been said, he walked swiftly round the grave to speak to her before she left the churchyard. She turned to him at once, and he could see the veil had done the mourners a kindness by concealing her waxen hard features.

'I hope you will forgive my forwardness in speaking to you like this, Miss Kempthorne,' he said, in a suitably quiet voice, 'but I would like to express my deepest sympathy at the loss of your uncle. I do hope you have been able to bear up.'

Behind the security of her veil, Deborah had been studying Nick as Laurence Trevennor was being lowered into the wet earth to be reunited with his wife. He certainly lived up to his reputation as an attractive man, and in his smart suit of clothes, standing straight, head and shoulders above the other men, he was hardly recognizable as the rough and wild youth she remembered. Deborah could see he thought himself an equal to any other man mourning her late uncle. The unquenchable fire in his sapphire-blue eyes had brightened up the dreary day and the boredom of the occasion as he'd stood opposite her, grim-faced, lazily holding his three-cornered hat and tapping it slowly against his knee. It seemed he had something on his mind and she would have given anything to know what it was.

Why were men like him, granite-faced, of a moody disposition, who always ensured they stayed one step ahead of the marriage bond, so attractive to women?

'Thank you,' she said to him now in response to his condolences. 'I… I fear it has been all too awful, Mr…?'

'Nancarrow, Miss Kempthorne. Nicholas Nancarrow. I knew your late uncle well and respected and admired him. I was born and raised in Gwithian. My father was Mr Trevennor's coachman.'

'Oh yes, of course. I remember my dear late uncle talking of you, Mr Nancarrow. I believe he held an affection for you.'

'I am honoured that you think so, Miss Kempthorne. I shall miss him greatly.' Nick felt uncomfortable to be commiserating with this gawky insincere woman, under the curiosity of the villagers who must be thinking he would be more aptly employed talking to them. They were his friends, some had been his parents' neighbours, and none was taken in by the Kempthornes' false show of grief. Nick knew that with

Laurence dead and Isabel presumed dead, they would be greatly concerned for the village with the Kempthornes residing there as influential gentry and its main employers. But Nick's first concern was to find out if Isabel really was in danger from the despised Kempthornes.

'May I escort you back to Trevennor House, Miss Kempthorne?' he said, keeping the power in his husky voice as he scanned the sky. 'The clouds are building up again and I fear we'll soon have rain. And you to the parsonage, Mistress Thomas, if you'll allow me,' he added gallantly as Charlotte joined them. He liked the Thomases, they had been good for the village since Perran had taken over the curacy five years ago when they'd been newly married; and they were only very minor gentry.

'Well I…' Deborah looked down doubtfully at the posy of rosemary she was holding, then at Charlotte as if to seek advice. Deborah had hoped to make an ally, for her own ends, of Charlotte Thomas, but despite Charlotte's kindly words and regular calls at Trevennor House after Laurence's death, Deborah was sure it was all pretence and felt she was being watched very carefully. Charlotte had made it quite clear she had little time for Edmund. Deborah wished she could tell the other woman to walk with her husband.

'Actually, Nick,' Charlotte said, with her habitual warm smile, 'the Reverend Thomas and I have been invited to Trevennor House for refreshment with the representatives of the other great houses and I hope to give Miss Kempthorne succour at this most grievous time. As my husband is presently occupied in a discussion with Mr Kempthorne, it would indeed be beneficial if you could kindly escort us to the house and out of the cold air. I am anxious for Miss Kempthorne not to succumb to a chill and we must remember the bereaved are most vulnerable to all ills. I have known Nick, Mr Nancarrow, for a number of years,' she ended by way of explanation to Deborah, in case the older woman thought her overfamiliar.

Nick thought Charlotte had spoken much of what she'd said as if she had a sour plum in her mouth. It was quite plain she didn't like Deborah Kempthorne. Nick gave her a little understanding nod. He did not want to escort Deborah Kempthorne anywhere but *out* of Trevennor House, but it would be the first helpful step in finding out the truth about the Kempthornes' true intentions towards Isabel and if indeed they had been responsible for causing the coach crash. He put on his hat and crooked each arm to bear the two black-swathed ladies out of the churchyard.

When they were on the doorstep of Trevennor House, Deborah could tell he was thinking again. She hoped it was about her, but thought it unlikely. She was the first to admit her own unattractiveness and she was several years older than he was. How could she keep his company without it seeming obvious or improper? She smiled artfully under her veil.

'As you were such a close acquaintance of my dear late uncle, Mr Nancarrow, perhaps you would care to come inside and take refreshment with the other mourners,' she said graciously. 'I feel Uncle Laurence would have wanted it.'

Nick accepted with a smile. He was gratified; he had not thought it would be so easy to gain entry into the house with the Kempthornes in residence. He had thought he would have to do it via the kitchens and Mrs Christopher, the housekeeper. He wanted to put back the ring Laurence had given him to show Isabel.

Nick was seated in the parlour amid the few dignitaries, who by their collective expressions were present purely out of respect for Laurence's memory, when Edmund arrived with Perran Thomas. Nick was engaged in a conversation with John Trevarthen, the steward and representative of the Bassets of Tehidy, about training a new pair of coach horses. Edmund raised his classic eyebrows to see Nick there but wasn't much interested in him. He made straight for Charlotte Thomas.

'A sad day for the village, Mistress Thomas,' he drawled.

'Yes, Mr Kempthorne,' Charlotte replied, returning his amused gaze with a stern look. 'In many ways.'

'Oh, I agree.'

Charlotte had moved away from the body of the mourners to pour a cup of tea for her husband. She didn't like being isolated with the table behind her and this predatory man in front of her. She knew precisely what kind of hunt he was engaged in. There wouldn't be a girl or woman safe in the village with him on the prowl. Her face showed her distaste.

Edmund found this added to the excitement of the chase. He was quite determined he would not leave Gwithian before she had succumbed to his charms. Before many weeks were out, he would turn her look of distaste to one of pleasure and anticipation for when she would next see him.

A movement outside the window caught Edmund's eye. Nellie had wandered into the garden after a cat and she was crouching down talking to it as she stroked its back.

'Mmmm...'

'What is it?' Charlotte demanded as he gazed out above her shoulder.

'Only that unfortunate creature you have so kindly taken under your wing,' he said innocently. 'I'll have some food sent out for her. Perhaps Mrs Christopher could find work for her in our kitchens.'

Charlotte's head whirled round and when she saw it was Nellie, she knew he was challenging her to keep the girl from him. 'Nellie has had sufficient food for today, Mr Kempthorne,' she said coldly. 'I saw to that myself. And she has enough work to keep her well occupied, I can assure you.'

'I was only trying to help, Mistress Thomas,' Edmund said. He sounded hurt but his eyes were twinkling.

'If you'll excuse me, Mr Kempthorne, I was about to get my husband a dish of tea.'

'Do forgive me,' he murmured, withdrawing. 'Your husband is a most fortunate man to have such a dutiful caring wife. I think I'll have a little brandy for myself.'

Charlotte was furious. Edmund Kempthorne had amused himself at her expense. Did he really think his good looks and sickening charm would get the better of her?

Deborah had lifted her veil and was sipping her tea as daintily as she could. When she could, she swept her eyes over Nick who was still talking to John Trevarthen. Nick was utterly relaxed and Deborah could see he wasn't in the least daunted by the company he was in.

Edmund saw the furtive looks Deborah was giving Nick. He was more than amused to think his plain-faced sister had designs on the good-looking cuckoo in their midst, and he was pleased. It meant she might transfer some of the obsession she had with him and how he ran his life.

After thirty minutes and little depletion of a table heavy with food and several bottles of wine, the brother and sister, the curate and his wife and Nick Nancarrow were the only ones left in the room. It was no reflection on Mrs Christopher and the servants' efforts to lay a good spread in memory of their late employer that the mourners left early but to show their disapproval of the couple who had inherited his property.

Deborah was pleased that although the room had almost emptied, Nick was still there. She listened attentively as he told Perran Thomas that he had no definite plans for the next few days but was soon to start training a pair of coach horses at Tehidy. She recalled the feel of Nick's coat sleeve as she'd held his arm when they'd walked to the house. In spite of her glove, she'd felt the material was rougher than the clothes her brother wore, but all the more masculine for that. She thought about what his skin would feel like. It set delicious feelings coursing through her vitals – and he was looking at her yet again.

'We'll see you in church on Sunday then, Nick?' Perran Thomas asked, picking up crumbs from his plate. He was the only one who had eaten a reasonable quantity of food.

'Of course,' Nick replied, as Deborah rooted her eyes on him and Edmund made a bad-mannered bored sound. 'I shall be back in my usual pew.'

'All the girls try to crowd into your pew when you're away, Nick.' Charlotte added. 'I expect they would like to sit beside you when you're here.'

'Oh?' Deborah said sharply.

'As a boy I carved my name on one of the pews,' Nick explained to her. 'The previous curate caught me red-handed and he was none too pleased. I received a thrashing from my father and from then on as a penance I was made to sit with my name in front of me, to remind me of how one should not behave in a holy place, and I've kept up the practice since.' Nick thought it was a feeble story but it made the Kempthorne woman take an interest in him.

Deborah gave a silly titter.

'I understand you visited my uncle every time you came back to the village, Nancarrow,' Edmund drawled. 'I hope we won't find your mark anywhere in our house.'

Nick thought the remark unworthy of an answer and gave a wry smile.

Edmund had been regularly sweeping his eyes over Charlotte and she had had enough. She and Perran had stayed to make up for the early departure of other mourners but she was determined on leaving now.

'If you will excuse us, Miss Kempthorne, Mr Kempthorne, the Reverend Thomas and I will have to take our leave to oversee our children's evening meal. They will be waiting for us.'

'Of course, Mistress Thomas,' Deborah said, rising to ring for their cloaks. 'You have been a great comfort to us but we can't have your little ones being neglected.'

Edmund hoped Nick would go too. Mary Ellen was in a back bedroom and should be quite ready by now to make him forget the funeral and the horrors of death. He wondered whether he should leave Deborah alone with Nick. He would have no real objection to the man being here occasionally before he slipped off on his travels again, if it meant that Deborah was less bothersome for a while. He had Nick marked down as a candidate to be parted from some money at the card table since he obviously could afford good clothes and the finest quality boots. But it would not do to leave the unlikely couple alone now. The servants were not fooled by the story of Mary Ellen's 'widowhood'. They might tolerate a gentleman's needs and indeed they seemed rather to like Mary Ellen who was friendly and kept out of their way. But they hated Deborah, who was cruel to them, and disapproval and gossip might spoil any chance of being popular in the village and accepted in society at Truro.

Edmund wanted to see Mary Ellen now! He fidgeted and tried to think of something other than his voluptuous young mistress.

Soon after the Thomases left, Nick suddenly asked if he might prevail further on their hospitality and use their water closet. Deborah lowered her eyelashes demurely and Edmund gave his permission, jumping at the opportunity to guide Nick to the room in question and out of the house.

'I'll show you the way, Nancarrow.'

'Please, do not trouble yourself, Mr Kempthorne,' Nick said pleasantly, but in a tone he hoped would not be argued with. 'I know the way.'

'Of course he does, Edmund, don't fuss.' Deborah did not want Nick to go yet.

There was no need for Nick to answer a call of nature and after a quick glance outside the parlour door to make sure none of the servants were about, he dashed up the elegant stairway and made straight for Laurence's bedchamber. He entered with a sense of reverence and gazed poignantly at the bed, now neatly made up, where his friend had died. The room felt horribly empty. Nick dug about in his coat pocket, took out the gold ring and put it back quickly in its original drawer.

He stood back to look at the battle scene of a bold painting over the fireplace. Instead of war-ravaged artillery and slain red-coated soldiers he saw the smashed coach and the bodies of

Phoebe Antiss, Ginny, Rickardson and the guard. But he did not see Isabel as he first had, bewigged, an ugly white face painted and blooded, twisted in terror. His mind moved further along the cliff, to Reskajeage Downs, and Isabel standing defiantly on the steps of Charlie's shack, her features hinting at their true loveliness and crowned with flowing honey-brown hair.

He saw the expressions and emotions she had portrayed on their lonely journey. Indignation that he had even touched her. Anger at his blistering verbal attacks. Shock and hurt as she'd plunged down the promontory towards the stream. Fear at the thought of climbing down the cliff. Grief over Laurence. The child-like quality of her face as she'd slept in his arms. Then, as they had grown to tolerate each other, sheer terror at meeting Gyver Pengelly, courage and triumph at killing the rat in Billy Noone's cottage, sorrow at the shipwreck and comfort for James Leddra.

He had not wanted to leave her at Crantock, but there was nothing else he could do until he was certain of her position regarding her safety.

There was a child's toy on Laurence's bed, a wooden doll dressed as a lady in an evening gown. An old toy of Isabel's? Put there in memory of her by a grieving Mrs Christopher? Certainly not by that hard-faced woman queening it in the parlour. He would have to go down to her now, and he hated the thought. He left the bedchamber hoping Isabel did not hate the thought of seeing him again.

He was thinking of her reasserting herself as a well-born lady in Kitty's house as he walked down the stairs and did not see a small child at the bottom until she spoke to him.

'You bin to the funeral?'

Nick was startled. 'Oh... um... yes.'

'My fathur said the old man should've died a lot sooner,' the little girl went on, matter-of-factly, her chubby hands held together and twisted in front of her swaying body.

There was no need to speculate who her father was, she even spoke in the same lazy way as Edmund Kempthorne. Dressed in a pale blue frock and petticoat and matching slippers, a cluster of red ribbons on the crown of her dark head, Nick thought she was quite the prettiest child he had seen. He sat on the lower steps and smiled, putting out a forefinger to touch her chin.

'Why do you think your father would say that?' he asked.

'Cus he was hard up fur money. I heard him talking to my mam. Said if the old man hadn't gone when he did he would've given him a helping hand. Wanted him to go up to see God a bit quicker,' the girl said innocently. 'My mam says my fathur's kind like that.'

'I see,' Nick replied, digesting the implications of this piece of information. 'Do you live here?'

'Aye, but only since a few days ago. We wus sent fur, from St Ives. Know it, do 'ee?' Nick nodded and she chattered on. 'Got fish as big as a ship there. I've got a bedroom and playroom all of me own here, but I have to keep quiet. Fathur's bought me lots of new toys. A hobby horse, a rocking horse, jumping jacks from the Frenchies and hundreds of dolls. I'm getting a nursemaid to look after me when me mam's busy. What your name?'

Nick smiled and told her, then asked, 'What's yours?'

'Morenwyn Leddra. I'm three, nearly four,' Morenwyn said proudly. 'How old are you?'

'Oh, about twenty-seven, I think,' Nick said with a wink. Her surname reminded him of the sailor he'd helped ashore from the shipwreck.

'Is that older or younger than old sourpuss?'

'Well, I don't know. Who's this sourpuss?' But he thought he already knew.

'Deb'rah. She's my aunty but won't let me call her that. She hates me and me mam. Mam says she's jealous cus she can't get a man of her own.' Morenwyn stepped closer and ran a fingertip round and round on Nick's knee. It tickled so much he took her hand and lifted her onto his lap. She wriggled about, all elbows. 'You're a fine man, Nick,' she chirped, staring up at him. 'Mam says a man would make her happy. You be a man for my aunty then p'raps she went be so sour and like me a bit.'

Nick wanted to laugh, but he restrained himself. Morenwyn felt warm and cuddlesome as she nestled close to him. He had never taken much notice of very young children before, not even Jimmy Rowe's, but this particular one would stand out in a crowd and was easy to take to.

'Tell me, Morenwyn, have you got an uncle?'

'Aye, Uncle James. Mam told me about him but we never see him cus he's always out at sea.'

Nick felt uneasy and hoped James Leddra would not take a notion to call at Trevennor House to see his sister, but he was sure the sailor would keep his word and not mention the two people he'd met in Trevellas Porth.

'Where's your mother, Morenwyn?'

'Upstairs, waiting fur my fathur,' she answered, putting her hands up to fiddle with her ribbons. Nick doubted that she ever kept still.

The parlour door opened and the Kempthornes appeared together.

'Ah, Nancarrow, now I see what has delayed you,' Edmund said, looking proudly at his daughter.

Morenwyn wriggled off Nick's lap and ran to him.

Nick got up and deliberately gazed warmly at Deborah who flushed crimson. She attempted to return the look but her smile did nothing kind to her hard face. Nick could tell she was interested in him but couldn't feel happy about it. She tried to speak kindly to Morenwyn who was in Edmund's arms, hugging his neck. 'Why don't you run along and see where your mother is, my dear?'

Edmund took the opportunity to escape to Mary Ellen. 'I'll take her up to the nursery, Deborah. Thank you for attending the funeral, Nancarrow. I understand you were here when our uncle died. I was sad to miss his last moments. Good day to you.' He put a finger and thumb into a waistcoat pocket and produced a coin which he offered Nick. 'For bearing the coffin.'

Nick held up protesting hands. He was offended. 'Not necessary. Laurence was my friend. It was an honour to carry him to his resting place. I was only too glad to be back in the area and to have the opportunity to bid him goodbye.' He moved aside to allow Edmund room to pass. Morenwyn's delighted chuckles were heard as she was borne to the top of the house.

'She's a dear little soul,' Nick said to Deborah.

'Yes, I'm very fond of children,' she lied. She was furious the little girl had wandered downstairs again. 'Morenwyn has lightened our heavier moments since Uncle Laurence's death.' She gave a small embarrassed cough. 'There is… um… no point in trying to hide the paternal half of her parentage from you, is there, Mr Nancarrow? Your face spoke clearly that you had noticed her resemblance to Edmund.'

'I hope if I have a child one day I'll be blessed to have one as delightful, and to love it as much as your brother obviously does Morenwyn, Miss Kempthorne.'

'I believe you… are not married.'

'No.' He smiled with his fullest charm. 'I am quite unattached.'

Deborah's face glowed deeper. 'I would appreciate it if you would not speak of the child as being my brother's. We are hoping for amicable relations with the local people and some may not approve of Edmund's… little indiscretion. At present we are keeping the little girl confined to the house. Hopefully in the future she will be able to go abroad in the village and the people will look kindly on Edmund for giving her and her mother a home.'

'I'm sure they will accept the situation,' Nick said soothingly. 'You have my assurance I'll say nothing about it. I thank you for taking me into your confidence. Also I thank you for your hospitality today but sadly now I must go. If we should meet in the future, please call me Nick.'

He held out his hand and Deborah shot hers out in return. It was big and heavy and felt clumsy enclosed in his fingers and her cheeks were so red they looked about to fry. She showed Nick to the door without ringing for a servant.

'Goodbye. Despite the sad occasion it's been a pleasure to meet you.' It was Nick's turn to lie.

'Wait, please, Nick,' Deborah urgently puffed out the words. 'I have a proposition to put to you.'

Chapter 13

Isabel had been surprised on meeting Kitty. She had been able to tell from Nick's smirking face that he was expecting it. He probably thought she had visualised a gaudily dressed, heavily rouged, common looking older woman with a voluptuous figure. But Isabel had hardly given the physical aspects of the woman she was being taken to a thought as she'd walked the cliffs, registering only that Gyver Pengelly had said Nick had lain with her.

Kitty was only three years older than Isabel at twenty-four, with tawny-brown eyes set in a pert pretty face. She wore a neat dress in pastel shades finished at the top with a snowy white lace fichu over an almost curveless figure. Her glossy natural red hair was worn in a 'sheep's head' of close curls and she shared Isabel's preference for wearing little jewellery. Kitty looked more like a clergyman's daughter than a woman who sold herself to gentlemen.

Nick had known that Isabel must be feeling at a disadvantage in her shabby clothes and sand-whitened shoes but as he looked at her, standing stiffly upright, her hands clasped before her, he was struck again by the change in her. The three days since the accident had turned her into a vibrant ethereal looking creature.

He'd lifted a palm in her direction. 'Kitty, this is Jenna Stevens.'

'Welcome to my house, Jenna,' Kitty said, her face open and friendly.

'Thank you,' Isabel replied, using her own voice.

Kitty's eyebrows shot up at the unexpected cultured tone and she turned to Nick for an explanation. Nick looked at Isabel with a mixture of contempt and amusement; trust you, he seemed to be thinking, to make sure Kitty knows at once you're not one of us.

'Actually, this is Miss Isabel Hampton of Truro,' he said, keeping an even voice. 'The late Laurence Trevennor's supposedly late niece. But for now we must think of her as, and call her, Jenna Stevens.'

Kitty's face worked with curiosity and there was a trace of excitement in her soft accent. 'I heard he'd passed away, but you didn't go over the cliff as was supposed then, Miss Hampton?'

'It was contrived to look that way,' Isabel said. She was pleased Kitty had called her 'Miss Hampton', it put them both in their rightful places and she knew Nick did not find it agreeable.

'Well, I suppose there must have been a good reason for it,' Kitty said, looking from Isabel to Nick and back at Isabel, 'but it can wait until later. Please sit yourself down and make sure you're comfortable. I'll get you something to eat and drink.' Then to Nick, reproachfully, 'I don't suppose you've bothered to make the poor maid a dish of tea, have you?'

Nick made a face and sat at the table, making a show of keeping his elbows off the flower-patterned lace-edged tablecloth. He'd been maliciously amused at Kitty calling Isabel a 'poor maid' but Isabel was wearing the face of a dignified lady and he couldn't tell if she'd been offended. Kitty was willing enough to give people their place but she never stood on ceremony for them.

'Benefit you took they boots off, Nick Nancarrow,' Kitty scolded. 'Never thought to use the scraper outside the door, did you? I can never keep a clean floor when you're about.' She put a small square table at Isabel's side and covered it with a lace cloth. 'I was some sorry to hear about Mr Trevennor passing away, Miss Hampton,' she said quietly, with genuine sympathy.

'Thank you, it was a great shock to me,' Isabel replied, keeping her eyes averted from Nick who was watching her closely.

'And losing your friend and servants like that too – must have been really awful for you.' Kitty eyed her shrewdly. 'By the look of you, you've been travelling rough since the coach crash. You must have been hurt. How are you now?'

'I do have a few aches and bruises left from the accident but nothing serious. My feet are rather sore.' A sudden thought made Isabel ask a sharp question. 'Did you know my uncle by any chance, Kitty?' She heard Nick's angry intake of breath and shot him a reproachful look. She didn't consider it an unreasonable question to ask this particular woman. Uncle Laurence had been a widower a long time.

'No, I've never been over to Gwithian, but Nick used to talk a lot about your uncle so I feel I know him in a way. From what I've heard, he was a very good man, a real gentleman. You must have cared for him very much.'

'I did,' Isabel whispered, suddenly choked by her loss. Embarrassed at displaying her feelings, she looked down at her lap and put a mental block between herself and the two others in the room.

Nick felt ashamed; it did not settle easily on a man so determined to stay emotionally free. Isabel had lost the last relative who had loved her and cared for her wellbeing and not once over the past three days had he told her he was sorry as Kitty had done. And at times he had treated her as badly as Gyver Pengelly would a stray dog. They had become quite close, sharing an unusual kind of comradeship on the cliffs, and then only a short time ago in the little cove he had behaved despicably towards her. He looked at her bowed head and couldn't blame her for hating him.

Kitty left Isabel to her grief and moved quietly about putting cups and saucers and plates of tiny cakes on the two tables. Then she took a position at the larger table which put her between

Nick and Isabel. She was aware of the strained feelings between them.

'Where's Talland?' Nick asked, breaking the mood.

'Out chasing about the dunes, I expect,' Kitty answered fondly. 'Wonder you didn't see him. He's too much like you, Nick, he likes to be wild and free and out of doors.' She turned to Isabel with a warm smile. 'Talland's my dog. He's a handsome great thing, a brown and white hunting dog, big and friendly and very protective.'

'I shall be glad to make his acquaintance,' Isabel said, putting aside her misery and smiling back. 'I've always enjoyed the company of dogs.'

'Talland's a good dog but nowhere near as noble and strong as Gutser was,' Nick chipped in, using a tone that implied the two women could not know very much about the animals.

'In your mind no dog in the world could match up to that creature you once had, Nick Nancarrow,' Kitty retorted, offering Isabel more tea and going to the kettle to refill the pot. 'Gutser! What a name to call a dog. It's about time you got yourself another one and next time choose one without a vicious streak in its nature.'

'I'll not hear a word against Gutser,' Nick said, banging his hand on the table. 'He was the best friend I've ever had. I never saw a finer looking hound in my packman days and he'd have guarded me with his life.'

Isabel thanked Kitty for the tea and caught her eye with a glint in her own. She said, conspiratorially, 'Gutser is just the kind of silly name a man would call a dog.'

The two young women laughed together.

Nick had not liked this; he and Isabel had engaged in a class war on the way here and now she had called Kitty successfully to her side in a gender war. Looking disgruntled, he said, 'Well, I can see you two are going to get along all right.' Pushing the plate of cakes away, he added moodily, 'Get rid of this fancy stuff and put some proper food on the table.'

'Yes, m'lord,' Kitty teased him with a mocking curtsey. 'If you've spent the last three days in his company, all I can say is you have my sympathy,' she told Isabel. 'What with his moods, his pride and his bad language.'

Isabel smiled, poignantly. 'It has been quite an experience, but I probably owe Nick my life.'

Kitty included them both in a look full of questions. 'Do you now? Well, I daresay you'll let me in on what's happened and your reason for being here. Then after that you'll no doubt welcome a hot bath, a change of clothes and a soft bed to rest on.'

Nick said, 'Just a good meal, a wash and shave for me, Kitty. Then I'm leaving. I have to get back to Gwithian for Laurence's funeral and I have things to do there.'

'I won't be able to go to Uncle Laurence's funeral!' Isabel said, her face stricken.

'I'll say goodbye for you,' Nick said softly, looking kindly at her. 'Then when you're able, you can do it for yourself.'

Kitty was amazed at their tale of the Antiss coach probably being deliberately run off the road and Laurence Trevennor's concern over Isabel's life and safety. She readily agreed to have Isabel stay with her until Nick had scrutinized the Kempthornes. But she said, 'Shame on you for dragging her across the cliffs, Nick!'

'I'm glad he did,' Isabel intervened. 'I had no idea how beautiful they are. And I'm grateful to you, Kitty, for being willing to give me refuge.'

Isabel stayed in the kitchen, warm and comfortable, as Nick went upstairs to wash and shave. He came back in clean clothes and she was dismayed to realize that he kept some of his personal things at Kitty's house. It spoke of a lasting relationship between the two.

When he made to leave, he kissed Kitty's cheek and both of Isabel's hands, giving her a lingering look before promising to get word to them on his observations at Gwithian in a few days' time.

Although that night she slept in a soft bed with fresh linen, Isabel was restless. The sea could barely be heard with the house situated behind the sand dunes and having thick walls and she had got used to having it in the background. But she knew what she really missed was having Nick's arms round her.

A great weariness and delayed shock from her many traumas overwhelmed Isabel after Nick had left and for the first two days she stayed mainly in the little bedroom given to her. Kitty tactfully left her alone but stayed about the house all day.

Isabel made up a full story of her life as Jenna Stevens, of being a lady's maid who was visiting a friend while her mistress was overseas. In this way, if anything of her true character slipped out, her manner of employment would explain it. Kitty told this story to her curious neighbours and it was readily accepted.

Nick had left the money Laurence had given him with Isabel, and Kitty had new clothes made up for her. The day after the funeral, she cheered Isabel up by bringing home from the village the few items that were to be her new wardrobe. The clothes were a good fit but Isabel wasn't particularly interested in them. After spending three days in the late Mrs Chiverton's shabby dress, the cut and quality of clothes didn't seem important any more. Isabel dressed and showed Kitty the effect for her to admire lest she was thought to be ungrateful then Kitty said she had to go out again for a little while. There was a slight look of challenge on Kitty's face and Isabel supposed she must be going to see one of the 'gentlemen'.

'You'll be all right for an hour or so, won't you, Jenna? Whatever you do, make sure Talland doesn't get inside the house and go near the room next to the sitting room. I'd prefer it if you didn't go in there yourself,' she said briskly as she got ready. 'The little table's laid in the kitchen for tea for you. I know you like to rest in there,' she smiled.

'You are very kind but you don't have to wait hand and foot on me, Kitty,' Isabel said. 'I know I would have expected it not so long ago but that side of my life is over with now. I want to learn to do things for myself. I've done a little cleaning and after watching Nick I have a rough idea how to lay a fire.'

'Very well,' Kitty said, pushing down the fingers of her mittens. 'When I come back I'll begin by teaching you how to cook. You can help me with supper.'

Isabel had only to put the boiling water into the teapot to make tea for herself. After doing this she sat and sipped and lingered, thinking back, as she often did, of the time she had spent alone with Nick. She wondered what he was doing. Whether he would soon have news for her. Whether he thought of her. When he would come back to Crantock.

She washed and dried her crockery and returned it to the kitchen dresser. She put the dish towel to dry above the fireplace. She plied the fire with more fuel, swept the hearth, and tidied up everything she possibly could to impress Kitty and express her gratitude. With nothing further to do, she thought of Mrs Chiverton's clothes still lying in a forlorn heap on her bedroom floor. She had insisted to Kitty that they mustn't be thrown away and Kitty had left them there, thinking she would change her mind. But Isabel felt they should be laundered and returned to Charlie and she wanted to do the task herself. She went upstairs to fetch them. When Kitty came home she would ask her advice on how to wash them.

As she passed through the hall, she heard a noise in the room next to the sitting room. She stopped, frowned and listened. There it was again. She'd thought Kitty's insistence on not letting Talland into the room was because she probably had her best furniture and ornaments in there. But Kitty had asked her not to go in there herself. Isabel was greatly curious. Was there some sort of secret behind that door? For a moment she thought her cousins had found out about her and were lurking in the house. But surely they would walk boldly up the path and bang on the front door. Isabel was suddenly worried that Talland had somehow got into the room. If he had broken anything, Kitty would think she had been careless in letting the dog in there and be cross with her.

Isabel opened the door slowly and called Talland's name.

There was no answering bark or scampering of heavy paws but a small voice said 'Hello' and Isabel clutched the door in terror.

'Who's there?' she said shakily.

'Come in,' the small voice said.

She went into the room and her eyes opened wide. Lying on a small bed was a child whom she could just make out in the darkened room. Isabel went closer.

'Hello,' the child said. 'You must be Jenna.'

'Yes, but who are you?' she breathed, staring at a boy with a slightly pale face lying on a bed of sheepskin and covered with one light cover.

'I'm Benjamin, Kitty's brother. Hasn't she told you about me yet?'

Isabel realized he shared Kitty's features, the same tawny-brown eyes and red hair. He was a handsome child even though his face was not perfect and he possessed a beautiful smile that had a haunting quality.

'I thought I'd heard Kitty talking to someone else,' Isabel said, smiling down on Benjamin, 'and supposed it was Talland. Now I come to think of it, it was an odd way to talk to an animal. And now I realize that the plates of food, the same as she'd given me to eat, which I thought she was putting down outside for Talland, must have been for you.'

'Speaking of Talland,' Benjamin said, 'would you go back and shut the door, please. He mustn't come in here. Then perhaps you'd like to sit awhile and talk to me.'

'I'd be delighted to,' Isabel said.

She carefully moved a chair nearer Benjamin's bed and sat down. The room was furnished as a bedroom. Isabel could think of no reason for Kitty not telling her about her brother and what this room was used for.

'Have you been ill, Benjamin?' she asked gently.

'All of my life, Jenna. My bones are too soft and they break easily, that's why I look like this.' He lifted the cover delicately and Isabel could see his middle was extended and his four limbs had obviously been broken often. 'I have to stay on this bed now for my own safety. I expect you think I'm about eight or nine because I'm so small but actually I'm fourteen.'

'Well, you're a very handsome fourteen-year-old,' Isabel said smiling, finding Benjamin easy to talk to. 'Have you and Kitty always lived in this house?'

'No, we came here about five years ago after Kitty came into a windfall. Before that we lived at New Quay, across the river. Kitty's so good to me, she's done everything for me since our mother died many years ago. Kitty said you are a friend she met back-along. I hope you can stay, Jenna. It will be nice having someone else to talk to.'

'I shall gladly come in here and talk to you, Benjamin. I don't know how long I'll be staying but it will be at least for a few more days. Is there anything I can do for you? Fetch you a drink or something?'

'No, thank you. Kitty does everything for me. She has to, you understand, with my condition; she knows how to move me. I usually have a nap in the afternoon, that's why the curtains are drawn. You get a good view of the River Gannel from the window.'

'I'm glad you have something interesting to look out at. Am I disturbing you? Would you rather I go and let you have your rest? I can come back later.'

'I want you to stay,' Benjamin said firmly. ''Tisn't every day I get a beautiful girl alone in my room.' Isabel laughed and didn't hear the door open and close. Benjamin's eyes told her someone had entered the room. Isabel got up and turned to face Kitty, blushing to the roots of her hair. Kitty was obviously furious with her.

Isabel moved away from the bed. 'I'd better go, Benjamin, I'll… um, come and see you again.'

'Good bye, Jenna,' Benjamin said in his small husky voice. 'Don't forget to come back, I'll be expecting you.'

Isabel went out and closed the door after her. She could hear Kitty settling her younger brother down to sleep in the gentlest of tones. She returned to the kitchen and waited to face Kitty.

When Kitty entered the kitchen, her face was dark with anger. She folded her arms and glared at Isabel.

Isabel gulped. She felt she had breached Kitty's hospitality but she still couldn't understand why she couldn't have been told about Benjamin.

'Why didn't you tell me you had a brother?'

'What gives you the right to go into a room I specifically asked you to stay out of?'

Isabel frowned. 'I heard a noise. I was worried that somehow Talland had got into the room.'

'Do you realise what Talland could have done to Benjamin if he'd gone into the room with you!' Kitty shouted angrily, clenching her teeth. 'He's a friendly dog and if he'd jumped up on Benjamin he would have broken every bone in his body! He would have killed him! Benjamin can break a bone simply by sneezing or moving too suddenly.'

Isabel stared stupidly at Kitty for a moment in sheer amazement then said coldly, 'If you are so concerned about Talland getting into Benjamin's room, why do you have a boisterous dog about the place?'

'You may have noticed that I don't allow him into the house. I'm a woman living alone except for a disabled brother. Talland protects us at night and gives peace of mind.'

'I understand that now, but if you had told me about Benjamin in the first place instead of being so secretive this wouldn't have happened. Why didn't you tell me? Did you think I would hurt him?'

Kitty unfolded her arms and sighed. 'I'm sorry,' she said tightly. 'I just get so worried about Benjamin. I was going to tell you about him when I found the right moment. The first two days you were here you were resting and grieving for your uncle. I thought you'd stay in the kitchen until I got back today and then I was going to tell you. I wanted to prepare you. I didn't want you going into the room and showing Benjamin any shock or pity. I simply *won't* have him upset.'

'What did you think I was going to do, Kitty? Run screaming in horror from the room. You must think I'm as shallow as Nick did at first. Perhaps I ought to leave here. Nick shouldn't have brought me here to intrude on your life. I'll go to my fiancé's aunts. They'll be angry at my deception but they'll let me stay with them until Captain Grenville returns. If I tell my magistrate acquaintances about my uncle's fears, my cousins will not dare to make a move against me, if indeed they mean me any harm.' Isabel's eyes were filled with tears. She couldn't take any more of being made to feel that she was a high-minded lady given only to cruelty and injustice. She got up and made to leave the kitchen.

'Don't go, Jenna,' Kitty said. 'You've made me feel very ashamed. Please sit down and let's talk. I'm very sorry for upsetting you.'

Isabel was doubtful. 'I'm sorry too, sorry that I disobeyed your house rule and that my uncle's suspicions have meant imposing on Nick and his friends. It doesn't seem fair that you've all been put out.'

'We're both upset, Jenna. Let's have some fresh tea and start again on a new footing.' Kitty gave a wry smile. 'Benjamin wants you to stay, don't forget. He's expecting to see you again.'

Isabel thought of the gentle-faced boy; she wanted to hear his unique voice and see his smiling face again. She sat down once more.

Kitty made the tea and joined Isabel at the table. 'Benjamin is all I have. He's the reason I work as I do. Our father deserted us when Benjamin was born and when our mother died I couldn't go out to work for long periods because he needs so much attention. There was a gentleman, he took a fancy to me and offered a way out of our predicament. I didn't think twice, I was only fifteen years old and all that mattered was Benjamin living in comfort and safety and having money to pay his medical fees. I saved for years to have this place built and the gentleman was very generous in helping me to furnish it. He died three years ago and two of his acquaintances approached me to take his place. They're both married and the arrangement suits me well. They live fairly close by and they each send someone to collect me and bring me back. It means I don't have to leave Benjamin for long. He still has to have the doctor regularly and I'll do anything I can to care for him properly. When Nick asked me if you could stay here, my only reservation was how you would react to Benjamin. I'm sorry if I upset you, Jenna. But I didn't know you. I had to do it my way. When I saw you in Benjamin's room, I was so afraid you'd upset him or had tried to move him. Even though I could see you were chatting comfortably, I overreacted. Do forgive me.'

Isabel had been staring at her cup and saucer while listening attentively. She looked up. 'I feel a little ashamed myself, Kitty. I think I overreacted too.'

'I think I know why in your case.' Kitty touched her hand and smiled understandingly. 'You went through a bad time with Nick up on the cliffs, didn't you? I know how stubborn he can be. He wouldn't have been slow in telling you how he felt.'

'He wasn't horrid to me all the time,' Isabel said loyally.

Kitty nodded. 'I've realized that too. Are we friends now? Will you stay?'

'I want to, Kitty. I feel safe here, but it doesn't seem fair. Now I know you have Benjamin in the house – what would happen to him if my cousins find out I'm here? They might hurt him.'

'Why should they think you're not dead? Everyone else seems to without question. Why shouldn't I have a house guest? Why shouldn't folk believe you're an old friend of mine? Even if you're seen and someone realizes you're a lady, well, I mix with the gentry, they'll only think you're something to do with one of my gentlemen. Furthermore, I just can't believe your uncle's suspicions. It's too fanciful. My first gentleman rambled on like that when he was dying, thinking folk were in the room when they weren't, imagining he was being poisoned. I like having you here, Jenna, honestly. I trust you with Benjamin now that you are aware of his condition and it will be good to know there's someone in the house to keep him company when I'm out. What do you say?'

Isabel gave a mighty sigh of relief. 'Put like that, I'll be happy to stay, Kitty.'

'I think there's one more thing we ought to clear up while we're bringing everything out in the open. What do you feel about my line of work, my gentlemen?'

'I'm not shocked or horrified if that's what you mean. I think it's a pity you have to do it but I admire your courage and your love for Benjamin. Others might have left him to fend for himself. If it wasn't for your dedication, I don't expect he'd still be alive now.'

'No, he wouldn't. Now that's settled, let's get some vegetables out of the spence so we can make a start on your first cooking lesson.'

Chapter 14

Gyver Pengelly shambled his sweaty hulk into Gwithian. He'd just spent some time with Nellie in the hovel she lived in and been told Deborah Kempthorne wanted to see him. Pengelly was in an expansive mood; Nellie had been good to him, the wreck of *The Bountiful* had been good to him and a meeting with Miss Kempthorne probably meant yet more money was in the offing.

He passed Trevennor House at noon, whistling a local jig and stopping to give attention to one of his huge dirty boots, the signal he was to give to show that he had received the message. Deborah was watching discreetly for him from an upstairs window. She moved away and sent for her cloak and hat.

'I'm going out, Edmund,' she told her brother, who had just risen from bed. 'I need a little fresh air to clear a headache before Nick arrives.'

'Mind how you go,' Edmund returned breezily. 'And if you see any of the villagers, Debs, try being civil to them. We won't make much of an impression if you keep your nose stuck up in the air all the time.' Deborah left the house on heavy feet and a loud, 'Huh!'

She met Pengelly at the appointed place, a lonely piece of dirt track, turning off to the left several yards further up the village street. The ground was wetter and more slippery than she thought it would be. She'd muddied her cloak and was in a foul mood.

'Why have you taken so long to see me!' she went straight in on the attack. 'I told that stupid girl to give you a message days ago.' Deborah was a little afraid of Gyver Pengelly and always used this aggressive tactic with him to disguise it and keep the upper hand.

'Sorry, miss,' Pengelly said, sounding anything but sorry. He knew the Kempthorne woman was likely to need him more than he did her and he held no respect for class, particularly pretenders to the title. 'So, what is it yer wantin'?'

'Do you want to earn some money?'

'Course I bleddy do! I ain't daft.'

'A lot of money.'

Pengelly ruffled his bush of a beard. 'Wantin' somebody else dead, are 'ee?'

Deborah glanced around to make sure they were quite alone. If anyone happened along she would scream and accuse Pengelly of dragging her here and molesting her for money. She had the evidence of muddy clothing to prove it. 'I'm worried about that girl, Nellie. She's a moron. She could spell trouble for us, talk about the real reason Isabel Hampton's coach went off the road.'

'No, not Nellie. She's a mite soft in the head but she went say nothin'. She only talks to folk I says she can.'

'She spoke to my brother last week and I've seen her talking to the village cats. Someone might overhear her saying something incriminating. And she spends a lot of time with that curate's sugar-sweet wife. I want you to get rid of her, Pengelly.'

'Get rid of Nellie!' he roared. 'I couldn't do that. I can use that maid, she went say nothin'. There's no evidence the coach went off delib'rate, I moved the rocks away.'

'We cannot afford to take the risk. If Nellie talks, there could be a noose round your neck and possibly mine. This way everything will be tidied up and we can get on with our lives and need never see one another again.'

Pengelly shook his head wildly. 'No, anybody, but not Nellie.'

Deborah pursed her thin cruel lips, raised her sagging chin and challenged him. 'Not even for one hundred guineas?'

'What?'

'One hundred guineas, Pengelly. Think of it. You'd have to plunder a lot of wrecks to make that much money. You could go away and start a new life somewhere. Get yourself a new wife and buy a lot of pretty girls… and I can always get someone else to do it for me.'

Pengelly licked his swollen blue lips. 'All right,' he snarled. 'But I'll do it my way. I won't have her sufferin'.'

'You surprise me, Pengelly, I didn't think you cared about anyone but yourself.'

–

For the last ten days Nick had been fitting the pair of coach horses he was training to pull the Bassets' four-wheeled chaise with all the different pieces of harness needed to get the animals used to the feel of them. Both the healthy black horses were about five years old and had been broken in for riding. Nick had ridden them before starting their training to get used to them and give them a chance to trust him. One horse, a quiet gelding with big open feet and what Nick termed 'a good shoulder', was ready to be introduced to the breaking-in cart, an ordinary cart fitted with extension shafts. For this the horse would wear a breast collar. Nick put it on slowly, talking to the horse all the time to retain its trust. When all was ready, the groom held the horse's head while Nick mounted the cart.

He tapped the gelding's rump with the whip and the next stage of training began. The horse began trotting without hesitation, it did not buck and seemed not at all nervous. After a short, well-paced walk round the paddock, followed by another longer one, Nick proclaimed the horse a 'natural' who would perform efficiently. He unharnessed it and led it back to the stables, making sure it was settled with a stable boy before making his way to the feed barn. The groom had got there before him and was sitting on a bale of hay. Nick sat on the next one.

As though on cue a chirpy kitchen maid appeared with their crib. She lingered about, trying to engage Nick in chit-chat but he didn't seem to notice. He pushed stray sandy hair away from his eyes and looked appreciatively at the food set on a pewter tray.

'A nice piece of horseflesh that gelding is, Sid,' he said, when the maid had gone back to her work. 'I reckon he'll be one of the best I've ever trained. 'Tis a good place to work, here. The Bassets, even though they're still in mourning, look after their craftsmen.'

'Aye, 'tis five months since Mr Francis died. Shame he never saw the alterations he wanted done to the mansion and the grounds finished first. We've lost a lot of gentry lately, all good men, what with yer Mister Trevennor. Never knew him meself.'

Sid was a freckled-faced man with a long bent nose and weak chin which refused to grow a beard. A year younger than Nick, he looked up to him because of his expertise with the horses. Horses were his usual topic of conversation followed closely by women and his latest conquest.

'Course, Laurence Trevennor was not as grand as the Bassets,' Nick said, 'but he was one of the finest men I've ever known. His successors are a right bloody pair, not that they plan to live at the house for long. You're lucky Mr Basset's got a son to carry on with his plans, Sid.'

'Aye, s'pose so.' Sid quaffed at an ale jug he had secreted behind the bale. He passed it on to Nick and brought up his second favourite subject.

'That there maid who brung our crib don't half fancy you. You'm all right there I'd reckon, Nick.'

'Not me, Sid. 'Tis you she's got her eye on,' Nick replied with a grin.

'Naw!' Sid exclaimed, spraying his shirt and waistcoat with ale. 'I've worked here nigh on twelve year from a stable boy and she's never given me as much as a second look, no matter what bait I dangle before her. 'Tis a fine looking stallion she d'see in you. She's looking fur a stud.' Sid leaned over and elbowed Nick with a wicked smile. 'Give it to her, will 'ee?'

Nick thought about it while eating a mouthful of fresh crusty bread, then answered slowly, 'No, I don't think I will.'

'What? Give up a chance like that? With all that bosom hanging out just fur thee? Yourn damned lucky you've got the looks to be so choosy.' Sid eyed Nick suspiciously. 'You're a funny bugger, you are, Nick Nancarrow. I know you don't prefer the company of men lest I wouldn't be sitting so close to you. You ain't married, I've asked 'ee. Got a sweetheart somewhere, have 'ee?'

Nick thought about this too while swigging from the ale jug. He pulled a long straw out of the hay bale and wound it round his finger. Finally, after keeping Sid on tenterhooks, he said softly, 'No, I don't think so.'

Sid did not think much of this answer and slapped his knee hard. 'What sort of an answer is that, boy! Good-looking man like you oughta know if he has one or no. I ruddy well would and whether she was good t'lie with.' Then Sid nodded his greasy head and looked knowingly. 'You have, haven't you? And she's given you a bit of trouble, eh?'

'Not a little trouble, Sid, a good deal of it. But she's not my sweetheart.'

'She worth it?'

'Aye, she's worth the trouble,' Nick said to the barn floor. He hadn't thought so at first. When he'd pulled Isabel's inert body round to him he would rather have had any other task in the world than the one given him by Laurence Trevennor. He would never have believed then just how much Isabel was to change.

He didn't need Sid's probing questions to be brought to thinking about her. He couldn't get her out of his mind. Not just because he had the task of finding out if her life was at risk.

He found he was continually going over every moment he had spent with her since he had discovered her at the coach crash until the noncommittal farewell he'd given to her at Crantock. There were moments when he longed to hurry back there to see what she was doing, how she was behaving, how well she was getting on with Kitty and Benjamin. But for now she was safe while he kept an eye on the Kempthornes… and every day that passed was one closer to Richard Grenville coming home and then Isabel could be put into his hands.

No matter how his thoughts of Isabel ran, they always ended up with remorse over his insensitivity. He'd thought about it often and why he'd acted that way in the cove, why he had not simply taken her into his arms and kissed her lovingly and seen if anything would have progressed from it. He had not wanted to be seen to be romantic, loving, making some kind of commitment to her, but few women liked being suddenly manhandled in any situation. No wonder Isabel had been so horrified at his actions. He wanted to make it up to her, to tell her he was sorry.

The harsh call of a peacock proudly strutting its way around Tehidy's subtropical garden brought Nick back to the present. Sid was waiting for him to go on but he forced Isabel's lovely face from his mind and talked of the horses.

'The first gelding will be easier to put through his paces but the other will be a good puller, I reckon. I'll tether it to a tree and encourage it to pull away until it's had enough of it. That'll put paid to it pulling the wrong way and putting the pair of 'em out of balance.'

Sid was impressed. 'Would never have thought of that meself. Something like that could keep a carriage under control and stop a nasty accident like the one at Deadman's Cove. Four dead, from Truro, I believe. Ever hear what happened to the horses, Nick?'

'They broke free and were all rounded up eventually and taken safely back to the Antiss stables in Truro.'

'Thank God for that. Hate to hear of good horseflesh going to waste.'

'Aye, me too.' Nick ate his crib and wondered what Sid would say if he knew he had been there at the scene of the Antiss coach crash.

'You going over to Gwithian again later on then, Nick?'

'I might.'

'On that mare loaned 'ee from the Trevennor stables?'

'I might.'

'I reckon you got some woman over there.'

'Just one I'm doing business with.'

Sid guffawed and slapped Nick heartily on the back, making the neck of the ale jug he was about to put into his mouth knock against his teeth.

'Well, boy, when you've finished doing business with this woman, send her over to me!'

Nick pressed his fingers to his bruised lips. 'Steady on, Sid. I might need these lips for kissing. Seriously though, I'm teaching a lady to ride, and believe me, you wouldn't want anything to do with this one.'

'Oh? A lady, eh? From what stables?'

'The lady or the horse?'

'The horse, you fool. But what's the lady like anyway?'

''Tis a horse from Laurence Trevennor's stables and the lady is his niece.'

'Not the one who died?'

'Sid, are you ruddy mazed? I've yet to teach a ghost to ride side-saddle. She's Miss Deborah Kempthorne who used to live at St Ives.'

'She paying you well?'

'Aye,' Nick replied, but he had not received a single penny so far.

'She a good learner then?'

'Ruddy useless. If you ask me she scares the horses.'

'She's pretty? Old? Young?'

Nick knew what Sid was leading up to. He snorted. 'She's plain-faced, cruel-hearted and built like a cart horse. Definitely not my sort of woman.'

Sid chuckled and made a lecherous gesture. 'They're all the same lying down.'

'No, they're not!' Nick blurted out, not liking that last remark. It brought a terrible sight to mind.

Deborah was nervous of horses and Nick was well aware that her proposition that he teach her to ride was a ruse to get closer to him. He'd never forget the first lesson. It had been a dreadful experience for him. She'd made him call at the house for her and made a great show of it in front of the servants. Mrs Christopher hadn't been too surprised when Nick had gone to Trevennor House after Laurence's funeral but her face was agog at the sight of him leading the new lady of the house out to the stable yard with her clinging to his arm, saying Nick this and Nick that, and he apparently hanging on to her every word. He wished he could have a quiet word with the housekeeper and tell her what he was up to.

His heart had sunk when Deborah dismissed the two stable boys. Without their help, actually getting Deborah onto the horse, a gentle, mature mare, and the largest horse in the stables, had been a most difficult manoeuvre.

When they were finally trotting through the village, he having to lead the mare by the reins because Deborah insisted she hadn't the confidence yet, they had passed Denny Rowe sitting up in a hedgerow near his home, as was his habit, to watch the village life pass him by and to sneak a quiet pipe of tobacco when Meena was busy and unlikely to catch him at it. Nick had wanted the ground to swallow him up. Denny had merely nodded at him and doffed his cap to Deborah. Deborah wouldn't usually have replied but she called back a loud 'Good day to you', seeming to want everyone to know she was abroad that day. Nick was glad the Rowes' cottage was not near the heart of the village and resolved he would never ride that way with his pupil again.

Thankfully Deborah was too nervous to ride for long but things had been worse for Nick when they got back. She had pretended to fall to the ground when he'd helped her down from the horse and she'd told him to help her into a stall so she could sit awhile.

'Just so I can return to the house in a calm state,' she had said in a deliberately shaken voice as she'd lowered herself none too gracefully onto a stool. 'I don't want Mrs Christopher to worry about me.'

Privately Nick thought Mrs Christopher couldn't have cared less about Deborah but she'd have plenty to think about if he was forced to linger in the stable with the woman.

'You did quite well for a first time, Miss Kempthorne,' he said. 'You will have to try to trust the mare. I've known Belle for years and she's never thrown anyone. A horse can tell when its rider is nervous of it. I understand Miss Isabel Hampton rode Belle often and she had no trouble with her,' he added, hoping to gauge something of how Deborah felt about her cousin.

Deborah's face stiffened and she smoothed down her riding skirt with taut fingers but she looked up at Nick from her ridiculously feathered hat with what she probably thought was a soft smile. 'Everyone is different, Nick. I'm sure I shall do better next time. You will have to be patient with me.'

She did no better the next time nor the one after that. All she succeeded in doing was getting Nick anywhere she could alone and, by the scowls he was receiving from some of the villagers, folk who were his friends and who had once trusted him, ruining his reputation for integrity.

Nick knew he'd find out nothing of what he needed to know from Edmund Kempthorne. Edmund had invited him to play cards and Nick had lost all the money he'd had with him; Edmund was a skilful cheater and just as skilful at keeping his thoughts to himself. Nick was still hoping the riding lessons would prove useful in getting information out of Deborah but he didn't want to get too close to her, that could mean unwanted complications. Isabel had told him she was an accomplished horsewoman and he wished it was possible to ride with her instead. The thought of holding and kissing Deborah, which he knew she was angling for, was most uninviting, but kissing Isabel's soft lips… and he had missed the opportunity.

Sid had been watching him while stuffing food into his mouth. 'You're off again,' he said, after the last swallow. 'Don't even blink an eyelid.'

'Eh?'

'You're thinking. Off in a world of your own. Got something on your mind, have 'ee?'

'That's right, Sid. 'Tis time to get back to work.' Impatiently he made for the stall of the second gelding. The sooner the task Laurence Trevennor had set him was over and Isabel came back from the 'dead' and got married, the sooner he could get on with his old life again, living free and easy and unhampered. He would dally no longer. After his work here was finished for the day, he would somehow force the Kempthornes' hand.

Chapter 15

Later in the day, when Nick turned up in the Trevennor stable yard as arranged, there was no sign of Deborah waiting for him dressed in her ill-fitting voluminous black riding clothes. A maid was sent to tell him that the mistress had been taken with one of her sudden headaches and requested his company in the parlour. Nick had taken more care with his appearance for this riding lesson which did not go unnoticed by the maid or her mistress.

'That will be all, Dorcas,' Deborah said, employing the softer voice she retained when Nick was about. 'I will ring if I need anything.'

'Yes, ma'am,' Dorcas replied dully, dipping her knee. She shot Nick a look of sympathy before leaving the room.

Nick was glad he did not receive any strange looks or cutting remarks from the servants here; Mrs Christopher and Wenna Sweet, the cook, had put their heads together and concluded there must be an ulterior motive for the attention he was giving their dreaded mistress. Mrs Christopher had taken him aside soon after the riding lessons had begun and told him that whatever he was doing, the household and the Thomases knew he was trying to look after Mr Trevennor's interests. It helped with what he had to do, knowing that some of the folk who'd known him all his life had retained their trust in him.

The parlour curtains were almost drawn and Deborah was reclining on a sofa with her feet on a green velvet stool. Her fingers were massaging her furrowed brow. The room, like the whole house since the Kempthornes' arrival, was gloomy and sinister and filled with the smell of Deborah's sickly perfume and stale sweat. Nick wanted to throw her outside and let in the two bloodhounds, which she insisted were to be kept outside when Edmund wasn't there. He wanted to thrust back the curtains and pull open the windows and let the clean fresh air fill the house that by right belonged to Isabel. He resisted the urgent need to take off his necktie and standing close to Deborah he put on a kindly smile.

'I'm sorry to find you unwell, Miss Kempthorne. May I suggest an infusion of rosemary tea? My mother and Mistress Trevennor swore by it for headaches.'

'How kind of you to be concerned, Nick,' Deborah said sweetly, 'but Charlotte Thomas was here a short time ago and made the same suggestion. She went straight back home and fetched some for me and I'm relieved to say the worst of the headache has lifted and I am beginning to feel quite comfortable.'

'Good, I'm glad to hear it.'

She had left off her black mourning clothes and was wearing a gown of pink with a muddy-green stripe over a silver-grey petticoat. Her hair was in a freer style than usual. A little rouge and paint on her lips did nothing to enhance her hard features.

'Did you have a good day at Tehidy, Nick?'

'Yes, thank you. The horses I'm training are shaping up nicely.'

'It's such a beautiful place. Quite sheltered now from the winds and elements with so many trees planted and growing on the north slope above the mansion, which in itself is a magnificent creation. They have the greyhounds there, odd-looking creatures but appealing I think, and those beautiful birds of paradise. There is also a bowling green and lake and the many and varied plants obtained from exotic countries. The excellent gravel walks do not get a lady's skirts muddy. It is paradise on earth.'

Nick raised his eyebrows at her lyrical description of Tehidy, knowing she had never been invited there and was unlikely to be in the future. He toyed with one of Laurence's snuff-boxes. 'You know Tehidy well then, Miss Kempthorne?' he said, baiting her. If he had to make advances to this despicable woman he wasn't going to be entirely gracious about it. It worked. Deborah looked most annoyed but did her best to hide it.

'I heard only the other day that the Bassets' steward was complaining at the amount of poaching perpetrated on the property. Forgive me, Nick,' she changed tack while struggling to get to a sitting position, 'would you like to sit down? I can offer you the drink of your choice. My brother has replenished the spirits table.'

'I wouldn't say no to a nip of brandy. You stay put, Miss Kempthorne, and please don't ring for someone. I can help myself.'

With the brandy bowl warming in his hands, he leaned back against Laurence's writing desk and looked at her from under his long fair lashes.

'Is Mr Kempthorne about this afternoon?'

'Did you wish to see him, Nick?'

'No, I was merely curious,' he looked right into her eyes, '... wondering if we are likely to be disturbed.'

Deborah flushed with pleasure and gave a noisy gulp. 'We shouldn't be.'

He walked to one of Laurence's many open bookshelves and ran a finger slowly along the spines of a row of books. 'Laurence always allowed me the use of his library. He was the main influence for my learning to read and write. I was wondering if I might borrow a book.'

'Of course you may, Nick. Take as many as you like.' Deborah rose awkwardly and tottered across the room and stood close to him. She watched his big rough hand flit from one thick volume of poetry to another. 'I don't know why Uncle Laurence didn't have a proper library made in one of the other rooms.' She eyed Laurence's zograscope, which he used to magnify specimens and detailed maps, his harpsichord and collection of flutes and guitars. 'I've always thought there was too much in this room.'

'He liked all his collections to be in the room he felt most comfortable in,' Nick stated, over her tilted face.

'You knew him very well, didn't you?'

'From childhood. I admired and respected him very much.' Nick took down a heavy book entitled *Olde Cornish Verse.*

'You are a romantic, Nick?'

He moved closer to her and smiled deeply. 'I'm told I can be.'

Her eyes were rooted to his. 'I can believe that.'

'Oh? Why is that?' he said in husky whispers, almost in her ear.

Deborah flushed again and lifted her wide shoulders in an embarrassed shrug. 'Well, I… you…'

It was the perfect moment for Nick to plunge in. He put the book down and moved just a breath away from her. His gaze held her full attention.

'Please don't take offence at what I'm about to say, but I've grown very fond of you.'

'Oh, Nick!' It was beyond Deborah's wildest hope. She moved a hand hesitantly forward and one of his moved to clasp it firmly.

'You don't mind?' he said softly through the thick air between them.

'Not one little bit,' she breathed, giving an unsightly shudder.

'Can I call you Deborah?'

'Oh, yes.'

'Deborah…'

'Yes, Nick?'

Nick's gut twisted but he had to say it. 'Can I kiss you?'

She said, 'Yes,' with a breathy sigh.

He put his other hand on her waist and bent his head forward for the kiss, the only one he had ever given that he was not looking forward to. Deborah allowed him to do all the work and he could not tell if she was unused to kissing or playing coy with him. She kept her eyes closed when he drew his lips away and then moved into his body. Putting her arms tightly about him she rested her face against his chest. He felt like a sacrificial lamb primed for the slaughter, but held her close. Her perfume had a heavy mildewed smell and her form felt heavy and cumbersome. He prayed she did not expect the situation to be taken to its fullest extent.

'I had no idea you felt the same way about me, Nick,' she said, in a deliberately sultry voice that grated more on his nerves than Isabel's first high-pitched squeals had.

He had given Deborah no encouragement during the riding lessons. He hadn't touched her unless he'd absolutely had to. He thought how readily he had taken Isabel into his arms even when he thought he'd hated her.

''Tis unthinkable,' he forced himself to sound sincere and romantic, 'me, falling in love with a lady. I never meant this to happen. I never meant to tell you. This morning I had made up my mind to send you a message saying I could no longer teach you to ride. I intended to stay away but couldn't… I can hardly believe you feel something for me, Deborah.'

'But this is wonderful,' she said, looking up at him earnestly, 'and I have something to admit to you, Nick. I know I should not have been thinking so but I felt attached to you right from the beginning, the day of Uncle Laurence's funeral. I tried not to fall in love with you. I thought there was no hope, knowing how you like to be a free agent and that I am a few years older than you are.'

'And it makes no difference that we aren't of the same class?'

'Age, class, what do they matter? Love can pass through any barrier.'

'You're right about that,' Nick said, but he wasn't thinking of Deborah. With bile rising in his throat, he uttered, 'Nothing matters except that we love each other.'

Deborah smiled and pouted her lips for another kiss. Nick looked into her dark eyes and saw only the spite and deceit that dwelt there. Lower down was her slightly arched predatory nose and finally the cruel lines that plunged downwards from the sides of her thin-lipped mouth. He could not believe that any man could find Deborah Kempthorne desirable. And Kempthorne was not even her name; would she mention that she was married and not available?

He kissed her again and this time she wrapped her arms possessively round his neck and let her passion run away with her. The well-rounded bosom pressed hard against him rose and fell as she panted. Nick wanted to run outside and gulp in lungfuls of fresh air. It was with much relief that the next part of his plan meant breaking away from her and stalking across the room. Deborah was alarmed.

'Nick, what is it?'

'It's no good, Deborah,' he said dramatically, raking a hand through his hair then banging his fist on the wall. 'I have no right to do this. What sort of a life can a working-class man with no money or a roof to call his own offer a lady like you? I can't ask you to give up all this and travel the roads with me as I search for work!'

'But, Nick,' she rushed over to him and flung herself against him. 'It doesn't matter. I have plenty of money now. We can live here together and you can ride the horses in the stable as owner and not trainer. I beg you, Nick, don't be too proud to say yes, don't allow anything to come between us. The people of Gwithian hold you in high esteem, they would like to see you sharing this house, we could be happy here.'

Nick put his hands firmly on her shoulders and made her look at him. 'Are you sure about this, Deborah? God forbid that I should ruin your life.'

'It won't be like that! I want you with all my heart, believe me, Nick.'

And you'll hang on to anything you want like grim death, Nick thought. 'What about your brother? He is sure to object.'

'Never mind Edmund. He can hardly object while allowing his common mistress and child to live in this house. Besides, he will probably be glad that I won't be taking so much interest in what he does. He's very dear to me and up until now he is all I've had. I practically brought him up and he constantly grumbles that I smother him. I don't think he will mind too much about us. Oh, please don't worry, Nick. It will be so wonderful to have the two men I love living under the roof of this grand house with me. What do you say, Nick? Oh, please let it be yes.'

Nick faked elation. 'I… I can't believe it! This is too good to be true. Is it all really this easy, Deborah?'

'Yes, yes, my dearest,' she said, laughing.

He thought that at this juncture he should pull her close and kiss her passionately and show he desired her body, but he was afraid she would think he meant it and want to go through with it. He brushed back his hair, saying, 'Phew, I think I need another brandy.'

'I'll get it for you, my love,' Deborah said eagerly.

Nick sat down close to the door and when she handed him the brandy, she sat at his feet and put her head on his knee. She ran her hands over the tops of his legs, making his skin creep as though it was covered with a thousand clammy insects.

Deborah was only dimly aware of running her fingers over Nick. Her mind was on other things. Edmund had been spending nearly all his time with Mary Ellen and Morenwyn and she felt that she was gradually losing him. Since Laurence Trevennor's funeral, her infatuation with Nick had grown to a painful intensity. She burned to possess him, this man with the restless soul that turned the heads of so many women and furnished them with impossible daydreams. And now she had triumphed over them, the women of the village who hated her and laughed at her, saying no man would look in her direction.

She knew Nick was not in love with her. No man had suddenly thrown himself at her feet before now, and a man like Nick would need some attractive bait before he did so. It must be wealth and position he was after. All those years of friendship with Laurence Trevennor had probably been to nurture the possibility that there would be a reward in it one day, something left him in Laurence's will. She smiled down at the Turkish carpet she was sitting on, a slow, malicious smile. By means of a generous bribe to the lawyer dealing with her uncle's estate, Nick Nancarrow would never know he had been willed the eight good stock horses in the stables.

Deborah knew also that Nick could be a hard man. He was not easily led or fooled and it would take a lot of cunning work to hold on to him. It all added to the thrill of capturing him. But she was nervous of him. There was a terrifying maleness about this man. He would not suffer fools, or schemers, gladly. Her hand froze and she pulled it away and sat up straight.

Nick was ready to put the last part of his plan into action. He placed a hand caressingly on Deborah's stiff hair. Taking courage again, she rested her face back on his knee.

'I will enjoy living the life of a gentleman, though by no means of course a conventional one. 'Tis a good thing that sharp-faced cousin of yours is dead and not able to share the inheritance.'

'Isabel? You knew her?' Deborah raised her head and stared at him suspiciously. If Isabel had not died, would he have tried this ploy on her?

'Saw her about as a child but only once as a woman. Sharp-faced prig, she was, full of airs and graces. Looked down on me, she did. Thought she was better than everyone else on earth. Not a patch on the woman you are, Deborah, my dear. I made a point of staying away when she paid Laurence a visit.'

'Did you?' Deborah purred. 'She was a bitch! She certainly thought herself superior to Edmund and myself and we were her cousins. Not once in the last ten years did she call on us at St Ives. We were not good enough because we lived a humble life in a small cottage and she flounced about in a grand mansion above the Malpas River at Truro, which I might add we were never invited to. Do you know what she did, Nick? She wormed herself so much into our uncle's good books and told so many lies about us he believed every word and disinherited us. We only have what we do because she is dead.'

Nick had never struck a woman in his life but he would have enjoyed slapping Deborah Kempthorne for her spitefulness and lies about Isabel. It was bad enough that he had to say awful things about her himself.

The distaste in his expression was no pretence as he said, 'You mean if she hadn't fallen over the cliff after the coach accident she would have inherited all this and you and Edmund would have had nothing?'

'Yes, my dearest, that is exactly what I mean.'

'That's terrible. 'Tis a good thing she went over the cliff, it did us all a great favour.'

'Yes, and to think the villagers felt sorry for her, that pasty-faced shrew. We have been deluged with letters of sympathy from the best families in the county. Some of the things they wrote about her were sickeningly sweet. Mind you, it may give us some useful contacts in the future. Her fiancé, Captain Richard Grenville, won't be told until he comes home for the wedding, but his two elderly aunts wrote to say they have actually gone into mourning for her. I could laugh when I think of how Edmund and I have inherited her fortune as well as Uncle Laurence's. We'll have to travel to Truro one day soon, beloved, and demand to be shown over the mansion.' Deborah's face glowed like a beacon. She took one of Nick's hands and put it next to her hot cheek.

'Has your cousin's body been washed up yet?' Nick leaned closer to study her harsh face for her reaction.

'No, not yet, but if or when it is I'd like to dance on her grave!'

'I suppose she really is dead. It would be a damned nuisance if she turned up and demanded the inheritance and her own fortune back.'

'She must be dead! What other explanation could there be for her disappearance? All the evidence implies that she fell over the cliff.' Deborah's face took on an evil tightness, her eyes narrowed and glared.

'She could have been kidnapped for ransom, I suppose, but,' Nick ran a finger down Deborah's cheek and said in a hushed tone, 'if it was never paid, she'd be as good as dead anyway.'

'If that bitch was to turn up,' Deborah snapped, 'I would take her for a walk and give her a helping hand over the cliff myself!'

'We could do that together,' Nick chuckled, as if he was enjoying the thought. 'I can see we are like-minded, my dear. I admire a woman who will stop at nothing to get her own way.'

Deborah was looking at Nick as if she was weighing something up. 'You needn't worry about Isabel Hampton turning up and spoiling things for us, Nick. I know for a fact she's dead. Her body was seen at the bottom of the cliff before it was washed away. I myself spoke to the man who saw it.'

Nick stopped his body from lurching. That man was Gyver Pengelly. Charlie Chiverton had told him that it was Pengelly who had brought the news of Isabel's death to Mrs Christopher. Deborah Kempthorne would surely have no cause to talk to Pengelly unless they were in cahoots over the 'accident'. Pengelly must have lied to be sure of getting his full blood-money. Here was the proof Nick had hoped he would never find.

'I'll do anything to get my own way, Nick. I have been treated badly and looked down upon all my life. I've known too many times when I have had to go without the things a lady of refinement requires to lead a respectable and comfortable life. I vow that I will never, never go back to that way of life again!' She shook with venom and Nick had to fight back the revulsion he felt. There was no doubt now that Laurence's fears had been justified and Isabel's life would be in deadly danger, if not from Edmund Kempthorne then his vile sister, if it was found out she was alive. He would have to keep a close watch over the Kempthornes, this revolting woman in particular. Unfortunately, now he knew the truth at last he wouldn't be able just to fade out of her life. She would be too curious, too jealous and too clinging to give him up and that could lead her to Isabel.

He needed an excuse to get out of this terrible choking atmosphere before Deborah expected him to make further advances. Even for Isabel's sake he could not do it.

'I suppose we will have to wait at least four months before we make our engagement known,' Deborah said, returning to a lighter mood. 'It would be improper and antagonize the locals if we did so with Uncle Laurence but two weeks in the grave, not that I intend to live in this stuffy village for good but I don't want bad feelings to follow us to Truro.'

Nick hoped his face did not betray his relief. He could easily believe Deborah Kempthorne was immoral enough to suggest he move into Trevennor House with her straight away. At least this way he hoped he could keep his friends in the village.

It was little Morenwyn who saved him further discomfort. A shriek and a lot of thudding noises followed by anguished screams were heard from the hallway. Nick and Deborah stared at each other for a moment then got hurriedly to their feet and rushed from the room to see what the commotion was.

They found Morenwyn lying crumpled and unconscious at the bottom of the stairs and her mother, hands flapping wildly in the air, in hysterics at the top.

'My baby! My baby!' Mary Ellen screamed over and over again.

The servants came running and Nick took charge of the situation, ordering Mrs Christopher upstairs to calm Mary Ellen and a young footman to fetch clean linen while he himself swiftly untied Dorcas' apron and pressed it against a gash bleeding at the back of the child's head.

'Here, take over from me,' he ordered Deborah. 'She needs a doctor urgently, the nearest is at Hayle. I'll ride there myself, it'll be quicker. Don't move her and cover her with a blanket to keep her warm till we get back.'

Chapter 16

'I've got something here you can read – for both of us,' Kitty said, with the small tremor in her voice that was there when she was excited. She had just returned from the village and could hardly wait to fling off her hat and cloak and dig a piece of folded and wax-sealed paper out of her basket. 'A friend of Nick's gave this to me just as I passed the shoemender's shop. It must be a message from him.' Isabel sprang to her feet from the kitchen table where she was struggling to make a perfect job of peeling carrots for a stew.

'How's Benjamin? Has he had his morning nap?' Kitty asked.

'Benjamin is fine. I had a little chat with him then he dropped off to sleep about half an hour ago.' Isabel took the letter from Kitty and peered at its back and front. There was no name or address on either side.

'Hurry up and open it,' Kitty said, hopping about, another of her habits. 'What does he say? Are you in danger or no? Does it say when he's coming back?'

'What did this friend of Nick's look like?' Isabel said at first, feeling the need to be cautious.

'Charlie Chiverton? He's an ugly little small man. Used to be an underground miner but does a bit of tin-streaming and free trading as a living now. Lives in a shack up on Reskajeage Downs. Don't worry, Jenna, he's a proper friend of Nick's.'

'He's the man Nick took me to after the coach accident.'

Isabel picked open the red unmarked sealing wax and spread out the piece of paper on the table. She recognized it as the paper her uncle had used and knew that Nick had gained access to Trevennor House. She marvelled at the exquisite handwriting on it and read out the letter slowly.

> *My Dear Kitty*
> *I trust this finds you and your friend in Good Health. I have found out here there is Great Malice aimed at your Friend. Take the Greatest Care. Will see you in the Near Future to discuss further.*

'It is signed with the initial N,' Isabel concluded, with a shudder. 'The letter makes it quite clear my cousins wish me harm as my uncle suspected.'

'Your cousins sound like a right nasty pair,' Kitty said to Isabel's doleful face. 'Don't worry about it, though. If Nick didn't think it safe for you to stay here he would have come himself instead of writing. He'll be here soon and we'll know more about it then.'

Isabel brightened at the mention of Nick coming back, then frowned and sighed, 'I still find it difficult to believe that my own kin wish me harm.'

'We'll stay on our guard. At least everyone in the village here is happy to take you for the friend of mine that I say you are.'

Isabel was staring at the letter, rereading it over and over as if she hoped she'd see something else written there. 'Nick doesn't mention my uncle's funeral… how it went.'

'Jenna,' Kitty said carefully, 'it seems indelicate for me to mention it but one of my gentlemen went to your uncle's funeral. He told me all about it. I can tell you what he said if you like.'

Isabel flushed. She had said she wasn't shocked at Kitty's line of work and this was true, but it was different discussing something Kitty had found out during the course of it. 'That would be kind of you.' To cover her embarrassment, Isabel looked again at the letter. 'I would never have thought that Nick could write as well as this. His lettering is quite perfect, artistic – unless of course he dictated it to someone who wrote it down for him.'

'Oh, that's Nick's handwriting all right. I've watched him write to Laurence Trevennor at this very table.'

'I would never have thought that Nick would have taken any form of schooling.'

'Why not?' Kitty asked, putting her pretty face at an angle that challenged Isabel's remark.

'Well, he's so wild and free in his nature. He must have been a lively child, always wanting to run about, not to sit still and learn the alphabet.'

'Nick's a very clever man, clever enough to know even as a boy that it was a good thing to have some learning.' Looking annoyed, Kitty used terse actions to clear away the carrots and peelings.

'Have I prepared enough for luncheon?' Isabel asked, looking at her closely.

'There's plenty for the three of us,' came the short answer.

Isabel was at a loss to know how she had upset Kitty. It reminded her of Nick's prickly moods and she wanted to ask if all working-class people were as sensitive as they seemed to be, but knew it wouldn't be appreciated.

'You were going to tell me about my uncle's funeral,' she said.

Kitty's mood took another swing and she looked at Isabel with sympathy. 'Do you want to sit down first?'

'No, I'm all right, Kitty. Please carry on.'

Isabel pictured Nick standing solemnly at the graveside as Kitty recounted what she had been told.

'I'm so pleased that so many of the villagers paid their last respects and it was good of the Reverend, Mr Thomas, to say a prayer for me too,' she said quietly, a few minutes later. 'It sounds as though all the local great houses were represented. I'm glad the Bassets sent someone. Some people consider them to be the county's foremost family and Uncle Laurence was always well received by them. My mother was a cousin to the late Mr Francis Basset's wife. Dear Uncle Laurence, he was greatly respected and he'll be very much missed.'

'That's what my gentleman said. He went into Trevennor House afterwards and said Nick was there too, looking smart and tidy, for a change, in a good suit of clothes. He knows Nick, you see, Nick trains all his horses.'

Even through her grief Isabel could not help saying, 'I would like to have seen that, Nick all dressed up.'

'Would you now?' Kitty muttered disapprovingly under her breath. She turned and raked vigorously at the fire to make the dead ash drop into the grate.

'I'm very sorry,' Isabel said to Kitty's back.

The other young woman swung round in surprise. 'Whatever for?'

'I'll be honest with you, Kitty, I don't know. I've known you long enough to realize you don't stay vexed for long but I don't understand your moods. You seem to get annoyed with me quite often, like just now when I mentioned my surprise at Nick's handwriting.'

'It wasn't that,' Kitty said, fiddling with the poker.

'What then?' Isabel said firmly.

Kitty glanced down uneasily. 'It doesn't matter. I don't want to upset you after talking about your uncle's funeral. It can keep.'

'No, Kitty. I don't need to be treated gently any more. If you have something you want to say to me then please say it now.'

'Very well,' Kitty said, holding up her head and saying rather severely, 'You talk about Nick a lot, Jenna. Too much, to be honest with you. You've been here over two weeks and it's just about all I hear from you. You ply Benjamin with questions about him too.'

Isabel knew she could not deny this and it occurred to her that perhaps Kitty was in love with Nick and jealous of the three days and two nights they had spent together. Tension crackled in the kitchen and threatened the friendship they were building up. Isabel did not want to quarrel with the woman who had so willingly taken her in, who was kind and generous to her, but because of her upbringing, she could not allow herself to be reprimanded.

'Why does it cause you so much concern, Kitty?' she retorted.

'Well, to begin with you are betrothed, soon to be married, and I don't hear nothing much about Captain Richard Grenville.'

'I've told you all about Richard,' Isabel said defensively, wanting to look away.

'Oh, I've heard about how you first met him at a charity ball in Truro's great assembly rooms. That he's a captain in the Navy, is the younger son of a baronet but was left a small fortune and property at Falmouth by his doting grandmother. That he loves the sea and spends most of his time on it. You've told me that you will live mostly at your estate at Malpas in Truro after you are married. You've told me the colour and style of your wedding gown, what flowers you have chosen to carry and where you are to spend the first days of your marriage.'

'Exactly!' Isabel said heatedly. 'I've told you everything about Richard.'

'No, you haven't. You've talked all around him but not about him. I don't know what he looks like, whether he's romantic, handsome, fat, old, has a sense of humour, and not once have you spoken of your plans for your future together.' Kitty was quite rattled and stood with her dark eyes blazing and hands on her narrow hips. 'Well? What does Richard Grenville look like? A hideous ageing sea captain with a peg leg and a large wart at the end of his nose?'

'No! He's as handsome as a storybook hero, he's young, tall and dark with a flashing smile. He's good and kind and witty and I was happy to accept his proposal of marriage because I was getting the better bargain!' Isabel's face was hot with indignation yet she could not remember the smaller important things about Richard Grenville while everything about Nick was emblazoned on her mind.

'Yes, but do you love him?' Kitty hurled at her.

Isabel turned sharply away and went to a window that gave a clear view of the snaking River Gannel. She watched a ship sail out of view on its way to unload limestone at Fern Pit, then said quietly, 'I've never had to consider whether I love Richard or not.'

Kitty moved up beside her and with all huffiness gone she put an arm round Isabel's waist. 'Do you like him?'

'Yes, I like Richard. He's a good man.'

'That's all right then. Many a good marriage has been founded on a mutual liking and respect.'

To Kitty, the matter was now closed. Isabel knew the point she had wanted to make but if Kitty thought she had been successful in taking her thoughts away from Nick, she was wrong.

Kitty said brightly, 'C'mon, m'dear, let's make ourselves a dish of tea. I know I could do with one. We'll have to burn Nick's letter, better leave nothing to chance.'

Isabel looked sadly at the letter. She wanted to keep it, to have something as personal of Nick's as his handwriting. It would help her feel secure. She didn't want to think about Richard, to worry that she might be at risk until she was his wife. The past could not harm her. She remembered only the good times with Nick and wanted to cling to them, and to anything linked with Nick. She read the letter again quickly. 'Will see you in the Near Future.' She fed it reluctantly to the flames and hid her face lest Kitty guess how soon in the near future she hoped it would be.

'I answered your question about Richard,' Isabel said, lifting down the tea caddy from a shelf of the dresser. 'But tell me, Kitty, are you in love with Nick?'

Kitty paused in putting saffron cake on a china plate. 'So that's what's going through your mind, is it? You think I'm jealous of you and Nick spending that time together so I had a go at you about Richard Grenville. I just wanted you to face your feelings for him and what you think you feel for Nick.' She looked up from the plate and she saw a guarded expression on Isabel's face. 'You can't have him, you know.'

A flicker of exasperation passed over Isabel's face and she breathed in heavily. 'I wish you were not always so forthright, Kitty.'

'In my profession I've had to learn a lot about what goes on in another's head and heart. Listen to me. You don't have to encourage the sun to rise in the morning and Nick is the same about his life. He has to travel about, he won't be tied down, he just can't be. He needs to be free as much as he needs air to breathe. Do you understand what I'm saying, Jenna?'

'You've made it perfectly clear, Kitty. You call me Jenna, my assumed name, but you think of me only as Isabel Hampton, don't you?'

'Up to a few days ago it's what you've been all your life. I'm worried for you, that's all. I can see all too easily the effect that being alone with Nick has had on you, and who can blame you? He's strong and masculine and so very good-looking – and completely unattainable. We all want most what we can't have, Jenna, that's one thing I've learned in my life, but some of the things we want we can never have. If you've got any romantic notions about Nick, my advice is to forget them. Apart from Nick's desire to keep his freedom, you come from different worlds; Nick hates yours and you would soon despise ours if you had to live in it for good. If Nick ever decides to settle down, it will be years away.'

'You're wrong in one of your remarks, Kitty. After what I've been through recently I've come to value different things and enjoy the simpler life of your world. Whatever the outcome of this strange situation, I can never go back to my old way of life, not as it was before.'

'You may have changed, but the facts about Nick remain the same.'

'What about you and Nick? Are you hoping if he does settle down it will be with you?'

'No. I think I was in love with Nick once, but it was a long time ago. He's more like a brother to me now, which is good, as all I've got in the world is Benjamin.'

A lump of jealousy that had lived at the bottom of Isabel's heart did not feel so heavy now. 'A brother? But I thought... when we came here you kissed...'

'Oh, that,' Kitty laughed and said unselfconsciously, 'We were lovers once but not for years now. We always kiss like that, out of habit more than anything, though it's so good to be kissed by Nick. But perhaps you know that.'

Isabel could have cried. 'No, I don't know,' she answered, feeling the truth with a keen regret.

'Well, that's just as well then.'

They sipped their tea and nibbled at thin slices of saffron cake, both glad the conversation was over and that their feelings for Nick were out in the open, although Isabel's not entirely. Kitty was content to have him as a friend and brother. Isabel knew now she was in love with him. She put aside the impossibility of his returning her love and of having a future with him and instead thought about Kitty sitting across the hearth from her.

'Would you like to get married one day, Kitty?'

Kitty smiled. 'I think you mean if a rich man who could provide for Benjamin and me asked, would I accept?' She shrugged her shoulders. 'I've had plenty of offers of marriage. Young men and old, some out of kindness, some wanting to reform me, as they put it. One of my gentlemen would marry me tomorrow, but Benjamin wouldn't be part of the arrangement and I won't have that. I might marry one day but right now I like my freedom, I like coming and going as I please.'

The same as Nick, Isabel thought, but did not voice it.

'Yes, you do have your freedom, Kitty. Looking back over my life, although I was fortunate enough to have wealth and position, loving parents and Uncle Laurence, I seem to have spent nearly all my life doing what was expected of me.'

'I wouldn't give a bean for the life of a lady. Many that I know of do everything at the whim of their fathers, husbands and then their sons, even their brothers. Being used at night when married, without the enjoyment side of it, some are beaten, even worse if their husbands have perverted minds, and then having to go about their social lives as though nothing bad is happening. Your life hasn't been bad at all really and at least you aren't going to marry a man who has been forced on you.'

Isabel tried to conjure up a feeling of being fortunate on that count but failed.

Talland ran up to a window. Kitty got up to open it so she could make a fuss of him and Isabel joined her. The dog was sandy and wet from the sea. He jumped up to his mistress and both women squealed when he shook out his shaggy coat. He begged their forgiveness from large, brown, appealing eyes and received a corner of saffron cake. After wolfing down the cake, he noisily lapped his water bowl dry and bounded off again.

'There goes another free spirit,' Isabel said, smiling after him.

'Aye, like someone else we know, eh, Jenna?'

Isabel thought she had annoyed Kitty again but no further chastisement came. 'Whatever happens in the next few weeks, I hope we will always be friends, Kitty.'

'Well, I second that, and Benjamin is happy that he's made another friend. I have to go out this afternoon. You can have one of your little chats with him.'

'That will be lovely, but sometimes I wish I didn't have to stay cooped up all the time,' Isabel said wistfully, looking out of the window and seeing Talland racing off up the Gannel.

'There's no reason why you shouldn't go out occasionally. Actually, folk will be more curious if you don't show your face from time to time. I'll take you up to the village tomorrow.'

Before she went into Benjamin's room, Isabel spent some time in thought, making plans as to how she would show her gratitude to Kitty and Nick's other friends who had helped her.

Following Kitty's instructions as to how to use the wash tub, dolly and mangle, she had laundered the clothes Charlie Chiverton had lent her herself. It had given her great satisfaction to accomplish a task that not long ago she would have thought fit only to be done by a menial. She had soaked herself from head to foot and made her hands red and chapped, but she had got the clothes hanging on the washing line and then caused Kitty much amusement by rushing outside every few minutes and grabbing at the clothes blown high by the wind to feel if they were dry. Kitty helped her with the more difficult task of ironing and told her how to place them near the heat of the fire to air them out. The clothes were now neatly folded on a chair in her bedroom. Isabel planned to return them to Charlie personally as soon as she knew it was safe to do so, and take some things to brighten up his shack and provide anything needed to make it completely waterproof. She hoped Charlie would see it as the act of a grateful friend and not as charity or condescension from someone who thought herself superior.

Isabel hoped Mundy Cottle would accept a copy of the Bible and after finding out exactly how many children she had, their ages and gender, she would ask Mundy if she could have a set of 'Sunday-best' clothes made for each one.

Showing her appreciation to Kitty was going to be more difficult. She was obviously well paid by her 'gentlemen' and lacked for nothing. Perhaps she could provide something to ease Benjamin's discomfort but she knew she would be stepping on sensitive ground even to suggest it.

She would have to be even more careful about showing her appreciation to Nick. It was all too easy to step on his pride and bring his scorn down on her head. She'd thought about a team of horses so he could resume his work as a packman or waggoner if he wanted to, but decided he would see it as too generous. He might not object to a dog to replace his beloved Gutser.

Benjamin was easy to talk to and a good listener. He had not been told the reasons for Isabel's presence in the house but he had sufficient perception to realize she was more likely to be a lady than a lady's maid. Isabel had admitted this during one of their earlier talks when he had asked her quite openly if it was so. Today she was able to discuss her ideas on how to thank those who had helped her. He had heard of Charlie Chiverton and Mundy Cottle from his conversations with Nick and agreed with her ideas for them and about the dog for Nick. For his sister he told Isabel of something Kitty had often talked about.

'Kitty won't expect to be given a gift but I can see you have your heart set on giving her something. She would love to have some exotic plants for the garden.'

Isabel said she would look into that as soon as she was able, then remarked on something different. 'You never have visitors here, Benjamin.'

'When we first moved here folk used to come down this way just to hurl insults at Kitty or try their luck with her. Then one of her gentlemen saw to it that they stayed away.'

Isabel was shocked at first when she'd realized Benjamin knew about his sister's 'gentlemen' but he explained that he'd guessed the truth himself from the taunts they'd received. He knew some of the ways of the world from long conversations with Nick, who had also taught him to read.

'I heard your voices raised this morning,' Benjamin said. 'I heard Nick's name mentioned. Was it something to do with you being in love with him, Jenna?'

'Benjamin!' she exclaimed but had to smile at his forthrightness.

'I get a lot of time to think lying here. I realized from the start how you felt about him. Kitty doesn't approve, does she?'

'Kitty thinks there is no hope of there being anything between Nick and myself. She thinks I should just forget about him and think about my fiancé, Richard Grenville.'

'Is that what you think too?'

Isabel hung her head. 'I don't think Nick could ever love me.'

'We can never be sure of anything in life,' Benjamin said, sounding like an old sage.

Isabel smiled to herself.

'Oh, don't you think that just because I've spent all my life lying on a bed and have spoken to few people that I don't know anything about human nature. No one is just what they seem to be on the surface.'

'Perhaps not,' Isabel said doubtfully.

'Do you agree with Kitty that you should only think about this Richard Grenville?'

'Well, I have agreed to marry him. One should not make that promise lightly.'

'You shouldn't enter into a life you don't really want either. It will only add to the heartbreak of the world and there's enough of that already, don't you think?'

'Seems to me that all I'm asked to do is to think,' Isabel replied glumly.

'Kitty's never spent much time thinking. She just gets on with the things she wants to do. She wanted a baby once and she had one.'

Isabel was startled. 'Should you be telling me this, Benjamin? Wouldn't Kitty have told me herself if she wanted me to know?'

'I think she would want you to know but she gets too upset talking about him.'

'Him? What happened to the baby?'

'He died, before he was even weaned. His name was Jeremy and he was the handsomest, brightest-eyed little baby you could ever see. He smiled all day and Kitty used to bring him in here with me so I could talk to him. How he would coo and chuckle. I missed him dreadfully when he died.'

'How did he die?'

''Twas a fever. Sudden, it was, on his little lungs. Nick was here when Jeremy died and he cried as much as Kitty and I did. Some folk didn't want Jeremy buried in the churchyard but Nick ran and fetched the parson when we knew how ill the baby was. The parson came and as he'd baptized Jeremy soon after his birth he said he had every right to be buried in hallowed ground.'

'Was Jeremy… do you know if Jeremy was…' Isabel couldn't get out the words she wanted to say.

'Nick's baby?'

'Yes,' she replied, feeling terribly embarrassed. 'I just have to know.'

Benjamin yawned, slowly and carefully, before answering and relieving Isabel of her burning curiosity. 'Jeremy was the child of one of Kitty's gentlemen. He was deliberately conceived and the gentleman was happy to go on providing for us. The other one did not object, or else she wouldn't have had the baby.'

Isabel thought she couldn't blame any woman for wanting Nick's baby, and she was glad that before the bright perceptive boy had a chance to read this in her face, he drifted off to sleep.

–

Across at Gwithian another young man was talking to someone about his sister. James Leddra had walked to the village from St Ives. He had recovered from his ordeal in the sea and had found another ship to sail on and was soon to leave Cornwall again. When he had learned that Mary Ellen and her daughter had moved from St Ives to live at Gwithian, in the house of the gentleman she favoured, he had thought at first not to go and see her, that she wouldn't want him turning up there and causing her embarrassment. But as he was about to go off to the other side of the world, and because he had so narrowly escaped with his life and might easily lose it in another incident on the fickle sea, he felt he ought to see Mary Ellen and his little niece while he had the opportunity, if only for a few minutes.

As he walked through Gwithian, James saw Denny Rowe sitting on the doorstep of the Leg of Mutton inn, an almost empty tankard beside him. Denny moved the tankard so James could pass through, and when James had been served he brought his drink back to the doorway for a chat.

'Not a local man then,' Denny said, squinting up at James's earrings and banging his inverted chest as he drew on his pipe. A string of tight coughs spluttered through the side of his mouth. 'Have to sit out here, 'tes easier on the breathin'.'

'Aye,' James sympathized. 'I'm a St Ives man born but not often there, hardly set foot on land for years till a few weeks ago when my ship went down near Trevaunance Cove with all hands lost.'

''Eard about that. Cryin' shame. Strange thing, isn't it? Bein' the sole survivor in a tragedy. 'Appened to me once, down the Purchase Mine. Went down with me shift, was the only one t'come back up again. Makes 'ee think, like there must be some special reason fur 'ee being spared.'

James nodded, a slight movement of the head, but enough for the two men of different ages and livelihoods to share the moment as though they belonged to some special brotherhood.

'I got kin in this village,' James said.

''Ave 'ee now? Who's that then?'

'They live in Trevennor House.'

'Oh?' Denny's head swung up sharply from his tankard, his rock-hewn face full of hostility.

'Not them Kempthornes,' James said hastily. 'I know how everybody do hate they.' He looked embarrassed. 'My sister, she lives there… with her little maid…'

James waited while Denny chewed over who lived at Trevennor House and what relationships existed there until he arrived at the correct people. James expected more hostility, or moral outrage, but Denny returned to his pipe without batting an eyelid.

'You look like yer sister, I can see it now thee've mentioned it. 'Tes none of my business what folk do. I've seen the little maid, she's as sweet an' dainty as a maid should be.'

'Thank you,' James said. 'I thought to call on them. I'm going away to sea when me new ship's made ready to sail – she's having a bit of work done on her. I don't want to make no trouble for Mary Ellen. What sort of welcome do you think I'd receive there?'

'Well, that Kempthorne woman! She'd rather spit on 'ee then pass 'ee by. He's not so bad, but I wouldn't like to say whether 'e'd 'preciate you turnin' up on the doorstep.'

James's expression told Denny he was torn about what to do. Denny added, 'But they're your kin. I'd go if I was you, yer sister might be glad t'see 'ee. I 'eard there was a bit of trouble concernin' the little maid.' Denny explained about Morenwyn's fall and how she was still unconscious.

James was deeply worried and braced himself for the walk to Trevennor House by buying another tankard of ale. 'Thank 'ee kindly,' Denny said. 'But will 'ee look up an' down the road a minute first?'

James did as he was asked. 'What am I s'posed to be looking for?'

'A woman about my age, as tiny as a buttercup with a little stern face that would frighten the Devil himself.'

'Can't see no one about anywhere.'

'Good on 'ee, boy. I'll 'ave that drink now. 'Tes the missus, you see. I promised 'er I'd only buy one drink. She'd chitter on me somethin' awful if she sees me with this one.'

James handed the ale over and scratched his head. 'P'raps you shouldn't have it then.'

Denny winked and swung his chin to the side. 'Nah! I promised I'd only *buy* one. Good luck with yer sister.'

James made straight for Trevennor House, but the closer he got, the more he dragged his heels. If the Kempthornes were as bad as their reputation then his sudden appearance could spoil things for Mary Ellen and Morenwyn, just when they'd found themselves in comfortable surroundings. If Edmund Kempthorne ever thought to offer Mary Ellen marriage and elevate her status he might think again if he was confronted with her rough and ready relatives. And if Morenwyn died from her fall, it might be just the thing to encourage Kempthorne to throw Mary Ellen out.

Not being able to bring himself to go to the front door, James had his eyes on the path that led to the back of the house and the servants' entrance when he heard a door being slammed and an outburst of crying. A maidservant rushed past him in a flood of tears with two more female servants running after her. The maid ran past James but the other two came to a halt after a few steps. James dived out of their sight behind the high wall and listened to them. It soon became apparent that the maid had fallen foul of one of Deborah Kempthorne's cruel moods. Despite Morenwyn's predicament there was no way James could ask to see Mary Ellen now. He turned about. One more drink with the coughing ex-miner and it was straight back to St Ives for him.

Chapter 17

Charlie Chiverton saw only the occasional person up on the cliffs, although sometimes he saw anything up to one hundred men escorting a long line of mules and mine ponies on the way to a smuggling run, or taking the contraband they'd received away to their hides. It was rare for him to see a gentleman. He was surprised to see one up here on Godrevy Head today. Charlie had come this morning to have a look at the sea to the west, to study the depth of the red stain flowing out to sea, marking the course of the waters from the Red River and giving the superstitious Charlie a sign of how well his alluvial tin workings would do.

Unsuitably dressed against the harsh buffeting winds, the man was standing in an exposed spot under the dawn light and looking across at the isolated Godrevy Island and its adjoining wild treacherous reef of rocks. The Stones stretched for a mile out into the surging sea. The gentleman was as motionless as the sketchy grey-tinged clouds that sat on the horizon in a luminous pink sky.

Charlie's first thought was that the man, who looked as if he had spent a night in heavy drinking, was going to jump the hundreds of feet into the ocean. It was not unknown for the insane, the despairing and the heartbroken to commit suicide along the stretch of wilderness coast where he lived. Those who did were usually young, as was the hatless dark-haired man Charlie was watching now. Charlie's wife had spurned another youth to marry him and he had leapt to his death from the very spot where this gentleman stood. So as not to risk another tragedy, Charlie moved up silently beside him.

'Ye all right, sur?' he asked in a soft voice with his pipe clamped between his worn teeth. He made ready to yank the other man backwards if he tried to jump.

The young gentleman's head spun round and he exclaimed through brandy-laden breath, 'What the hell…'

'Sorry if I did frighten 'ee, sur. I don't expect to see nobody up 'ere this time o' mornin'. Not thinkin' of jumpin', are 'ee?'

'No, no,' the gentleman expressed astonishment. 'I suppose you could say that I'm up here because I'm so very glad to be alive – or rather, that someone else is alive. I needed to be alone to think things through.'

Charlie's canine face was screwed up against the wind. He blinked hard to get a clear picture of the other man's face and recognized him from Laurence Trevennor's funeral. Edmund Kempthorne's features were not so handsome now, blotchy from the salty blast of the sea and lack of sleep and in need of a shave. He was leaning with both hands on his walking cane, his knuckles blue with cold. Charlie felt an instant dislike for him. His instinct told him this man was a master of deception and could never be trusted.

'Oh, why's that then? If 'ee don't mind me askin',' Charlie said.

Edmund looked at Charlie for a moment. He didn't care who the shabby little man who had suddenly appeared beside him was, he needed someone to confide in and this stranger would have to do.

'It's my little daughter. Three days ago she took a bad fall down the stairs, from the very top. It's a very tall stairway, the main one of Trevennor House. She was knocked unconscious. If it had not been for my sister's riding instructor who was in the house at the time she might have died. He knew what to do and rode at once to fetch a doctor. The doctor was able to come straightaway to attend to her. She was unconscious up until last night and we didn't know if she had suffered any brain damage. Thank God, the doctor says she is very fortunate. Given time and sufficient rest, she should make a complete recovery.'

'I'm sorry about yer dattur but glad to 'ear she'll be all right. Just a tacker, is she?'

'She's three years old. People say that Morenwyn is the living image of me,' Edmund said proudly. 'I adore her. I don't know what I would have done if I had lost her.' His face twisted with emotion and he turned his head to stare at the lonely island across the sea.

Charlie saw Edmund in a different light now. He knew he was not married and it was unusual for a gentleman to acknowledge his illegitimate offspring. This one clearly loved his child, too.

Edmund suddenly gave a tremendous shiver and realized he was freezing cold. He pulled his inadequate coat in tight and his teeth began to chatter. 'Brr, I… I'm f-freezing. I… I didn't realize there was so little shelter. Are you by any ch-chance on your way to Gwithian? We could w-walk there together. I would appreciate the company. Perhaps you would tell me your name.'

When given the opportunity, Charlie liked to chat and he was curious about this young man. He pulled off the ragged tartan scarf round his neck and offered it to Edmund who took it and wrapped it gratefully round his own. Charlie puffed on his pipe, he had acquired a knack of keeping it lit in even the foulest of weather. Edmund looked at him enviously, he did not seem at all cold, but then Charlie did look as if he had grown an extra layer of thick skin.

'You learn to keep warm livin' up near the clouds,' Charlie said, as though he'd read Edmund's thoughts. 'I'm on my way nearly to the village. I'll be followin' the Red River up-aways to my tin-streamin' workin's upstream. You get particles of tin in the waste that runs into the river from the copper works, you know. I shall 'ave a good day today cus the sea's a deep red.'

He ignored Edmund's look of puzzlement and went straight on, 'My name's Charlie Chiverton and I reckon thee to be Mr Edmund Kempthorne and your good lady sister to be Miss Deborah Kempthorne. That makes 'er ridin' instructor a friend of mine, Nick Nancarrow. 'E's a good man, is Nick. Got an intelligent 'ead on 'is shoulders.' Charlie would not normally tell anyone, even folk whom he knew, any of his business, but it might prove useful to Nick if he could glean what this gentleman felt about him.

They turned their backs on the double island in the sea, immediately feeling more comfortable with the wind behind them. Edmund was still shaking with cold but managed to control his jaw.

'I shall always be grateful to Nancarrow,' Edmund said, rubbing his arms vigorously to help his circulation. 'I had no idea it was so fearfully cold up on the cliffs,' he added breathlessly.

'Well, you got the force of the Atlantic Ocean blowin' all the way across from America hitting 'ee.'

'If I plan to come up here again I will remember to wear warmer clothes and a lot more of them.' Edmund wrapped his arms round his body and beat his hands on his upper arms.

''Tes 'an'some up 'ere in the spring and summer. Try again in a few days if there's a hot sun and no wind.' Charlie plodded along sure-footedly a little way in front.

'I may even bring Morenwyn up here on the first warm day after she has recovered.'

'Went 'urt 'er none. Fresh sea air'll 'elp 'er to thrive.'

Charlie helped Edmund along by pointing out the safest passage for his soft-booted feet to take, avoiding pits and rabbit holes, kicking aside small rocks that he might trip over.

'Do you live in this area, Chiverton?'

'Ais, got my own little shack on Reskajeage Downs back-along the cliffs aways. Lived there fur years, 'twas where I took my missus back to the day we was married. She were a fine 'an'some woman. I loved 'er dearly but she died many a year ago now. Never 'ad no children, mind. She would 'ave loved littl'uns, would 'ave made a good mother. She were a ruddy good wife. Worked as a bal-maiden when I went down the mines and alongside of me when I took to tin-streamin'.'

Edmund looked at Charlie and there was a quiver in his voice as he said, 'You really do appreciate the ones you love when you lose them, or think you are going to lose them. I hate death, the very thought of being buried under the ground. I can never bring myself to look at a dead body.' He shuddered then stumbled over a low ridge of rock weathered into a honeycomb appearance that was just sticking out of the ground. Charlie helped him up and waited for him to brush himself down. Their passage was very slow and it was a long walk back home for a soft-living gentleman in thin clothes.

'I'm not familiar with this area, Chiverton. Whereabouts is Reskajeage Downs?'

'Aw, 'bout a mile or two, mebbe more on from Godrevy Point where we wus standin' jus' now.' Charlie didn't want Edmund Kempthorne to know exactly where he lived. 'I usually walk 'cross the cliffs rather than the roads. There's some hellish drops along the way, you 'as to know where to put yer feet.'

'My cousin Miss Isabel Hampton was killed along there in a coaching accident, at a place the locals call Deadman's Cove. Did you by any chance see anything?'

'I came across it 'ours after it 'appened. The bodies 'ad been taken away by then and looters 'ad picked the wreckage clean, nothin' left but a few sticks fur kindlin'. Some pretty pieces of wood. I'd like to 'ave seen the coach in one piece, 'tes a rare and wonderful thing t'see on the roads.'

'Apparently my cousin wandered away from the wreckage and fell over the cliff, but as far as we can tell no one actually saw her fall.'

'On this part of the coast the roads are never far from the sea. She could 'ave fell, but then she could 'ave bin pushed over by the looters, poor soul. I've known a few to go over in my time – men, women, children, horses, dogs, cattle. Some of 'em must 'ave bin pushed.' Charlie wanted to get off the subject of people falling over the cliff and spoke of something different. 'What with so many ships going down along this coast, I've had some good pickin's over the years.'

'You sound as though you've had an interesting life, Chiverton. You say you know Nick Nancarrow?'

'Aye, known un since 'e was a young 'un. 'E was born 'n' bred in Gwithian.'

Edmund had good reason to be curious about Nick. He saw him as a fortune-hunter; what other reason could there be for the handsome drifter to declare his love for his plain-faced, bad-tempered sister? Edmund had no intention of allowing anyone to drain his newfound fortune away from him, even though he was grateful Deborah spent so much time preening herself in front of her bedroom mirrors and having fittings for new clothes that she took less interest in his affairs these days. She certainly meant to snare Nick Nancarrow for the marriage altar. She was having arrangements made to have her first marriage, which had never been consummated, annulled. What Deborah didn't know was that Edmund had told her lawyers not to go ahead with the proceedings. When Nancarrow saw he was getting nowhere he would soon wander off out of their lives.

'Nancarrow was a close acquaintance of my late uncle's, did you know that?'

'Aye, Mr Trevennor was a fine gentleman and well respected in the village. He weren't too proud to pass the time of day with me and he treated my wife like a lady. It was natural for him and Nick to become friends.'

'I understand Nancarrow is a drifter, but he seems straightforward, honest and hard-working.'

'He is that.'

Edmund stopped. With his dark eyes screwed up against the wind and flying grit, he stared into Charlie's bloodhound eyes. Charlie met his gaze squarely and clenched his fists which were stuffed inside his pockets, immediately on his guard.

'Tell me, Chiverton, if you were me, would you be concerned if Nancarrow was paying court to your sister? He is, after all, much younger and of a different class, but she is quite taken with him.'

Charlie's overgrown eyebrows flew up and he burst into a fit of coughing to cover his amusement. He had seen Nick the day before and had taken a letter from him to be passed on to Crantock. Nick had said the Kempthornes were an evil lot and he had to stick around to keep an eye on them. He hadn't mentioned what his tactics were concerning Miss Deborah Kempthorne, but then no man would want to admit that, even if he did have an ulterior motive. Charlie knew why Nick was acting in this uncharacteristic way and didn't envy him having to make up to that ungainly spiteful woman. Charlie thought that by now Nick must be wishing he had tried to get the information he needed about Isabel Hampton's safety from the brother instead. Strange though, the way Nick had spoken about Isabel Hampton. Almost as if he had grown fond of her...

Bringing his coughing under control, Charlie cleared his throat, turned away to spit on the ground and wiped moisture from his eyes. A lonely gull appeared in front of them, flying in a haphazard line as it was battered by the wind at their back. It finally won the contest and veered off towards Godrevy Island.

'Life's sometimes a bit like that gull just now,' Charlie said. 'A man chooses to fly against a fearsome wind – in Nick's case, declarin' 'imself to a lady of quality who'd be expected to spurn 'im an' send 'im rightfully packin' – but sometimes the force of the wind, and even the tide can be overcome and won. I daresay the lady could do a lot worse than Nick, if that's the way the land's lyin'.' Charlie hoped that would do to help Nick's cause along.

'Really?' Edmund said, surprised at the poetic note in Charlie's speech. He made a mental note to remember that some of these dirty unkempt persons were not as unintelligent as they looked.

'My fear is that Nancarrow is a fortune-hunter and seeks only to relieve my sister of her half of our recent inheritance.' And I have plans for her half as well as mine, Edmund thought easily.

'Naw, not Nick. He went be int'rested in fancy livin'. He's prob'bly jus' took a likin' to Miss Kempthorne. Better Nick courtin' 'er than someone who's really after 'er money.'

'I do hope you are right, Chiverton. My sister seems to have her heart set on Nancarrow and all I want is to see her content.' But Edmund was still unconvinced that he did not have a rival for the family fortune.

He was thoughtful as they took the last few steps off the cliff path and stepped onto the fine sand of Gwithian beach. The wind was not so buffeting as they moved closer to the village but Edmund was even slower walking over the shifting sand. He tut-tutted at the discoloration of his boots caused by the walk across it two hours earlier and thought how desperate he must have been over Morenwyn's fall and grateful at her recovery to have made his way along unknown paths not knowing where he was going.

'I wonder that I did not get lost,' he murmured to himself.

Charlie heard and understood. 'Aye, 'tes easily done.' He dug in his pocket and pulled out a tiny carving of a dog, perfectly whittled from a chip of wood. ''Ere, sur, p'raps you'd like to take this to yer little maid. I made it out of a bit of mahogany driftwood I found on this beach. It might cheer 'er up a little.'

Edmund was visibly moved and Charlie felt that Laurence Trevennor need not have feared for Isabel Hampton's life from this man. He was the sort who might make threats when backed into a corner but he wouldn't have the courage to carry them out.

'This is very kind of you, Chiverton. I'm sure Morenwyn will treasure it, it is just the kind of thing she likes to play with.' Edmund searched in his pockets to give Charlie something in return and took out a tobacco pouch with silken drawstrings. 'Please accept this for your pipe, it contains the finest tobacco. I have much enjoyed our talk, it seems a pity to leave it here. I am ravenously hungry – can I invite you to join me for breakfast?'

Charlie sucked in fresh cold air through his hewn teeth and looked amazed. He had never been invited into a gentry house before, not even by Laurence Trevennor. Half of him wanted to go but an unwise comment might put Nick's plan in danger, and perhaps the young gentleman was hoping to catch him off his guard and have him reveal more about Nick.

'I do thank 'ee fur the tobacco, Mr Kempthorne, sur, but I went 'ave no breakfast if 'ee don't mind, though 'tes kind of 'ee t'ask. 'Fraid I 'ave to get on to my workin's. Got a young boy there to 'elp me out and I do like to keep an eye on un.'

'As you please. I hope you have a good day's work.' Edmund gave him back his scarf and Charlie went on his way, carefully putting the tobacco pouch into a hidden pocket inside his ragged coat. He would smoke his gift at his leisure when he got home. He was bursting to see Nick again and find out what he had discovered and how much he was suffering at the hands of yet another lady of the class he so despised.

Edmund tramped up and down the dimes, walking along the foot of them when he could. Although it meant having more sand blown into his face, it was the quickest route back to Trevennor House. If he kept his eyes on the church tower, he would not stray and become lost. Once at home, he would change out of his bedraggled clothes, return himself to his usual smart veneer and check on Morenwyn. Then after he had eaten a hearty breakfast he would see what he could do about his other hearty appetite. Mary Ellen had been in a state of shock since their child had fallen and would be of no use to him for a few more days.

He reached the road and was not far from home. Looking down the village, he thought of Nellie living somewhere along the way, all alone in her hovel. He smiled. He would walk down that way later in the day.

Chapter 18

If Charlie had accepted Edmund Kempthorne's invitation to breakfast with him he would have met Nick leaving Trevennor House after enquiring about Morenwyn. Nick was pleased that the little girl was expected to make a complete recovery and decided that he would soon make his way over to Crantock. He was mightily relieved to get away from the stuffy confining atmosphere the house now bore and Deborah Kempthorne's clinging attention. As far as he was concerned, the Kempthornes had ruined Trevennor House and he was angry about it. He hated them touching and rearranging Laurence's things, things that now belonged to Isabel. He headed for the village's one alehouse to refresh his throat before returning to Tehidy.

He saw Jimmy up ahead of him walking fast and shouted to him. Jimmy turned round, saw who'd hailed him and carried on walking.

'You in a hurry, Jimmy?' Nick said, catching up with him.

'Aye,' was the only reply, and grudgingly given.

'Is it Marion's time?'

Jimmy stopped abruptly. 'Aye, but 'tis no concern of yours.'

'I know why I'm getting this frosty front,' Nick said, blocking Jimmy's way.

'You're a traitor, Nick Nancarrow,' Jimmy hissed. 'A traitor to the village and worse still, a traitor to Mr Trevennor who made no secret of the regard he had for you and how he felt about they Kempthorne parasites. But now here's you, a man who pretended to be Mr Trevennor's friend for years, making up to they rotten folk and Mr Trevennor barely put down in the ground. What's the matter with 'ee, didn't you get a mention in the will after all your returning visits?'

Nick grabbed Jimmy's coat collars and yanked him close. 'Is that what folk in the village are saying about me?' He was venomous and shook Jimmy until he got an answer.

'Aye, 'tis, and you can damned well leave go of me.'

'You've known me all your life, Jimmy Rowe. We played together as boys in the grounds of Trevennor House. You know how much I respected Laurence Trevennor, how much I cared for him. I thought we were friends, but friends trust each other and if they see a friend behaving in a peculiar way they should know he has a good reason for it.'

Nick thrust Jimmy away and strode off, his feelings hurt and bruised. He had not expected all the villagers to give him the benefit of the doubt while he played up to the Kempthornes; he understood their resentment and could cope with their hostility. But he'd thought those who knew him well would have thought better of him.

Jimmy ran after him. 'I'm sorry, Nick. You just said what Mother's been saying about you, that we should trust you, that what you're doing is your way somehow of helping the village. The Kempthornes are threatening to sell the sheep and most of Mr Trevennor's land and most of we will be out of a job, many out of their homes. We can always try the mines for work but we prefer to work out in the good clean air, not ending up like Father has with his chest. Everything's looking black today – I'm sorry I took it out on you.' Shamefaced, Jimmy nervously held out his hand and after a moment's hesitation Nick accepted it.

''Tisn't an easy job I'm doing, Jimmy, and I can't tell you no more than that.'

'Aye, fair enough,' Jimmy sighed. 'I'll make sure the word gets around the village, careful like.'

'You best get on to Marion. Is she having a bad time? A man doesn't usually leave his work…'

'Aye, Mother sent for me. I'm that worried…' Jimmy's eyes filled with tears.

Nick sighed heavily. He rested a hand on his friend's arm. 'I don't s'pose I can do anything but get in the way. I'll call in on you later.'

'Aye, thanks. The women are with her, along with Mistress Thomas. I just hope and pray…'

Nick walked Jimmy to his garden gate then made his way back to his original destination. He was in none too good a mood and was enraged when barred from going under the thatched roof of the Leg of Mutton by the last man on earth he wanted to see.

Gyver Pengelly was leaning heavily against the doorjamb with a huge arm stretching across to the other side. He sniggered and slavered. He did not speak, just loafed there with a stupid look on his hideous face, as though he was savouring a secret he badly wanted to divulge. Nick was in no mood to be thwarted in his plans. He would not be denied access to the inn like two other men who were standing warily at a distance with their hands crammed in their pockets waiting for Pengelly to move out of the way.

'Get out of my way,' Nick ordered coldly.

Pengelly hee-hawed and fingered his persistently dirty beard. 'Huh! Thought you'd 'ave bin too damned proud t'drink with the likes of we! I 'eard thee've gone up in the world, prefer to sup with the gentry now. Didn't take 'ee long to wheedle yer way into the big 'ouse now ole Trevennor's dead!'

Nick was determined not to hear any more but Pengelly puffed up his barrel chest and overhanging paunch and shouted louder, 'Got a fancy fur that Kem'thorne lump of a female, 'ave 'ee, eh? She's not a pretty little thing like that wench you 'ad with 'ee recently. What 'ave thee done with 'er then? Got 'er laid up somewheres waitin' fur yer next visit? Wonder what she would say if she knew you're beddin' that bitch down the road.' Pengelly howled with laughter. 'P'raps someone oughta tell 'er. Tell 'ee what, Nancarrow, if I see 'er I'll do it fur 'ee!'

The two other men backed away. They had no wish to be caught up in a brawl if Gyver Pengelly was one of its participants. Pengelly was known to pick a fight most days of the week and Nick Nancarrow had a fearful temper when roused, he had never walked away from a fight in his life.

Nick was seething with anger but today he turned round and walked away. He did not relish the insults that would be thrown at his back but he did not want Pengelly to keep spouting about Isabel with the jealous Deborah Kempthorne living in such close proximity.

'Told 'ee 'e was too proud to drink with we!' Pengelly snorted at the two men who were astounded at Nick's retreat. 'Gone all soft 'n' dandified now 'is 'ands 'ave bin roamin' over a lady. I reckon Nancarrow's gone as soft as the body of the whore 'e sees at Crantock!'

Nick whirled back round, his blood boiling with rage and fear cutting at his breath that Pengelly might have seen Isabel with Kitty.

Pengelly jeered at him. 'I might make me way over there one day, Nancarrow, if I can find enough pennies t'make up 'er fancy price.'

So he hadn't been to Crantock but Nick couldn't stand his vile talk. 'Shut your filthy mouth!'

'You gonna do it, Nancarrow? Do 'ee want t'fight me?'

'I'd like to beat you straight into Hell!' Nick hissed with passion.

'If it's Hell you're talking about,' came a calm voice from a new spectator, 'may I suggest a fair fight to determine the outcome of who is going there.' It was the Reverend Perran Thomas. 'A wrestling match, perhaps. I used to like to wrestle myself but since I've been married I've had problems with my back.'

Pengelly inserted a crude innuendo but the young curate either didn't hear it or allowed it to ride over him. There was a gleam in his eyes. 'I do enjoy a good wrestling match, so may

I put it to you both that you take part in a contest that can be overseen for its fairness?'

''Tes a good notion of yourn, Rev'run, sur,' Pengelly slurred, remembering gleefully how he got away with cheating the last time he wrestled with Nick.

'Fine by me,' Nick murmured through clenched teeth.

The landlord and his few other early customers could be seen lurking behind Pengelly.

'Round the back of your establishment, landlord?' asked the Reverend Thomas eagerly. 'So as not to offend any ladies who may pass by this way.'

''Tes all right with me, sir,' came the landlord's answer.

Word quickly spread, as it always does when excitement is afoot, and soon a small crowd had gathered in the flagstoned yard at the rear of the alehouse. The landlord ordered his young son to sweep the yard thoroughly and remove all stones and small debris that might hurt the wrestlers in a fall. Then he and some of the men put down a padding of sawdust from the barrel he kept filled to sprinkle on his taproom floor. When that was done to the curate's satisfaction, they laid out a circle with ropes. A low but excited hubbub of voices issued from those outside the ropes as Nick and Pengelly stepped inside them.

The two wrestlers did not have their wrestling jackets with them but the landlord was a big man and was able to provide a wrestling sash from his own collection for each contestant. These were worn over one shoulder and across the body to provide grips for the wrestling holds.

Jackets, kerchiefs, shirts, boots and Pengelly's long filthy waistcoat were taken off. Well-developed muscles were flexed while discreet wagers were passed behind the curate's back.

The crowd of fidgety men, women and children continued to grow outside the ring. The landlord's wife and a serving maid openly compared Pengelly's grimy, hairy, repugnant body with Nick's handsome physique. They admired the excellent symmetry of his body, his sinewy muscles as they rippled beneath smooth and bronzed skin, his strong and supple limbs.

The Reverend Thomas chose two men from the crowd whom he knew to be honest and true to make up the three sticklers required to umpire the match. He held his silver-plated timepiece in his hand as he addressed the contestants.

'You know the rules,' he said, in a voice quite different from the one he used for sermons. 'A "back" is scored when a man has been picked up by his sash and dropped flat on his back so that at least three of his four pins, that is the shoulders and hips, hit the ground simultaneously.'

'Eh?' Pengelly said vacantly, shaking his head as if it was full of troublesome fleas.

'At the same time,' Nick informed him sarcastically.

The women tittered, provoking some of the men to mutter at them to shut up or clear off.

The Reverend Thomas went on, 'The first man to "back" his opponent wins the match. However, if a back is not made, a point will be awarded for every pin down at the end of two ten-minute rounds. If the score is level then a further round of five minutes will be wrestled to find the winner. No grappling on the ground. All throws must be made from a standing position. Marks will be given against a wrestler who breaks any rule, resulting in a point being deducted from his score.'

He paused and Nick put out his hand for the traditional handshake before the first of the hitches but the curate started up again.

'I entreat you both to wrestle fairly in the spirit of the great Cornish wrestlers who have gone before you. Those who followed our king, Henry the Fifth, to Agincourt, those who won a great sporting carnival at Calais, France, at the invitation of King Henry the Eighth, Lyttleton Weyworth who wrestled before King Charles the First. Noblemen and clergymen have made wrest—'

'Damn yer bloody blubbing!' Pengelly snarled as he pounded the ground. 'Get on with it!'

Nick was just as impatient to begin and shot the curate a black look.

'Yes, well then, shake hands and begin!'

Nick held out his hand again. He knew he would not get a sporting handshake from Pengelly and was prepared for the brief contact of their flesh, nor was he surprised the other man started immediately with a foul move when his right hand gripped Nick's sash at the shoulder and took fingers of flesh with it. Pengelly laughed in his face, he knew Nick would not complain. With his face screwed up against the pain, Nick got a firm grip on Pengelly's sash at the back.

'Scat un back, Nick!' encouraged the landlord.

It was what Nick had in mind. Putting his weight on one foot, he stretched out the other and hooked it behind Pengelly's leg to sweep him off balance and onto his back. Pengelly was as strong as an ox, he stood firm, tightened his grip on Nick's shoulder and spat in his face.

'A mark against you, Pengelly!' Perran Thomas shouted and scribbled on the inside leaf at the back of his prayerbook. 'Break and begin the next hitch.'

Pengelly pushed Nick forcefully away before he could lower his leg and bring it back on the ground and he only just managed to keep his balance.

'Too much beddin' of women is your trouble, Nancarrow. Can't 'ee stand up straight?'

Nick wiped the spit from his face, breathed in deeply and advanced with his hand out for the traditional shake before each new hitch. Pengelly shrugged it off.

All wrestlers had a favourite hitch and Nick liked to crouch and dodge about to get his own and prevent his opponent from getting his. The spectators were silent as they watched, heads bobbing and ducking to catch every move the wrestlers made. They held their breaths as Pengelly muttered to himself. He could not get a hitch and Nick was taking his time to move on him. Five minutes passed slowly. Then Nick cut through the air so rapidly and perfectly he hitched the ox's sash, turned his back on him, applied his right heel to Pengelly's right ankle, then bending forward to make a hip throw, he swung his right leg outside Pengelly's and sweeping back on his heel drove Pengelly's legs clear off the ground and dropped him on his back. It happened before Pengelly could blink. Nick did not get three pins down on the sawdust but he stood back satisfied with the two points he had scored.

'Shame, shame, nearly 'ad un then, Nick,' someone said.

'Shut yer mouth, bastard!' Pengelly snarled.

'Now, now, no bad language,' remonstrated the Reverend Thomas, wagging a trim finger.

Pengelly said something so foul the parson turned beetroot red and hoped none of the women and children present knew what it meant.

The round was over and Pengelly stood slumped and sulky-faced. He glared at the faces around him, resenting their comments on Nick's fine style and throw.

Pengelly could wrestle well and his Cornish pride rose to the fore. His fair play in the second round surprised Nick but he did not lose his concentration. The points and advantages were divided equally between them in the next ten minutes. At the end, the Reverend Thomas conferred with the other two sticklers and after an anxious minute he announced the match a draw. Murmurs went round from Nick's supporters and Pengelly beat his chest like a madman, making the serving maid go white with fear. The Reverend Thomas called for the deciding five-minute round.

'I'll get 'ee now, you rotten young sod!' Pengelly boomed.

'You won't win this time, not even by cheating, you scum,' Nick retorted, his hands spread out, wishing he could put them round his enemy's neck.

'No talking,' a stickler warned.

Soon after the handshake, the two men got a grip on each other's sash. Pengelly leaned in and rammed his corkscrew thatch under Nick's chin, making him choke. The Reverend Thomas slapped Pengelly's thick arm when he refused to break the foul move and he gave way grudgingly. On the next hitch, Nick went straight for a 'flying mare', gripping Pengelly's sash at arm's length, one hand above the other, then pivoting on one foot to face the same way. Pulling hard with both hands, he moved forward several paces, picking up speed until he gained good momentum. He stopped abruptly, arched his back, pulled on Pengelly's weight to hit his buttocks and carried the brute up over his bowed head and shoulders and dropped him on his back.

Pengelly smacked the ground amid a hail of cheers but managed to hold his brawny shoulders off the ground. He blasphemed and kicked out, hitting Nick's knees and bringing him down. Grabbing his shoulders, Pengelly smashed one of his knees into Nick's face. Nick's bottom lip split open and blood spurted from his nose. He yelled in pain and anger and two men from the crowd leapt forward to prevent the match degenerating into a vicious brawl.

'One more action like that, Pengelly, and you will be disqualified!' Perran Thomas said angrily.

Pengelly howled back curses.

There was no handshake before the next hitch. The adversaries made contact, hanging on and staring into each other's eyes. Pengelly got the advantage of an arm lock, immobilizing Nick's left arm in his sweaty right armpit while Nick's hand gripped his flabby shoulder. Pengelly puffed his vile breath into his face.

'I swear I'll find that maid of yourn an' 'ave 'er yet, Nancarrow,' he leered.

Nick howled in rage, then drew on his years of wrestling experience to counter Pengelly's vice-lock arm by stepping quickly across his front with his left leg and thrusting his hip against his bulging middle. Forcing his trapped arm forward through the lock, Nick hooked his right shoulder in the crook of Pengelly's elbow, pivoted round and lifted his hulk over his hip and put him on his back again. This time all four pins were cleanly on the ground and the spectators' cheers echoed up and down the village.

Panting heavily, Nick tried to wipe the blood and sweat from his face. It was difficult with so many hands thudding congratulations on his back. The landlord's wife pushed folk aside and handed Nick the dish towel she had draped over her shoulder. He took it with a nod of thanks and buried his face in it. Money on the wagers began to pass hands and those without any exchanged verbal promises.

'Congratulations, Nick,' Perran Thomas said brightly. 'You contested and won a fair and talented match – on your side, that is.'

Nick emerged from the dish towel with an enormous smile on his face. He had been afraid of what the villagers, his lifelong friends, were thinking of him 'courting' Deborah Kempthorne. Judging by their reaction today, and after what Jimmy had not long ago told him, he was sure that Meena Rowe had been busy with rumours of him 'being up to something'. Nobody argued with that tiny old woman for long. Nick stayed still while the landlord's beaming wife retied his ruffled hair.

'You've given us gathered here a good deal of pleasure.' Perran Thomas stuck out his hand and pumped Nick's. He put out a leathered, buckled foot and pointed at Pengelly's defeated form. 'It is a great pity this man is not a sporting fellow but then I do not consider him a true Cornishman no matter where he was born.'

Shouts of 'aye' went up and the landlord offered Nick a large tankard of ale. He downed it in seconds to more cheers and backslapping then received some ardent kisses from most of the women there.

Some money was pressed into the palm of his hand.

'Just a little collection fur 'ee, boy, to show our appreciation,' the landlord said with a cheery grin.

'Thanks, all of you,' Nick said, feeling humbled, 'But 'twas a pleasure for me.'

'Not much of a prize but you deserve something.'

Nick made his way towards the rest of his clothes. He wanted to get away before Deborah Kempthorne got word of what had been going on and demanded to know how and why it had happened and fussed over him with her deadly scent and cloying arms. He couldn't bear such a spectacle to take place in front of the villagers.

A scream and a yelled warning made him whirl round and he saw Gyver Pengelly hurtling towards him like a raging bull.

Nick flattened the beast with one crushing blow of his fist. As he shook his skinned knuckles, Pengelly sank into oblivion.

He came round several minutes later. He rubbed at his swollen chin and shook his head to clear his vision. He raged when he saw he had been dragged out of the alehouse yard, down past Trevennor House, the parsonage and the church and dumped on the dusty road where it ran out through the village. He had aches and pains all over his body; some of the villagers had taken the opportunity to get even with him for past hurts.

He vowed his revenge on Nick and Gwithian as a whole.

Pengelly hauled himself up and shambled on down the road, heading for Nellie's shack. She could clean him up a bit. Suddenly he couldn't stand the thought of her staring at him from her huge blank eyes. It was the only thing about her that he couldn't get fully under his control. He usually slapped her about a bit when she stared at him, and she would surely stare at him today with these cuts and bruises. He made himself fume at the vision of her inside his head, until he wanted to see those colourless eyes blank for good. It put him in just the right mood to earn the vast sum of money offered to him by that Jezebel, Deborah Kempthorne.

Nick went straight to the Rowes' cottage, afraid of what news he would hear there. There was an eerie silence as he went through the gate, along the pathway and lifted the back door latch. He sucked in his breath and braced himself.

Jimmy and Denny were standing at the foot of the stairs. Jimmy was holding his small son in a tight grip, his baby daughter was lying on her back in her crib by the hearth, making no sound as she watched her hands moving about above her eyes. Nick was about to speak but Denny put a finger to his lips for silence.

A stern female voice was heard from the bedroom overhead. It was Meena's. 'Now like we told 'ee before, Marion, one more mighty effort and 'twill be all over. Now, push! We can't do the job for 'ee!'

There was a cry of real anguish from Marion. Denny wrung his hands and checked a fit of coughing. Jimmy pressed his lips to his son's head to stop himself from crying. Nick clenched the table top.

Marion filled the cottage with the sounds of someone bearing all the pain and effort of the world on herself. The two little ones started to cry, bawling mournfully for their mother and the danger she was in.

Jimmy could stand it no longer. He thrust his son at his father and ran up the stairs. Nick went to the baby girl and picked her up gently and cradled her in his big arms.

The children stopped crying. Jimmy stayed his foot on the top step. There was a new cry. Weak at first, then louder and lustier than its brother's and sister's had been. There was another cry from Marion, the triumphant cry of a mother. Then an outbreak of female chatter as those on their feet upstairs got on with the things that needed to be done.

Jimmy came back slowly down the stairs to his father's side. Nick joined them. The three men and two children waited in eager anticipation for the news. They shifted their feet. They glanced at each other, afraid to speak.

At the top of the stairs Meena's tiny head peeped round the wall. She grunted at what she saw. 'What are you lot standin' about like that down there for? Haven't any of 'ee got somethin' to be gettin' on with?'

'Mother…?' Jimmy got out in a throaty plea.

Meena's face broke into a huge smile which screwed her face up like a field vole's. 'Bring us up a kettle of water, then put un back on fur a huge pot of tay. We'm got a brand new baby boy up here and a mother with a mighty thirst.'

Jimmy gave a whoop so loud it startled his two older children into crying again. He kissed their heads, he kissed his father, he even kissed Nick, then he danced around the kitchen.

Denny wiped a tear from his eye, grinned at Nick then passed him his other bawling grandson to pacify while he took the kettle upstairs.

Nick was at a total loss what to do to stop the children crying. Jimmy had turned to jelly and was sitting down, rocking backwards and forwards, crying and laughing at the same time. Nick looked at each screwed up little face fighting to be heard the loudest in each of his arms. Denny stayed upstairs talking to Meena and Nick got no sense out of Jimmy when he spoke to him so he took the children outside.

The new environment caught the little ones' interest and after a few fits and stops they both settled back happily into Nick's arms. He wondered what Deborah Kempthorne would say if she could see him now; even more, he wondered what Isabel would think of him. He didn't feel as awkward as he might have done; he'd seen Morenwyn Leddra quite frequently before her fall and she was always asking him to pick her up.

Charlotte Thomas emerged from the cottage. 'Let me give you a hand, Nick. I'll take little Mary.'

Nick gratefully handed over the baby girl. 'Thanks,' he said. 'I didn't realize babies could get so heavy. Everything all right up there?'

'Yes, it's all over at last, and with a successful outcome, thank God,' Charlotte replied, smiling down at the baby held so naturally in her arms.

'I overheard Meena telling Denny she had quite a bit of trouble, he was a big 'un,' Nick said seriously, shaking his head at this mystery of childbirth.

Charlotte smiled at Meena's terminology and Nick's bafflement. 'All's well that ends well.'

Nick was busy trying to adjust Boy Jimmy's wayward outer clothing and she looked up under his bent head. 'What has happened to you, Nick? Your face is as battered as the new baby's.'

Nick grinned wryly. 'You should see Gyver Pengelly's.'

'So that's it, is it?' Charlotte said disapprovingly but resignedly. Fighting seemed to be the way of some men. 'Was anybody else involved?'

Nick looked away cagily. 'There were a few onlookers about.'

'Perran? Was my husband there?'

Boy Jimmy coughed and Nick made a great display of patting his back.

'So Perran was there.' Charlotte looked at the baby girl. 'I don't know. What can we do with them?'

'What's the new baby going to be called?' Nick asked to cover his embarrassment.

'Joshua!' came the reply, and a heavy hand thudded on his shoulder. Jimmy was jubilant, dancing all round the yard and up and down the garden path. 'It means God is my strength. I had a quick look at him, he looks just like me.'

'Aye, and I suppose that's all that matters to you,' said Meena tartly, but smiling all over her tiny face as she took the little boy from Nick. 'Git yer ale down 'ee an back off to work while thee still has a job to go to.'

Nick's arms felt light and empty with the children gone. He had never understood a man's delight at becoming a father before, at receiving a huge responsibility, a millstone round his neck. But perhaps that was not the way to look at the birth of a child. He downed three bottles of ale with Jimmy, one after the other, and before he left for Tehidy he proudly agreed to be one of Joshua Rowe's godfathers.

Chapter 19

Charlotte Thomas followed Pengelly's route to Nellie's home some sixty minutes later. She was feeling pleased with some arrangements she had made for Nellie and was on her way to tell her. Before her marriage, Charlotte had lived in a little village on the outskirts of Camborne. She had farming friends there, a large secluded concern, and they had agreed to give Nellie a secure Christian home in return for light labour about the farm and her gift at calming animals. Charlotte could now get Nellie away from the malignant Gyver Pengelly and the amorous threats from Edmund Kempthorne. Her friends would keep an eye on Nellie and make sure she was never abused again.

Perran, too was pleased with the arrangement and had business later this afternoon in the Camborne area. Charlotte would get Nellie packed up, take her back to the parsonage and put her into new clean clothes, and then Perran would take her to the farm. The sooner the better, to get her away from those who only wanted to take cruel advantage of her. And if Charlotte had to, she was prepared to lie to Nellie and say it was Gyver Pengelly's wish that she go.

When she reached the little bridge that spanned the Red River, Charlotte stopped to pick a few early pale primroses from the wayside; they were Nellie's favourite flowers. The simple gift was to help put Nellie at her ease, along with the sweetmeats in Charlotte's purse. Nellie would be nervous and probably frightened of leaving her home, the rough shack where she'd been born and bred.

The sun was hot and the air still. Charlotte pulled a silk bow off her dress to tie round the flowers. Nellie would think it was her birthday, the first day of June, which the villagers marked with affection by bestowing little gifts on her. They had always been generous to Nellie. She had not starved since her grandmother's sudden mysterious death and Charlotte knew that if only Gyver Pengelly and the like would leave her alone, she could have lived quite happily in Gwithian in her own way.

Charlotte walked for some minutes then turned off the road and made her way along a narrow path, trodden down in many curious twists and turns through rough grass. Nellie lived out of sight from the road but it wasn't long before Charlotte saw the shack up ahead, a small square building with a low roof which was kept in a reasonable state of repair by local men. Weeds, brambles, ivy and long grass grew all around it and purple-headed periwinkles. There were usually some animals in the vicinity and Charlotte was surprised not to see any of Nellie's stray cats lolling about in the sun. It was a quiet, peaceful scene, yet something did not feel quite right.

A shriek from inside the shack made Charlotte stop abruptly and drop the bunch of wild flowers.

'No, no, Mister Pengelly, I don't want it!' Nellie screamed in fear.

Charlotte flew towards the door.

–

Nellie begged Gyver Pengelly, who was holding her cruelly by the scruff of her neck, to let her go. 'It tastes 'orrible, Mister Pengelly, I can't eat it.' Pengelly slapped her face, not for the first time since he'd got there, and shook her by the fistful of dress he had clutched at her neck. 'Eat it, you bitch! 'Tes the first time I've cooked a meal fur a woman in me life an' you aren't grateful to me! Eat it!'

He forced her jaw open and scooping up fingerfuls of a stew-like mush from a wooden platter tried to get her to swallow some. Nellie threw back her head and yelled in fright and pain.

'Why won't you eat?'

'Me gran told me never to eat nothin' bitter,' Nellie wailed, struggling. 'I promised 'er. She ate somethin' bitter an' 'orrible afore she died an' made me promise afore she went never to do the same. She wus good to me an' you 'ave t'keep a promise to the dyin' or they'll come back an' git yer an' take yer to 'ell.'

''Tes not bitter, it's good fur you. Now eat it or I'll break yer blasted neck!'

Pengelly bent Nellie back across his knee and pushing cruel fingers down her throat he made to pour the food into her mouth.

-

Edmund Kempthorne sauntered down the road not long after Charlotte had, whistling gaily and swinging his cane. He had spent twenty minutes talking quietly to Morenwyn before eating a satisfying breakfast. Then suddenly overcome with weariness after his three nights of worry, he had slept all morning, unaware that his sister's intended had been engaged in a bitter wrestling match elsewhere in the village. Deborah didn't know about that either yet. She'd been taken with a sudden blinding headache during the night and was still lying abed. After Edmund had risen, he had enjoyed a quiet luncheon by himself. He had then considered propositioning Dorcas as she'd nervously cleared away the dishes, but if he made a play for the servants in the house Mary Ellen would make him suffer by withholding her favours. His thoughts turned to Nellie. It was a lovely day for an afternoon stroll...

When he came to the bridge he saw that some of the primrose clumps on the road's verge had been disturbed and prodded them with his cane. The likely thief was Nellie, he decided. So she had passed this way recently, hopefully in a homewards direction. He sauntered on. He had heard Nellie was partial to sweetmeats and had a box of them in his pocket. He also had a few shillings made up of several pennies in a pouch; she'd think herself very rich if she accepted them.

Edmund glanced up at the sky and smiled at the friendly sun, then looked thoughtfully down at the flowing red-stained water under the wood at his feet and remembered his meeting much earlier in the day with the odd-looking tin-streamer. He had given Morenwyn Charlie Chiverton's carved dog and she hadn't let it out of her little hand since. Edmund thought what a wonderful day this was turning out to be. He strolled on and was soon following Charlotte's path through the rough grass.

Charlotte rushed into the dark manky smelling shack. A scream was already leaving her throat as she saw Nellie bent over Pengelly's knee with food slithering down her face. She was gagging and then coughed wretchedly; the next moment she was being violently sick.

'Let her go, you savage!' Charlotte yelled.

Pengelly thrust Nellie away and kicked her viciously in the stomach. Nellie cried out and scrambling to her feet lurched towards Charlotte.

'It's all right, Nellie. He won't hurt you now that I'm here. What was he trying to do to you?' Charlotte held the trembling woman close to her, keeping her eyes rooted on Pengelly who stood glaring at her, panting.

Nellie was crying and complained like a child who felt hard done by and had found an adult comforter. ''E wus tryin' to get me to eat somethin' 'orrible, Mistress Thomas. Said 'e'd beat me if I didn't, but it's too bitter. Say I didn't do nothin' wrong!'

'You did nothing wrong, Nellie.' Charlotte tried to sound calm while edging herself and Nellie towards the door. 'You don't have to eat anything if you don't like it. What were you trying to give her?' she demanded of Pengelly.

''Twas just a drop o' stew, not that 'tes any of yourn bizness!'

Charlotte could smell something pungent rising from Nellie's face. It reminded her of the strong damp smell of a certain fungi and suddenly Charlotte knew with horror why Nellie's grandmother had died unexpectedly of stomach cramps. Fear and revelation must have shown on her face because Pengelly roared and lunged at the women. Charlotte and Nellie ducked away from him; he stopped and turned by the door, blocking their exit.

'Let us out of here at once,' Charlotte said, as sternly as she could through her fear.

'You can't prove nothin'!' Pengelly shouted at her.

Charlotte eyed the platter, still bearing the evidence. 'All I want to do is to take Nellie out of here to the parsonage and get her cleaned up. Now please move.'

'And leave you to go straight to a magistrate?' Pengelly grinned evilly. 'You'd get medics or some such to look at my stew.'

'Why should they believe me?' Charlotte said, gulping but keeping a calm tone. 'You could say Nellie cooked it.'

'They'd b'lieve thee afore me! And that wench may be a simpleton but every country maid d'knaw what's poison and what ain't. I reckon I'll have t'keep both of 'ee quiet.'

Charlotte shook with terror, but said contemptuously, 'Then you'll find yourself at the end of a hangman's noose.'

'Not if I can get far away enough from here first.' Pengelly stalked towards them. 'That woman's mad, I'll make it look like she murdered thee then took 'er own life. She'll be the one to 'ang, in remorse like.'

'Keep away!'

'Is Mister Pengelly going to hurt us?' Nellie whimpered.

Charlotte could see one chance for Nellie. Pengelly couldn't grasp them both at the same time if Nellie was pushed across the room. Charlotte pushed with all her might. 'Run, Nellie, run! Get help!'

Pengelly hesitated, his outstretched arms swinging both ways but deciding on the parson's wife. He could still make it look like Nellie killed her. He lunged and caught Charlotte's hair, knocking off her hat and yanking her towards him. Nellie looked about in despairing bewilderment then ran out of the shack shrieking.

Charlotte screamed and struggled and Pengelly laughed. 'Don't thee feel nice an' soft after that ragged creature.'

Nellie saw Edmund Kempthorne and ran wildly at him. ''Elp! 'Elp! 'E's killin' 'er!'

Edmund raced up to her and pulling her flailing hands down shouted into her face, 'Who's killing who?'

'Mister Pengelly! Mistress Thomas!'

'What?'

Edmund pushed Nellie aside and ran to the shack. He found Gyver Pengelly bending over Charlotte's still body and cried out in anguish. 'What have you done to her, you swine? Get back, get back, or I'll kill you myself!'

Pengelly laughed. 'An'what's a fine gen'leman like you goin' to do to me, eh? I could turn yer bones to jelly. I'll say that mad woman killed you and 'er.' He thumbed at Charlotte's body.

Enraged to real violence for the first time in his life, Edmund lashed out again and again with his walking cane. It bit into Pengelly's flesh and made him howl like a demented animal. The cane broke and Pengelly snatched the stump from Edmund's hand. Edmund whipped up a length of rope lying on the ground and slashed it across Pengelly's face, adding to the damage caused by Nick and the vengeful villagers. Something hit Pengelly in the back; he glanced over his shoulder and saw Nellie throwing sods of earth at him. Edmund Kempthorne's soft features were distorted with rage and horror and Nellie looked as if she had lost all reason. Pengelly didn't like the odds. With an oath he grabbed the plate of stew and ran out of the shack and off, whipping his hand across Nellie's face on the way.

Edmund ran to the doorway, wishing he'd had his small hand gun with him. He could have despatched Gyver Pengelly legally in self-defence and the defence of these two women. Nellie had hit the ground from Pengelly's final assault on her. She shook her head stupidly and getting unsteadily to her feet tottered to her wrecked home.

'Is she dead, Mr Kem'thorne?' she whined from a badly bruised and swollen face.

Edmund was staring into space, as if he didn't quite know where he was and why he was there. He didn't answer but turned his head and looked down at Charlotte lying crumpled on her side, half under the makeshift table. He groaned. He couldn't bear to look at her if she was dead, and it would be too awful if that lovely, desirable young woman really was dead. But he couldn't order Nellie to go to Charlotte, she was unlikely to be able to tell the difference between her being alive or dead.

Moving very slowly, Edmund lowered himself down on his haunches and steeling himself to look under the table but not actually at Charlotte, placed his trembling fingers on her neck. When he felt a pulse he cried out in relief.

Nellie was looking at him with the perplexity of a child. Edmund shuddered; these two women on whom he had designs had been terribly hurt and he felt a sadness and a measure of responsibility for them. He gently pulled Charlotte out from under the table. Her head rolled to face him as he held her in his arms. 'Charlotte,' he said softly. Her hair was all over her face. He smoothed it away, saw with more anguish the ugly mark left from the blow Pengelly had knocked her out with. 'Charlotte…' He looked around for water to splash over her face but there was none. He called her name again and her eyelids moved. He traced a delicate fingertip down her face and she stirred. It took a moment for her to come to and when she did she stared at him from immense dark eyes, his face red from his fight, but smiling, gentle.

She struggled to sit up and he helped her, keeping firm arms about her. 'What happened?' Her speech was slightly slurred. 'Where's Nellie?'

'She's here, she's not hurt. Shush now, don't talk.'

'Pengelly! He—'

'He's gone, I fought him off.'

Charlotte blinked, still feeling dazed. She could only lie against Edmund's warm body. 'You saved our lives,' she murmured.

'Yes.'

She thought for a while, then her tone was snappy. 'You need not think yourself noble, Edmund Kempthorne. If you were here it meant you had come to use Nellie, even if you have since redeemed yourself.'

'Yes.' He smoothed back a feathery strand of dark hair.

Charlotte gathered her wits and made to stand up. Reluctantly, Edmund withdrew his arms and helped her. Then he and Nellie half carried her home to the parsonage.

–

Edmund called at the parsonage the next day to ask after Charlotte's welfare. She was badly shaken but rather than rest in her bedchamber had insisted on lying on a sofa in the parlour. Perran, delighted to welcome the new and unlikely hero of the village, ordered tea for three and chattered as he vigorously stoked up the fire to keep his wife warm and comfortable.

'We can't thank you enough, Mr Kempthorne. Without your timely intervention there would have been two more funerals in the village and one would have been for my own dear wife.'

'It was providence that I happened to be out for an afternoon stroll and saw Nellie running for help,' Edmund said, presenting Charlotte with a beribboned bunch of snowdrops and keeping his eyes fully upon her. 'My uncle cultivated a large patch of these beautiful flowers in the garden of Trevennor House,' he told her. 'They have flowered by the thousand this year.'

'They are lovely, Mr Kempthorne,' Charlotte said, raising the posy of miniature white bells to her nose.

Perran took the snowdrops from Charlotte to place them in water and bid Edmund take a seat. Edmund took a chair, the nearest he could to Charlotte, and continued to gaze at her steadily. He could do this quite openly in her husband's presence because Perran Thomas was doing the same thing, adoringly. She gazed back at Edmund for a moment and he knew she had not told her husband just how close he had been to the hovel yesterday afternoon when he'd discovered her predicament.

'I'm so glad to see you are recovering, ma'am,' Edmund drawled, stroking a light fingertip under his chin in a suggestive manner. 'It was a dreadful experience for all of us yesterday, but for you especially.'

'I just need a day or two of peace and quiet,' Charlotte said, her hand moving unconsciously to where she had been struck.

'That vile man, what is going to be done about him?' Edmund said, suddenly getting angry. But there was a nervous note in his voice. He was terrified at the thought of running into Gyver Pengelly while out alone.

'I'm afraid we will be unable to bring the man to justice,' Perran said, just as angrily, making the fire roar up the chimney.

'Oh?'

'It is most unfortunate, Mr Kempthorne,' Charlotte replied. 'My husband would have made sure Pengelly was not only apprehended but detained in custody but when Nellie is questioned she becomes confused about what happened. Pengelly will say she went mad for no reason and she was the one who struck me. Despite my pleas to her, she swears Pengelly never meant her any real harm. We are worried that if Nellie is questioned severely she will unknowingly say something to incriminate herself. She could end up in court. In the end my husband decided not to alert the authorities. I'm afraid there is nothing we can do, unless...'

'Unless of course you will corroborate my wife's story, Mr Kempthorne,' Perran took up the theme from his wife.

'Oh no! I mean, I'm not very good myself under that sort of thing, interrogation... I'd get all mixed up and could make things bad for Nellie and she's suffered enough as it is.'

Perran and Charlotte exchanged looks. Charlotte was not surprised at Edmund's response, but Perran was. He didn't know that Edmund Kempthorne was afraid of the local folk discovering that he had been at Nellie's shack yesterday with the express purpose of taking advantage of the simple-minded girl. It would provoke a scandal. Perran concluded that Edmund was terrified of Pengelly, of the retribution he might try to mete out if he testified against him. Both Charlotte and Perran realized it would be futile to plead with Edmund. They didn't approve, they were angry about it, but Edmund had saved Charlotte and Nellie's lives.

There was an uneasy moment of silence then Edmund asked meekly, 'Um, what is to be done about Nellie? Surely she cannot go on living in that shack.'

'Do not be concerned about Nellie, Mr Kempthorne,' Charlotte said somewhat tartly. 'My husband has taken her to a place where she will be safe and well cared for, a secret location of course. She will soon forget all about Gwithian and her past ordeals and will live out the rest of her life in contentment.'

'I'm relieved to hear that, and very pleased for her,' Edmund said in a small voice.

A maidservant brought in a tray of tea and a message for Perran.

'There's a parishioner waiting to have a word with me, my dear,' Perran said. 'Will you pour the tea please, Mr Kempthorne? My wife is not up to it. I shall be but a few minutes.' He went out of the room after the maid and left the door slightly ajar.

Edmund did as he was asked in silence, placing a cup and saucer close to where Perran had been standing, one next to his chair and the last on a small table where Charlotte could reach it. He stayed close beside her. Her face was swollen and bruised where she had been struck and tiny tendrils of her soft hair were sticking to it. He wanted to smooth her hair away and kiss that tender place.

'I meant what I said about Nellie,' he breathed softly.

'We know you do, Perran and I.'

'Then you do not think too badly of me?'

'Whatever you do, whatever you are, Mr Kempthorne, I shall never forget that you saved my life, and Nellie's. You could have run away. Gyver Pengelly is a terrible man, everyone is afraid of him – with perhaps the exception of Nick Nancarrow, and that strange little tinner friend of his.'

'You are very kind,' he said in a husky whisper. 'Do call me Edmund.'

Charlotte sighed a little impatiently. 'I shall always be grateful to you, *Mr Kempthorne.*'

Edmund understood what this meant. 'You have a good marriage?'

Charlotte did not blush. 'Yes, I have. Perran and I are more than husband and wife, we are soul mates. We love the part of each other that will live for all eternity, but even if we did not...'

'Forgive me. I shall leave.'

Charlotte smiled. 'Sit and drink your tea, Mr Kempthorne. I shall enjoy the company of a friend.' Edmund resumed his seat and smiled with his easy charm. 'Friends it is then, and I am honoured that you think of me as such.'

'How is little Morenwyn recovering from her fall?'

'She is much better, thank you, ma'am. I was more frightened over her mishap than at the thought of being at Pengelly's mercy.'

'That is only natural, Mr Kempthorne.'

Edmund lounged back comfortably. 'You know that I'm her father, don't you?'

'One only has to look at her. It is a shame that you and her mother have not married, but nevertheless I admire you in a small way for supporting them both. Do you not think, however, that for Morenwyn's sake you ought to make your union with her mother lawful and right in God's eyes?'

Edmund was rather amused. He shook his head. 'We all live under different laws, do we not?'

'But there are consequences to be faced for everything we do. Anyway, I shall be very glad to have Morenwyn here to play with my children, if that is agreeable to you and her mother. A child needs the company of other children, a time to play and grow and learn to socialize. She can do that here.'

'You are very kind, Mistress Thomas, and I'm sure Mary Ellen will be happy for Morenwyn to come, but was there an edge of warning in what you said at first?'

'Yes, Mr Kempthorne. What I meant was that others may not receive her. I understand you intend to set up permanent home at your larger residence at Truro. Your little girl will feel rejected and terribly unhappy if she grows up to be shunned by society there.'

Edmund looked down into his empty cup thoughtfully. 'Mmmm, you have given me something to ponder on.'

'I hope you will make the right decision.'

'For my daughter, whom I adore as you do your husband and children, I intend always to make the right decisions.'

Perran returned. 'That was one of the Trevennor shepherds,' he said gravely. 'He thought we ought to know that Gyver Pengelly is going about laughing about yesterday's events. Pengelly is saying he believes he can get away with anything. I fear what he might get up to next.'

Chapter 20

Isabel had left the house at Crantock a few times now. Avoiding all signs of other people, she had wandered across the nearby beach and over the dunes that gave the house such a dramatic backdrop. She usually ended up on the cliff and would stand and gaze longingly into the distance, back the way she had come into Crantock, hoping to see a tall sandy-haired man striding confidently towards her, but Nick never appeared.

Yesterday she had walked to the Gannel, just a short distance. She'd been unable to go far on the beach because the tide was fully in, so she'd backtracked and mounted the high sand dunes. Trudging through them somewhat dejectedly she took her time getting onto the cliff and moved sluggishly on to Polly Joke, looking out for the scraggy cattle that came to drink from the stream that ran to the sea.

Everything seemed to run to the sea, Isabel thought as cold sea breezes ruffled her hair, but why? To challenge its unforgiving mastery? Happy to be an infinitesimal part of its majestic vastness? To be wild and free, to roam at will? On her way here she had made a wide detour to avoid the cliff's edge where she had stood with Nick watching the surf and tide bombarding Crantock's beach. That had been a special moment. It would have made her feel acutely lonely to be there without him. Yet what did that matter? Wherever she was on this wild rugged coastline, close to the sea that raged its way into the deserted little cove today, she thought of Nick.

She scrambled back up on the cliff and searched every rocky exposed headland, every part of the twisting path she had trodden with him, but as before there was no sign of him. The journey they had made together had taken place only a few short weeks ago, but it seemed like a lifetime now and she could hardly bear to go on looking for him.

'Wishing he was here won't make it happen any quicker,' Benjamin said, smiling kindly at her glum expression, which was in startling contrast to the health and vigour her walks had given her face. He moved his hand carefully to brush the back of one of Isabel's.

She delicately touched his hand with her fingertips. 'But it's nearly a week since we got his letter, Ben. He said he would be here soon. Something must have happened. Something must have gone wrong.' Ben took his hand away and she got up to pace his room.

'Don't worry so much, Jenna. Nick will be here by and by. You can trust him, you know that.'

Isabel stopped to stare out of the window, her mouth in a tight line.

'Is she sulking again?' Kitty asked her brother as she popped her head around the doorway.

'She is,' Benjamin answered, grinning.

'Right, miss! Benjamin will be all right on his own for a little while. You put this cloak on. I'm taking you up to the village. A change of scene will do you good and give you something else to think about.'

'I only want to know what's going on,' Isabel said, somewhat moodily, after they had secured the house and left Talland roaming about close by. 'I want to know whether I'm in danger or not, that's all.'

'Is that so?' Kitty replied, sounding unconvinced. 'Never mind that now. Spring is in the air, 'tis a lovely day. Make the most of it.'

Isabel enjoyed the walk up the steep muddy track that led into the heart of Crantock. She had always been used to lots of people around her, servants, Phoebe, Ginny, and those she'd socialized with. It was quite different to be in the company of just two people and a free-spirited dog, although she admitted it gave her plenty of time to think about Nick and daydream.

She looked with interest at the cottages and shops as she and Kitty went along and watched a farrier putting a new shoe on a horse until Kitty pulled her on. She was fascinated by all the different sights, sounds and smells and lapped them up, knowing they would have meant nothing to her in what she now thought of as her 'old life'. She laughed at a gaggle of honking geese following a small girl and boy with dirty little faces but was offended by two rough-looking sailors whom Kitty saw off with a hurl of verbal abuse. She apologized to Isabel, explaining it was one of the things she had to put up with when people knew of her profession.

Isabel chatted briefly to a young mother working at a hand loom in the doorway of her cottage with her many small children playing about her feet. The weaver said she liked to work there for the better light and the opportunity it gave her to talk to folk who passed by. Isabel couldn't stay long in any one place, it was too risky, and reluctantly moved on. Another woman was making besoms from broom twigs in the fresh air and Isabel could smell beer brewing in every other cottage.

Some of the people they passed on their way blatantly shunned them while others gave Kitty and her 'friend' a cheery greeting, including a stout woman who looked as though she would be attractive to the eye if she hadn't been wearing such severe clothes and a concealing hood.

'She's a Methodist,' Kitty explained as they went on, making sure no one held them up for a long conversation. 'There's a few of them hereabouts. She always has a word for me even though she's condemned my manner of living to my face. I admire her for that.'

Isabel looked after the woman with mixed feelings. 'The people I used to mix with wouldn't even speak to one of them.'

'Why's that then?'

Isabel was careful to drop her voice. 'The incumbent of my parish says they are nought but a sect. They have taken too many ideas upon themselves and criticize the Church openly. They're beginning to influence the people so much that some are beginning not to attend their parish churches and would rather pack themselves into the mean meeting houses the Methodists are building all over the county.'

Kitty sniffed as she picked up her skirts above her ankles to avoid soiling the hems on a muddy patch. 'Sounds like nothing but prejudice to me. They seem all right; well, most of them. Course there's always some who go too far and spoil whatever others are trying to do. 'Tis reckoned they put their money where their mouth is where Christianity and charity are concerned. Anyway, John Wesley is an Anglican clergyman himself, so I've heard.'

'He ought to know better,' Isabel said stiffly. 'And Methodists aren't the only ones to be charitable.'

Kitty could not help laughing. 'Are you so sure you're not prejudiced yourself, Jenna? Perhaps you should keep your judgement on him until you've heard him preach. He comes to Cornwall nearly every year. We could go together, might be interesting.'

'I do believe you're teasing me,' Isabel returned, 'and suddenly I feel rather ashamed. I've just remembered Mundy Cottle's a Methodist and she's a wonderful woman. Nick teased me about her too.'

'I think it's about time I had someone I can trust to be quiet to come down to the house and speak to Benjamin. He can't make up his mind about God and spiritual matters if he never hears about them,' Kitty said thoughtfully.

As they walked, Isabel was thoughtful too. If Kitty considered it was safe for her to walk through the village, she thought she might venture further along the cliffs when out alone, retrace more of the steps she had taken with Nick.

‘’Tis difficult for you, isn’t it?’ Kitty said shrewdly. ‘Being forced to live a different way of life to what you’re used to. You probably don’t know whether you’re coming or going.’

‘It hasn’t been easy but I’ve enjoyed much more than I’ve hated. It’s the way I think and feel that’s so puzzling and strange. I feel almost elated one moment and very low the next. Oh, look at that!’ They had come to the centre of the village where a holy well with a conical stone roof stood.

‘The holy well? Have you never seen one before? The village actually boasts two wells, we passed the other one on the way up from the house. ’Tis called St Ambrusca’s well, I’ll show it to you on the way back.’

‘No, Kitty, the holy well is interesting but I was referring to the man in the stocks close beside it. Phoebe Antiss once had a little pet monkey and he looks just like it. I wonder what his crime was.’ Kitty viewed the scrunched-up figure of the old man sitting on a bench, his body draped over where his legs filled two of the six holes of the heavy stocks.

‘Jack Rejerrah? Thieving, not paying his debts and drunkenness are the usual reasons he’s in there. The other day he was put in for swearing and relieving himself in front of a lady whose carriage was held up in the mud while passing through the village.’ Jack Rejerrah was spattered with wet mud, a trickle of blood was on his bristly chin where a stone had been thrown at him. There were several stones at the foot of the stocks. He was fast asleep and snoring with a loud bronchial wheeze.

‘It looks like he’s been in there for a long time.’

‘Spends most of his life in there. You get so you don’t notice it any more. Don’t worry, the parish constable will probably let him out soon.’

‘Good day to ’ee, Miss Kitty.’

A deep rough voice from behind them made Isabel start and a sharp twist of dread clutched the core of her stomach. She recognized that voice. The women turned round together.

‘What do you want?’ Kitty asked hostilely as she reached for Isabel’s hand.

'Only want t'wish 'ee both a good day,' Gyver Pengelly boomed, his oily mouth distorted in a snarl. 'You an' yer friend. No law 'gainst it, is there? Only tryin' to be civil.' He was leering at Isabel who instinctively backed away, taking Kitty with her. 'Who's yer friend then? Seen 'er afore somewheres.' Pengelly licked his fat wet lips.

'None of your business.'

Pengelly was holding a gin bottle round the neck. He took the last swig and threw it away. He looked bruised and battered and had obviously been in a fight.

Kitty pulled Isabel further away. She was worried. Gyver Pengelly had seen Isabel up on the cliffs with Nick and he was greatly interested in her. She fervently hoped there would be no trouble and damned herself for bringing Isabel this far from the house.

Pengelly was not going to give up. He went round the back of Kitty and paced alongside Isabel. 'What's yer name then, me 'an'some?'

'I don't have one,' Isabel retorted, trying to control her trembling.

'Huh! Everybody's gotta name.' He stared at Isabel's stricken face and she winced when he gave a tremendous roar. 'I mind 'ee now! Yer Nancarrow's woman! Well, yer name went be Nancarrow, I can count on that. That swine went never git married.'

Kitty thrust Isabel round to her other side and walked faster. She was heading them towards the farrier's shop where she might be able to grab a hammer and beat Pengelly off if necessary.

'Get away from us, Pengelly! We don't want your company.'

Isabel looked round Kitty at Pengelly, as if she wanted to challenge him. Kitty held her arm tighter. 'Get ready to run!' she hissed.

'What's that?' Pengelly bellowed. 'Planning to run away from me? Not yet, you don't.'

He edged in closer to Kitty, forcing the two women to veer round in a wide circle until they found themselves back at the stocks. With brute force he suddenly tore Kitty away from Isabel and threw her aside to land across Jack Rejerrah.

'Now, my pretty little thing, 'tes jus' you 'n' me.'

He expected Isabel to scream and try to run away but she stood her ground and folded her arms. To be scared when she herself was threatened was one thing but to harm her friend and the unfortunate old man in the stocks…

'How dare you treat her like that! Don't you come near me, not one little step, or you'll be sorry you were ever born!' Fury gave her courage even though this brute made her skin crawl with revulsion and fear. At that moment she was almost as glacially calm as she looked.

A crowd of curious onlookers had formed, drawn by the shouting, but Isabel doubted if any man among them would come forward to face up to Gyver Pengelly on her behalf. He leered in anticipation.

'Now I'll know what those lovely red lips Nancarrow kisses tastes like.'

Isabel choked back the bile rising in her throat and braced herself. As his massive hands reached for her shoulders, she brought a knee up sharply in his groin. He let out a mighty howl and bent double, whereupon Isabel locked her fists together and smashed them down on the back of his neck. He hit the dirt on his knees at her feet. Isabel jumped back, rubbing her bruised hands. Kitty had scrambled to her feet and watched the felling of Gyver Pengelly with open-mouthed astonishment. Then she leapt forward and gave him a vicious kick in the backside which sent him sprawling on his face.

'Where on earth did you learn to do that?' she asked Isabel incredulously, the excited tremor in her voice pronounced.

'Aye, you gave un what he's deserved for a long time, maid,' a woman said from the cheering crowd.

'I… I saw two stable boys fighting many years ago, one did it to the other and it… just came naturally to me,' Isabel gasped, hardly able to believe herself what she'd done. She was cradling her painful hands and trembling all over.

'By the look of un someone worked un over afore he came into the village today,' a man laughed.

The Methodist woman came forward and placed a comforting arm round Isabel's shoulder. ''Twas just like David the shepherd boy bringing down Goliath. Do you know the account from the Bible, m'dear?'

'Yes… but I'm glad I don't have to cut off his head.'

'Would serve the bugger right,' the shoe repairer put in with relish.

'Now, now, brother,' the Methodist woman scolded. 'Let's hear none of that sort of talk. We're all the Lord's children, even him.'

'Devil's child more like,' someone else muttered.

Pengelly groaned, tried to get up but slumped down again with his giant paws massaging the back of his neck. Too much alcohol and the beatings he'd got in Gwithian the day before had taken their toll.

Another man, a miner by his clothes, stepped between Isabel and Gyver Pengelly. 'Nothin' good went into creatin' 'im,' he said harshly. 'Well done, maid. You've put us men to shame but if any of you others are with me we'll drive un out of the village.'

Cries of agreement sang out and the miner nodded in satisfaction. 'You women all go on 'ome or be about your business, and you, Kitty, get yer friend 'ere off 'ome too.'

Kitty was grateful to the miner. She led Isabel quickly away from the crowd before any awkward questions could be asked. As they walked back to her house, they heard Gyver Pengelly bellowing amidst the shouts of the men, about ten brave souls in number, as he was driven out of Crantock in the opposite direction. Jack Rejerrah had not stirred during the commotion and slept on peacefully.

'Did I let my real voice slip through?' Isabel asked, a worried frown creasing her forehead.

'No, but folk can tell a cut above the rest. They'll probably think you've got some airs and graces from working as a lady's maid. I can't wait to tell Nick about this,' Kitty said, breathless with excitement. 'Gyver Pengelly has terrorized the North Cliffs for years.'

'I hope he doesn't come looking for revenge,' Isabel said nervously.

'He won't dare show his damned ugly face around here for a long time to come,' Kitty laughed.

'But he'll be thinking about me after what I did to him. If he gets too curious it could lead to someone realizing or finding out who I really am.' Isabel felt strangely elated now the immediate danger was over but she put her remarks to Kitty with an edge of fear in her heart.

'Oh, don't worry, Pengelly's far too stupid to work it out by himself.' Kitty sounded light-hearted as she led the way into the security of her house but for a moment her face was coated in doubt. She hoped Nick would not be much longer in coming back.

-

In the spacious sheltered garden at the back of Trevennor House, Edmund Kempthorne had got the servants to put out two comfortable chairs. He was lounging back next to Mary Ellen as they fondly watched Morenwyn playing quietly with her family of dolls on a thick rug on the lawn. At that moment Edmund was perfectly serene. There was nothing to tell of his daughter's fall down the stairs except for the bandage swathing the top of her pretty head. His sudden heroics over Gyver Pengelly had pulled Mary Ellen out of her nervous stupor about Morenwyn's accident and she had come to him with her usual vigour. People in the village were saying that Gyver Pengelly would be too ashamed to show his face in Gwithian for weeks and by that time Edmund intended that he and his family would be living at Truro. Anyway, even if Pengelly did turn up,

Edmund had no inclination to wander the village, with Nellie gone and no opportunity forthcoming from the parsonage.

Deborah Kempthorne was watching the cosy little scene out in the mild weather from inside the house. Every time her brother raised the hand of his mistress to his lips, her hard features tightened. Every time her niece's happy piping little voice reached her ears, she snorted angrily.

Deborah was furious at Pengelly's botched attempt to despatch Nellie and she couldn't take part in the hero-worship Edmund was getting from Mary Ellen, and to a lesser degree even from Mrs Christopher and the other servants. The servants were very fond of Nellie and Charlotte Thomas and hated Gyver Pengelly. They were rather proud that their new master, who was nowhere as demanding and bad-tempered as their hated mistress, had saved the two women by beating off the vile brute. Deborah had always wanted things to go well for Edmund but she was jealous of his popularity. The only bright spark to come out of the incident over Nellie was her being packed off somewhere, already apparently forgetting about her 'friendship' with Gyver Pengelly. At least Deborah didn't have to worry any more about the simple-minded woman saying something that would incriminate her in the Antiss coach tragedy.

Morenwyn left the rug and went to her parents. Edmund lifted her onto his lap. Deborah scowled as he and Mary Ellen made a fuss of her and made her chuckle happily. Edmund would be calling for the nursemaid soon to take Morenwyn upstairs for a nap while he and Mary Ellen snuggled down in another room.

Deborah hated the cosy domestic scene. What a pity the brat hadn't died in that fall! She went to her dressing table and stared at her reflection in the glass. With Nellie out of the way, she could now turn her attention to getting rid of that harlot outside and her obnoxious spawn.

Chapter 21

The next day Isabel stood by Talland's side on Crantock beach. They were out early, watching an ocean full of white horses as far as the eye could see. She was learning the sea's moods, a huge living creature, sometimes a monster, never to be mastered, but irresistible, compelling. Even on calm days it was restless on this coast, always had a heavy swell. It called to a deep part of Isabel that she had never known existed; she believed now she would always want to live near it.

The tide was ebbing away, the great rollers rising tall but falling back in defeat, and with each one went Isabel's hopes that Nick would come today. It seemed that all she did now was do battle with her feelings for him. She gazed dispiritedly at the part of the cliff where she and Nick had stood and looked down. It was hard to imagine that she had once hated him, had berated him at every chance.

Talland never stayed still for long and after a few impatient whines, which were ignored, he barked at her and finally she threw the stick he had plonked down at her feet. Then she laughed and made up her mind to make the most of the freedom she had. In two weeks' time Richard Grenville would disembark at Truro and she would have to 'come to life' and face the Kempthornes' wrath at her deceit. Soon after that she would be married.

She raced Talland to the dunes, scrambling barefoot up the spilling sands and running down again in long sinking strides. Her skin tingled and her eyes glowed, her hair streamed out behind her in a honey-brown cloud. Then they wandered in and out of the caves at the foot of the cliffs, the rock in places glowing a glorious green and copper red.

High up in the cliff, gulls were nesting and while they tolerated one or two big black crows that occasionally flew too close to their homes, they didn't like the intrusion coming from below. Isabel wasn't concerned over the territorial birds, they were too far away to harm her except for spotting on her head or clothes and she was too carefree these days to care about that. She studied the deep blue shells of millions of mussels that clung to the lower parts of the cliff, but she screamed shrilly and made Talland bark in alarm when they entered the last dark cave and two noisy pigeons suddenly flew out and startled her.

The girl and dog next ran alongside the tidal river of the Gannel as it was being rapidly emptied of its sea water. Two more dogs appeared and Talland ran about with them. Isabel followed the river's twisting bank; the water was low enough to paddle in in some places but it was always too dangerous to swim in. The sea had left the rest of the beach in rippled sand and various sized pools; the deeper the water, the deeper the colour blue. On the other side of the river, Pentire Point East stretched out as a headland, with New Quay reaching the other way inland.

When he got bored with his companions, Talland chased after Isabel. She envied the dogs their lifelong freedom. The trek she had made with Nick had awakened a thirst for the outdoors in her blood. She had asked Kitty if she could acquire a horse for some much-needed exercise but Kitty had deemed it inadvisable. Few ordinary young women were accomplished riders and it would draw attention to herself.

Isabel knew her restlessness came mainly from a deep-rooted longing to see Nick again. To hear his voice, even to have him swear or hurl an insult at her. To feel safe with him nearby. She was desperate to see him again even though she knew it would break her heart, because she could never have him. She watched the receding sea and sighed for the man who might as well be all the way across the Atlantic Ocean, he seemed so far away from her.

Talland whined, as if he wanted to tell her that if she remained still for much longer she would become too cold. Taking his sympathetic hint, she walked slowly back over the dark wet sand, paddling through some of the freezing cold water pools. The scruffy dog padded along a little in front of her, asserting his independence, but occasionally glancing back to make sure he was heading for where she intended to go. Isabel retrieved her shoes from where she'd left them on a path at the back of Kitty's house, and then meandered along it, following the course of the Gannel again. It was a narrow rising path sheltered on both sides by dead hawthorn bushes that were covered with ivy, and gorse bushes just waking up from their winter sleep and showing touches of small golden flowers. Isabel sniffed them and liked their almond smell. After a while she realized Talland was no longer with her.

At the end of the narrow pathway she came to green fields and a low bank leading down to the beach where black sea-weeded rocks jutted out of stony sand and driftwood lay dotted about. Way across the river was a high bank with the occasional cottage nestled in it. Isabel realized that if she had waited down on the beach for the tide to recede further, she could have carried on walking right up the side of the Gannel. She kept to the path and soon the stony stretch of sand she had looked down on was behind her and what seemed miles ahead was wide golden ridged sand and the snaking river. The river was so low she could not believe she had watched large fishing boats on it and cargo barges carrying limestone, coal and earthenware to unload at Fern Pit or three miles up at Trevemper on a flood tide.

Everywhere was quiet, no one was about, she was gloriously alone.

A solitary white swan floated up the shallow water remaining in the river and Isabel clambered down the bank to survey its graceful passage. Her melancholy had gone and she followed the footprints on the hard wet sand left by two gulls. She felt a sense of adventure, the kind of feeling that had been 'corrected' out of her as a child. She balanced one foot in front of the other on the sand ridges as she proceeded upriver, and on skirting a wide pool of sea water she was splashed by a playful Talland who had decided to rejoin her. Capitulating fully to the mood, she took off her shoes, hitched up her petticoat and waded in and out of the pools, laughing as the dog dashed about sending up sprays of cold water over her.

Kitty had warned her to be very careful if she ever ventured up the Gannel. The tide came in and out rapidly, 'always like a lion, never like a lamb', spilling out over the river bank and covering the sand where she was, and all that she could see, completely.

Isabel lingered in several spots, letting time tick by, but scanning the river often and when she did fancy it was filling up again she kept close to the bank or the rocks where she could easily climb out of danger. She was unconcerned, knowing the bank and fields would give an easy walk all the way to Kitty's back door.

When she came to the wide wooden bridge that gave a short cut to wagons and pedestrians travelling to and from New Quay and Penpol Creek she sat on its edge for a few minutes then ran across its flat boards and back again, not wanting to risk being cut off on the wrong side by the tide. In a short time the bridge would be completely submerged and a stranger would not know of its existence.

Talland barked and led her into Penpol Creek where five small boats were moored in a few inches of muddy water under a high, tree-lined, grassy bank. No one was about on the jetty and the only sign of life was the smoke issuing from a ragged looking cottage set well back. There was a ladder running up the bank under the cottage and Isabel pictured happy urchin-like children scrambling up and down it in play. But today it seemed everyone was keeping out of her way and she was glad of the fact.

She and Talland investigated the boats, all of them black-stained at the bottom and brightly painted on top. They found nothing interesting or threatening and chose one painted red and blue and named *Tyak Mor* in white lettering to sit and dream another hour away in.

Isabel closed her eyes and shut her mind to the scolding she would get from Kitty for staying out so long. She was savouring these moments for the times when she would be tied to a grand house, a husband she did not love, a nursery, and a social life that no longer held any appeal for her. She would try to remember the tangy salty ocean air and the sun that warmed the fragrant wild flowers and leaves, the clean embrace of the wood smoke from the cottage; the swish of the wind stirring the spindly trees on both banks of the creek, the distant churn of the ocean and the nearby trickles and lapping of water, the calls of the seabirds. There was the homely smell of Talland's musty coat which he refused to have groomed, his snores as he snoozed with his nose in her lap. When she needed to in the future, she would retreat here. Isabel put her hand in her pocket and touched the tiny conical shells she had taken from the little smuggler's cove. She would be sure to take them with her as part of her cherished memories.

She retreated now from the possibility of her life being in danger, from the talks Kitty thrust on her about Richard Grenville. Isabel had tried to think about her fiancé, to make plans for her future with him. She had spoken to Kitty and Benjamin as though she was looking forward to it, but she knew Benjamin at least wasn't fooled. The way Kitty went on about Richard Grenville, it seemed she thought their future marriage was more important than the fact that two people could be capable of plotting her murder, people who even now were probably spending vast quantities of her money. Isabel squeezed the shells in her pocket and instead of thinking about the shame and hurt of what had happened in the cove, she substituted a tender embrace, a gentle kiss, soft romantic words. Then she retreated completely into her own small world of here and now and the need to see the man she knew she loved and could never have. More time ticked slowly by.

Talland jumped out of the boat and Isabel's eyes sprang open. He had made a terrific splash. Back to her full senses, she felt the boat rock alarmingly. It was floating fully on its mooring rope and she knew the tide was rising faster than she had imagined. She tried to pull the boat on its rope up to the bank to scramble ashore but it wobbled so much she was afraid of falling into the water. She could not swim and was gripped with panic. Looking over the side of the boat, she realized she could wade to the bank with the water up to her thighs if she was quick about it. Talland had swum to the bank, only a few lengths away, and ran up and down it, barking encouragement to her.

Hitching up her skirts to an unseemly height, her shoes held high, Isabel slipped over the side of the boat and waded ashore. It seemed that with every step the water grew an inch and she was soaked through to the waist when in utter relief she threw her shoes onto the grassy bank and scrambled up beside Talland.

She was cold, muddy and scratched but she told Talland it was a small price to pay for being safe. She would hasten home and dry herself and change, hoping to avoid Kitty and a severe scolding.

A curious noise further along the creek and across the tidal river made her look that way and she was surprised to see a wagon coming across the bridge. The sea was nearly up to the level of the bridge and would soon cover the path the wagon would need to take. Surely it was too dangerous to attempt a crossing now. Kitty had told her how some folk had met their deaths trying to race the river and according to legend the spirit of one drowned man was said to haunt it.

Isabel waved frantically. 'No! Go back!' she shouted, running along the bank. 'It can't be done. It's too late!'

Her pleas were futile, carried away on the wind and lost in the distance. If the wagon was washed off the bridge, it would plunge into deep, swiftly moving water. There would be no chance of the people swimming to safety, the undercurrents would drag them down and wash them out to sea in a matter of minutes.

It was a nightmare. The tide suddenly swirled over the bridge and the driver of the wagon, whom Isabel could see was a stout man of about fifty, tried to stop his two brown nags and get them to back up but the icy cold water whipping about their hooves sent them into a panic and they reared up. The driver shouted terrified orders. The woman at his side, probably his wife, screamed and screamed. Talland barked madly and Isabel screamed too.

The water rose and surged. One of the wagon's back wheels was floated off the bridge as though it was happening in slow motion. Isabel watched in sheer horror as the wagon, the two horses and the two people were sucked off the bridge and sank into the whirling sea water.

In only a few moments there was no sight of the wagon, the horses or the people, but Isabel could still hear their terrified screams. They were calling to her, shouting to her to save them. But how could she? She screamed back at them to stop and put her hands over her ears.

Rough hands took her shoulders and turned her round and were pulling her away from the edge of the bank. They were trying to drag her down with them! Trying to take her in their arms and hold her tight and take her to join them in their watery grave. Why should they do that? She wanted to live, to see Nick again. She wanted Nick.

'Nick! Nick!'

'I'm here, Isabel! I'm here, my love. 'Tis all right. Look at me, be still and look at me.'

She heard his voice, somewhere far away, breaking through her horror. Then his voice was in her ear, tender, gentle. He was smoothing back the hair that had fallen wildly about her face and lifting her chin to look into his deep blue eyes.

'Nick! Is it really you? Are you really here?'

'Yes, Isabel, my dear beloved. I have you safe in my arms now.'

Her eyes wide in disbelief and fear that she was dreaming, she looked up into his face. It was true. He was really there, his wonderful handsome face looking caringly down on hers. Only then did she feel his strong arms about her. The cold white fear left her and she buried her face into his chest and cried wretchedly.

There was a small boathouse on the bank of the creek and gathering her up, he carried her into it. He sat on a barrel and held her very, very close, stroking her hair, caressing her soft wet cheek. Talland sat still and quiet at their feet and they waited together for her distress to die away.

Nick stroked Talland's head then ordered him home to guard the house.

Isabel clutched Nick's shirt and used it to wipe at her eyes. She was shaking. Nick edged himself out of his coat and wrapped it round her.

'Did… did you… see?'

'Aye, I saw,' he replied quietly, shuddering at the memory. 'There was nothing anyone could do for them. It was foolhardy to try to cross over with the tide coming in so fast.'

'They were so frightened. I… I hardly saw their faces yet I could see their fear. I'll never forget it. Oh, Nick… those poor people.'

'Hush, Isabel.' He nestled his face on the top of her head.

'I wanted you to be here… and then you were… I wanted…' She looked up earnestly into his eyes. 'How did you know I needed you, Nick?'

He had been rubbing her arm gently and moved his hand to cup her chin. He could feel a small quaver there and looked into her eyes, so grey, bright and startled.

'Kitty was worried with you being out for so long. I could tell by your tracks you had to be along here somewhere. I wanted to come days ago, but Edmund Kempthorne's little daughter took a bad fall down the stairs and I was the one who went for the doctor.'

'Morenwyn? I've heard about her but have never seen her. Is she all right now?'

'Aye, thank the Lord.' Nick hesitated, sighed and went on with distaste, 'I'm afraid Deborah Kempthorne thinks I have a liking for her, she's so jealous she would have been suspicious if I'd left before Morenwyn had safely recovered. She made out she was distressed and needed me to lean on. I've been worried about leaving you for so long, Isabel. Recently I fought with Gyver Pengelly because he was making threats against you. I was afraid he would see you here and Kitty's just told me he did, yesterday, but you and the villagers saw him off. I should have come before, but if I didn't turn up for work they would have asked in Gwithian where I was and Deborah Kempthorne would have been too curious… I've let you down, Isabel, I'm sorry.'

She looked deeply into his handsome features. 'You haven't let me down, Nick, and you're here now. Is Kitty very angry with me?'

Nick smiled at her. 'Yes, hopping mad. She was worried Pengelly had come back and kidnapped you.' He then said on a stern note, 'I was worried about you too when I arrived at the house and Kitty told me you'd been out all morning. I'd hate to see you hurt.'

'I'm sorry, Nick,' and fresh tears brimmed in her eyes.

He gently wiped the tears away with his shirt and smiled again. 'Kitty will be fine when she knows you're all right, she cares about you. So do I. I'll take you back in a few minutes. Kitty's had to go about her business and Benjamin's sleeping, he doesn't realize you've been out for so long.'

'Dear Ben, I'd hate to think I've been worrying him. Nick, why didn't you tell me about Benjamin before we arrived at Kitty's house?'

'Kitty never talks about him to anyone but me, I was the only one she allowed to see him. I thought it was her place to mention him after I'd gone.' Nick suddenly held Isabel tighter and she clung to him. She could feel his warm breath in the hollow of her neck, it gave her a lovely shivery feeling.

'I've got a lot to tell you, Isabel,' he said.

'Would Edmund and Deborah really wish me harm if they knew I was alive? The note you sent suggested Uncle Laurence's fears were well-founded.'

'I'm afraid so. I don't trust Edmund at all and I'm certain Deborah would try to kill you.' Nick sighed heavily. 'Oh Lord, I hate that woman, her sort's the scum of the earth. I've got close to her, you see, I'm supposed to be teaching her to ride.' Nick couldn't bring himself to tell Isabel just how close he had got to Deborah Kempthorne, the things he'd been forced to say, that he'd had to hold and kiss her. He held on to Isabel's slender, softly rounded body and drank in the beauty and femininity of it.

'What shall we do?' Isabel asked. She did not feel frightened at her own fate at that moment; she was too stunned by the tragedy she'd just witnessed and felt so warm and safe in Nick's arms.

'We'll talk about it later, with Kitty,' he said, just wanting to stay where they were, as they were.

She gently touched his split lip with the tip of a finger. 'Did that dreadful Pengelly do this to you?'

Nick grinned as he relived the memory of Gyver Pengelly hitting the ground from his last blow. 'He slept for hours after what I did to him,' he boasted, then he was full of concern. 'Did he hurt you?'

Isabel looked at her hands and smiled. 'I thought I'd broken all my fingers striking him, they hurt for hours afterwards.'

Nick took her hands and kissed them, lingering over them.

Isabel stirred and touched his bruised lip. 'Does this still hurt?'

''Tis nothing that a kiss wouldn't make better,' he whispered huskily.

She felt a new power surge through her, vibrant, raw and strong. It filled the core of her being. She knew she had captured a little part of this elusive man. She softly kissed his sore lip, taking her time as he had done over her hands, then pulled back and smiled.

A shiver ran up Nick's back. She was about to ask another question but he wanted her touch again and he lifted her head forward and kissed both of her lips with both of his. It was a sensation so sweet, so delicate, mingled with the taste of her tears. He kissed her again. For the first moment under his full onslaught Isabel became rigid but she quickly surrendered and returned his intensity.

'We'd better go back to Kitty's,' Nick said softly when reluctantly he brought the kiss to an end.

'You don't have to go off straight away, do you, Nick?' Isabel asked fearfully.

'No, my love. I don't have to get back to Tehidy till tomorrow.'

He helped her onto her shaky feet. 'Why are you so wet? Did you fall in the water?' He laughed lightly as she told him about her and Talland's adventure on the *Tyak Mor*.

'Nick, hadn't we better tell someone about the people who drowned?'

'No, there were folk on the other side of the river who witnessed what happened. We won't talk about it to anyone but Kitty. We can't afford to draw attention to you, Isabel.'

On the way back they chatted about her conversations and friendship with Benjamin so they wouldn't have to think about the people and horses who had perished on the bridge.

Talland was sitting dutifully on guard outside the house. There was no sign of Kitty having come back yet. They looked in on Benjamin who was still sleeping peacefully. Nick led Isabel to the kitchen and put her beside the hearth to warm through. He took a bottle of brandy from the dresser cupboard where Kitty kept it and poured out some for Isabel which she drank with shivering hands and much coughing.

Nick patted her back, told her the brandy would set her up properly again, and kissed her soundly.

When he finally let her go to drink his own brandy, she pulled the wet uncomfortable clothes away from her legs.

'I'm going upstairs to change out of these clothes. Can you make a pot of tea, please, Nick? I could do with a dishful rather than more brandy.'

'Want any help?' he said in a low voice, lifting a handful of her wet skirt.

'Only with the tea,' she replied, looking at him squarely but with a light smile.

Nick suddenly became serious and for the first time Isabel saw that he was embarrassed. 'Isabel, I'm sorry about what happened in the cove before I brought you here. I behaved very badly. I did and said things I had no right to. I was impatient… I shouldn't have reacted the way I did.'

She couldn't tell his exact reason for being sorry, whether it was for his insensitivity or because she was betrothed to another man. It didn't matter. They were here together, for now, and she was content with that.

She changed quickly, not bothering to wash off the salt water; that could wait until later. She wanted to spend as much time alone with Nick as possible before Benjamin woke up or Kitty came back.

Nick looked at her lingeringly. 'I've made the tea. Do you want something to eat?'

'No, thank you.'

'Do you want to talk?'

She shook her head.

He held out his arms. 'Then come to me.'

She went straight into his arms and into a passionate kiss. It was different this time. It took Isabel's breath away and filled them both with desire. If she moved just a breath away from him he pulled her back, his deep sapphire eyes begging for understanding.

'I don't have to go back until tomorrow. When Kitty comes back, can we go somewhere to be alone? Will it be all right this time?'

Her grey eyes were warm and smoky. 'Yes, Nick.'

'Are you sure, Isabel? That it won't be something you'll regret?'

She held him tighter. 'It's all I'll ever want, Nick.' As they kissed again the door was suddenly pushed open, letting in a draught. They both looked round. Kitty stood in the doorway of her kitchen with her arms folded firmly and a face set in wild-weather fury.

'And what, may I ask, is going on here?'

Chapter 22

Nick saw Kitty coming towards him and sharply turned his back on her. He cursed himself for staying so long in one place, the place she knew he would go to. She reached him and stood at his side.

'I came here to be alone,' he said tersely.

'No need to take that tone with me,' Kitty replied loftily, 'and don't forget this is also my special place.'

'I'm sorry,' he murmured, truly humbled.

They were in the churchyard which stood high up between the Gannel and the village and was easily seen from the front of Kitty's house. They were standing in front of her baby son's well-kept grave. A posy of primroses, freshly picked and put there that morning in a little clay pot, gave it a poignant charm. Kitty read the name on the wooden memorial plaque as she always did. Then she linked her arm through Nick's and moved in close to him. He clasped her mittened hand.

'I've always cherished the dream that Jeremy would have grown up to be proud of you,' she said, keeping her eyes on the little plaque. 'Having no father to rear him, he would have needed a man to look up to.'

'I'll make sure he would have done,' Nick said, and Kitty knew it was a promise. 'What do you want with me, Kitty?'

'I want to talk about Jenna – Isabel.'

'I don't.'

'You must, but not here beside my baby's resting place.'

They walked away slowly, arm in arm, out of the churchyard, away from the view of the sand dunes, sea, beach and the River Gannel. The village was buzzing with people, all talking about the tragic drownings. Kitty commiserated with those of her neighbours who talked to her, but having witnessed it, Nick felt sick to the gut and remained stonily silent. When they reached the other end of the village, dusk was falling and they were quite alone. Nick leaned against a granite stone stile. Kitty sat on the bottom step. Nick sighed. Now would come the lecture, and it came at once.

'You're angry with me because I stopped you from claiming your prize,' Kitty began harshly.

'I'm bloody angry with the way you went on about it. Anyone would think I was about to carry Isabel upstairs there and then. You know I wouldn't do such a thing with Benjamin in the house.'

'Don't tell me you didn't have something planned for a later date. When you turned up today you said you didn't have to go back until tomorrow but now I've upset your little plan and you're going off tonight.'

'It's none of your business! Isabel had just gone through a terrible experience and you really embarrassed her. That was bloody cruel! And I'll have you know I don't think of making love to her as a prize. She's not a damned wrestling match! Isabel's more to me than just some willing woman to be lain with.' He had said his piece and felt better for it.

Kitty, however, had not finished with him. 'I'm sorry for upsetting her, I didn't know about the drownings then. I'm glad you think something more of her than I've supposed of you but it was a shock to come in and see the two of you like that. 'Tis a good job I came home early and put an end to your scheme or you would have ruined the poor maid's life.'

'What are you talking about?' Nick said crossly, trying not to explode.

'Do I have to remind you that Isabel is betrothed to another man and will be married to him in a few weeks' time?'

'What of it?' Nick was acutely embarrassed and it cut him deep to have the beautiful moments with Isabel shattered and held up to criticism. What would have been a truly wonderful loving experience would have remained private between them, should have remained private. And what was Kitty talking about? Ruining Isabel's life? By making love to her? He had made love to many women and had never been accused of ruining their lives. And Isabel wasn't an innocent waiting for her wedding night… A tightly closed shutter sprang back in his mind. 'The next thing you'll be telling me is that she's a virgin.'

'She is,' Kitty said firmly.

He looked at her. 'Tell you that, did she?'

'No, she knows what I do for a living but we've never talked about such things. I've got to know Isabel very well since you turned up with her in my house that day. Nick, where men are concerned Isabel is totally innocent,' Kitty said emphatically, 'and very loyal. If anything happened between you, she could never bring herself to marry Richard Grenville. You would leave her feeling she'd betrayed him and hankering after you. And you're not about to offer her marriage, are you, Nick? Even if you did, think about it. What could you offer her? A life of wandering about, then when the babies came along setting her up in a poky little cottage somewhere and she rarely seeing you, thinking you probably resent her for curtailing your precious liberty. Is that the sort of life you would want for her? You'd be too proud to accept or borrow money from her, even to set yourself up in a business of some sort, and you wouldn't allow her to spend her money on supporting you both, would you, Nick?'

Nick listened attentively to every word that Kitty said, grim-faced, stiff-backed, with a mounting gloom. He stared at the night-blue sky, clear and cloudless, and for the first time he didn't feel free, comfortably, soulfully free, free to light up the world and leave it by morning like the pale yellow moon. There was no golden glow round the moon this evening, just a thick black circle.

'Isabel's a lady. She's used to a totally different world than we are. She's been born and bred to marry into her own kind and would not thank you for dragging her down. She talks of wanting to leave her old way of life behind when this trouble with the Kempthornes is over but her recent ordeals have blinded her to her good sense. Life is different and rather exciting despite the dangers, and like so many women who've come across you, Nick Nancarrow, she's fascinated by your good looks and strong character.' Kitty was out of breath and drew in the cool evening air. 'I believe 'twas a good thing I nipped things in the bud before they went too far between you. I'm very fond of Isabel, Nick. I don't want to see her hurt.'

It was a long time before he spoke. His voice was lost and sad. 'I've had women of Isabel's class before, they meant nothing to me and I was no more than a distraction to them. But I feel different about Isabel. She's different to any woman I've ever met... I should have known she had never lain with anyone before. I should have known Isabel's not a liar. It accounts for...'

'For?' Kitty could just see his face, it was easy to read. 'I see, so it nearly happened before.'

Nick stood up straight and paced the dew-covered grass in front of Kitty. He stopped and faced her. 'Just before we arrived at your house, Kitty. She shook me off, quite forcibly. Poor sweet Isabel. I offended her, I must have frightened her so much, yet she forgave me...'

Kitty got up from the cold stone and rubbed at her cloak. 'I know there's a special feeling between you and her, Nick. 'Tis only natural after what you've been through together.' She was sorry for him. What could she offer him? 'When things get back to normal, when Isabel's fiancé arrives and she gets married, perhaps you can keep some sort of friendship going.'

'Like training her coach horses?' He sounded bitter.

Kitty wound her arm round his. 'You will keep things on a proper footing from now on, Nick?'

'Aye,' he consented wearily, kicking the lowest step of the stile.

'We'd better get back to her and Benjamin before it gets dark. She must be awful upset, what with the drownings and you going off suddenly and me following you. We don't want her worrying about us. You are coming back?'

'I have to, for a little while. There's no doubt Isabel's in mortal danger from the Kempthornes. We have to decide what to do next, where's the safest place for her to stay.' His mind flew to Trevennor House, to the loathesome couple who held sway over it now, to Deborah's darkened face as he'd told her he would not be seeing her that evening. He thought of the contrast in her and her innocent honest cousin. He thought of the elderly gentleman on his deathbed. He whispered to the memory, 'You had no idea what you asked me to do, Laurence...'

–

Under that same pale moon, Edmund and Deborah Kempthorne were walking the short distance home from the parsonage. Although she had sulked all day because Nick would not be with her tonight, Deborah was aglow inside, having confided in Charlotte Thomas of her future wedding plans. The two women had discussed gowns and marriage duties and even nurseries, but Charlotte hadn't seemed enthusiastic and Deborah knew it was not just from the shock of her near death at the hands of Gyver Pengelly. Deborah hadn't cared much, she liked to gloat over the identity of her bridegroom, knowing every woman in the parish would wish to take her place, and if she had bored the parson's wife, that pleased her too – anything to make her life uncomfortable if Edmund was being spurned.

Edmund had been bored all evening. Deborah had inveigled the invitation and he had consented to attend in order to maintain their status in the village and in the hope of getting near Charlotte again. He had kept up the chit-chat with Perran Thomas, who seemed to have no more desire to have his company than Edmund did his, while Deborah had monopolized the attractive curate's wife. He was glad when it was time to leave and he could go to Mary Ellen.

Deborah suddenly gasped. A man was sprawled in a drunken heap in front of the gate to Trevennor House. It was Gyver Pengelly. He was splattered with mud and horse dung from a passing cart and his own vomit. He sensed someone was there and heaved himself to a sitting position. On seeing the Kempthornes, he filled the night air with obscenities, shouting at them to give him money for ale.

Deborah hastily looked up and down the village. No one else was about and she told Edmund to ignore the brute and hurry inside. Pengelly was furious.

'Yer not too proud t'talk to the likes of me when yer wants some dirty work done, woman!' he bawled, trying to get to his feet but falling back in a heap.

'What's he talking about?' Edmund asked, unafraid of Pengelly in his drunken state and curious enough to forget Mary Ellen for the moment.

'Take no notice of him, Edmund,' Deborah replied crossly. 'The man is drunk and an imbecile. Come, we will go in by the servants' entrance.'

'Where's Nancarrow tonight then, eh? With his other woman?'

Deborah went rigid, her face worked instantly from outrage to livid jealousy. She kicked Pengelly viciously on the shin.

'What do you mean by other woman?' she screamed at the top of her voice.

'The 'an'some lookin' woman I've seen un with,' Pengelly leered. 'Saw 'er meself only yes'day. A piece o' quality if ever I saw one too.'

'What woman?' Deborah shrieked, shaking alarmingly.

'For goodness sake, Deborah!' Edmund shouted at his sister. 'Can't you see he's only taunting you? How many ladies do you think Nancarrow's courting? He told you he's busy at Tehidy tonight and that should be good enough for you. Get inside the house at once and I'll get rid of this man. And be quiet, you'll wake up the whole village.'

Deborah could see Edmund was about to throw a bigger temper than she had. Still shaking with outrage, she stalked into the house without another word. Edmund's anger had caught Pengelly's attention. He looked up at the young gentleman through blinking eyes. Edmund threw some coins at him.

'Get to your feet,' he said icily, confident he had paid for Pengelly's co-operation. Any information he might gain would be useful to get rid of the fortune-hunting Nick Nancarrow when the time was right. 'If Nancarrow has another woman, you can tell me all about her and I'll be the one to deal with it.'

When Pengelly had got up, Edmund forgot his new kid gloves and pushed the shaking hulk up the road. He was not going to hold the conversation outside his own front door.

–

The road was hard and dry the next morning and Nick concentrated on the clip-clop of the horse Deborah had authorized for his use from the Trevennor stables. He had ridden through Portreath and was on the road near the coast at Reskajeage Downs. Before returning to his work at Tehidy, he was going to call on Charlie Chiverton.

The night before in Kitty's kitchen, he and Kitty had agreed that Isabel should remain where she was. Isabel had listened silently to the discussion. Her face had paled when Nick had told her he would be leaving almost immediately, but she had said nothing and kept her eyes on the table as her two companions settled her immediate future.

'There's no reason why folk round here should think she's anyone but who I said she is,' Kitty had insisted, glancing uneasily at Isabel's bowed head. She had never seen her so dejected. 'There's no reason why they should think Miss Isabel Hampton is still alive either.'

'What about Gyver Pengelly?' Nick asked. 'He's seen Isabel twice and he was almost certainly responsible for the coach accident. He was the one who said he saw her body and he knows that's a lie.'

'But even if he puts two and two together, and that's unlikely with his dumb brain, he can't admit it, he daren't talk about it. He would be hanged for being involved in the deaths of Phoebe Antiss and her companions. You haven't got time to take Isabel anywhere else, Nick, and you can't keep making up stories about who she is. Her fiancé will be home in two weeks. I think she'll be quite safe here, specially if she stays close to the house and keeps Benjamin company, and you keep an eye on the Kempthornes during that time.'

'Is that agreeable to you, Isabel?' Nick asked softly.

Isabel raised her head and said numbly, 'Perfectly.'

'Right then,' Nick said, getting up to go. 'I'll get Charlie to pass on a letter to you in a week's time.'

Nick had spent the night lying awake in a farmer's barn where he had obtained permission to stall his horse. He had gone over the days and nights spent on the cliffs with Isabel and over every minute spent in the boathouse in Penpol Creek. At dawn he had saddled up and left, his face drawn, his life suddenly feeling empty, and the thought of seeing Deborah Kempthorne again even more repugnant. He couldn't bear the thought of her cloying arms contaminating his neck and her cruel lips seeking his after kissing Isabel. But after he'd seen Charlie and done his day's work, for Isabel's sake, he'd have to endure it again.

–

Charlie Chiverton was up as early as Nick. Outside his clifftop home he stretched and yawned, cleaned his worn teeth with the side of a dirty finger and threw oats into the pot of water boiling over the outdoor fire for his breakfast. He rubbed his work-blackened hands in the fresh crisp air and screwed his bloodhound face at the sky to see what the weather would be like that day.

'A good day, cloud building up and rain by night, quite cold, I d'reckon,' he said to himself.

He broke off a piece of the outer rim of an abandoned wagon wheel he had found on the road and pulled out some of the spokes to encourage his fire. Then he wedged the remains of the wheel into his pile of firewood, marvelling at what some folk were careless enough to throw away.

He was sitting down on the bottom step of his shack with his bowl of porridge when he was brought back to his feet. He put his breakfast aside. Gyver Pengelly was striding towards him.

'An'what can I do fur thee, Gyver?' he said bluntly.

'Got a brew goin', 'ave 'ee, Charlie? 'Tes bloody damned cold an' I'm sure I can smell a kettle of tay,' Pengelly answered, squinting through his beaten face. There was dried blood on his black beard and even though Charlie wasn't given to cleanliness, he had never smelled anyone so foul before.

''Elp yerself,' Charlie said, sitting down with his porridge again. He passed Pengelly the wooden bowl that had been his wife's. 'There's oats in the pot.'

'Very civil of 'ee,' Pengelly muttered, helping himself to tea and porridge.

'What's brings you along 'ere then?'

'Oh, jus' out fur a bit of a walk.'

'You look like you've been through all the wars of the world.'

'Huh! 'Twas nothin'. I'll get my own back soon enough.'

'Bin doin' a spot of wrastling, so I've 'eard.'

Pengelly made a howling noise. 'I'll get that bastard an' all!'

'Nick knows 'ow to watch 'is back.'

'Well, we'll just 'ave t'see about that, won't we? Where's 'e to now?'

'Your guess is as good as mine.'

'Not with the wealthy bitch from Gwithian, I knaw that much.'

'Then you know more than me.'

Pengelly poured the dregs of the watery porridge down his throat, wiped his beard with the back of his hand and dropped the bowl down with a clatter. He looked at Charlie with a glint of amusement, paused over his mug of tea, grinned, then drank it down in one gulp with a mighty belch.

Charlie watched him carefully, fully alert even though he appeared quite relaxed.

Pengelly threw his mug so it hit the bowl. 'Tell me, Chiverton, do 'ee think p'raps Nancarrow was spendin' the night with that sharp-faced 'Ampton woman, though I must say she's a pretty wench in ordinary garb.'

Charlie made a mental note that his knife was readily to hand in his belt. He looked perplexed.

''Ampton woman, Gyver?'

'You d'knaw the one I'm talkin' about. The lady from Trurah who was s'posed to 'ave died in that coach smash back-along. Old man Trevennor's hoity-toity niece.'

'You been on the grog, Gyver?'

Pengelly smirked and spat. 'I reckon you know what I'm talkin' about. I said I saw 'er body down the cliffs but I lied. Miss Deb'rah Kem'thorne paid me well to get t'ridst of she. All the rest on the coach died but I never got round to seeing if she was dead. When word got round she must've gone over the cliff cus bits of her dress was found on the gorse, that's what I thought too an' that's why I said I saw 'er body, but of course there was no body.'

'Go on, Gyver, it seems you 'ave a story you want to tell,' Charlie said quietly.

'Last night I was talkin' to Mr Edmund Kem'thorne. We talked about the wench I saw with Nancarrow up on the cliffs near Portreath the mornin' after the coach wus wrecked. A tall woman, with soft brown 'air and a pleasing shape who talks well. Like the woman I saw with Nancarrow's whore at Crantock. Where else would Nancarrow suddenly get a woman from unless 'e 'ad rescued 'er from that fine gentry coach, does thee think, Charlie?'

Charlie put down his bowl and shrugged his shoulders. 'Even if what you say is true, 'tes no concern of mine.'

'Aw, I reckon you could tell me a thing or two about it.'

Charlie looked at the stinking hulk coldly. 'And what if I can?'

Pengelly rasped on his beard with one paw, and grinned. 'I 'aven't come 'ere after information, Chiverton.'

'Aye, I know that.'

The air was electric between them. Pengelly's hand went inside his waistcoat but Charlie got his knife out first. 'I wouldn't if I were you, Gyver. This knife 'as been sharpened on men's windpipes.'

Pengelly got clumsily to his feet and faced Charlie as he stood on the step. 'Now you wouldn't want to cut up an old friend, would you, Charlie?'

'You're friend to no one, Pengelly.'

'What do you think you're going to do, pointing that knife at me?' Pengelly laughed nervously.

'Get a bit of information out of you, Pengelly, if you don't want to feel the sharpness of it. Did Kempthorne pay you to kill me?'

'Now, Charlie, there's no need to talk like that.'

''E did, you ruddy swine. What's Kempthorne up to now?'

'How should I knaw?' Pengelly growled.

'You can't work out anythin' by yerself, can you, Pengelly! Kempthorne wants the 'Ampton woman to remain dead and wants any witnesses out of the way who can say diff'rent. I suppose 'e intended to send you on to Crantock after you'd finished with me. He's not the sort who could stomach doin' away with someone 'imself. Am I right?'

Pengelly's blotchy fearful eyes narrowed and he shouted a profanity. Then he turned his head and vomited over the fire. Charlie came down the steps and stood cautiously at his side, waiting for him to finish. But while he was still spewing, Pengelly whipped out his knife and lunged at the hand Charlie held his knife in. Charlie cried out as Pengelly's blade made a long inch-deep cut above his wrist and his own knife fell out of his grasp. Pengelly went in for the kill but Charlie hurled himself backwards and fell at the foot of the steps.

Pengelly stood over him and laughter roared from his belly. 'Not quick enough fur me that time, Chiverton.' He wiped his hairy chin. 'And do forgive me awful manners.'

Charlie's eyes bored into Pengelly's while he pulled off his neckerchief and wound it round his slashed arm.

'Not much point in doin' that,' Pengelly boomed. 'I'm gonna give thee a few cuts to join un.'

'You're not man enough,' Charlie spat.

'Well, I'll just see 'ow loud you can squeal.'

Charlie was counting on the fact that Pengelly would want to torture him to death rather than despatch him with one swift throw of the knife. He read the human hulk right. Pengelly came at him with the knife tight in his fist ready to plunge into his gut. Charlie held his breath and waited. When Pengelly was bending forward close to him, the knife an inch away from his vitals, Charlie brought his two feet up into Pengelly's huge middle and thrust him away.

Pengelly staggered back. He kept hold of his knife but a moment later he was howling and gagging on his own blood. He had fallen back onto one of the strong wooden spokes of the wagon wheel and it had entered deep into his back.

Charlie flung himself to his feet and knocked the knife from Pengelly's hand. 'Looks like I've got the advantage now, Gyver,' he said, friendly like, but with a grim face.

Pengelly struggled to get off the spoke. It wasn't a pleasant noise that reached Charlie's ears. 'Help… me,' Pengelly pleaded.

'Yes, I'll help you. It'll be a pleasure. This is for the folk on the coach and the danger you've put Miss Isabel Hampton in.'

With that Charlie's face looked like a friendly puppy's, but it betrayed his intentions. Pengelly's eyes grew to twice their size as slowly Charlie raised his foot. Pengelly howled in terror. Then Charlie put his foot on Pengelly's chest and plunged it forward.

Chapter 23

Nick had headed his horse across the clifftop from the road and was trotting back along the route he had taken with Isabel from Charlie's shack when he saw the little man running towards him. Nick picked up speed and, when he reached Charlie, threw himself from the horse.

He grabbed Charlie by the shoulders, dwarfing him as though he was a little boy come to him hurt. Charlie was panting and there was blood seeping from his arm and blood across his shirt front. 'What's happened, Charlie?'

'Gyver… Pengelly… tried to kill me… Isabel Hampton's in danger… the Kempthornes know she's alive…'

Nick exhaled a long breath. 'Where's Pengelly now?'

'Over the cliff… with a wagon spoke through un. 'E was some powerful man to drag…'

'Thank heavens he's dead! But are you hurt badly, Charlie?'

'Naw, 'ad worse 'n' this out workin'. I'll stitch it up meself later. Never mind me, boy. I was on my way to Crantock to warn the women. I take it you'll be going there now. What do 'ee want me to do?'

'You go on to Gwithian,' Nick said, tightening the kerchief to stem the bleeding from Charlie's arm. 'If you go to the parsonage, I'm sure Charlotte Thomas will bathe and bandage this and from there you can see what the Kempthornes are up to. I'll go back to Crantock and get Isabel away to safety and have someone come to stand guard over Kitty and her brother.'

Miles away along the coast Isabel trudged her way wearily through the sand dunes. She was heading, almost without realizing it, for one particular spot on the cliff. It would have been quicker to go along the beach and climb up, but she was in no hurry to get there, or back to Kitty's sympathetic looks and soothing words and Benjamin's quiet understanding of yesterday's events.

She had hardly spoken a word to Kitty since the other woman had torn a strip off her and Nick for kissing in her kitchen and she wished she did not have to stay under Kitty's roof for these last few days until Richard arrived home. It wasn't that Isabel was ungrateful to Kitty for her shelter and friendship, she knew that everything Kitty had done was in her best interests. But Kitty had cheated her out of the crowning moment of her life, and Isabel had nothing to say to her. It was unbearable. Not until she could get away from Crantock and resume some semblance of her old life would she be able to try to forget the man she loved so desperately.

All was quiet and lonely up on the cliff. There were no wheeling birds today to give her a sense of freedom. She was out in the open, all the wildness of Nature about her, but she was a prisoner. Prisoner to her future, prisoner to her memories of Nick's kisses and caresses, her want and need for him. Their rapturous moments together yesterday had been spoiled and he would not bother to recapture them against Kitty's watchful eye or disapproval. When he had left last night, he had given her only a polite goodbye. Those moments could not have meant the same to him as they had to her.

Isabel was now on the spot where she had stood with Nick and watched the waves race one another in a frenzy onto Crantock beach. The depth of her pain was almost too much to bear, but she could not move from this bitter-sweet spot. She was rooted in the memory of a moment too wonderful.

She heard a dog barking and smiled fondly. Talland had come after her. He bounded into sight and lay at her feet, caught for a moment in her desolation. Then he lifted his head and leapt up, edging close to Isabel. She looked round to see what had startled him. Moments later a figure came into view, following the way they had come. She saw at once it wasn't Nick; she watched intently and her breath caught in her throat when she recognized who it was.

–

Deborah Kempthorne had not had a wink of sleep all night. Despite Edmund's reassurances that he had spoken at length to Gyver Pengelly before seeing him out of the village and Pengelly had said he was only taunting her, Deborah was intensely jealous of the very thought that Nick had another woman. She had wanted to send someone over to Tehidy and see if Nick was really there but Edmund had put his foot down and refused to allow her to give the order. He had pointed out she would ruin everything with Nick Nancarrow if he knew he was being spied on and surely she didn't want to risk that. He would be off on his travels again, and a handsome man like Nick would soon wheedle his way into another wealthy lady's affections. But Deborah wasn't going to leave things there. She would demand Nick give up his job at Tehidy and move into Trevennor House and be in charge of the stables where she could keep her eye on him at all times, and she would do away with his uncharacteristic coyness about sharing her bed.

She was going to tighten her grip on Nick and reassert the hold she had over her brother. Edmund and Mary Ellen had had a vociferous quarrel last night ending with him storming off and sleeping in another room. He had gone out early this morning and Deborah had seen him talking to a village wench; presumably he was off somewhere now making up for his lost night. Now would be a good time to go to Mary Ellen's room and try to bribe or threaten her out of the house and out of Edmund's life.

Deborah made her way along the short corridor and tried Mary Ellen's door. The child had just gone to breakfast with her nursemaid and Mrs Christopher, so her mother would be quite alone.

Mary Ellen was heavily asleep, and by the strong smell of brandy in the room, under the spirit's influence. Deborah closed the door softly and moved to look down on her. She took a vicious pleasure in seeing the first wrinkles appearing around Mary Ellen's usually splendid eyes, a few grey roots in her wealth of shining hair. In a few years' time Edmund would be looking for someone younger; getting rid of Mary Ellen would do him a favour, he could remember her as she was.

Deborah prodded her arm and whispered, 'Mary Ellen…'

The other woman did not stir. Deborah moved closer and shook her. Mary Ellen was too deeply asleep and the smell of brandy was all about her. Deborah looked at the nearly empty bottle.

'How much of this did you drink?' she hissed irritably.

There would be no bargain made with this woman today. Even if Edmund stayed out all day, Mary Ellen would have such a massive hangover she wouldn't be capable of understanding any proposition. Deborah looked at her closely. There was a certain hardness on the pretty face which Deborah knew was reflected on her own. Mary Ellen would not give up her man easily, one who was also the father of her child. She was probably hoping Edmund would marry her some day, perhaps for the child's sake, and set her up as a lady. She would never let go of Edmund. She would run straight to him and tell him of any attempt to pay her off, and Edmund would be furious. But Deborah couldn't let anyone else have one of her men.

She held Mary Ellen by the shoulders and shook her violently. The only response was a rolling of the head and a small moan. Deborah let her fall back on the pillows. She stood still for a few moments listening for sounds of anyone moving about upstairs, but all was quiet. The only sound was Mary Ellen's heavy breathing in the dark clammy room.

Deborah set her face and pulled a pillow out from under Mary Ellen's head. She put the pillow down over her face and pressed hard. It was so easy. Resistance came only at the end when Mary Ellen put up her arms and clutched desperately at Deborah's, but only for a moment. Even when all resistance stopped and Mary Ellen's arms fell down to the bed, Deborah kept the pillow where it was for another few minutes, just to be sure.

She put the pillow back under Mary Ellen's limp head and tidied her hair round her blue face. Mary Ellen looked quite peaceful apart from her colour.

Deborah left the room but kept her hand on the door and looked back into it. 'Mary Ellen!' she called out. 'Are you awake yet? I want to talk to you about that child of yours.' Deborah waited, as if for a reply. Then she mumbled, 'Drunk again, I'll have to leave it until later.' She added to herself, and I might just take your daughter for a little walk later this morning, it's time I took an interest in her...

–

Nick charged into Kitty's kitchen where she was stirring soup on her brick oven. He grabbed her arms and whirled her round. A spoon clattered on the floor and Kitty gave a cry and stared at him dumbly.

'Where's Isabel? Where is she? In her room, in with Benjamin?' There was a hopeful note in his voice but the urgency in it alarmed her.

'Why? What's the matter?'

Nick gave her an impatient shake, making her tawny eyes grow in size. 'For goodness sake, Kitty! Where is she?'

'Out walking. I tried to keep her inside but she was determined to go. I can't keep her locked up.' Kitty was alarmed now. 'What's happened, Nick?'

He let her go and rushed to the door. 'Which way did she go?'

'I don't know,' Kitty wailed. 'She hasn't spoken much since yesterday. I just let her go, Nick. It would have done no good making her mope round the house all day.' Kitty ran after him and she grabbed him by his jacket. 'What's happened? Is it the Kempthornes? Are they after her?'

'Not yet I hope, but they know she's alive and living here. Charlie was attacked by Gyver Pengelly a short while ago and Pengelly was paid by the Kempthornes to come here and kill Isabel.' Kitty stifled another cry. 'Charlie's hurt and Pengelly's dead but I'm worried the Kempthornes might have sent someone else here to make sure Pengelly does his job properly. You pack her things, Kitty. I'll find Isabel and get her away from here as soon as possible.'

Outside, Nick thought hard. He pictured the solitary boathouse at Penpol Creek. But would Isabel go there alone so soon after the drownings?

'Talland went off through the dunes a little while ago,' Kitty said. 'He usually follows Isabel.'

'I'll search the dunes and the cliff and pray to God she went that way. If she comes back before I do, make her stay in her room and lock the doors.'

–

'Good morning to you, Isabel. If I may say so, you look exceedingly well for a corpse.'

'How did you find me?'

'By means of a mutual acquaintance of ours. A miscreant by the name of Gyver Pengelly. He was spitting fire about another acquaintance of ours – Nick Nancarrow. He talked about Nancarrow having a woman. I questioned him and realized it was you. Pengelly was able to tell me where you were.'

Isabel was amazed at how calm she felt. She looked steadily ahead. 'How did you find your way along here?'

'I watched your friend's house – a pretty woman, incidentally, who does service for some gentlemen I know. I saw you leave her house. I didn't want you to see me so I waited a while and happily the dog followed you and I followed him. I was curious to see you, dear cousin, but I confess I am even more curious to learn why you thought it necessary to fake your own death and disappear these past few weeks. You even missed our dear late uncle's funeral.'

Isabel lifted her head higher and said coolly, 'Uncle Laurence believed I was in danger from you and Deborah. Was he justified in his suspicions, Edmund?'

Edmund smiled at her with boyish charm and then feigned a look of hurt. 'What a thing to say, Isabel. I know you and Deborah did not like each other,' he smiled again, adding a hint of malice, 'but I thought you and I were not averse to each other's company.'

He moved two steps closer. Isabel stood her ground. She felt uneasy but was not afraid. She knew the cliffs better than Edmund, knew the best way to move quickly over the wild terrain, and she had Talland with her. He was a big dog, could be fierce and protective. He had positioned himself between her and Edmund, his body alert and his ears pricked.

Isabel studied Edmund. He was dressed in soft muted colours with a lacy neckcloth, silk shirt, buttons all over his long-tailed coat, thick braid adorning its wide cuffs. Only his leather riding boots with strong soles were suitable for travel across the cliffs. He took off his feathered blue tricorn hat and held it lazily in one hand. He was a handsome man, she could not deny it, and his look of steady determination in place of suave sophistication enhanced his refined features today.

His dark eyes emerged from the secretive shadows of their lids and slowly looked her over from head to foot. Clearly, Edmund approved of what he saw.

'You've changed, Isabel,' he said in a voice that drifted towards her.

'More than you can possibly imagine, Edmund,' she replied. 'You have too.'

'It must be because I'm living off the old man's money. Deborah and I were looking forward to making use of yours as well – until now.'

'It has given you a certain air of confidence,' she said, keeping her chin high.

'I enjoy living at Trevennor House,' Edmund drawled. 'It's not as grand as your mansion in Truro but we intend to move in there when all the legal matters have been finalized.'

He spoke as if Isabel were actually dead. Her uneasiness broke into a tiny burn of fear. She looked at Talland then back at Edmund with an unspoken warning in her eyes. He glanced at the dog who growled threateningly. Edmund smiled smugly, put his cane in front of his feet and rested both hands nonchalantly on it.

Everything was so still. Isabel could hear her own breathing and heart pounding and the small clicking noises Edmund was making with his tongue inside slightly parted bps.

'Do you know, Isabel, my dear,' he said, his voice sultry, 'I have always believed you were a rather beautiful creature under your haughty exterior. Looking at you now, I can see I was correct. It seems that living a rough life among the common people and taking in all this fresh sea air has agreed with you.'

'How kind of you to say so,' she returned acidly.

'Are you still untouched?'

Isabel did not dignity the question with an answer. A few days ago she might have blushed but after being disturbed with Nick by Kitty, she felt immune to maidenly embarrassment.

'I was thinking of the time you must have spent getting to know Nick Nancarrow,' Edmund went on lazily. 'My sister was all over him from the day of the old man's funeral. It seems women find him irresistible. Is that how you find him, Isabel?'

'It is no concern of yours, Edmund, if I have lain with half the men of the village of Crantock.'

Edmund straightened his back and their eyes locked. He said spitefully, 'He has had quite a passionate affair with Deborah.'

Isabel pursed her lips, put her head to one side and smiled wryly.

Edmund laughed. 'So you don't believe me. Well, I suppose she is too awful for that sort of sacrifice, even to save your precious life…'

The last three words hung in the air. Isabel did not move a muscle.

'Are you paying him well to keep a watchful eye on us, Isabel?'

'No, Nick is looking out for me because Uncle Laurence asked him to shortly before he died.'

'How unfortunate that he found you alive at the coach accident and chose to keep you that way.'

'I take it you paid that Pengelly brute to wreck the Antiss coach and bring about my murder?' Isabel said harshly.

'No, that wasn't me, cousin, but Deborah. I would not have been so calculating, I would have been content simply to have tried to relieve you of part of your fortune in some other way.'

'And what do you intend to do now, Edmund?'

He grinned, flashing his teeth. 'Kill you, of course.'

Ice gripped Isabel's heart, but she asked resolutely, 'Why?'

'Because I have to, simple as that. It is a pity to have to do it.' Edmund shuddered violently. Isabel was surprised at its intensity. His voice changed to a pained, childish whimper. 'Deborah's idea failed and I came here to make certain Gyver Pengelly did not fail me, but for some reason he hasn't appeared yet. Deborah doesn't know I'm here, she'd only interfere. She'd be so jealous to know that Nick Nancarrow is involved with you. I have to be sure you really die this time, Isabel, sure for myself. But I hate death, hate the very thought of it. I could never crush a beetle or even swat a fly. I hate the sight of anything dead.'

'Then why kill me?' Isabel attacked his fears. 'It will only haunt you.'

'I couldn't do it except for one reason.'

'Whatever the reason is, Edmund, can't we talk about it? There must be some sort of arrangement we can come to. You've said I've changed. Yes, I have, so much so that I can never go back to my old way of life. I don't want to live in a mansion and wear the finest clothes and go to balls any more. I want only a simple life. I'll agree to anything that you want—'

'No!' Edmund snarled, his face growing ugly. 'I want you dead and out of the way for Morenwyn. I don't trust you, any more than you could trust me or my revolting sister. I won't risk going back to being poor again ever! I want my daughter to live the way you were brought up. She's the only person I care about, the only one I love, and I'll do anything for Morenwyn. Anything!' He threw his cane down.

Talland moved towards him and growled. Edmund placed his hat carefully on the ground; he seemed oblivious of the dog and kept his eyes on Isabel. He stabbed a finger at her. 'I'd even kill someone. You!'

Isabel jumped back and Talland snarled. 'I'll tell the dog to attack you if you don't go away from me at once!' she screamed.

She didn't have to give Talland the order, he lurched forward at the sound of her distress. Edmund pulled a small pistol from inside his coat. Isabel screamed. Talland leapt and Edmund's hand was thrust upwards; the pistol went off and was sent spinning away. It hit the ground and slid to the cliff edge where it fell onto a rocky ledge a few feet below. The shot had sounded in Talland's ear and in agony he ran off yelping.

Isabel could see the pistol but she reckoned Edmund was probably too frightened to climb down after it. Her one chance lay in the fact that she was fitter than he was and could most likely outrun him.

She was unprepared for him snatching up his cane and lashing it cruelly across her legs. She lost her balance and fell, landing heavily on firm grassy ground dotted with small rocks. She was dazed but pulled herself upright and held her shoulder.

Edmund stood in front of her, gloating. 'I still have the advantage, cousin. It's over the cliff for you. I never intended to shoot you. The gun was to encourage you to move to a convenient spot on the cliff where I could push you off. I don't want to have to look at you after you've met your end.'

Isabel shook her head to clear the dark floating spots before her eyes. Her voice came breathlessly. 'You won't be able to coax me to go anywhere. You are too used to soft living, Edmund. I am probably just as strong as you are.'

Edmund jabbed the end of his cane painfully into her chest. 'But I do have the advantage of this, Isabel, my dear.' He made another vicious attack on her legs and she screamed, drawing her knees up tightly. 'Try running away from me now,' he laughed. A salacious smile spread over his face and she instinct-ively wrapped her arms round her legs. 'Nothing can save you now. Your death is certain this time but before I do anything about that I'm going to beat you almost senseless so you can't struggle and then I'll indulge myself. If Nancarrow hasn't—'

'Get away from me!' Isabel shouted, snatching up a big stone and hurling it at him.

It hit him in the chest. Before he could use the cane again, Isabel grabbed another rock but Edmund was too alert and knocked it out of her hand. She cried out and he raised the cane to bring it down across her head.

Isabel made to defend herself and as she looked up at him her eyes widened. 'Nick!'

Edmund chuckled, a horrible throaty noise. 'Oh, you can't fool me like that, my dear. I'm not going to turn round so you can kick out or bring a rock down on my head.'

His expression turned to one of horror when he was hauled violently off his feet by the back of his coat collar.

Chapter 24

Edmund was choking and turning purple before Nick hurled him down to land some distance from Isabel with a body-jarring thump. Nick picked up the cane, broke it in two over his knee with an angry grunt and threw the pieces down.

'Laurence was right about you disgusting Kempthornes!' Nick shook with rage. He lifted Isabel to her feet and held her protectively round the waist without taking his eyes off Edmund for an instant. 'I'm going to get the law on you, Kempthorne. I'm going to make sure you hang.'

Edmund sat where he'd landed and rubbed at a bruised arm but he was smirking. 'No one would believe you, Nancarrow, the word of a common drifter against a gentleman.'

'They'd believe me,' Isabel cried, clinging to Nick with one hand and pointing the other at Edmund. 'I'll tell them the whole story about how Uncle Laurence asked Nick to take care of me because he was afraid that you and Deborah would harm me. I'll tell the authorities everything you've just told me.'

'I won't let you deny my daughter her rightful place in society,' Edmund snarled, his face livid and ugly.

'You'd have done that yourself soon enough anyway,' Nick said in sharp, clipped tones. 'You'd have gambled it all away and left Morenwyn with nothing.'

'I would not!' screeched Edmund. 'How dare you talk about her, she means nothing to you! I want everything for Morenwyn and that means her money,' he jabbed a taut finger at Isabel, 'and I'll make sure Morenwyn gets it.'

Edmund got slowly to his feet, his nostrils flaring, his breathing heavy. Then quick as a weasel he charged them with his head down, arms spread out, trying to ram their bodies towards the cliff edge.

Nick swept Isabel aside but he was caught by Edmund's sweeping arm and sent to the ground. Edmund howled in rage at his failure and made for the cliff edge. Nick was puzzled until Isabel shouted, 'There's a gun on the ledge down there.'

Nick got quickly to his feet. He was faster and more steady moving than Edmund, he grabbed Edmund's arm and struggled to hold him. They slipped precariously to the cliff edge, barely keeping their balance.

Her heart pounding, Isabel edged closer to the men, looking for an opportunity to help Nick.

Nick pulled Edmund to the ground, trying to pin down his arms but his own arm ended up under Edmund's body, pressed agonizingly on a sharp-edged piece of rock. Nick cried out and lost his grip. Edmund scuttled away, intent only on getting his gun. Desperation lent him courage and he lowered himself down onto the ledge while Nick scrambled to his feet. As he advanced on his quarry, Edmund snatched up his gun and pointed it at Nick's chest with a leer on his face.

'You die, Nancarrow!'

With his eyes fixed on the gun, Nick shouted, 'Get back, Isabel, run to safety.'

She did not move.

Nick launched himself at Edmund's body and Edmund fired. The bullet seared Nick's shoulder. He didn't feel the pain or the bruises he received where he hit the narrow ledge of rock, ending up with Edmund's legs pinned under his chest. The gun flew out of Edmund's hand, down into the ocean.

The upper part of Edmund's body was hanging out over the cliff. Below him the rushing waves thundered into the black rock a hundred feet below. Edmund struggled and squealed in abject terror. Nick grabbed his belt with his good arm but with Edmund flailing about he could not get a good grip.

'Keep still, Kempthorne,' he warned, but his breath had been knocked out of him and his voice was barely audible.

Edmund screamed and screamed. He could not hear Nick, or Isabel as she shouted to him to stop struggling. The beat of his heart pounded in his ears, his face filled with blood. Wave after wave of terror engulfed his brain. He couldn't breathe. He gulped for air. His bulging eyes could see only the foaming ocean, his ears could hear only the roar of the sea. If the water did not get him, the rocks would. Deadly, enormous, they were inviting him to come down and die on them. He screamed for Deborah.

Isabel tore off her cloak, hitched up her skirts and climbed down to Nick. She got on her knees beside him. Edmund's wild struggles were making him slip from Nick's desperate hold; with each crazed movement he was working free. Isabel got a handful of Edmund's coat and then cried out as it was torn from her and Edmund disappeared from sight.

Cautiously she looked over the ledge. Nick wriggled forward and followed her gaze. They stared in shock and disbelief at the bloody sight of Edmund's body, half on a rock, half in the ocean.

Nick gathered himself up and taking Isabel's hand led her up onto safer ground. He picked up Edmund's abandoned hat and they retreated inland from the cliff edge for a few yards, then sank to the ground. Nick lay on his back with his eyes closed. Isabel rested her head on his chest and he put his battered arms about her.

'Are you hurt badly, Nick?' she asked after a moment.

He opened his eyes and traced a finger along her furrowed brow. She looked into the shade of blue that no depth of sea or sky could match. 'Thank God you're safe,' he breathed. He gingerly touched the wound on his arm and winced, then grinned. Isabel's heart went out to him. ''Tisn't too bad,' he said. 'No bullet in it, just scored the skin.' He gently ran his finger down Isabel's cheek. 'Don't worry, I'll live. What about you? Are you all right?'

'Yes, I wasn't hurt,' she said with a soft smile.

'You're forgetting this.' Nick tenderly touched the grazed and bruised swelling on her temple. 'You've collected a lot of bumps and bruises over the last few weeks.'

'It's nothing. I am not as soft as I was in the old days.'

'The old days… they were only a few weeks ago, seems like years now.' He became very serious. 'I was worried out of my mind about you, that I wouldn't get here in time…'

'How did you know Edmund had found out about me?'

Nick told her about Charlie's fight and Gyver Pengelly's demise. Isabel shuddered but wasn't sorry about the brute's fate.

'Is it all over now, Nick?'

'Nearly, Isabel, nothing can hurt you now. You can come back from the dead. There's only that witch, Deborah Kempthorne, to face and that will be a pleasure.' Nick picked up Edmund's hat which he had thrown onto the ground beside him. 'And it will be a pleasure giving her this,' he added grimly, twirling it on his fingers before tossing it away from them.

Isabel laid her head back on his chest and he held her close. 'It's all over so suddenly.'

'Aye,' Nick said soberly, 'all over…'

Isabel felt a lump in her throat and clung to him tighter.

A few minutes later they were walking back to Kitty's. They did not touch. Neither spoke. Nick walked with his head down, his hands behind his back holding Edmund's hat. Their steps were slow, as if they wanted the short journey to last for ever.

Kitty ran to meet them from her doorway, hopping about as she hugged them both. They told her what had happened and she ushered them inside like a broody hen and filled them with tea and brandy and bathed their wounds.

'At last you're Miss Isabel Hampton again,' Kitty said as she gently wiped a clean cloth over Isabel's grazed temple. 'Be funny not calling you Jenna anymore.'

'Well, make sure you call me Isabel. I'm not Miss Hampton to you, Kitty,' Isabel said.

'You must send word to Richard Grenville's aunts, let them know you're really alive and well.'

'Yes, I suppose I must,' she replied, but she could only meet Kitty's elation with a sinking heart. Nick glanced at her then looked away.

'So you're off to Gwithian in a little while, the pair of you, to tell Deborah Kempthorne the game's up?' Kitty said to Nick.

'Aye.' He looked steadily at Isabel. While they were here, she was still under his care, dead in the sea as far as the Grenville family were concerned. 'We need a little time to recover first.'

Kitty hovered about, not leaving Isabel and Nick alone, but Isabel knew there was nothing they could say to each other that would change anything. She said forlornly, 'Ben's awake, I think I'll go in and talk to him for a little while.'

–

Trevennor House had had an unexpected visitor earlier that morning. Mrs Christopher opened the door to a young man who stood somewhat nervously on the back kitchen doorstep. Mrs Christopher was in something of a flap and it didn't help to have a stranger in rather foreign dress suddenly turning up. 'Yes, what is it? Did the doctor send you here?'

'Doctor? No, I believe me sister's living here and I wondered if I could see her.'

'Sister? What's her name?'

'Mary Ellen Leddra. I'm her brother, James.'

Mrs Christopher gasped and clapped her hands to her bosom. Tears filled her eyes.

'She does live here, doesn't she?' James asked in alarm.

Mrs Christopher could only nod.

'Has something happened to her?'

'She's dead,' Mrs Christopher whispered. 'I'm afraid she was found… I'm sorry…'

'Dead? But how? What happened?' James shook his head disbelievingly. 'I don't understand.' His face set grim, he put his hand on the door frame and lifted a foot over the doorstep. 'Can I come in?'

Mrs Christopher nodded and showed James into the main kitchen where the rest of the servants were gathered in a stunned huddle. They had been discussing Mary Ellen's sudden death when James had knocked on the door.

'This is Miss Mary Ellen's brother,' Mrs Christopher informed them, drying her tears on a well-pressed handkerchief. 'She told me she had a brother.' She turned to James and motioned him to sit at the huge table. 'You're a sailor, I can tell by your appearance.'

James ignored the invitation to sit down. 'What happened to Mary Ellen?' he whispered, bitterly regretting now that he had not called on her the last time he had come to Gwithian.

'It only happened a short time ago,' Mrs Christopher explained, looking about guiltily as though she was afraid she might be overheard. 'The doctor's just left. She died in her sleep, so the doctor said. It's what Miss Deborah, she's the lady who owns the house jointly with her brother since Mr Trevennor died a few weeks ago, well, she suggested that to the doctor and he agreed with her.'

'Suggested? You don't sound convinced that's the truth.'

'Well, Dorcas there,' Mrs Christopher pointed to a maid who was peeping through a door that led to the rest of the house, 'she saw Miss Deborah at Miss Mary Ellen's bedroom door, calling to her that she wanted to speak to her about her little maid, Morenwyn. Dorcas went into Miss Mary Ellen to draw back the curtains and let in the fresh air, that's how Miss Mary Ellen likes – liked to start the morning, in a nice bright room, and to see if she wanted her breakfast in bed. But Dorcas had a bad fright. Miss Mary Ellen was dead, all gone blue in the face, but as warm as you and me. Dorcas was so shocked she couldn't call out or move for ages, she just sat there with Miss Mary Ellen and that's when she saw this in her hand.'

Mrs Christopher held out a tiny scrap of lace. 'It's from Miss Deborah's dress, the new one she only wore for the first time today. Dorcas ran to me at once. I told the mistress and she sent for the doctor. We wanted to see what he would say but he wasn't much interested and soon left. All of us here think Miss Deborah could have done away with Miss Mary Ellen and we were just discussing what to do about it. We're all for walking out on the Kempthornes but we don't want no trouble from Mr Edmund. He might even accuse one of us of killing Miss Mary Ellen but not one of us would have harmed her, she was always pleasant to all of us.'

James had listened to the housekeeper with his head in his hands. 'I should have come before,' he groaned, sinking down on a nearby chair. 'I didn't know whether to or no with Mary Ellen moving out of St Ives to this grand house. I thought she might not have wanted a ragbag brother turning up and spoiling things for her. I'm off to sea again in a day or two and it didn't seem right to just go off. I thought I'd come and ask at the kitchens about her. I never expected...'

'I'm so sorry,' Mrs Christopher said, biting her lip. 'If only Nick Nancarrow was here. He'd know what to do.'

James looked up sharply. 'Nick Nancarrow?'

'Do you know Nick?' Mrs Christopher asked, her face showing that her hopes were rising.

'Aye, I do, he saved my life a few weeks ago. My ship went down on the rocks at Trevellas Porth.'

'When was this exactly?'

James pinpointed the day and Mrs Christopher frowned. 'Wonder what he was doing there? That's two days after Mr Trevennor died. Nick disappeared straight afterwards and didn't reappear until the funeral.'

James looked about uneasily and Mrs Christopher raised an eyebrow, but he had nothing more to say, he had promised not to mention seeing Nick with his young woman friend and had said too much already. 'Do you think this Miss Deborah will let me see Mary Ellen and my niece?'

'I don't know. She's a terrible woman,' Mrs Christopher bleated, beginning to cry again, and the other servants echoed her last remark.

Wenna Sweet, the cook, continued, 'Since the body was discovered, Miss Deborah's ordered Morenwyn's nurse to sit with Miss Mary Ellen and has kept Morenwyn close beside her. We've all been keeping an eye on her, we don't trust her, you see. We're waiting for Mr Edmund to come home.' Wenna Sweet coloured. 'That's the little maid's father. He adores her and would never hurt her. Then we thought we'd all leave.'

James looked at each of the servants and they all nodded it was their intention to leave. 'Well, if there's the smallest chance that woman might hurt my niece I won't let her stay in this house.' He got to his feet with a loud scraping of chair legs.

Mrs Christopher's face creased with worry.

'But—'

'Quick!' Dorcas said from the doorway. 'She's trying to get Morenwyn to put her cloak on. She says she's taking her out to meet her mother!'

James pushed past Dorcas and ran the length of a long passageway to confront Deborah Kempthorne. Morenwyn was wailing that she didn't want to go outside and Deborah was pulling and pushing her, insisting that she should obey.

'She's not going anywhere with you!' James cried.

'Who on earth are you? How dare you enter my house!' Deborah shrieked.

'My name's James Leddra, brother of the little maid's dead mother and that makes her my niece. I'm not satisfied with what the doctor said about Mary Ellen's death and I'll not have Morenwyn staying under this roof or going anywhere with you.' Morenwyn ran to Mrs Christopher who picked her up and hurried her away to the kitchen, the rest of the servants putting themselves in one united body in front of them.

'You have no right to come in here and say such things or make demands. The child is my brother's child and in his absence I am in charge of her. Get out of my house at once, all of you,' she screamed at the servants. 'You're all dismissed! And leave the child here with me.'

'Not on your life,' James said menacingly. 'She'll not meet the same fate as her mother did today at your vile hands, woman.'

'I could have you jailed for saying such a thing to me. Get out! Get out all of you!'

'Aye, we're only too happy to go,' Mrs Christopher said bitterly, peeping over the other servants' shoulders. 'And we're taking Morenwyn with us. You're a cruel, evil woman, Deborah Kempthorne, and I pray justice will be done and you'll come to a bad end.'

'I'll have you hanged for kidnapping. Now get out! Get out! *Get out!*'

When James, Mrs Christopher, Morenwyn and the rest of the servants were assembled outside the front gate of Trevennor House, James said, 'That woman is mad, if you ask me.'

'Mad and evil,' Mrs Christopher said with passion.

'Will she come after us?'

'No, I don't think she'll be able to. I've seen her get in a rage like that before and it will bring on such a bad headache she won't be good for anything for hours. I've got a suggestion to make, James Leddra. We can't stand like this out in the cold. Let's go next door to the parsonage. The curate's wife is a good and sensible woman, she'll know what we ought to do and Morenwyn will be happy and safe playing with her little ones.'

Charlotte Thomas was not shocked to see so many people trooping up to her front door looking for refuge. She had half expected the servants at Trevennor House to walk out en masse since the Kempthornes had moved in but she was shocked at their tale of Mary Ellen's death. Perran was out on parish business but she took charge with confidence, knowing she could appeal to Edmund Kempthorne's better side when he finally came back. She knew he would be devastated that his sister could have murdered his mistress. She sent a stable boy with a letter to the constable at Hayle informing him of the suspicious death.

The servants of Trevennor House were uncomfortable standing about in the parsonage parlour, so Mrs Christopher sent them to the kitchens to help with the parsonage staff's duties, warning them sternly not to go outside the house. Morenwyn, who was fidgety and anxious, was taken upstairs with her nursemaid by Charlotte and settled in the nursery with her own brood.

When Charlotte returned, Mrs Christopher said, 'We can't thank you enough, Mistress Thomas. You don't know what it's been like these past few weeks, Mr Trevennor would turn in his grave.' And she burst into tears.

Charlotte comforted her and looked at a thoughtful James Leddra. When she caught his eye, he apologized. 'Sorry, ma'am, but I was wondering if the portrait in the hall of Trevennor House is of the late Mr Trevennor.'

'Yes, it is,' Charlotte answered. 'It was painted many years ago when Mr Trevennor was a young man. Why do you ask?'

James had Charlotte and Mrs Christopher's full attention. 'You're all friends of Nick Nancarrow's, aren't you?' he said uncertainly.

'Yes,' Mrs Christopher replied, frowning in curiosity. 'I've known him since he was born and raised here in Gwithian. His father was Mr Trevennor's coachman and Nick grew up to be very close to my late master. What's this all about, James Leddra?'

'I saw someone with Nick on the day of the shipwreck, a tall, pretty woman with the same features and same colour eyes and hair as the man in that portrait.'

Mrs Christopher was puzzled then stunned. She looked at Charlotte in disbelief. 'Miss Isabel!'

'She told me her name was Jenna Stevens but there was no mistaking she had a lady's bearing and a good voice under the one she used. Nick asked me to keep quiet about seeing them together.'

'Miss Isabel's alive!'

Charlotte thought things over out loud. 'Mr Trevennor spoke privately to Nick just before he died. Nick disappeared soon afterwards. Miss Isabel was said to have died the same day but her body was never found. Gyver Pengelly said he saw her body but he can't be trusted. You know a ring was missing from Mr Trevennor's bedchamber on the day of his death, Mrs Christopher, and you assumed one of the Kempthornes had taken it but it was returned to its place on the day of the funeral, the day Nick was back. And our gardener said Gyver Pengelly was spouting about Nick having a fine woman when they wrestled that day behind the alehouse.'

Mrs Christopher took over. 'And Nick's been acting some peculiar making up to the vile woman, but I always knew I could trust him. It must have something to do with Miss Isabel.'

'His way of protecting her?' Charlotte said. 'If the coach crash wasn't an accident… if Deborah Kempthorne is capable of murdering Mary Ellen and seemed to be trying to harm Morenwyn…'

'I don't know what you're talking about,' James Leddra said, 'but it sounds like there's been some strange goings on here.'

'We don't know all there is to it either,' Mrs Christopher said.

'Where can I find Nick Nancarrow now?' James asked, heading for the door.

'He's got a job over at Tehidy but he hasn't been there last night or today. Deborah Kempthorne sent one of the stable boys over to send for him at once but I told him to report back to me seeing as Miss Mary Ellen was dead. I know about a… certain friend he sometimes keeps company with at Crantock, he could be found there, a quiet house tucked in on its own down from the village by the sand dunes.'

'I'll find it,' James said, preparing to leave the room. 'I'll go there now. He ought to know what's been going on here, to keep away from Trevennor House. Will you ladies be able to cope if Mr Kempthorne turns up demanding to see his daughter?'

'We can deal with Mr Kempthorne,' Charlotte said. 'He's different altogether from his sister. He loves Morenwyn and would do nothing to harm her. I'm sure I can get him to agree to letting her stay here until this matter is cleared up. Can you ride, Mr Leddra?'

'No, ma'am, I aren't too good on me land legs, never rode a horse afore.'

'Get one of the stable boys to saddle up my mare. You can ride behind him, she'll get you to Crantock in a short time.'

'If that Jenna Stevens is there, ask her if she's really Miss Isabel Hampton,' Mrs Christopher said in a small, frightened voice. 'And if she is, tell her to be careful. Mr Edmund may be better than his sister but if you ask me they Kempthornes are an evil pair.'

Chapter 25

'So you'll be leaving us soon,' Benjamin said, his quiet voice much softer than usual.

Isabel gently smoothed damp red hair away from his tawny eyes. He looked sad and small and so vulnerable today. She placed the lightest kiss on his cheek. 'What makes you say that, Benjamin?'

He gave her a weak smile. 'Well, there's been a lot of coming and going for a start, Nick leaving last night and then arriving so suddenly again. I'm very sensitive to the mood of this house and to Kitty's moods. I'm not always sleeping when she thinks I am and I'm more aware of what goes on than she believes. I usually say nothing because I don't want her to worry that I'm worrying over something.'

'Oh, Ben, you're one of the strongest people I've ever met.' She looked sadly around the room; she would miss her daily visits here. She was surprised at the intensity in his dark eyes when she looked back at the boy.

'Jenna, if that's your real name, am I as strong as Nick to you?'

Isabel glanced down Benjamin's frail body and back to his fine face. She used her own voice this time. 'You're as strong as Nick but in a different way.'

Benjamin's eyes grew slightly larger and he blinked his fine lashes. 'I'm honoured to hear you say that, a lady paying me a compliment.'

'I'm no one special, Benjamin.'

'You are to me. I've fallen in love with you,' he said, his voice dropping and his cheeks flushing, but he looked directly into Isabel's eyes.

'I'm honoured to have you say that to me,' she said, her eyes misting over. She kissed him softly again.

'Well then, I've said it, I was determined I would before you left,' and Benjamin seemed to grow older and more pleased with himself with every word. 'I'm so glad to have been a part in your adventures, whatever they are. Will you tell me now? What your real name is and the real reason for Nick bringing you here?'

Isabel stroked his cheek tenderly, soft and warm from his blush and his delight at his announcement. 'Of course I will, it's something I've wanted to do since I first met you. My name is Isabel Hampton. I live at Truro and my uncle lived at Gwithian. A few weeks ago he was very ill and I was on my way to see him but the coach I was travelling in was run off the road. That's when I met Nick properly for the first time. He saved my life then and saved it again today.' She went on to give Benjamin a full account of her life since the fateful day her uncle had died.

Benjamin's eyes were alert and excited when she'd finished. 'I wish I could have seen you beat down that Gyver Pengelly fellow,' he chuckled but added in concern, 'Everything else must have been quite awful for you, Isabel.'

'Not all of it. The worst thing was the deaths of my friend, Phoebe Antiss, my maid Ginny, and the two coachmen, and my not being there when my uncle died and was buried. But without all this happening, I wouldn't have met people like Charlie Chiverton and Mundy Cottle, and you and Kitty.'

'And Nick.'

She looked straight ahead and not at the boy for a moment. 'And Nick.'

'Do you think love can't cross the divide, Isabel?'

It was her turn to redden. Benjamin had a way of talking and looking at a person as if he was reading their innermost thoughts. 'What divide are you talking about, Ben?'

'The one between you and Nick.'

'But Nick and I are friends now, we no longer hate each other.'

'I wasn't talking about that. I know you're in love with him and very deeply. I've listened to you talk about him and watched your face when his name's mentioned. You wouldn't have missed those two nights and three days on the cliffs with him for the world, would you?'

'How well you have come to know me.' She added wistfully, 'There's no hope for Nick and me, there can be no future for us together. We could never cross the class barrier to begin with.'

'It's thoughts like those that are part of your problem,' Benjamin said, looking at her deeply. 'You don't have to have this heartbreak, you know, Isabel.'

Isabel was about to ask him to explain himself when Nick entered the room. 'We'll have to go soon, Jenna.'

'Isabel,' she corrected him. 'I've just been telling Benjamin all about myself.' She kissed the boy's hot brow. 'I'll come back to see you very soon, Ben, I promise you.'

He smiled, a small light movement of his soft features that was specially for her. 'I'm so glad Nick brought you here. You've brightened up my life in a way you'll never know, Goodbye, Isabel.'

'Goodbye, Benjamin. See you in a little while.'

'She's a remarkable woman,' Benjamin said to Nick the moment she'd left the room. 'Don't you think?'

'Aye, she is,' Nick agreed, somehow feeling embarrassed under the boy's inscrutable eyes.

'And growing more beautiful every day.'

'That too.' Nick shuffled his feet.

'I love her very much.'

Nick was amazed at the blunt statement. 'Do… do you?'

'Yes, and I wouldn't let her slip through my fingers.'

'Oh, well, I… I have to go now.' Nick headed quickly for the door. 'You have a little rest, Benjamin.'

Benjamin fluttered his lashes to say he would, then smiled before closing his eyes.

Isabel hugged Kitty, promising to let her know the outcome of her trip to Gwithian as soon as possible. Nick was waiting silently at the door as she put on her cloak when he saw two figures hurrying towards the house. Bidding the women to wait inside, Nick went to meet the visitors.

'Nick Nancarrow,' James Leddra hailed him from the foot of the path.

'Who…?' Nick looked from the man with gold earrings to the boy beside him whom he recognized as coming from Gwithian's parsonage stable. He was holding Charlotte Thomas's mare.

'Don't you remember me? James Leddra. From *The Bountiful*. You saved my life in Trevellas Porth a little while back. I'll never forget you.'

'James Leddra! What on earth are you doing here?' Isabel had been peeping out from behind the curtains of a window and recognized James before Nick did. She rushed out of the house, sending Kitty in a spin, and pushed past Nick to meet the sailor. 'How did you find us? Why are you here?'

Nick came up behind her. James looked at each shocked face. 'Hello, Nick.' He inclined his head to Isabel. 'Miss Isabel.' He didn't wait for fresh shock to register on their faces that he knew who she really was. 'Mrs Christopher told me I could probably find you both here. The parson's wife lent me her horse and stable boy to get me here quickly. I turned up at Trevennor House this morning to find my sister, Mary Ellen, was dead, almost certainly murdered in her bed by Deborah Kempthorne a short time before. Me and Mrs Christopher took my little niece, Morenwyn, and all the servants there over to the parsonage till the constable arrives. They're hoping if the child's father comes home he'll agree to letting her stay there till all's sorted out. We all thought 'twas best to try 'n' find you both and tell you what's happened.'

Isabel shook her head as she took in the news. Nick whistled through his teeth. 'Edmund Kempthorne won't be going home,' he said grimly. 'A short time ago he tried to kill Isabel and me and he went over the cliff. We couldn't save him.'

'Well, that's one thing we don't have to worry about then,' James said harshly, grief over his sister's death striking him hard now the urgency of his errand was over. 'The maid will be better off without him as a father!'

'I'm sorry about your sister, James,' Isabel said, touching his arm.

'Thank you, miss.'

Kitty had moved up to the gathering. 'Then there's only the Kempthorne woman to see to now,' she said, putting Edmund Kempthorne's hat into Nick's hand.

'Aye, and I'll enjoy doing that,' Nick said, with some of the venom he felt for the woman.

Isabel hugged Kitty again and went to the horse Nick had been using. It was one she had often ridden herself on excursions with her uncle. She stroked its forehead and momentarily rested her face against its strong neck. It was good to see something familiar again, something connected to her uncle. She was as able a rider astride a horse as she was side-saddle and astride was how she mounted. Nick made a wry face and swung up behind her.

James Leddra had not followed them, he was too busy eyeing Kitty, not expecting to find a lovely creature in a silk gown here. Kitty folded her arms, stared him out and then looked across at the couple waiting on the horse.

'Hadn't you better be going?' Kitty asked the sailor tartly.

'Aye… aye… good day to 'ee, miss…'

James mounted Charlotte's mare self-consciously and awkwardly with the aid of the stable boy. Isabel started the journey back to Gwithian at a confident trot. Nick sat close to her, his hands resting loosely on the tops of his legs. The stable boy urged the other mount on after them. James Leddra looked back over his shoulder at the redhead standing sedately on her garden path. Kitty tossed her head and went back inside.

'I reckon he'll be finding his way over here again before he finds his way back to sea,' Nick said in Isabel's ear as they rode through Crantock under the scrutiny of the villagers who were about.

'James?' she half-turned her head and their faces were close together. 'Why?'

He gazed into her eyes before she turned back to watch the road. 'Didn't you see the way he gawped at Kitty just then?'

'No… James and Kitty? I don't think Kitty will welcome that, shell soon send him off with a flea in his ear.'

They were clear of Crantock and Nick put his arms round her waist. Isabel leaned into him. He laughed. 'Flea in his ear? I can tell you've been around Kitty for a while. Miss Isabel Hampton would never have said that.'

'The old Miss Isabel Hampton doesn't exist any more,' she said vehemently.

Nick didn't answer that. He thought he knew better than anyone how much Isabel had changed. She was no longer a haughty madam who thought she had the right to demand her own way in all things, who had once railed against him for simply touching her. She had been humbled. Now she was warm, caring, feminine. All these things had been only just under the surface, but it had taken some very rough treatment and a whole new way of life to bring about the changes. Nick wasn't proud of his part in that; but he had hated her then. Now his feelings were far from that.

'Things should work out quite simply for you now,' he said. 'Edmund's dead, he can't hurt you. Gyver Pengelly's dead, he can't be paid to hurt you. And even if the authorities refuse to believe Deborah Kempthorne was responsible for Mary Ellen's death, the suspicion will follow her. She wouldn't dare make a move against you. You are strong and confident now, you don't need anyone to keep an eye on you until… for the next few days…'

Until Richard Grenville came back. The time in which Laurence Trevennor had asked him to ensure the safety of his beloved niece. Nick couldn't bring himself to say it. Even if she still needed a protector, he wouldn't be able to bring himself to remain in that position after today, after they had confronted the evil witch at Gwithian.

Isabel knew what Nick had been unable to say and she felt him move away from her.

She hid her disappointment. 'I'm so glad James and Mrs Christopher got Edmund's daughter away from Deborah. She's always hated children.'

'That woman hates the world,' Nick muttered. He was utterly relieved not to have to play the suitor to her again.

'Edmund said you were pretending to be interested in Deborah.'

'Well, I couldn't find out anything from him, he played his cards too close to his chest. I didn't think for a moment I would fool him by showing an interest in Deborah but it was the best way to get close to her, to find out what she really felt about you.' Nick ground his teeth. 'She said she wanted to dance on your grave, that if you were alive she'd push you over the cliff herself and make sure of it. She meant every word of it.'

Isabel shuddered, but she wasn't much interested in how her cousin felt about her right now. 'Did… did you kiss her?'

'What's that got to do with anything?' Nick snarled, snatching his arms away from her.

Isabel was reminded of his behaviour up on the cliffs in their early travels. Were things between them reverting to the way they had been then? 'Nick, please, I'm sorry, I shouldn't have asked you that. I didn't mean to upset you.' Tears pricked her eyes.

Nick looked at her stiff back. 'I'm sorry I snapped at you. But what I had to do with that woman… it was an awful experience.'

'You…?'

Nick made a choking noise. 'I couldn't have done that, even for you, Isabel.'

She stayed quiet as they cantered on, glancing back every so often to see if James Leddra and the stable boy were keeping up with them.

'I'm sorry if I've upset you, Isabel,' Nick said, when they were riding the coastal path along Reskajeage Downs. She didn't reply and he uncurled his fists and put his hands on her shoulders.

'I was thinking of all the people that have suffered because of me,' she said. 'Phoebe, Ginny, Rickardson and the guard. Did I tell you the guard had only been taken on that day? Then there are all the good people that have been put out on my account. Charlie and Mundy Cottle, Kitty, Benjamin, and most of all you… all the things you've had to do for me. And Deborah is a most dangerous woman, she couldn't have been fooled either into thinking you really cared for her. She might have done anything to keep you in her clutches, she still might.'

'Isabel, slow down, will you?' She did as he asked, but only after they had left Deadman's Cove, the scene of the accident, behind. 'You can hardly blame yourself for Deborah's attempt on your life. And you haven't put my friends out. Charlie, Mundy and Kitty were only too glad to help, and as for Ben, you've made a huge difference to a lonely young man. They all like you very much, you're their friend too now.'

'And what about you, Nick?'

'Laurence was my friend and a fine man. I would have done anything for him.'

'And I am your friend now, Nick?'

'That goes without saying, doesn't it?' he returned moodily.

Isabel was silent. How much of a friend did he consider her?

The riders got off their horses before they reached Gwithian village, the stable boy taking both mounts and walking them on in front. They didn't want to advertise their presence and alert Deborah. Charlie Chiverton met them outside the village.

'I've been keeping meself out of sight,' Charlie told Nick, ignoring the others. 'I seen all the servants, the young 'un and this man 'ere,' Charlie tossed his head at James, 'trooping into the parsonage, then 'e goin' off on Mistress Thomas's 'orse. Nothin's stirred in the big 'ouse. No one's gone in or come out.' Then Charlie looked closely at Isabel, he was not quite sure who she was.

'Hello, Charlie,' she said, offering him her hand. 'I'm so pleased you weren't hurt too badly by Gyver Pengelly. I've washed the clothes you lent me, I shall return them to you as soon as I can.'

'So 'tes thee, Miss Isabel,' Charlie said, shyly shaking her hand. 'You look quite different.'

'We'll go to the parsonage first and hope Deborah Kempthorne doesn't see us,' Nick said, impatient to get on.

'Well, if she's lookin' out of a window she went recognize Miss Isabel,' Charlie said, falling in with Nick's long strides. 'What 'ave ye done to 'er, boy?'

'I haven't done anything to her,' Nick returned stonily.

Isabel turned from James Leddra's sympathetic eyes and concentrated on keeping up with the other two.

Charlotte saw the four of them coming and admitted them into the parsonage herself.

'Miss Isabel, how good to see you again, and looking so well,' she added, taking in the young woman's changed looks. 'I'm so sorry you've had to go through such an ordeal. I'll be glad if you and Nick, and Mr Leddra and your friend,' she glanced at Charlie and made a mental note to send for hot water and towels to clean his bleeding arm, 'would all step into the parlour so we can piece the whole story together. Mrs Christopher is waiting anxiously in there.'

'And Morenwyn?' James asked respectfully.

'She's upstairs in the nursery with my children and the nurses. Don't worry, she's quite happy. She's used to her mother being indisposed and her father being away for long periods of time. He'll be the best one to tell her what's happened to—'

'He's dead too,' Nick interrupted ungraciously and received a withering look from Isabel.

'He tried to kill us but lost his own life,' Isabel explained.

The little gathering was unprepared for Charlotte's reaction. A small strangled cry passed her lips, her face went white and she clutched at the hall table. James reached out to prevent what he thought was going to be a faint. Charlotte used his arm to steady herself but stayed resolutely on her feet.

'You should not have told her like that,' Isabel remonstrated with Nick.

He apologized to Charlotte. 'I'm sorry I shocked you, Mistress Thomas. Can I get you something?'

'No, no,' Charlotte forced a sort of smile. 'I'm sorry. But after everything that has happened it has been a shock. You see, I was in a similar situation myself only a few days ago. Gyver Pengelly tried to kill me and Nellie. It was Mr Kempthorne who saved our lives. I wouldn't have believed he'd try to kill anyone. He… he didn't seem capable of it. Please, let's go into the parlour.'

Isabel obeyed immediately to lessen Charlotte's distress and embarrassment. She opened the parlour door and Mrs Christopher, who was looking anxiously out of a window towards Trevennor House, dropped the curtain and rushed to her with outstretched hands.

'Miss Isabel! Oh, Miss Isabel, thank God you're still alive. You don't know what it's been like these past weeks. If only I'd known you were still alive.'

Isabel took the housekeeper to a sofa and sat holding her hands. 'I'm sorry about all that's happened, Mrs Christopher. But it was necessary that everyone believed I was dead.'

'It's been a nightmare since Mr Trevennor died,' the housekeeper sobbed. 'If only I'd known you were alive,' she repeated, 'the last few weeks would have been bearable.'

'I couldn't take the risk and tell you,' Nick said, going to them and putting his arm round Mrs Christopher, 'it might have put you in danger. You do see?' She turned and cried in Nick's arms. 'It's nearly over now,' he said soothingly. He looked at Isabel. 'In a little while Miss Isabel and I will go up the road and confront Deborah Kempthorne.'

Isabel got up and went to Charlotte who was standing by a table touching the petals of a vase of snowdrops. Edmund Kempthorne had passed them into the parsonage that morning before he'd left for Crantock.

'Are you feeling better now, Mistress Thomas?'

'What? Oh, yes. I'll have these flowers removed, they make the air heavier to breathe.' Charlotte had overlooked some of Edmund Kempthorne's shortcomings but she wanted nothing from a common murderer, a man who had obviously been as evil as his sister. 'And how are you, Miss Isabel?'

Miss Isabel. She looked at Nick, holding Mrs Christopher who was clinging to him, he gazing sightlessly over her head. Now folk knew she was still alive, was she to be Miss Isabel to everyone again? She couldn't wait to go next door and enter Trevennor House, her rightful home, and turn out her remaining cousin, the vile woman who had plotted and so very nearly succeeded in her murder. *Miss Isabel.* When she saw she had come back from the dead to claim her inheritance, what would Deborah Kempthorne call her?

Chapter 26

Nick stalked into the parlour of Trevennor House, thrusting back the door and making it jar to a halt. The curtains were drawn, shrouding the room in almost darkness. He could see the clumsy shape of Deborah Kempthorne stretched out on a sofa, a hand laid across her brow. He strode towards her, grimacing at the distasteful odour of her headache powders, scent and perspiration.

Deborah moaned as if from afar. 'Who's there?'

'It's me.'

'Nick?' She tried to get up but fell back clutching her head in agony. Her headaches were genuine; probably the only thing about her that was.

Nick went round to the windows, roughly pulling open the curtains.

'Wh-what are you doing?'

He began opening the windows, as wide as they would go, letting in the cold air.

Deborah tried and failed to sit up again. 'Oh, Nick. Please close the curtains… my head… What are you doing? You're making a draught.'

He ignored the muffled pleas from the sofa, returning to his station in front of it. Deborah lowered her hand and opened her eyes with a squint. She could not see Nick well. 'Come closer, I can't see you properly.'

Nick stood his ground, his hands resting on his hips, his face stern. The better light showed up the woman's full ugliness.

Deborah struggled and this time she managed to sit up, groaning and holding her head. She tried to pat her hair back into place but succeeded in bringing down more of its straggly ends. 'Where have you been, Nick? I sent for you hours ago. What time is it?'

'About midday.' He spoke sharply.

Deborah screwed up her face and tried to focus on his face. Her cap fell off and she was forced to wipe spittle from the side of her mouth. Her hands flapped about the sofa until she located a handkerchief which she dabbed at her lips then patted over her face. Nick's mouth tightened at the sight.

'I've had a terrible morning,' she said in a complaining voice. 'Mary Ellen was found dead and the servants are accusing me of having something to do with it. Then some awful sailor turned up saying he was the child's uncle and took her away. I dismissed all the servants and then this wretched headache came on. I've been lying here in sheer agony waiting for you to come to me.'

'What a pity.'

'Are you all right, Nick? You sound strange. But things are better for us now with Mary Ellen out of the way. Why don't you sit down beside me? I want you to hold me.'

'I've brought someone to see you, Deborah.'

'Oh no, who is it? I'm in no fit state to receive visitors.'

Nick looked across to the doorway where Isabel had been standing, listening. Deborah followed his gaze but could see only the hazy outline of a tall, slim female. 'Who are you? What do you want?'

Isabel crossed the room and stood beside Nick. Coolly, she said, 'Hello, Deborah.'

'What?' Deborah's eyes shot wider and she shook her head and stared until her vision cleared. 'Who are you? You sounded like… you can't be…'

'But it is. Your cousin Isabel Hampton, back from the bottom of the ocean.'

Forgetting her agony, Deborah jumped up and looked closer. 'You're an imposter! You look a bit like Isabel Hampton but she wasn't so—'

'Beautiful,' Nick supplied.

Deborah gaped at him. 'What are you doing with this woman in my house, Nick?'

'My house, Deborah,' Isabel said coldly. 'I did not perish that day of the coach accident. Nick saved my life, he took me to safety where you could not hurt me.'

'I don't believe you. It's not true!'

'Every word is the truth,' Nick said with relish. 'I took Isabel to safety then I came back to Gwithian for Laurence's funeral, and kept coming back here with the intention of keeping an eye on you and your wretched brother, to find out if you meant harm to Isabel as Laurence suspected. It didn't take long for me to find out the truth, did it?'

'Uncle Laurence? What's he got to do with this?' Deborah's voice was becoming shrill.

'I was Laurence's friend, remember. He trusted me but did not trust you and Edmund. He knew you wished Isabel harm. He told me what he suspected and asked me to look after her. That's what I've been doing, with the help of my friends, these past few weeks. I've got friends, Deborah, Isabel's got friends. That's something you don't know about, is it? Everybody hates you!'

Deborah thrust her hands to her head and shook it from side to side. 'I don't believe a word of what you're saying. I don't know what's the matter with you, Nick. You said you loved me.'

'Love you? I loathe you, the sight of you, the sound of your voice, the death-laden smell of you, the very essence of you. You are the most evil woman I've ever had the misfortune to meet.'

Deborah let out an animal-like scream and fell back on the sofa. 'No, she's dead… that woman's not Isabel, she's dead…

you came to me as a fortune-hunter believing she was dead, she was seen…' Realization hit her at last. 'He lied.'

'Aye, Gyver Pengelly lied when he said he saw Isabel's body. Now he's dead too, dead and in Hell, the proper place for him.'

Deborah's face took on a reptilian appearance. 'You won't get the better of me! Edmund will be here soon. He'll put things right. He won't believe that I killed Mary Ellen. He'll say Dorcas killed her, she was the one who found her. No one will believe a servant over a lady. There is no evidence to say I had anything to do with it.'

'They'll believe me, Deborah Kempthorne,' a quiet voice said from the doorway.

Those in the room looked to see who had entered. Charlotte Thomas was there, holding out a piece of white lace with dark hair lying on it. 'I believe Dorcas. This is the piece of lace she found in Mary Ellen's dead hand. It comes from your dress, torn off in her last bid for life. I've just been upstairs and studied the bed. These dark hairs were lying across Mary Ellen's body. They come from your head, they fell out as you bent over her and suffocated her to death. And I have more evidence. Last night my husband overheard your brother talking to Gyver Pengelly. He told me what passed between them. We thought it was just the ramblings of a drunkard then, but now I can see it was another plot to find Miss Hampton and kill her. I have sent for the constable. He will be here shortly to take you into custody.'

'No! I don't believe you. You're all trying to frighten me.' Deborah looked wildly from face to face. 'Edmund will sort things out and if that creature you've brought in here really is Isabel Hampton, he'll make sure she really dies! She won't take all this from us. Edmund won't let her! He won't!'

'Edmund has already tried to kill me,' Isabel said calmly. 'He found out I was staying with friends of Nick's at Crantock and followed me along the cliffs early this morning. But his plan failed. Nick saved me again and Edmund tried to kill him. Edmund got what he deserved. He fell over the cliff. We did try to save him but he struggled too much. He's dead.' Isabel held out Edmund's hat. 'He's the one in the ocean, Deborah, and we saw his body, Nick and I, lying down there, smashed on the rocks.'

'No! You're lying! You can't come back now and say these things to me!' Deborah launched herself at Isabel but Nick stepped between them and pushed her violently away. She howled like a wolf and ripping a brooch off her dress threw herself at Nick. 'I'll mark your handsome face! No woman will ever look at you again.' The brooch scored a line down his cheek before his hands could grip her arms. She spat and struggled, screaming hysterically, lashing out with her feet, trying to wrench herself away. She was completely out of control. The brooch fell out of her hand and Isabel kicked it away.

Nick grunted with the effort to restrain her. Isabel tried to clutch one of her arms and Charlotte rushed forward to help. Deborah delivered a kick in her direction and Charlotte was knocked off her feet.

'Push her down on the sofa, Nick,' Isabel cried.

'I'm trying to!'

Isabel reached across Nick's arm and managed to grasp a handful of Deborah's thick hair. She twisted her head round and slapped her cousin's face soundly. Deborah was stunned and sank to the sofa, her screams reduced to a whimper, her chest heaving.

Perran Thomas came in with the constable and some of the male servants. He went straight to his wife. 'The constable will take over now, beloved.'

Deborah Kempthorne was trussed up and led away, shouting abuse and threats. Outside she had to run a gauntlet of booing villagers who had got wind of events from the sacked servants.

Perran put his arm round Charlotte but he was looking at Isabel who was gazing alternately at Nick and the familiar things in the room. 'Come, my dear,' Perran said to his wife, 'there is nothing left for us to do here now.'

Isabel went to Nick immediately after their tactful withdrawal. 'Your face…'

''Tis nothing,' he said softly, becoming aware of his stinging cheek. 'Are you all right?'

'Yes, but… it was almost worse than up on the cliffs with Edmund.'

'Aye, I hope justice will be done to that woman. I'd hate to think of her going free to wreak more evil on the world.'

Isabel made to put herself in his arms but he moved away. 'It will be good to see Laurence's things back in their proper places, to get the smell of the Kempthornes out of the house for good.'

Isabel swallowed her disappointment. 'Mary Ellen must still be here. I'll see she's buried in the churchyard. I've never met her… there'll be no point in looking in on her…'

'No, best not to.'

'I think I'll go up to Uncle Laurence's room, where he died. Will you come with me, Nick?'

'I'll wait down here. You need to go alone.'

Isabel sat quietly on her uncle's bed, reliving the happy memories of childhood days spent at Trevennor House with him. She tried to picture the conversation he'd held with Nick against the plump pillows. Uncle Laurence breathless, patient, as Nick looked at him in disbelief at his request. Nick agreeing to go and do the errand for the one man he cared for in the class he seemed to despise, but not looking forward to it, a chore to interfere with his solitary, drifting life. Uncle Laurence had been right to be afraid for her, but he could have had no idea of the consequences of his fears.

'The man you sent to help me has changed my life, uncle,' she whispered through her tears.

She found Nick waiting for her by the front door and they returned to the parsonage without saying a word.

Morenwyn was in the parlour, hiding behind her nurse's skirts and refusing to be introduced to her seagoing uncle. Her face was puckered and she was about to burst into tears.

Isabel looked at the little face so reminiscent of Edmund's. She whispered to Charlotte, 'This seems to be too much for her, I wouldn't like to see her frightened or upset.'

Nick moved slowly towards Morenwyn. 'Hello, Morenwyn. Do you remember me? It's Nick. I've seen you often at Trevennor House, the big house next door.'

Morenwyn's dark eyes lit up and she left her nurse and went to Nick with her arms out. Nick picked her up and she wound her arms round his neck and buried her face against his shoulder. Nick turned so she was facing James. 'You see that man sitting there, Morenwyn?' he said softly, stroking her hair.

She nodded with big nervous eyes.

'Well, he's your Uncle James. He's a good man and a friend of mine. You're not afraid of a friend of mine, are you?'

Morenwyn shook her head. James gave her a big grin and she allowed him gently to pat her hair but she clung to Nick and would not move her head away from him.

'And you know your nurse, and Mrs Christopher and Mistress Thomas?' Nick took her round in a circle to see each smiling, encouraging face and the little girl nodded each time. 'Well, the other lady in the room, the pretty lady who came in with me,' Nick took her to face Isabel, 'is a friend of mine as well. She's called Isabel and she's your cousin. Say hello to her, Morenwyn.'

She didn't speak, just stared, so Isabel said 'Hello' and held out a hand to her. Morenwyn lifted her head from Nick's shoulder and kept staring. 'You look a bit like the old man's picture,' she piped.

'He was my uncle, Morenwyn,' Isabel said. 'Would you like to come to me? Just for a little while?'

Morenwyn thumped her face back against Nick's shoulder. 'I want my mam and my fathur.'

'I'm afraid your mam and father have had to go away, Morenwyn,' Nick said gently. 'They sent Isabel to come here to look after you. I expect you will be living with her from now on.'

Isabel's eyes widened. She hadn't thought about her little second cousin's fate before now, but she said quickly, 'Yes, you can come and live with me, Morenwyn, and your nurse can come too. We're part of the same family and we'll have lots of fun together. Would you like that?'

Morenwyn's face screwed up to cry. She had the little wooden dog Charlie had carved for her clutched in her hand and dropped it. Isabel picked it up. 'I know the man who made this for you. We could ask him to make some more, a whole farmyard of animals.' She held out the dog and Morenwyn took it back. Her tears stopped. 'Would you like to come to me?' Isabel said, holding out her arms. 'Just for a minute. Then you can go back to Nick.'

Morenwyn looked up to Nick with pouting lips. He grinned cheerily and said, 'Go on, princess. I'll be right here. Isabel is a kind lady, she won't hurt you.'

'I don't want to go to sourpuss. She frightens me,' Morenwyn said.

Nick mouthed to Isabel, 'She's talking about Deborah Kempthorne.'

'You won't have to go anywhere near her again, Morenwyn, I promise. She's gone away too and will never come back to Trevennor House.'

Morenwyn was finally convinced and gingerly held out her chubby arms to Isabel. Isabel took her, a bit uncertainly at first, she had never held a child before, then she cuddled her in close and Morenwyn held up the wooden dog. 'Will the man make me a cat?'

'I'm sure he will,' Isabel laughed gently. 'He's about here somewhere. I'll ask him for you in a little while.'

Morenwyn rested against Isabel's neck. 'I want my mam,' she whispered.

'I know, Morenwyn,' Isabel whispered, trying to hold back tears of her own. 'Would you like to go and play with the other children now?'

'Yes, please.'

Nick came forward and kissed the top of Morenwyn's head and Isabel kissed her hot cheek. The nurse carried the sad little girl out of the room.

Isabel was worried. 'I hope I said and did the right things.'

'Rest assured you did, Miss Isabel,' Charlotte told her brightly. 'You were perfectly natural with her.' Isabel looked at Nick for confirmation and he nodded.

'She's very fond of you,' she said.

'Aye,' he sighed, 'I saw a lot of her, she was always running about Trevennor House. Poor little mite, what a life she had to look forward to, but I reckon her future will be better now despite losing her parents.'

Isabel looked at James Leddra. 'I'll be happy to give Morenwyn a home but as her uncle it is of course for you to say where she goes.'

'I'm grateful to you, Miss Isabel. I couldn't look after her the way Mary Ellen would have wanted. I'm a seafaring man, the best I could do is pay some family to look after her.'

'She'll be safe with Isabel,' Nick said firmly. Charlotte and Mrs Christopher nodded silently, they could both see the new strength Isabel had acquired in the weeks since her uncle's death.

–

Kitty was surprised to see James Leddra coming up her pathway again that day. She met him before he could knock on the door. 'What are you doing here? Has something gone wrong?'

'Nothing's wrong, Miss Kitty,' James said bashfully. 'Miss Isabel was anxious for you and your brother to know what's happened. She and Nick are tied up with the constable at the moment and then she has to settle the servants back into the house after my sister's body is taken away, so I said I would come back to tell you.'

'You mean you asked Nick if you could come instead of him,' Kitty said somewhat haughtily, making no move to invite him into the house. 'I thought you had a niece to see to.'

'She, um, didn't know what to make of me. The poor little soul has had an upsetting day. She's going to stay at the curate's house tonight, she's got his young'uns to play with there.'

'And you thought you'd come over here because you're interested in me. I'm not for sale to just anybody, James Leddra.'

James looked as though Kitty had blown him back down her path. 'I... know that. I didn't come here to try my luck, Miss Kitty, but like you said, I am interested in you. Few women have caught my eye like you have.'

'Well, I suppose you'd better come in and tell me what happened at Gwithian then, seeing as you've ridden all that way over here again. The stable boy can amuse himself for a while.' Kitty looked down at James's feet and frowned. 'You'll have to take those boots off first and come in quietly, I don't want my brother being disturbed. I'll tell him myself later.'

–

Nick came to Isabel in the churchyard in the growing darkness. She was standing beside her uncle and aunt's double grave, dressed in black in a dress borrowed from Charlotte, able to show she was in mourning at last.

Isabel saw he was dressed and packed for travelling. 'You're going away?'

'Aye, Charlie's leaving in a minute, he's got the pleasant task of telling the fortunate Mrs Gyver Pengelly she's now a widow. I'll be leaving with him. I've spoken to the constable, done all I can here. It's time I moved on. Have you been saying goodbye to Laurence?'

'Yes.' She paused before going on. 'I hate saying goodbye.'

Nick studied Isabel's pale loveliness then looked down at the grave. 'I reckon he would have been pleased with the outcome.'

Isabel sighed. 'He wouldn't have wanted so many people to die. I'll have his name put on the headstone. I don't suppose Deborah and Edmund would have had it done once they'd moved to Truro.'

'He can rest in peace now.'

'I found a copy of Uncle Laurence's will in his bedchamber. He left you his horses, Nick.'

Nick smiled. 'That was just like Laurence. I won't take them.'

'But Uncle Laurence wanted you to have them. You said earlier today you would do anything for him; you can't go against his last wishes for you.'

Nick thought. 'I'll take a couple with me, think about taking up as a packman again.'

Isabel said carefully, 'With Uncle Laurence gone, I've got no one left but Morenwyn.'

'She's lost her parents today but I'm sure you'll be able to make it up to her. She needs a woman's love, James was right about not being able to look after her properly himself.'

'A man who can't stay put in one place,' she mused. 'I hadn't seen Morenwyn before today, she's a pretty little girl. I shall give her the home Edmund wanted her to have.' She touched Nick's arm. 'Do you have to go?'

He looked at her evenly. Kitty's words about Isabel's future echoed in his mind. 'Aye,' he dropped his voice. 'I reckon I do.'

Taking her hand from him, she nodded; this man could only be happy with his total freedom and he wasn't interested in her personal plans. 'Your other horses will be here waiting for you when you want them.'

Nick took something small out of his jacket pocket. 'I keep meaning to give this back to you.'

'My ring. Have you kept it on you all this time?'

'Aye. Well, I think that settles everything.' The wind pulled at his hair and rustled the trees which lined the graveyard. 'Goodbye, Isabel.'

He held out his hand and she put hers into it. 'Goodbye, Nick. Thank you for everything.'

He bent his head and kissed the back of her hand briefly. One more look and he left her there alone.

Chapter 27

About two weeks later, a young man, a stranger, turned up at Trevennor House late at night. His arrival sent Mrs Christopher into a dither. She forgot to offer to take his hat and cloak and showed him into the parlour then rushed upstairs to the nursery. Isabel was just coming out of the room, closing the door very slowly.

'Miss Isabel!'

'Shush,' Isabel put an urgent finger to her lips. 'I've just got Morenwyn off to sleep. Nurse is sitting with her and I've promised to come back in a little while. Tomorrow we're going to see Charlie again. He's promised to have something new carved for her by then. She's really looking forward to it.'

'Poor little maid, bless her. She's afraid that since she's lost her mother and father she's going to lose you too. I thank the Lord she's got you, Miss Isabel.'

Isabel made her way to her own room. 'I'm going to retire myself in a little while. I've felt pleasantly tired since the walk we took along the beach this afternoon.'

'You shouldn't spend so much time outside,' Mrs Christopher chided, following on her heels. 'You've got a wild streak in you these days, if you ask me.' Isabel stopped at her door. 'What did you want to see me about, Mrs Christopher?'

The question sent the housekeeper into her dither again and she pulled on Isabel's arm. 'Oh, yes! There's a gentleman come to see you. It's Captain Richard Grenville.'

'Richard! Here?'

'Aye, he said he got your letter and he's sorry to call at such a late hour but he felt he had to come at once.'

Isabel felt a moment of panic. 'Mrs Christopher, I know this will sound a strange question, but what does he look like?'

Mrs Christopher was completely taken aback. 'Don't you know? He's your betrothed.'

'I know but I simply can't remember. It's as though he belongs to another time, another life.'

'Well, he's a fine looking man, tall and dark, I believe. I was so surprised to know who it was myself I didn't stop to have a good look at him. Silly really, he was bound to come here sometime, I suppose.'

'I'd better go down then,' Isabel murmured.

Mrs Christopher frowned at her simple dress, slightly crumpled from the walk across Gwithian beach and made grubby by Morenwyn's sticky hands. 'Aren't you going to change out of that dress first?'

She tut-tutted when Isabel said in a surprised voice, 'Whatever for?'

'But it's your young man downstairs, he's a gentleman. You haven't put on one of your fine gowns since they arrived from Truro, and that was only a few then. Don't know why you sent for them in the first place.'

Isabel sighed impatiently, lifting her eyes to the ceiling in an expression Mrs Christopher had seen often in another young man who'd frequently called at this house in the past, a man with a wilder nature and not such particular ways as the one waiting downstairs.

Isabel squared her shoulders and leaving Mrs Christopher to shake her head and mutter, she pattered down the stairs and walked into the parlour in business-like fashion.

Richard Grenville had been stroking and talking to her uncle's bloodhounds and had got them in a playful mood. He left them immediately, ordering them firmly to lie down as he held out his hand to Isabel. She put hers on his and he kissed it lightly, then she took it away.

'It was good of you to come, Richard, but you should not have troubled yourself at such a late hour. All manner of vagrants and cut throats are abroad at this time.' She furtively studied his face to see if she remembered anything about him and, with the wariness she had acquired since her adventures, to make sure he really was Richard Grenville. It was like looking at someone she vaguely knew from her childhood. 'Please sit down,' she said. 'Can I offer you anything?'

Richard Grenville considered his fiancée with humorous dark eyes. 'My dear Isabel, I set foot on land but four hours ago. I went straight to my aunts' house and was regaled with the accounts of your adventures along the North Cliffs. They showed me your letter to them – they are most put out that you have not called upon them since your sudden rising from the dead.' He let out a hearty laugh, one that belonged to a seaman working only with other men. 'And there was me believing you were waiting for me to come back to marry you, concerned only with the wedding lace.'

Isabel could not help but respond to his smiling face, his dark complexion made even darker by exposure to sea winds and burning sun. 'I hope you are not angry with me too, Richard. Please do apologize to your aunts on my behalf but I hope they will understand that I have been in no mood for socializing and I will not leave my young orphaned cousin who has had a greater need of me.'

'I am not in the least bit angry with you, Isabel. Rather, you have me greatly intrigued.' He surprised her by pulling her to her feet and wrapping his arms about her. 'I like your smile, it is much more open and friendlier than I remember.' He brought his face to hers and kissed her lips. He would have made the embrace longer and more intimate but Isabel struggled out of his grip.

'Come, my dear, no need for coyness. Our wedding date is but a few days away now.'

'I have something to say to you, Richard,' she said firmly.

Richard put his head slightly to the side and his eyes were full of wicked glints. 'I know all about the time you spent with the handsome man – Nancarrow, I think his name was. If anything happened between you, I don't really mind, as long as he hasn't left you with child. These things are understandable, Isabel.'

'Oh, are they, Richard? Well, nothing like that did happen though I don't suppose you kept yourself to yourself while you were at sea.'

'Surely you didn't expect me to,' he said, laughing. 'You are not that naive, are you, Isabel?'

'I was naive, Richard, but not now. As for what I expected of you, the fact is I hardly gave you a second thought.'

'Oh.' He looked crestfallen but only for a moment. 'You've acquired quite an acid tongue, my dear, but never mind, I rather like the idea of returning from sea to find my wife has completely changed every time. It will make for a less predictable kind of marriage.'

Isabel stood very straight and looked determined. 'Richard, listen to me closely, I will have no argument on this. I am not going to marry you.'

'You're not—'

'I'm sorry but my mind is quite made up. I cannot marry you and I hope you will be gentleman enough not to make a fuss. I've cancelled the wedding plans and nothing you can say will make me change my mind. From now on I intend to live here quietly with my cousin. I realize of course I owe you recompense for breach of promise and I hope you will accept my mansion and grounds at Truro.'

Richard stared at her for a few moments then nodded his head and gave a huge grin. 'I thought you'd say that somehow. Well, no matter, we weren't in love or anything and one bride is as good as another to provide a man with a home port and a family. Pity though, I should have liked to boast about you to my comrades.'

Isabel was suspicious. 'You are very understanding, Richard.'

'It can be a life of danger and sudden misfortune at sea, my dear. You learn to live with it and accept it and adapt to it and we must all look to our own destiny. You may keep your property, Isabel. As long as I can feel a ship's boards under my feet, I shall be content.' He gave her his endearing grin again. 'Actually I rather think the old aunts will be somewhat relieved that you don't want to marry me. Word has got around about your adventurous spirit and I don't think they knew how they were going to cope with it. You're the talk of the county, my dear.' Isabel found his amusement infectious and laughed with him. 'Thank you so much, Richard. You have made telling you so much easier, in fact almost a pleasure.'

'You said in your letter you wanted to see me as soon as possible and I thought I might as well ride over and get it over with. I will take you up on your earlier offer now, if I may, and would gladly accept a large tot of rum.'

When they were seated and chatting amiably, Richard winked and said, 'I rather think on my next leave from the briny I will be looking forward to my nuptials again. Since your "demise", the old aunts have been cultivating another young lady for me.'

Isabel had been thinking that if her circumstances had not changed, this attractive man wouldn't have made her a bad husband. She lifted her glass of wine to his glass of rum. 'I'm sure that whoever that fortunate lady is, you will make her a fine husband.'

–

Isabel rode through Crantock, delighting the villagers she had known briefly by acknowledging each one with a friendly greeting. Jack Rejerrah was in the stocks and rolled his drunken head when she called to him, a stunned look on his wizened face. Isabel didn't linger, she couldn't wait to see Kitty and Benjamin again.

Kitty's house was ominously silent. Isabel felt a sense of foreboding as she dismounted and tethered her pony to the garden gate. Talland was sitting outside the back kitchen door with his great head down heavily on his paws. He didn't jump up excitedly when he saw her but plodded towards her with large sad eyes, whimpering when she knelt to stroke him. Isabel looked up sharply. The windows at the front of the house were curtained over. She ran to the door, didn't knock, walked straight in and made her way to the hub of the house, the kitchen.

Kitty was sitting there, dressed in black, beside the fire in the chair she had first put Isabel in. She looked up and smiled wanly.

Tears sprang to Isabel's lashes. 'Benjamin?'

Kitty looked into space. 'I found him when I woke this morning. It was peaceful, in his sleep.'

'I'm so sorry.' Isabel put her arms round Kitty and they hugged and cried.

'I should have come before this,' Isabel said as she made tea. 'I would love to have spoken to Benjamin again. But Morenwyn wouldn't let me go. She was afraid I would leave her like her mother and father. I left her playing at the parsonage and she doesn't realize I've slipped away.'

Kitty smiled through tear-soaked eyes. 'Your first duty is with that little maid, like mine was with Benjamin. You came on the best day for me, Isabel. It's good to have a friend here. I need that right now. I hope everything has settled down for you. Tell me all about yourself. When are you going back to live in Truro? I'm still waiting for my wedding invitation.'

Isabel put her cup down. 'You won't be receiving one, Kitty.'

'I've gathered that much. Well? Why not?'

'I'm going to live at Gwithian from now on, for good. I'm making a home for myself and Morenwyn there.'

'And what did Richard Grenville say about that? I take it you've seen him?'

'Richard came to Trevennor House as soon as he'd come ashore. His aunts had told him the story of my "death" and sudden reappearance. He was fascinated by the whole affair and couldn't get over how I've changed. He said he liked the idea of having a wife who might have changed for the better every time he came home.'

'And then you told him you didn't want to marry him. I thought you might do that. What did he say?'

'He was very good about it, he said it was all the same to him because we weren't in love or anything. I offered to settle my Truro mansion on him for breaking off our engagement but he refused. I shall keep it for Morenwyn, then she will have the opportunity of making up her own mind what kind of life she'd like for herself when she grows up. I've been very careful making out a new will. I've settled a large sum on Morenwyn and after her the rest goes to charity. I don't want her to grow up being in the same position as I was.'

'That's very sensible.' Kitty looked at Isabel in approval, she hadn't credited her with much common sense when she'd first met her. 'I must say I like the sound of Captain Richard Grenville. He must be a good man to have let you go like that, no anger, no recriminations. I'd like to have met him.'

Isabel grinned. 'Richard will soon be snapped up by someone else. You'd like a bevy of sailors turning up at your door, would you, Kitty?'

'Oh, you mean James Leddra. I had quite a shock with him turning up here again that day. He's got a certain charm for a simple sailor but I won't be counting the days till his ship docks again in Cornwall.'

A silence grew and Kitty waited for the inevitable question. 'Have you seen Nick?'

'Only briefly. He called to see if James Leddra had told me everything. Have you seen him?'

'Not since that day.'

'So he doesn't know you've decided to live at Gwithian.'

'No, not that it would make any difference.' Isabel moved quickly on to something else. 'While I mainly called to see you and Benjamin, I thought I'd collect the clothes Charlie Chiverton loaned me. I'll take them back to him and take Morenwyn with me. Charlie makes little carved animals for her, I think she'll love to see where he lives. I called in on Mundy Cottle on the way here. I wanted to show her my gratitude for helping me, as I want to with all of Nick's friends who helped me. I was almost too afraid to ask if I could have a set of Sunday-best clothes made for her children. But I should have known I needn't have worried over Mundy, she said working clothes would be more practical and if the good Lord wanted to provide for her family through me, who was she to argue with Him. I'm going to take Charlie a few little things for his shack. It's too late to do something for dear Ben, but I'd like to do something for you, Kitty, if you'll allow me. Please say you will.' Isabel wiped tears from her eyes and Kitty smiled encouragingly.

'Ben didn't need anything, Isabel, but you gave him so much in the few weeks you were here. He had someone else to talk to, to keep him company, someone to listen to his dreams.' Kitty's eyes overflowed. 'Pour me another cup of tea, will you, please? I think there's some saffron cake on the dresser shelf. I haven't had a thing to eat today.'

'Would you like me to stay with you, Kitty? I'm sure Morenwyn will be happy to stay with her nurse and Mrs Christopher if I go home and explain that I'm staying with a friend just for a little while.'

'No, I'll be all right, Isabel. I've had Benjamin to myself nearly all his life and want it to be that way until the funeral. Then after that perhaps I could stay at Trevennor House for a while until I adapt to life without him. My gentlemen can do without me during that time. Who knows, I might decide they can do without me for good.'

'It will be wonderful to have you stay with me and you must stay as long as you like.' Isabel took Kitty's hand and squeezed it.

'Don't take this the wrong way, Kitty, but if you don't want to work for a living, I have enough money to provide for you well for the rest of your life. I could do it for all of Nick's friends.'

You have his friends but not Nick himself, Kitty thought. Perhaps I shouldn't have interfered…

'We'll wait and see what happens, shall we? But I'll always provide for myself.'

'As you please… Can I go in and see Ben?'

'Of course. I left his curtains open. He liked to look over the river… you go in by yourself… just the two of you, he would have liked that.'

Chapter 28

Kitty was out on the beach when Talland barked and ran away from her. She watched the tall fair-haired man who was waving and running towards her but did not go to meet him. He had a dog with him, not quite fully grown, a smooth-coated creature, mainly white, with a long face. Talland chased it round the beach in a circle then it stopped to make friends.

'So you've come at last,' Kitty said, keeping her eyes on the dogs. 'I thought I might have heard from you at Christmas but winter's come and nearly gone again, Nick Nancarrow.'

His face was pained. 'I don't know why but I went into the churchyard first to visit little Jeremy and it was a shock to see Benjamin's grave there beside his. When did it happen, Kitty? If I'd have known…'

Kitty walked along the bank of the Gannel. 'There was nothing you could have done, Nick, and I didn't know where to send word to. Benjamin died about a month after you left, peacefully in his sleep.'

Nick put his arm round Kitty's shoulders and kissed her forehead. 'I'm sorry, Kitty. Thank God he didn't suffer at the end. How are you coping without him?'

'I'm getting used to it, all my friends have been very good to me. I'm just grateful I had Benjamin for so long. What have you been doing with yourself – apart from getting a new dog?'

'I took up as packman around the county and beyond.'

'But not down this way?'

'No.'

Kitty looked back at Talland scampering about with his new friend. 'So, what's the dog called? He's an ugly little thing, hope he hasn't got a vicious streak in him like Gutser had.'

'It's a she and her name's Cassie and she's as gentle as a lamb,' Nick said petulantly.

'I'm glad to hear it and I'm glad you've given her a decent name.' Kitty eyed him critically. 'Getting lonely, were you?'

Nick ignored the question. 'Things the same as usual with you?'

'No, actually I'm getting married at the end of the summer.'

'Are you indeed! Not James Leddra by any chance? I knew he'd taken a strong fancy to you.'

Kitty scoffed. 'A woman doesn't want to marry a man who's like a ship passing in the night.'

'One of your gentlemen then?'

'No, someone I met… when I was staying at a friend's house last year.'

'Are you deliberately trying to be mysterious, Kitty?'

'No,' she replied. 'He's a gentleman, I first met him while I was staying with Isabel after Benjamin's funeral. I shall be selling the house here if you're interested.'

'What would I do with a house?' Nick said, gazing up the river.

'You have the money, you've been putting your earnings away for years and never spending much. You must have a tidy sum if you decide to settle down.'

Nick grunted and sighed. 'How is Isabel?' he said, as he sighted the turning into Penpol Creek.

'She's living at Gwithian now.'

'For part of the year?'

'For good.'

'Oh? Does Grenville mind? Then I suppose he's at sea for most of the time.'

The tide was out and the rock pools were getting too wide to skirt round so Kitty turned back, bringing the sea wind fully in their faces. Against the noise of the surf she said glibly, 'Isabel didn't marry him.'

Nick walked straight into a pool of freezing cold water. 'Damnation! Why not?'

'She wasn't in love with him.'

'I knew that, it doesn't explain why she didn't marry the man.'

'Oh, Nick,' Kitty said despairingly, 'Isabel's changed. She sees things in a different light now, you should know that too.'

'What's that supposed to mean?' He kicked at the hard sand, sending it towards the two playful dogs.

'Don't growl at me, Nick Nancarrow. Those few weeks spent in hiding from the Kempthornes changed Isabel so much she couldn't possibly go back to her old way of life. Why don't you go over to see her?'

Nick stopped walking. 'You're dancing to a different tune, aren't you?'

'I was listening to the wrong one back-along. I should have known better.'

They walked on to the house, Kitty humming gaily to herself, Nick in a stony silence.

'I won't have your dog in the house, even if she is as gentle as a lamb.'

'Cassie wouldn't come inside anyway, she likes to run free.'

Inside, she asked his dour face, 'Well, are you going to see her?'

'You know I always make my way back to Gwithian when I'm in these parts,' he replied, scraping back a chair and flopping down at the kitchen table.

Kitty glared at his boots. 'Anyone would think I didn't have a scraper outside my back door. But Laurence Trevennor is not there now.'

Nick thumped the table. 'Then I'll go visit his grave!'

Kitty was not going to fish any longer. 'So, you did fall in love with Isabel then?'

''Tis none of your damned business!'

Kitty saw to the fire and banged plates on the table.

Nick winced. 'I'm sorry, I shouldn't have shouted at you. I'm upset over Ben.'

'Benjamin allowed Isabel to make him happy, Nick, just like little Morenwyn is. You should see them together, there's laughter at Trevennor House again, would be more if Isabel's life was complete… with the man she loves. You don't need me to tell you how she feels about you, do you?'

'No… well, I was hoping she cared for me after the time we spent in Penpol Creek and here in your kitchen. It's not as easy as that, Kitty.'

'Some things are as easy as just reaching out and receiving them, Nick.'

–

Nick next called on Mundy Cottle. Mundy clucked all over him and made him sit down, hurrying to fetch her cooking pans.

'I'm not hungry, Mundy.'

'Eh? What's the matter with you then, boy?'

'I've just come from Kitty's at Crantock, she fed me well to bursting before I left.'

'Oh, I see,' Mundy said, not hiding her disappointment. 'Perhaps your little dog would like a bite to eat. It doesn't have to stay out there.' She threw a biscuit outside for Cassie.

'And how's she at Crantock then?' There was always a slightly disapproving tone in Mundy's voice when she spoke of Kitty.

Nick gripped the back of a chair, tipping it backwards and forwards impatiently. 'She's becoming an honest woman later this year, she's getting married.'

'I'm glad to hear it, 'tis one step in the right direction to walking the straight and narrow. Sit yourself down for goodness sake, Nick. You haven't been here five minutes but you're already eager to be on your way.'

Nick did as he was told with a heavy sigh. 'Have you heard that her brother, Benjamin, died?'

'Aye, bless un. Only knew about un from what you told me. He sounded a good little boy, God rest his soul. Still, no more suffering for un now.'

'Aye, it was quiet there without him, even though he never made a sound. It's quiet in here today with your children all out.'

'Most of 'em are at work, the rest out doing chores, probably playing before they come back in. I have another little maid calling here now, you know.'

'Oh?' Nick had a good idea who she was. 'Morenwyn's her name, a handsome dark little thing she is too, she loves to play with my young'uns. She comes with Jenna – Isabel I call her now. Some funny goings on all that was. You did a good job looking after she though, must have been really frightening at times. Isabel talks about you a lot.'

'Does she?' Nick sounded impatient. Was Mundy going to dig away at him like Kitty had?

Mundy picked at her nails. 'Aw, glad to get her off your hands, were 'ee then?'

'I was glad when the whole thing was over but as far as I'm concerned Isabel and I are friends.'

'I'm glad to hear it. She's a fine handsome woman. The folk of Gwithian are some glad to have her living there and taking care of her late uncle's interests instead of that other lot. You going on to see her later?'

Nick raised his eyes in exasperation. He knew he had better not say no. 'Probably.'

Mundy moved off to her cupboards and started taking out food. 'I'll make you a meal anyway… she didn't get married like she planned, you know. P'raps when you get to Gwithian you ought to stay around for a bit…'

-

Charlie Chiverton was sitting outside his shack, puffing on his pipe, unperturbed by the sharp wind whistling round him, whittling away on a piece of stick. He held up his craftwork.

''Tes goin' to be a sheep, 'tes fur the little maid—'

'Living with Isabel in Gwithian,' Nick finished for him as he dismounted from one of his horses.

'Knaw about that, do 'ee?'

'Aye, I've heard about nothing else all day. I'll help myself to a mug of your terrible coffee but I don't want anything to eat.'

Charlie looked at Nick's two horses. 'Tradin' goin' well, is it?'

'Aye.'

'Fine animals, too good fur packhorses. You must cause a stir everywhere you go.'

'I try to keep myself unnoticed.'

'A fine lookin' man like thee will 'ave some job doin' that. Nice lookin' dog you got there. There's a few scraps knockin' around somewhere if she's 'ungry.'

Nick threw Cassie a crust of bread and poured himself a mug of coffee.

'I 'eard the Kempthorne woman went to the rope just as she deserved,' Charlie said, using the point of his knife to dig out the appearance of fleece on his work. 'Talk 'bout she's 'ardly died down round 'ere yet.'

'Aye,' Nick said grimly, sipping the bitter coffee and making a face for two reasons. 'I watched her swing. Stood right at the front of the crowd so she could see me. She died kicking and screaming, cursing me and Isabel and anyone to do with us. I reckon Hell itself won't be prepared for that woman.'

''Tes all over now. Time to put it in the past.'

'I don't waste my time thinking about her,' Nick said, settling back on the shack's steps.

'Well, there's plenty of other women to be thinkin' about. Did I tell 'ee Isabel comes over 'ere to see me?'

Nick breathed out heavily. 'You did.'

'Isabel's a fine lookin' woman too, some different to the one you brung 'ere last year.'

'Yes, I know, I've seen that for myself,' Nick returned irascibly.

''Ow come thee went off on yer travels again then?'

'Charlie!'

'She didn't git married, you know, but you could have put a spoke in that idea like the one I put in Gyver Pengelly's back if thee'd 'ad a mind to. I think thee did. Why didn't 'ee then?'

'I'm beginning to wish I'd never come back!'

'Gah! I knew you'd come back and not just because you usually do. Well, what are you wasting yer time 'ere fur? Would serve 'ee right if she didn't keep waitin''.

Nick put his hands up in exasperation and got up. 'Keep your horrible coffee, Charlie Chiverton. I'll come back and see you another time.'

'Just a minute. I've nearly finished here.' Charlie held up the perfect figure of a sheep. 'There, you might as well take this and give it to the little maid.'

'What makes you think I'm going to Gwithian?'

Charlie pushed out his lips and looked down his nose at Nick. 'Where else would you be goin'?'

–

When Nick reached the little bridge at Gwithian he saw the tiny figure of Meena Rowe coming along the middle of it. She lifted up her head and gazed at Nick from the confines of a black bonnet that looked much too big for her.

Nick grinned. 'Didn't you see me coming, Meena?'

'Course I did, but I got better things to do than gawp at travellers. I'm on my way to Jimmy, to give him his crib. Men! They forget everything and want a woman running after them all their lives.'

Nick had dismounted and Meena turned up her tiny face for him to kiss.

'I don't want anyone running after me, I like to take care of myself.'

'We'll see.'

'What does that mean?' Nick asked, becoming defensive.

'Back this way, aren't you?'

Before Nick could argue again that he always came back to Gwithian, Meena pointed at Cassie perched across the back of Nick's other horse. 'What's the matter with your dog? Got a broken paw?'

'No, she likes a ride every now and then.'

Meena moved closer. 'Mmmm, looks half starved to me.' Then she turned on Nick. 'So do you. We'll expect you for supper, will have a nice bit of local mutton stewing then, I know you're partial to its taste.'

'Meena,' Nick exclaimed, 'I'm not hungry. In fact I've eaten so much today I don't care if I never see another morsel of food for a week. How's the family?'

'They're all right, if you're intent on changing the subject.' Meena lifted her chin and tightened her shell-like features.

'And the baby, Joshua?'

'He's thriving, not much of a baby now but you can soon see that for yourself.'

Nick was feeling uncomfortable under Meena's all-seeing eyes. 'Would you like a ride to the fields, Meena? I'd like to see Jimmy again.'

'You can see him by and by, I reckon you got other folk to see first.'

Nick waited for his fourth barrage on Isabel that day but Meena was already walking away. She called over her shoulder, 'See you at supper then, Nick, but if you've got other plans, another time will do… and you don't have to come by yourself.'

Nick waved to the tiny old woman and watched her thoughtfully until she was out of sight. She hadn't mentioned

Isabel residing permanently in the village, she'd judged correctly that he knew already. It seemed all his friends were resigned to his fate, but did fate have the same mind?

Chapter 29

Nick moved on and saw Morenwyn in the parsonage garden playing with the four Thomas children, sheltered from the wind by the boundary wall. They were all wrapped up well against the cold and had two nurses in attendance. Nick leaned on the wall from the saddle and called Morenwyn's name.

'Nick! Nick!' She came running, the nurses and the rest of the children following on her heels. 'Are you coming in to play with us?'

Nick had an assortment of five small faces all looking up at him, the youngest child just about able to toddle on its chubby legs. Morenwyn had grown in height and was even more pretty. 'Perhaps later, princess. Here, I've got something for you.'

'What is it?' a boy aged about six asked bluntly. He put his arm round Morenwyn protectively.

'It's all right, Barnabas.' Nick grinned at him as Morenwyn's nurse nodded her approval. 'It's Nick Nancarrow, remember? I'm Morenwyn's friend. I've got something for her, from another friend, Charlie Chiverton.'

'Has he made something for me?' Morenwyn asked, standing on tiptoe to see.

'Is it another animal for her?' Barnabas demanded, reaching up his hand.

'Aye, it's a sheep this time.' Nick passed it to the nurse who gave it to Morenwyn who was immediately surrounded by her playmates.

Morenwyn passed through them and dropped Nick a perfect curtsey. 'Thank you for bringing it to me, Nick.'

Nick smiled to himself; he knew who had taught her to do that. 'I'll come back later, Morenwyn, and show all of you my new dog.'

He met Charlotte Thomas as she was leaving Trevennor House. 'Nick! How good to see you. How are you? You're looking well.'

Nick looked deeply at the attractive young lady. 'I am, thank you, Charlotte. I've just been talking to Morenwyn and your children over the garden wall.' He glanced discreetly at Charlotte's swollen middle. 'If it's not indelicate to mention it, I see congratulations are in order.'

'Again,' Charlotte added emphatically with a twinkle in her eye. 'I was just having a word with Mrs Christopher. She'll be delighted to see you. I'm on my way home to tell the nurses it's time the children were back inside.'

'A bit of cold weather won't hurt them. Never did me any harm.'

'No, you're the living proof of that,' Charlotte replied with a smile.

Nick wanted to ask a question in his usual confident manner, but he had had too many searching and knowing faces peering back at him today and it came out all hesitantly. 'Is, um, Isabel not at home?'

'No, she is not.' Charlotte watched Nick's face closely and saw it fall. 'But she's not far away. She's taking a walk along the beach. These days she's just like you are, Nick.'

'Eh?'

'Always wanting to be outdoors. She'll be back in time to take tea with Morenwyn.'

Nick looked down as he shifted his feet. 'I'll go in and have a word with Mrs Christopher then.'

More shouts of 'Nick!' and offers to fill him with food greeted him in the large busy kitchen. He relented because he knew he wouldn't win and ate a yeast bun fresh out of the oven while being watched by all the adoring female staff.

'I shall get as fat as a cat if I keep this up,' he grumbled. 'Aren't you women satisfied unless you're plying a man with food?'

'No, but then,' Mrs Christopher looked at him pointedly, 'food is not the only way to a man's heart. Miss Isabel is out walking.'

'Mistress Thomas told me,' he sighed heavily.

'She never married that sea captain or whatever he was.'

'I know that too.' Nick felt the women he was with were beginning to close in on him.

'She's some good to us, Miss Isabel, we wouldn't know what to do without her, would we, Cook?'

Wenna Sweet agreed and put another fat yeast bun on his plate.

Nick broke it in half, intending to give it to Cassie when he was outside again. 'Morenwyn's growing well and looking very happy,' he said conversationally.

'Oh, she is,' Mrs Christopher said enthusiastically. 'Miss Isabel is like a proper mother to her. Will make a good mother to her own one day.'

Nick looked all round the kitchen. He had a good idea what they were hoping he would say. 'I might have enough time to see her briefly before I go on again.'

'Oh, you haven't got business elsewhere, have you?'

'I thought I might ride over to Tehidy and see how the coach horses I was training are getting on. I did rather go off and leave them suddenly.'

'You mustn't leave us yet, Nick, you've only just got here.' Mrs Christopher was looking outside. 'Your dog is getting restless. I think she'd like a run along the beach. What do you think?'

Nick got up suddenly. 'Oh, very well, I'm going! I'm beginning to feel crowded in here and I've had enough ear-bashing for one day.'

'Shall I give the order for the stable boys to see to your horses?'

Nick gave Mrs Christopher a long thoughtful look. 'Better not. I might be riding off again quite soon.'

As soon as he'd gone, Mrs Christopher turned to the maid. 'Dorcas, tell the stable boys to put Nick's horses in their old stalls.' Then she and Wenna Sweet went to the larder to prepare a feast.

–

Nick ordered Cassie to lie down and keep quiet. He watched Isabel at a distance from behind the security of a sand towan. Gwithian's beach was much longer than Crantock's but straight and wide and he had spotted her instantly. She was at the water's edge, moving back as the tide rolled in more and more with each thundering wave, her hair streaming out in a honey-coloured mass. Cassie edged forward and Nick put up a restraining finger. What was Isabel thinking about? Her times spent here with Laurence? Regret that she had not married Richard Grenville? The time spent with himself on that fateful journey that had changed her life so much?

Isabel was thinking about Nick. She thought about him every day and every night. Mostly she thought about the two nights she had slept with his arms round her, strong and warm, making her feel safe.

She hadn't seen or heard from him for over a year now, and she still felt the biggest part of her life was missing. If only she hadn't fallen in love with him. Phoebe Antiss would have said, 'Granted he's tall and handsome and possesses brilliant eyes and some wonderful wild ways, but he's not the only man in the world, dear heart. You'll soon meet another.' Isabel had given herself time to see if this was true, but her feelings for Nick had only grown stronger, her need for him cutting into her with a deeper longing.

There had been a steady stream of young gentlemen flocking to Trevennor House when news of her broken engagement had got round the social circles. She was an heiress and after her enforced adventures something of a curiosity. When she had not returned their interest, many had still clamoured at her door besotted by Kitty, not caring about her background and profession, and Kitty had taken a fancy to one in particular and agreed to marry him. Kitty wanted to settle down and have a family. So did Isabel, but only one man could fill that need.

One day Nick would come back to Gwithian… wouldn't he? He always had before. He had grown very fond of Morenwyn, surely he would come back to see her. No one seemed to know where he had gone and what he was doing, not even Charlie Chiverton. Why didn't he write? Send just a little note to tell someone he was keeping well? It was such a long time. Surely he would come… She had waited for him before like this out on the beach and cliff.

Isabel didn't hear the small white dog yapping its way towards her. A big wave rushed in and soaked her feet and she ran backwards, splashing her cloak and dress. 'Oh dear, what will Mrs Christopher say? She'll scold me for getting my good shoes wet.'

'Tell her 'tis none of her business.'

She spun round and got another soaking as she stood and stared.

''Tis good manners to say goodday to a body.'

She didn't want to speak. She just wanted to run into his arms and hold him tightly to be certain he was really there.

'Well, if you won't speak to me, say hello to my little dog. Cassie, say hello to Miss Isabel Hampton, the lady of Trevennor House.'

Isabel glanced at the dog who was diving at the incoming waves. 'It's… it's a much better name than Gutser.'

'So you remember that name. Is that all you've got to say?'

Isabel blinked, but Nick was still there. She had looked forward to this for so long that now he was here she didn't know what to say. She felt shy and awkward, the way only a man like Nick Nancarrow can render an otherwise strong and confident woman. She thought she would have seen him trotting up the village or striding towards her, his wild hair spilling behind him. But here he was and she had practically walked backwards into him.

She moved out of the cold water and onto firm sand. 'Have you been back long?'

'Not long in Gwithian but I've called on Kitty, Mundy and Charlie since I've been back round here.' He lowered his head, stern-faced. 'Aren't you pleased to see me?'

'Oh, y-yes, of course I am. Morenwyn will love to see you, she talks about you a lot. I hope you can stay, Nick.'

'Do you, Isabel? For how long?'

'For as long as you like.' She was still staring at him, as if she believed he wasn't really there with her.

He loved the warm smokiness of her wonderful eyes but he wasn't sure how she felt at him being there. 'I'll probably stay for a while…'

'If you haven't got somewhere to stay you're welcome to sleep in the stables like you used to do,' she added quickly lest he think she was playing the lady. 'You would be very welcome to stay in the house but it wouldn't be seemly.'

'I'll find a place to lay my head if I stay that long. I must say I didn't expect to come back and find you unmarried.'

'There was no reason for me to marry Richard Grenville and I would have made him very unhappy eventually.'

'No reason, Isabel? I find that a curious thing to hear you say.'

'Will you ever realize that I've changed?' she said almost desperately. 'That the time we had together gave me different outlooks and values? At the end I saw I didn't need to marry someone I didn't love just for position or because he made a desirable husband. Oh, you make me so mad sometimes, Nick Nancarrow!'

His face darkened. 'I only asked you a simple question. I didn't come here to be told I'm stupid, Isabel Hampton.'

'Then why did you come here?'

'I'm damned if I know!'

'Oh, that's definitely the Nick Nancarrow I know. Pig-headed and rude.'

Nick's patience was on a short fuse. He had not wanted this to happen. A verbal tug-of-war. But then things had never been put right with Isabel from the time Kitty had disturbed them in her kitchen. They had both felt embarrassed and Kitty had added guilt to the feeling. Guilt probably on Isabel's part that she was betrothed to another man, guilt on his that he was only going to use her. But that wasn't true. Being with her would have meant the world to him.

He asked softly, 'When did you decide that you weren't going to marry Richard Grenville?'

Isabel was feeling crushed at their argument. She frowned. 'Does it matter, Nick?'

He touched her hair and all her hopes came tumbling back. 'I think it does, for both of us.'

'It was from the day I first spoke to Benjamin. He made me see how I really felt.'

'Then when you agreed to make love with me you didn't feel you were betraying Grenville?'

'No, I knew I could never feel anything for Richard. I knew you cared a little for me, you were so kind and attentive in the creek. I wanted to give myself to you and I wanted to take from you too. I had hoped and dreamed that something might have come out of it, but I felt at that moment that I could have lived on the memory for ever.'

Nick put his hands firmly on Isabel's shoulders and looked right into her. 'I felt more for you than just caring for you, Isabel. But Kitty came back and made me feel I was about to cheapen you, that I was only looking for a casual encounter with you. Believe me, it would have been more than that.'

Isabel's eyes were full of hope as she looked back at him. 'Kitty made me feel underhand and ashamed, as if by behaving that way with you I was somehow being ungrateful to her.'

'Dear Kitty, she thought at the time she was doing the right thing, bringing up Richard Grenville as an uncrossable bridge between us, but it wasn't true. I don't believe we would have come together without there being something wonderful and lasting between us. I love you, Isabel.'

'Oh, Nick,' she cried and flung herself into his arms. 'I've spent all this time since you left me longing for you to come back and say that.'

Nick rested his chin on her head and told the ocean, 'All that wasted time...' Then he brought his lips to Isabel's and kissed her as though he was trying to make up for all that lost time in one moment.

They strolled along the shore, holding one another tightly as if they never wanted to let go.

Isabel said, 'I thought you would have fought to the last breath to stay independent.'

'That's not independence, Isabel. Being afraid to love and commit yourself to someone, that's only running away. Besides,' and he looked at her, grinning cheekily, 'I'd be a fool not to marry the woman with the best legs in Cornwall.'

Isabel laughed and reached up to kiss him. 'I wonder what Uncle Laurence would say? To us falling in love.'

Nick nodded his head in satisfaction. 'He'd be absolutely delighted, I reckon, and he'd approve of us getting married as soon as possible.' He picked Isabel up in his arms and whirled her round. 'We've got a lot of lost time to make up for and I want to provide Morenwyn with another garden full of children to play with.'

'Nick Nancarrow!' She kissed him, overwhelming him with her passion and urgency. 'Then let's hurry up and tell Morenwyn and all the others that you're staying.'

'For ever!'

'For ever...'